LINGER

When wounded souls collide, anything
can happen—even love.

P. J. O'DWYER

Black
Siren
Books

New York

PRAISE FOR THE AUTHOR...

Novels Written by P. J. O'Dwyer

SATIN AND STEEL
WOMEN OF LAW ENFORCEMENT SERIES

Linger

THE FALLON SISTERS TRILOGY

Relentless

Defiant

Forsaken

HUNTER'S MOON
WESTERN MYSTERIES WITH HEART SERIES

Claimed

Black Siren Books

331 West 57th Street
Suite 510
New York, NY 10019
www.blacksirenbooks.com
inquiries@blacksirenbooks.com

This book contains an excerpt from the forthcoming book *Deadrise*, the second book in the Satin and Steel, Women of Law Enforcement Series by P. J. O'Dwyer. This excerpt has been set for this edition only and may not reflect the final content of the forthcoming edition.

Printed in the United States of America

LCCN 2015914511

ISBN 978-0-9848997-9-1 (trade cover)
     978-0-9848997-8-4 (e-book)

Cover design by Patricia Schmitt [Pickyme] www.pickymeartist.com
Interior layout and design by P. J. O'Dwyer

Visit the author's website: http://www.pjodwyer.com

To my daughter, Katie, may God bless you and keep you safe as you pursue your dream job in law enforcement. You are *my* real life heroine.

DEDICATION

Freedom comes with sacrifice. No one knows this more than the men and women—both past and present—who have served in the United States Armed Forces.

And it is with the utmost respect I dedicate *Linger* to these brave individuals and their families, who struggle each day with separation, financial hardship, debilitating physical and mental injuries such as PTSD, and, finally, to those who gave the ultimate—their lives—so that we may live in liberty as our forefathers intended.

Thank you.

ACKNOWLEDGMENTS

To my editors, Amy Harke-Moore and Madeline Hopkins, as always, without you this story would not be possible.

Thanks to my gifted illustrator, Patricia Schmitt, your insight is uncanny. All I have to do is imagine it.

A special thanks to Colonel David Ridlon, US Army (Retired), for his knowledge in regard to that branch of the military. As always, any and all mistakes are my own.

My heartfelt thanks to my family, the "Fabulous Four"—my father, Turk Divver; his wife, Pat Moran; my brother, Joe Divver; and my favorite cousin, Danny Divver. Thank you for making my dreams a reality. Love you all.

To Tom and Chris Morse, also dear cousins of mine, thank you for allowing me the opportunity to bring to life Memory Maker. Over the years I've loved every moment that I have vacationed in your lovely mountain oasis and knew someday it would be the perfect backdrop for Brit and Colt's story.

And to all my fans, I hope you enjoy *Linger*, the first book in the Satin and Steel, Women of Law Enforcement Series. You inspire me every day with your steadfast support!

Chapter One

*D*RIZZLE, MORE AGGRAVATING THAN A DRIVING RAIN, smeared Brit Gentry's windshield when the wiper blade squeaked across the glass. Brit clicked it off and growled. She'd picked a lousy day to travel Interstate 68. The only thing lifting her spirits was the jagged notch cut into the ridge of Sideling Hill. Like an open jaw, it allowed the flow of vehicles to pass from the east and into the west. She again pressed the gas, eager to put more miles behind her, when suddenly her Pathfinder slid onto the shoulder, kicking up rocks. With her heart in her lap, she pulled back on the steering wheel.

Slow down.

Brit eased off the accelerator. Smashing into the side of the Allegheny Mountains, although tempting, wouldn't bring highly decorated Afghan war veteran Sergeant Beau Crenshaw back from the dead.

Nope. But she wouldn't have to live with the guilt of killing him, either.

Brit's fingers skimmed the semi-automatic inside the pocket of her driver's side door. She hadn't wanted to bring it, hadn't wanted to look at or handle another firearm, but black bears thrived in the mountains. If she ventured out once she made it to her getaway in Deep Creek, Maryland, she would need the added protection. The sentimental piece of metal had been her father's and the first gun she'd ever fired. She'd almost tossed it into the Chesapeake six weeks ago—a watery grave the perfect resting place for everything and everyone who had ever caused her pain.

The sky grew darker, fog rolling in as she approached the town of Cumberland. The wind picked up, buffeting her SUV, making it a challenge to keep from swerving into the next lane. The interstate, now more circuitous, cut a path high above the old brick city once known as the gateway to the west. Brit would usually crane her neck to catch a glimpse of the ornate spires of the courthouse and the churches that seemed to stretch toward the heavens. But not today. Her hands remained clenched on the steering wheel, the gorgeous fall colors of October dull and muted through the murk.

Trucks whizzed by on her left, a wall of dirty water spraying her windshield. She hit the wiper again, along with the washer fluid, and fishtailed. Gritting her teeth, she counter-steered until she regained traction. *Damn it, Brit, get a grip.* She was normally rock steady in all situations. She couldn't fall apart—not with her job. Only Brit had been slowly succumbing to an all-out breakdown since that night in March on the Chesapeake, during the maiden voyage of a Sun Odyssey 33i sailboat she never expected to own

Since then the hits just kept coming. Brit shook her head in defeat. Sergeant Beau Crenshaw and a little thing called a financial disclosure investigation had been the cherry on top of the melting tower of ice cream that was her life.

Brit swallowed, the pressure from the elevation lessening in her ears. The highway narrowed. The usual two-way traffic, reduced to one heading west in two lanes. Fringed with dense trees on both sides, westbound 68 and its constant grade, either on the incline or decline, could be treacherous with the slick roads. Brit needed to get past the two idiot truckers up in front who were playing cat and mouse with each other.

She signaled and pulled around the semi into the left lane, its height making it difficult to see the road up ahead. Brit pressed down on the gas pedal and flew past him. A dark compact car behind her seemed to have the same idea and came up on her bumper, then eased off. Damn good thing. One tap of the brake and he'd find himself fishtailing or in a three sixty.

Brit put her sights on the next truck ahead in the right lane. It was a double tandem—two trailers hauled by one lonely cab. Now *that* made her nervous. It was like a train on a collision course.

A white pickup flew by in the right lane, then zigged over in front of her. Brit tapped the brake, holding her breath. *Shit.* Not good. The idiot better not try that around the—

Too late.

The pickup darted in front of the tandem, and Brit tensed. Air brakes screeched and the trailers tottered on their wheels before swinging across the highway like a giant metal gate.

Brit sucked in air and jerked her Pathfinder onto the shoulder. With dense trees to her left and the skidding semi to her right, she squeezed through. Tree branches struck her driver's side window like spears. They clunked and scraped her SUV, the uneven ground bumping her up and down until she was able to pull back onto the highway. Something clipped the right rear of her quarter panel. She stiffened at the crunch of metal on metal. The SUV spun, and a hot flash of panic radiated up her chest. Like a merry-go-round, everything whirled—trees, roadway, the semi—except for a black projectile coming toward her at lightning speed.

I'm going to die.

Brit shut her eyes tight, waiting for the impact that would shatter her bones and tear her flesh. *God. Let it be quick.*

Her SUV stopped, rocked a few times until she sat at an angle, motionless in the right lane. A thunderous clap came from somewhere— maybe behind her—the ground shaking. Brit's eyes popped open. The awful groan and whine of metal bending and twisting echoed around her. The black projectile she now knew to be the compact lay flipped on its roof on the left shoulder, smoke billowing from its hood.

With Brit safely insulated behind the downed semi, vehicles on the other side collided, one after the other. She tensed at each deadly impact, crunching metal and shattering glass echoing all around her until only the sound of her erratic breathing remained. Her head fell back against the headrest, her eyes closing while she worked through the sharp pains radiating up her back.

She was sore but alive.

Her eyes opened, and she scrabbled for her cellphone sitting in the console. Shaking fingers stabbed at the keypad, #77. She knew the call would go to the closest state police barrack and didn't hesitate.

"Multi-car pileup, tandem on its side on 68." Her breaths came in waves, and she squinted against the fog. She tried to find a mile marker, anything, when a wisp of fog thinned and lifted. "There's a sign." She squinted at the yellow background and black lettering. "Caution. Truckers steep descent," she almost shouted into the receiver.

"Ah . . . you're going to have to be more specific than that."

"Triangulate my phone!" Brit scrubbed her face hard. That's all she had. She couldn't say when the next exit would come up. This wasn't a frequently traveled route for her. Brit swung her head around toward the wreckage on the shoulder. She couldn't determine the make of the compact. "Possible fatality." Brit got out. The highway in front was a proverbial ghost town, the fog enveloping her in its misty shroud. She turned behind her and gasped. Flames shot above the semi, left to cool on its side. "Vehicles on fire." She clicked off, hoping they'd taken her seriously about the triangulation thing, and threw her phone onto the driver's seat. Thinking better of it, she grabbed her gun and shoved it into the back waistband of her jeans. There was no way to know how many lay injured or dead beyond the semi. Like a rockslide, it filled the highway from shoulder to shoulder, making it impossible to get to those who were now keening and shouting for help. Fire and EMS were on their way. If the semi was leaking fuel, it could be a ticking time bomb. Staying away from it was her best option. Brit put the agonizing voices out of her mind and bolted toward the compact.

She'd do what she could until the emergency responders arrived. Then hightail it out of here. No way was she staying for the media circus that would ensue or for the boys from the Cumberland Barrack. That was all she needed—to be recognized and linked to a deadly pileup and possibly the only survivor. They'd blame her. Find some way to pin this tragedy on her. Why not? They'd love to parade her photo on national TV. They'd been doing just that in the weeks since the shooting.

Brit edged around the compact and crouched down. With the windows blown out, she'd know if the driver survived. The quiet unnerved her—not even a moan. With her hand on the frame, she peered inside. Her shoulders slumped when she found the vehicle empty—until she noticed the missing windshield and the shards of broken glass glistening on the gravel shoulder. Brit skirted the wreckage. Her hands began to tremble at the blood and dark hair embedded in a spidery chunk of windshield lying in the grass. Her breathing became erratic. She clasped her hands together and tried to control her airflow.

In, out, in, out.

That night on the hill came flooding back. The grisly hole in Crenshaw's forehead, his wide-eyed stare, the blood.

Get it together, Brit. Find the driver.

Right. Probably up in the tree line. Cold and wet from the constant drizzle, Brit shivered at the prospect and hugged her draping black sweater around her. A trendy style, it had kept her comfortable in the heated SUV but wasn't functional out in the elements. Neither were her lacey cami and thin straight leg jeans. And her footwear—forget it. She loved fashion— craved it more than most women because of the uniform. Glancing down, Brit cursed the perfectly coordinated outfit she'd chosen this morning and her lack of good sense. She wouldn't get far traipsing through the woods in her high-heeled tall suede boots.

She'd do her best.

Brit rounded the mangled metal and headed up the grassy, wet incline. She hovered at the tree line. "Hello!" She took a few steps into the low brush, its leaves a golden brown, rubbing against her legs. "Are you hurt?" Brit shook her head. Now that was stupid. She knew whoever it was would be in bad shape, if they had survived.

No answer, except for the pitter-patter of rain hitting the crown of trees above. Brit moved deeper and grimaced at the suction her designer boots made as they sunk into the mud.

Whatever. She could replace the boots. Pulling her heel out of the muck, Brit swatted at low-lying branches. If she could help this person she would. She continued through the woods, cupping her right ear. Still nothing. The wail of sirens grew more distinct. *Thank God for modern technology.* They'd be here soon, faster than she wanted if she continued to search in vain for a victim she felt sure was no longer of this world.

Turning around, she then maneuvered back the way she came. Her vehicle was maybe fifteen yards away, parked at an angle in the far right lane where it had finally rested. The pickup that had caused all the problems had vamoosed. Lucky for him.

Brit crossed the highway, grabbed her phone from the seat, and hopped inside where she'd left her Pathfinder still running. She snagged the gun digging into her back, juggled it and her phone, and lifted the lid to the center console. She placed the gun inside, shutting the lid with a *thunk*. Brit clicked her seat belt and did an inventory of her truck. Suitcases were scattered in the back from the impact and a small cooler lay on its side in the passenger footwell. She righted it and then angled her head to check her driver's side mirror. Brit lurched backward, her unexpected scream, shrill and so unlike her, drowning out any conscious thought except—*holy shit*!

Heart racing, eyes widening, she tried to decide if he was man or beast. But it was the pistol aimed at her center mass that had her going into survival mode. She reached for the top of the center console, debating about her weapon.

I'm as good as dead if I go for it.

Her door flew open. Brit's eyes darted toward his hairy face.

"Move over," he shouted.

Her hands went up. "Okay." She eyed Sasquatch—head full of curly raven hair, bearded, broad, and bleeding from his forehead and a hole in the knee of his jeans. *Huh?* If this was the guy from the compact, she'd have thought he'd be in worse shape, considering the condition of his vehicle.

"Move it." He used the gun as an extension of his arm and waved it at her before he snatched her phone from her hand.

Brit's eyes narrowed when he shoved her only means of communication into the left front pocket of his windbreaker. *Awesome.*

He jerked the gun at her, his meaning clear.

"Going." With one hand up, the other unlatching her seat belt, she did her best to climb into the passenger seat, which was difficult with the cooler taking up most of the footwell.

He slid into the driver's seat, moaning when his butt hit the leather. Slamming the door, he kept the gun trained on her. "Where we going?"

Brit, with both hands up now, pressed back into the door. Was he kidding? He wasn't going anywhere with her. She eyed the door handle. Damn boots. She'd skate on her heels onto the highway like a skittish deer, and he'd shoot her in the back.

"Hospital?" She shrugged, hoping he'd consider his injuries, especially the jagged pieces of glass glittering from his knee. "Got a lot of tendons running through there." She pointed toward the gaping hole in his jeans covered in blood.

"No hospital." His hand shook on the wheel, and his eyes seemed to fill with pain or . . . was it fear? "Where were you going?" His voice was razor sharp.

"Shopping." It was lame. But the only thing that came to mind. Must have been the stupid outfit she chose to wear today.

He glanced into the backseat, then narrowed in on her. "Try again."

Brit stared him down. She wasn't telling him.

He took a deep breath. "So you're a hard a—" Her cellphone, still clenched between his dirty fingers, rumbled.

She knew the sound. Brit only hoped whoever was texting her wouldn't give up her identity.

He looked down, a smile curling his lips as he read the text out loud. "Did you get the combo to the cabin?" He glared at her. "Bob from Deep Creek Railey Realty."

Brit slumped against the seat, relieved Bob Dawson hadn't mentioned her name.

"Secluded?" He looked down his nose at her.

"What?" It came out bewildered.

"Your cabin."

Brit took a needed breath through her nose. "You need a doctor." Keeping her hands up, she pointed toward his left temple and the bloody knot bulging at his hairline. "You could have a head injury."

He snuffled. "Don't much matter. I'm on borrowed time anyway."

Great.

The sirens increased in intensity. Sasquatch shook his gun at her and put the vehicle in drive. He peeled wheels, fishtailed, the guardrail looming toward her before sideswiping it with the SUV. Brit slapped her cheeks hard with both hands and sucked in air. "What the hell?"

He grunted. His lips quirked, shrouded in the forest of black whiskers. *Asshole.*

She didn't need this, and to think she'd tried to save his ass back there.

"Look. You can take the truck, drop me off at the exit." She pointed toward an approaching green sign; the words *Exit 34, Route 36, toward Frostburg* whizzed past. *Damn it.*

She wasn't taking him to her lakefront mountain home. Maybe Bob called it a cabin. But that's what he called everything up there. This guy would think he'd kidnapped some wealthy heiress. Which she wasn't—not even close.

"Never been to Deep Creek."

Was he kidding?

This wasn't a vacation, especially not for him. She needed to heal. He needed to heal, too. But—

Wincing, he repositioned his butt in the seat. "Know anything about first aid?"

"No!" It came out angry, exasperated, and she regretted it immediately. Rolling her lips in, she angled her body away from him, her blond hair falling past her eyes concealing—she hoped—her true feelings. She couldn't afford to incense him, though her own blood—that was still on the inside where she wanted to keep it—was boiling mad.

A pair of green eyes tunneled into her. "This is happening, Brit Gentry. So deal with it."

Her mouth dropped open with disbelief; real fear trickled to every recess of her body. He *had* been following her, knew her name. Her stomach roiled. There was no hiding who she was. He'd have that gun trained on her until he decided to take the kill shot.

Brit swallowed hard "How do you know who I—"

"Buckle up." He hooked his chin toward her, steadying the gun with his left hand against the steering wheel as he drove. He yanked at his seat belt, then came up short when it locked. "Son of a *bitch*." He jerked it a few times like a nervous rider on a roller coaster before it clicked in place.

She guessed he'd learned his lesson about the usefulness of seat belts. Brit tried not to smirk while she fastened hers. She raised her hands again, hoping he'd relax, especially with the gun.

His shoulders leveled off, and he settled into the seat, his face set and determined.

"Can I put my hands down?"

"In your lap where I can see them."

Brit complied. There would be no more finagling her freedom. He wanted her for a purpose, all the more reason to start strategizing her escape—or his demise.

Sasquatch had more to worry about than a malfunctioning seat belt. First chance she got, she'd put a bullet between his eyes.

So much for deluding herself about the gun—she was a professional killer. One who, given the command, could squeeze off a fatal round at a hundred yards with dead accuracy.

Only this time, this Maryland State Police counter-sniper was on her own.

Chapter Two

*D*EEP CREEK REMINDED COLT RIVERS OF HIS HOME IN Montana, where he was hoping to end up when this thing played itself out. He wasn't doing too good at making that happen though. His ribs hurt like a son of a bitch, which told him from experience he'd cracked a few when he landed on the shoulder of the road.

But he'd drawn a tall straw when one of the guards, sympathetic toward his story, smuggled an untraceable gun into the US Disciplinary Barracks—his home away from home in Fort Leavenworth, Kansas, for the past four years.

He'd waited patiently for the one opportunity that would bring him closer to freedom. That chance event happened three weeks ago when they'd chosen him and a few other inmates to help with the trash.

Colt could still picture the garbage truck driver's wide-eyed expression when he'd swung into the passenger seat wielding a loaded gun. His gaze was glued to the weapon, deadly and pointed at his head. He hit the gas.

The driver knew, just like everyone else, that the guards weren't armed. Even if they had caught on, Colt was the man with the gun. He guessed they figured him to be a compliant inmate who'd serve out the rest of his nine years. The government's way of rewarding him for being a model prisoner. They were wrong.

And so was his buddy Seth Gentry.

His recon wasn't the best without the usual technology—cellphone, computer. Didn't matter—he had a gun and Seth's sexy wife. She'd lead him to her husband. Probably on some fancy business trip. He'd been to their house on the water. Nice digs, even a sailboat.

Didn't take a genius to figure the bastard had been living lavishly since retiring as a decorated Army Ranger—nor a degree in finance to know where he'd come by the money.

Looked like he kept his lady in the finest fashions, too. But she had one thing on Seth—compassion. She could have easily said the hell with this and driven off after the accident, instead of traipsing through the woods searching for an injured driver. But it wouldn't have changed the outcome for Brit Gentry. She was going to be in his company with or without an interstate pileup. Just happened sooner rather than later.

He had to give her credit. Most women would have flipped out. No, she wasn't the hysterical type or even your normal type, for that matter. She was pissed, pissed at him. *Well sorry, lady, for ruining your little vacation*, but he'd had a bad four years thanks to her husband.

Colt passed a Maryland State Police Barrack on the right, his jaw tightening. "How much farther?"

"Two miles on the right. Sang Run."

Damn, that sucked. He was hoping for seclusion. Having the state boys within walking distance meant she'd be stapled to his hip.

He made the right, noted the gas station on the corner and the Mexican restaurant on the left, his stomach groaning. He hadn't eaten since leaving his hidey-hole in the Kansas forest. Food hadn't been a priority over the past few days. Getting from Kansas to Maryland had been. Now that he was here, he needed food bad. Passing out wasn't an option.

"What's in it?" He nodded toward the cooler that had been crowding her shapely legs into a corner of the footwell for the last half hour.

"Eggs"—she gave him a lift of her brow—"probably broken after the accident, bacon, milk, orange juice, and muffins."

Colt's mouth watered. "Will you make me something to eat when we get to your place?"

She shrugged. "You're the man with the gun."

Right.

Brit pointed toward the left. "Marsh Hill Road."

Colt took the turn. They passed a ski lodge on the right with condos on the left facing the lake. The narrow road wound up the mountain. Small cabins, tucked under trees ablaze with fall color, faced the lake. More cabins built into the mountainside were perched on the right.

"Which one's yours?"

"A mile up on the left—Memory Maker."

Colt snorted. Oh, this would be a memory all right. A bad one.

He passed more homes—not cabins. They seemed colossal.

"It's after Sun Drenched Cove."

What the hell kind of place was this? They named everything. That should have been his first clue the Gentry cabin wasn't your simple four walls and maybe a fireplace like back home.

"Right here!"

Colt hit the brake, the seat belt slamming into his aching ribs. "Thanks for the advance warning," he snapped and took the sharp turn down a gravel drive.

He did a double take. *Son of a bitch. Make that two colossal luxury homes.* He drove by a building with large windows, spied what looked like a pool, then parked in front of the main cedar-shingled house with several gabled roofs.

"I think I've been more than accommodating." She made a careful sweep of her arm indicating her truck.

Colt didn't miss the edge to her voice. Or, he turned toward her, the way her brows snapped together when she was mad. Like when he'd asked her about first aid. Which was something she was going to have to help him with—like it or not.

"Until I'm a hundred percent, I expect to be short-tempered."

She twisted her face at him like a disagreeable child. "I don't plan on being in your company that long."

"I'm the man with the gun, remember?"

Her lips thinned, and she reached for the door.

"Hold up." He grabbed her arm. "I'll come around and let you out."

"*Okay.*" She dropped back against the seat, folding her arms across her chest.

Swinging open his door, he got out. Maybe a little too fast—everything tilted. He waited for it to pass, relieved Brit was still in the car and not witness to how weak he really was or how the pain rocketed through his body.

He shut the door and limped around the SUV, his gun trained on her. Opening her door, he seized her forearm, surprised by the firm muscles of her arm, and helped her out and over the cooler. In her four-inch-heeled boots, she came to the tip of his nose. He was six three. Calculating her height in his head, that would make her of average height—five six or so. With her cool attitude, upper body strength, and height, he wouldn't discount her ability to cause him trouble.

She eyed his hand, then lifted her chin. Irritated brown eyes, fringed with long lashes, pierced him. "You think you can back off and give me an inch of space to move, Mr. . . . ."

Giving her his name could prove problematic. He'd use his old bird dog's name. "It's Beau."

Her eyes closed, her expression becoming pained like she was riding out a migraine or something.

"What's wrong with you?" He pulled his head back, a little irked. He'd loved that dog.

Her lashes fluttered open, and she took a deep breath. "I take it that's not your real name. How about I call you John?"

His lips quirked. "That's not very memorable." He nodded toward the sign above the door, *Memory Maker*.

She jerked her arm away and bent down and grabbed the cooler. She stepped around him and onto the landing of the portico. "You're not someone I want to remember," she slung over her shoulder as she worked the combination lock on the door, cursing when it didn't budge.

Colt, keeping her accounted for, went to the back door of the SUV and snatched her suitcase and another smaller bag. He scanned the back cargo area. It was empty. After locking her sleek new bronze-colored Pathfinder—yeah, he'd checked out the factory sticker inside the driver's door jamb—he pocketed her keys and came up behind her, feeling a tad guilty for all the damage he'd caused her shiny new car.

"You have the right house?"

"Yes," she growled. "It's the combo."

"Did you get the new combo?"

She turned and gave him a lift of her brow, then gave him her back and punched in a different code. She yanked on the handle. It didn't budge.

"How about a window?"

She elbowed past him, stepped off the portico, and crunched through leaves until she stood in front of a window, minus a screen. She pressed in on the corner until the window frame, set on a crank, popped. She pried it open the rest of the way.

Colt dropped what he had and hobbled down the step, ready to follow behind.

Brit hoisted her leg over the sill. "I'll come around and unlock the door."

Like hell. He reached for her arm. She dodged him and disappeared inside, shutting the window. A lock clunked into place.

Shit. Colt hobbled back to the porch and aimed his gun at the lock when he noticed a green beacon of light flashing on the combination pad.

Green means go.

He gripped the knob. It turned. He flung open the door and entered into a foyer. Beyond the entrance, it opened to a massive great room, floor to ceiling stone fireplace, view of the lake, and no Brit until she came from a doorway to the right, looking guilty.

She tipped her head, her eyes widening. "You got the door op—"

"What's in there?" Colt shoved the gun into the back of his waistband and snagged her shit. Throwing the cooler and small bag on the long bench to the left, he then shut the door. When it locked behind him, he gripped the handle to her suitcase and strode toward her. The quick movement shot daggers through his knee. He gritted against the pain, grabbed her arm, and pulled her into the room. He hit the light.

In the middle of the room sat a king bed, blankets pulled down, fluffy white towels sitting in a neat folded pile on an overstuffed chair to the right with a matching ottoman.

"I thought you'd like to take a shower and get some rest after you eat."

Colt thought about that for a moment, tried to calculate the time—it was possible—and then called bullshit. The towels were too perfectly folded, the washcloth done up like same fancy napkin. She'd been up to something.

"Uh huh." He let her arm go. "Here's your suitcase." He handed it to her.

"I sleep upstairs."

He shook his head at her naiveté. "Don't know how many bedrooms you have in this swank mountain retreat, but you're sleeping with me."

She said nothing and walked out.

To hell with it. Brit Gentry would find out soon enough who he was and what he wanted.

"And the name's Colt Rivers." He spun on his heels, trying to get a glimpse of her face to see if she recognized his name. But he only lost his balance in the process. He reached for the dresser, her laughter floating back to the expansive bedroom. Surrounded by sky blue walls and honey-colored trim, he took a deep breath, trying to work through the pain, and then shuffled across the carpet.

No more nice guy.

Chapter Three

COLT. BRIT CLENCHED HER TEETH WHILE HE SHUFFLED behind her with the gun. He was full of himself, that was for sure, and presumptuous. She wasn't sleeping with him. She got it. He needed to keep her close and accounted for. Fine. He could tie her to the chaise next to the bed and, if he was lucky, she'd still be there when he woke up.

Unzipping the soft-sided cooler, Brit scanned the extravagant, oversized gourmet kitchen with its large island that incorporated a chunky bar for eight. Her eyes landed on the butcher block of knives sitting on the far counter, facing the pool house complex.

"Think you're fast enough?"

Brit turned to find Colt leaning against the tall kitchen cabinet bordering the great room with a TV remote in one hand, his gun in the other. He eyed her, then the knives more than ten paces away.

If she hadn't been so consumed with their sleeping arrangements—and sleep better be all he had in mind—the butcher block with its array of knives, from meat cleaver to paring knife, would have been her first stop. Not the cooler with eggs and bacon he'd coveted with desperate hungry eyes on the drive here.

Why should she care if he was hungry?

She didn't know him, didn't like him, and was his hostage until she could come up with a sensible plan of attack or escape.

Damn him. She was leaning more toward escape now. He wasn't as frightening as he had been at first sight. He was . . . gruff. His pain would account for that, like he said. But he'd been kind to her, even polite—the whole hostage thing notwithstanding, of course.

Will you make me something to eat? Not, *You will make me something to eat.*

Well, she was hungry, too. Probably why she was having a hard time deciding her next move. But one thing *was* clear. He needed to believe he had her trust. That she could identify with him and his troubles. Whatever the hell they were.

Feeding him was a good start. "Kind of at a disadvantage without the knife." She held up the bacon in its plastic packaging. "You want to do the honors?"

His lips twitched. "Go ahead. I'll sit right here and watch." He hobbled toward one of the stools at the bar and dropped his hulking frame onto it with a moan. He rubbed at the drying blood above his eye. It didn't look near as bad as it had when the blood was bright red and oozing. She didn't know how hard his head was. But if it was as resilient as the man, he probably only had a mild concussion and a whopper of a headache.

He'd survive. Strike one for her.

"Eight seats not enough?" He scrutinized the intricately carved wooden table with twelve matching chairs that sat in the dining room adjacent to the great room.

"It's an investment property. We rent it out." As soon as the words left her mouth, Brit cringed.

Damn it, Brit. Stop talking.

Although if he knew her name, he'd done some research about the "we." Maybe. Okay, she wasn't positive of the amount of intelligence he had on her, and asking during the drive up seemed pointless. But unless the guy lived under a rock for the past six weeks, he'd have read the headlines or watched it unfold on the news. Funny thing. He could pass for one of those adventure types that lived off the land—sure smelled like one, anyway. So the rock thing might not be too far off.

Too bad for her she'd be his company for the foreseeable future, as her plan of escape had been foiled when the touchy lock to the front door decided it liked the last combination she'd entered. Lucky for her she'd had enough sense to snag the disconnected cable box from the TV in the great room. The only TV in the house that was still hooked up to cable since *she*—there was no "we" anymore—had been in the process of changing over to satellite at the urging of the realty company.

Last thing she needed was him hooking it up and catching the nightly news. He hadn't gotten around to asking how the TV worked, but it was on his mind. That she'd gleaned from the remote he carried in and placed on the counter.

She'd continue to ruminate over the cable box's impromptu hiding spot, under the bed he'd be sleeping in, until she could safely retrieve it. Brit cleared her mind of it for now and rounded the center island. She eased the paring knife out of the butcher block, mindful of the watchful eyes behind her, and sliced open the bacon. She laid it out on a plate and stuck it in the microwave. Next she started a pot of coffee. She liked tea, but she got the feeling this guy drank coffee—black. The bacon popped and sizzled, the smoky aroma making her mouth water. Brit took a skillet from beneath the cabinet and stood when she caught him smiling.

"What?" Her hand landed on her hip.

"You're efficient."

She nodded toward the gun—very deadly and still in his hand, leveled at her. Now would be a good time to make him consider her feelings. Or rather what she wanted him to believe were her feelings. "Nervous mostly."

He eyed the gun, then her, and shoved it into the waistband of his jeans. "Better?"

"Thanks." She set the skillet down on the cooktop, skirted the bar and grabbed an earthenware mug from the cabinet above the coffeepot. She kept her back to him, her attention drawn to her SUV and her own gun so close but inaccessible. *Shit.* Her police ID and agency-issued chest holster were tucked inside the spare tire compartment in the back. He wouldn't know to look there. Getting her keys from him could solve all her problems—she could just leave. She certainly didn't need another shooting investigation on top of the one she already had. "How do you like your coffee?"

"Cream and sugar."

An exasperated smile curled her lips. This guy was becoming a true contradiction. Usually she was spot-on at reading people—him not so much.

"Settle for milk?" she called over her shoulder while she filled the mug, adding two teaspoons of sugar, and caught him fooling with the remote.

"Yep." He held it up. "How do you work the TV?"

"Waiting on DirecTV. It's not hooked up." She rounded the island toward him and dug out the half gallon of milk in the cooler, hoping he bought her excuse. She added a generous amount, tossed the spoon in the sink, and handed it off to him. "It's hot."

"Appreciate it." He set down the remote, a frown tugging at a pair of sculpted lips, and cupped the mug with both his hands. They were large and lacerated and caked with dried blood. He took a sip. "Good." His voice was throaty with what she believed to be sincere gratitude.

"Uh huh."

There was something about his eyes. Sad. Best not to look too deeply or she might be tempted to ask why. Not that she didn't have a boatload of questions for him. There'd be plenty of time for that, she supposed. Only he needed to be receptive to her inquiries. Brit put it aside for now and added some butter to the pan and started cooking the eggs on low. The timer went off on the microwave, and she checked the bacon, starting it back up for two more minutes when he snuck up behind her.

Brit gasped, raised her arm on instinct, and swung.

Colt clenched her wrist. "Whoa. I thought we had an understanding?"

"Understanding?" She glared at him. "You commandeered my vehicle, sideswiped it." Then she jammed her finger at him. "Now you're holding me hostage."

"There's no need to get hostile."

He actually looked offended.

"Hostile?" She yanked her arm from him and punched open the microwave, grabbing the tray of bacon. "*Shit.*" She dropped the searing plate on the granite countertop, her fingers and palm stinging.

His arm went around her. His chest, a wall of muscles, pinned her against the countertop, and he dragged her to the right.

"No!" Confused, hand throbbing, chest tightening, Brit thrashed.

"Crissake. Chill." He turned on the sink and grabbed her wrist, shoving her hand under the cold water.

The relief was instant, and Brit relaxed in his arm. Her fingers grew numb while rust-colored water filled the porcelain farm sink. It was a mix of his blood and grime from his hand.

The amber color grew deeper, redder. *Oh, God.*

It's a hallucination, Brit. Stop it.

She couldn't. It happened once before, a few days ago, when she'd taken a shower. Brit began to tremble.

"Whoa. What's wrong with you?" He nailed her with a pair of widening eyes.

Brit couldn't catch her breath. "I-I can't . . ." Her legs crumpled beneath her, the edge of the counter loomed. Colt caught her, her temple missing the corner by degrees. He lowered her to the tile floor.

"Shit," he hissed under his breath. "You're having a panic attack."

Brit leaned against the cabinet, her mouth tingling, hands and feet going into spasm.

"Don't move." Colt got to his feet and opened and slammed drawers.

Damn my life. She knew what was happening. The agency psychiatrist had warned her about these episodes. Being held hostage certainly wasn't helping.

Colt came down on his haunches, his hand cradling the back of her neck. He placed a paper bag over her face.

Brit flinched. "Wa-wait."

"Just breathe."

She raised shaky hands and cupped the bag tight over her mouth, the bag crinkling in and out every time she took a breath. She didn't know what to make of him. His knee that was very close to hers had begun to bleed again through the hole in his jeans.

"Why?" Her voice echoed from inside the bag. She turned her head toward his in bewilderment. "Why are you doing this?" She meant taking her to begin with. But there was this caring side to him that didn't fit the profile of an abductor.

"How ya doing?" His eyes lingered over her face.

Brit kept the bag tight to her cheeks, taking easy breaths. The tingling was subsiding, but she was still light-headed.

"God, just answer the question." Her voice was agitated and hollow through the brown paper.

He stood and gave her his back with the gun shoved in the waistband of his jeans. Any other time, she'd be able to wrestle it away. But not now. Just standing would be a hazard.

He turned and scrubbed his face hard. "I don't get off on hurting women."

Brit's brows snapped together, and she yanked the bag from her face. "How a-about scaring them, Sa-Sasquatch."

"Sasquatch?" His mouth twitched—not a smile. That he'd reserved for his green eyes that gleamed down at her with amusement. "Put the bag back over your face before you pass out."

"I have a razor if you're interested." Her words were muffled through the bag. She gave him a smug face—not that he could see it. But it made her feel better.

He rubbed the scruffy beard, saying nothing about the razor, and nodded toward the cabinet. "I'll help you set the table."

God I need to take a chill pill.

That had probably been what he was about to do before she tried to take a swing at him. Being a CADI—a person who has caused an accidental death injury—sucked. The label would stick with her forever thanks to the agency's shrink. Even if they exonerated her, she'd probably never be back on the exclusive S.T.A.T.E. Team she'd fought so hard to become a member of. She wasn't the bold, unwavering Brit her team members had come to count on.

Brit scooted and inched her back up the cabinet, trying to get her legs under her.

Colt gripped her arm. "Take it slow."

Together they awkwardly brought her to her feet with Brit holding the bag to her face.

"Tell me who you are." Her words were demanding, yet her voice sounded weak through the paper bullhorn she had pressed to her face.

"The one who's going to finish getting this grub on the table." He led her past the stove.

Brit frowned at the eggs' stiff centers. "You need to turn them off."

"I'll get it." Colt pulled out a chair to the dining room table for her. "It's food. That's all I care about."

Brit eased herself down, wary.

He moved into the kitchen, turned off the eggs, and pulled out two table settings. He set down the plates and silverware and grabbed his coffee from the island, placing it next to one of the plates. After doling out eggs and dropping several pieces of bacon on each of their plates, he sat down.

He took the bag she still had plastered to her face and winked. "I think you're good."

Heat rode up Brit's cheeks. She'd been so concerned with his movements, she'd forgotten about hers.

"Not as long as you have that gun." She gave him a meaningful look.

"Would you have taken me with you without it?"

It was a fair question. She didn't know. "I might have taken you to a hospital if you didn't want to deal with the paramedics on the scene."

"I told you no hospitals." He took a sip of his coffee. He kept his eyes on her and pulled out the gun. He popped out the bullet in the chamber and sat it down on the table between them. Next he disengaged the magazine, shoving it in his back jean pocket. He laid the gun between them and scooped up the last bullet.

"Make you feel better?"

Brit rolled her lips in. "Not until you tell me what you want with me."

Colt took a bite of his eggs. "Eat. We can talk later."

Her stomach grumbled. Fine. She nibbled her bacon, giving him covert looks while they continued to eat in silence. Or was it more a quiet strategy session on both their parts? Maybe not too quiet the way he choked his food down. No way was that going to be enough for him.

Brit stood.

Colt's hand shot out, and he snagged her arm. "Where you going?"

"*God*, will *you* relax. How about a muffin and some more eggs?"

His grip lessened. "If it's not too much trouble."

Trouble. No. They'd both do better if he had a full stomach. Hunger could be like a hair trigger. She didn't need him pulling his. Of course that was a moot point as long as the ammunition stayed in his pocket.

"No trouble."

Colt's hand remained latched on her arm. "This isn't how I planned it." His eyes held hers for a brief moment before he let go of her.

Brit turned away from him and grabbed for the bag of muffins on the counter. He loved to give her just enough to make her crazy with speculation. She didn't know him, didn't think she'd ever seen him in her life. She certainly didn't recognize his name. And his bullshit line irritated her. He knew *her* name. This thing sounded pretty planned to her—maybe not the pileup.

She threw two muffins in the toaster and fried up three more eggs, ignoring the mild stinging of her hand. She set the feast down next to him and took her seat.

"Thanks." He smashed his muffin into the eggs, sopping up the warm, runny yokes, and shoved it into his mouth like a vagrant.

Brit toyed with her food, now cold and unappetizing. She forced what she could down, irritated she forgot her tea, and doubly pissed she was going to have to ask permission to get up, based on his behavior the last time she made a move to stand.

The guy was jittery as hell.

"I forgot my—"

Red and blue strobe lights filled the kitchen, and Brit's stomach clenched.

Colt jumped up, his chair clattering backward to the hardwood floor. He grabbed for the gun. "You call the cops?" The words ripped from his throat, his eyes darting from her to the kitchen window.

"At the accident scene! Your car looked like a crushed tin can." Brit pushed away from the table and stood. "Didn't know you weren't worth saving." She tottered backward on her heels and then straightened, remembering the gun was unloaded.

He must have realized it, too, the way his face dropped. But he still had the magazine and single bullet in his back pocket. Brit clutched his hand with the gun and relied on her training.

"What the . . . ?"

Brit ripped the gun from his grasp before he could react. She sidestepped him, her destination the front door.

"Don't." Colt blocked her and grabbed her arm. Their gazes locked. "You got a nice place here, house on the Chesapeake, and a pristine sailboat." He cocked his head. "You own them free and clear?"

"That's none of your business." Stunned, she brushed past him, contemplating his all-important question.

Damn him. Brit shoved the gun inside the back of her jeans.

Did he know about the little financial disclosure investigation she had going on with the state? Or the fact she'd murdered an unarmed man?

Brit gnawed her bottom lip, flipped on the porch light—it was dark now—and opened the door.

Chapter Four

*S*HIT! COLT PACED THE KITCHEN, CAREFUL TO KEEP himself concealed. Lot a good it did if she turned him in. But the look on her face when he'd mentioned her extravagant lifestyle seemed to strike a chord. He hoped enough for her to keep him around.

The gun had been a calculated move—he had no choice but to give it up. He needed her to start trusting him. Having her lithe body cave in his arms with her struggling to breathe was the last thing he'd expected. She'd been fighting him seconds before.

He wanted to kick Seth's ass for putting him in this position.

The knock came. She seemed to fumble with the lock. The door creaked open. Colt's breathing slowed, his heartbeat echoing in his ears. He moved a little toward the kitchen window. The metallic yellow letters affixed to the cruiser glistened in the rain, *Maryland State Police.*

Shit.

"Hey, Pete."

Fuck. Colt rested his head up against the refrigerator and grimaced. *Son of a bitch. She knows him.*

"Brit." The trooper's word was abrasive.

"Guess I owe you an explanation." Brit cleared her throat.

"Could have stayed to give your account."

"Make things easier on the accident reconstruction team," another trooper added.

"I know. I wasn't thinking."

The door creaked again. "Wanna tell us what happened?" Footsteps shuffled on the hardwood floor, and Colt ducked down, moving past the kitchen window toward a side door and another refrigerator. He pressed his back up against it, eyeing the doorknob and the woods beyond.

"There's not much to tell. A white pickup cut off the tandem. I slipped through on the shoulder before the trailers flipped on their sides."

"What about the car on its roof?"

"Couldn't locate the driver." She took a deep breath. "I wanted to stay, but I had a splitting headache by then, and . . ." Her voice was remorseful.

"Under the circumstances I can see why you—"

A phone rang the same time Colt's back jean pocket vibrated. *Shit.* He grabbed her phone.

"You need to get that?"

Colt gnawed on the inside of his mouth while the incessant ringtone vibrated his hand.

"Ah . . . it'll go to voice mail." She sighed. "How many fatalities?"

"We lost three at the scene. And we got two critical at Sacred Heart. The fog was too thick to call for a medevac to shock trauma."

"God, I'm so sorry."

When the ringing stopped, Colt peeked around the refrigerator. A shadow grew larger on the wooden floor of the dining room. His chest tightened.

Shit. They'll be in the kitchen before long.

"We are, too. All right. Anything else you remember?"

"That's about it."

"You up here by yourself?"

"Yeah. Looking to clear my head."

"I gotcha."

Two sets of shoes shuffled against the floor, growing fainter. "You think of anything, give us a call."

"Sure. Have a good night." The door clicked shut.

Colt waited until one door then the other slammed shut on the cruiser before he ducked down and headed toward the dining room.

Brit rounded the corner. "I—"

Colt shook his head, his meaning clear. He wasn't going to engage her in conversation until the cops were up the steep driveway. He waited until the rear lights disappeared around the bend where the indoor pool complex sat.

"You know them personally." Colt cocked his eyebrow.

She swallowed, wetting her lips. "Only Pete. He-he has a home on the other side of the lake."

Maybe. But he'd picked up on a few things during that limited conversation. She seemed to know more than your average citizen.

"What would you know about accident reconstruction?"

She only stared back at him with those gorgeous brown eyes of hers. *Damn it.* He couldn't decide if she was frightened of him—which she should be—hiding something, or just being obstinate.

Either way, she needed to know this wasn't a game. He pulled out a chair and grabbed her arm, sitting her down. "Answer the question."

She ripped her arm from his grasp and rubbed her biceps. "You're hurting me." Their eyes connected. Hers were filled with contempt. But it was the pout taking shape on those perfectly formed lips of hers that told the real story, and he hated himself in that instant.

"I don't want to, Brit. *God*, I don't want to." He pulled out another chair, positioning it directly in front of her, and sat down. "Please, answer the question."

Her eyes blazed back. "You seem to know everything else about me."

He leveled a hard gaze at her. "Some, not all."

Brit's head fell back, and she closed her eyes. "My dad is retired Maryland State Police Commander Joe Dodd," she said like she was in pain. Well, pained she had to divulge the information.

Colt clenched his jaw. It wasn't the name. He didn't know this Joe Dodd, didn't care that he was who he was, except *Daddy*—if he found out—wouldn't like Colt holding his daughter hostage.

That wasn't going to happen as long as he had her phone *and* any other means of communication she could get a call, text, or email out from.

"So why didn't you turn me in?" Colt arched a curious brow at her.

She shook her head, chin dipping slightly, fingers digging into her palms.

"Because I'd rather give you whatever it is you want and make this thing go away—make you go away—without some grand circus with the state police." Brit lifted her head. "I don't need the drama."

"I piqued your curiosity, then?"

Her eyes beaded in on him. "You wanna tell me what's going on here?"

Colt stood, taking her up with him, but with less force. "First, give me a tour."

She held her ground. "So I can give you an advantage."

"I gave you the gun."

"Unloaded." She cocked her head. "I guess you forgot that little detail when you freaked out and grabbed it off the table," she said, giving him a self-satisfied look until her gaze swept over him.

"What?"

"You're still bigger than me."

He wouldn't be surprised to learn she knew a thing or two about self-defense, judging by the tight muscles in her thighs and arms. But he'd been trained by the best. Plus, it was true, size mattered, and he certainly had that over her.

Colt motioned for her to go ahead of him, and then started with the first door by the entrance. He peeked in—powder room. The window where she'd tried to give him the slip. The next door along the wall was shut and . . . He tried the doorknob. Locked. He then took a closer look and noticed the keyhole. "Where's the key?"

She gave him a look that said *Die.*

"Not talking, huh?" Colt reached into his pocket and pulled out her set of keys. He eyed the lock and found what he thought was the matching key and slipped it in. A smile touched his lips when it turned.

He swung open the door and flipped on the wall switch. It was a walk-in coat closet and catchall with shelving. He brought her into the closet and dug through a stack of empty boxes, mismatched remote controls to TVs, cables, extension cords—those might be handy—and a small tool set. He flipped it open and decided the silver box filled with a multitude of things Brit could use as a weapon would remain in the closet, along with the set of knives from the kitchen and anything else he found she might arm herself with.

Perfect—his closet, his stash. Taking the extension cord, he led her out and shut the door, locking it.

Brit's eyes flitted to the cord in his hand and then to Colt. "What do you need that for?"

"To take a shower."

Confusion lined her pretty face. "I don't understand."

She'd figure it out soon enough. He led her around the corner of the wall toward the bedroom when he caught the empty phone jack. "How many land lines in this house?"

"In every bedroom."

"How many bedrooms, including phones?"

"Eight counting the complex." She pointed toward the olive-colored building across from the parking pad. "But no phones."

Nice. While he'd been doing time, Seth and his new wife were amassing a fortune and living the high life. Colt leaned against the door jamb. He guessed with cellphones there was no need to incur a phone bill. Although the Gentrys could afford it. A sharp pain shot through his chest, and he winced. His ribs were killing him, each breath an exhausting exercise he'd rather not perform. He grimaced at that. Living was preferable to dying, so he'd deal with the pain. The shower would ease some of it. He'd more than likely have to threaten Brit with his brute strength to get her to wrap his ribs and clean out his knee. Colt's jaw tensed. It wasn't who he was and it pissed him off.

Tomorrow he'd do a sweep of the entire complex—and that was how he saw it—with two full flights of stairs, either going up or down, and a posh indoor pool house with more bedrooms located across the parking pad. A wave of exhaustion came over him. He didn't resemble that Army Ranger sergeant who could sweep an entire Afghan village in a few hours with his elite fighting team. This thirty-eight-year-old body needed a few hours' sleep in the worst way—and to heal.

Damn. After a car wreck that could have easily ended his life, he should be thankful to be alive. He took a labored breath.

I am.

He wasn't going to make things easy on Seth by dying in shame. He moved Brit into the darkening bedroom and sat her down next to the pile of towels on the ottoman. He flipped the light on at the nightstand, a warm glow filling this side of the room.

There was only one way to keep her accounted for while he got washed up. He eyed the extension cord in his hand and grimaced at the thought of having to tie her up after what he'd witnessed in the kitchen earlier.

He couldn't do it.

Damn, the woman was becoming a pain in his ass. "You're taking a shower with me. Clothes are optional."

Chapter Five

BRIT SAT STONE-FACED ON THE TOILET OF THE EXPANSIVE bathroom with its oversized jetted tub while Colt kicked off a pair of worn work boots, taking a pair of bloody white socks with them.

He'd sat her there, directly in front of the shower door, fully dressed after she'd taken a combative stance with him about the shower thing.

"Don't make me regret my decision not to tie you up." He gingerly lifted off his gray T-shirt. "I'm thinking one panic attack is enough for the night."

Brit's gaze traveled up his narrow waist, the swirls of soft dark hair covering a well-defined stomach and chest until she locked onto a pair of interested eyes.

Shit. She'd been checking him out.

"Change your mind?" He unbuttoned his jeans and slipped out of them, along with his underwear.

"No," she choked back and turned her head.

The glass shower door thumped open and then closed with him chuckling amidst the spray of water from the showerhead. Brit peeked over her shoulder. Rivulets of water cascaded down the door. Even with the distorted view, she could still make out his naked body, and her own shuddered with awareness.

This is not happening, Brittany Dodd Gentry.

Colt Rivers was a bruising, hairy goliath—not her weekend fling. Jeez, she'd never even had a fling. Seth was the only man she'd ever slept with, the only man she loved. Too bad for her, she hadn't put her detective skills to good use when she'd first met him. She'd been blinded by the gallant, highly decorated and recently retired Army officer and basking in the glow of becoming one of the first female Maryland State Police counter-snipers at twenty-six. Marrying him, at the time, seemed more blessing than curse. *Ugh.* She had horrible taste in men.

Brit eyed the closed door to the bathroom. This was insane. There was nothing keeping her from bolting. She cursed at the criminal lathering up in the steamy shower she coveted for herself.

Brit glanced over at the unloaded gun he'd taken back from her and left sitting on the vanity. He'd stored the magazine and bullet in the closet, along with the set of knives and any other item she could use against him. But her keys remained in the front pocket, the silver flower keychain poking out, catching the light from the overhead fixture.

She needed her own gun with actual bullets. It would be the leverage necessary to get him to spill about the money she couldn't account for. Getting the brass off her back about that would be one less thing she'd have to worry about. He was keeping her on a string like a marionette, refusing to talk about it.

Brit gave a covert glance at the shower. He was busy shampooing his hair. She inched her foot toward the jeans, taking her eye off him when the toe of her boot snagged the pant leg.

"Not thinking of leaving?"

Brit jerked, pulled her foot back, and swung her head toward him. "No," she said through clenched teeth.

Colt wiped away the steam from the shower door, his distorted face unreadable.

Damn it.

She might as well resign herself to the fact she'd stay rooted to the toilet seat, afraid to move a muscle until he told her to. There was no way to get the key, open the door, escape to her truck, and retrieve her gun before he flew out of the shower in all his nakedness and caught her.

Okay. First she needed to keep her mouth shut. She'd already told him more than he needed to know, especially about her father.

Of course, he'd peppered her with questions. Like why she seemed prone to panic attacks.

Newsflash. I'm your hostage!

But it was more than that. She'd fled to the mountains for a reason. To get it together. That wasn't likely to happen. In fact, Sasquatch had only added another element of stress. Finding out who he was, what he *did* know about her, and his mysterious question about her finances was the only reason she remained glued to a toilet seat that was hurting her ass.

And, yeah, most women might flip out having a gun shoved in their faces and being carjacked and held hostage.

But she wasn't most women.

The door popped open, steam furling into the bathroom. Brit got one look at his muscular, hairy calf and turned her head. He rustled behind her, the friction of terry cloth against bare skin making her anxious.

"You can look."

Brit gritted her teeth. He made it sound like she wanted to. Okay. Maybe she did but without him knowing or judging her reaction. "You better be decent."

He gave a deep-throated laugh and bent down close to her ear. "I'm decent."

The intimate rasp of his voice unnerved her. He was way too close, too . . . She turned her head and swallowed. Too naked with only the towel wrapped around his narrow hips.

"Do you want to get a shower before bed?" His eyes lingered on her face.

"I didn't think I was allowed."

"I don't see any restraints on you."

Yeah, well, he was still a lot bigger, even with her jujitsu moves. Brit eased her body off the toilet seat, wary. "You going to watch?"

A sly smile curled his lips. "Not unless you want me to."

His words made her stomach flutter with unexpected awakening, and Brit moved away from him. "The only thing I want is my suitcase."

"Can't do that, sweetheart." His mouth twisted with what she thought was indecision. "Tell me what you need inside it."

Brit closed her eyes for a moment and took a deep breath. The thought of him digging through her lingerie with his rough, barbarian hands was, well, embarrassing. Fine. It was what it was. "Underwear, running bra"—no way was she going to be forced to sleep next to him without it—"flannel pajamas."

"Anything else?"

Yeah, now that she thought about it. "There's a pair of men's pajamas for you in the chest at the end of the bed."

His lips quirked. "Appreciate you thinking of me."

Right. He knew damned well she was thinking of herself.

"I'll be in the bedroom gathering your things." He scooped up his clothes, including her coveted set of keys, and slipped out, shutting the door.

Brit's legs shook. She'd like to blame it on the odd position she'd been sitting in. But with everything she'd endured over the past several weeks, she knew differently. Brit took a seat on the toilet again. She couldn't afford another attack and waited for the dizziness to pass. She stood slowly and then balanced on one foot and unzipped her boot and then the other, tossing them onto the floor. She slipped off her sweater and the lacey cami. Her body grew cold, the hot shower awaiting her that much more appealing. She stripped off her jeans and shirt.

The door creaked open. Brit sucked in air, holding her flimsy camisole to her chest, and tried to cover up her lacey bra with its plunging cups. She relaxed a fraction when only Colt's hand reached inside the bathroom with her clothes and toiletry bag—that was half open—dangling off his fingers. Brit snatched her belongings. Figured he'd go through those, too.

The door shut, and Brit set her clothes down on the toilet seat. She gathered what she needed from the bag, her shampoo—not the leftover bar of soap from a recent guest Colt had used for his entire body—conditioner, and soap. Starting the tap, she tested the water with her toes and unhooked her bra. The straps slipped down her shoulders, and she took it off along with her thong before stepping under the hot spray of the shower. She let the water pulse along her back, which had stiffened up, and washed her hair. There would be no luxuriating in the steamy warmth. Brit quickly scrubbed the grime and nervous sweat from her body and stepped out, relieved the water hadn't turned blood red.

Grabbing a clean towel, she dried off, combed her hair, and slipped on her underwear and the pajamas. She unscrewed the lip balm from her bag and applied a thin layer. Squaring her shoulders, she then grabbed her stuff and opened the door. Colt sat on the edge of the bed still in the towel, tearing a bedsheet into strips.

"What are you doing?" Brit dropped her things on the chair. Before he was done, he'd have them barricaded in with police bullets chipping away at the furniture. "Stop destroying my house."

"It's a lousy sheet, Brit. I'll buy you a new one," he slung back.

Brit looped around the ottoman and froze. Sweat dotted his brow. Odd for a man who had just taken a shower in a house that was only now starting to warm up. He must have found the thermostat outside the bedroom.

"What's wrong?"

A pair of distrustful green eyes nailed her. "Don't act like you care about me."

She shouldn't. But he'd helped her earlier today. She frowned. Although she'd probably had the panic attack *because* of him.

Brit took the sheet from him. "I'll tear the rest."

He nodded, grimacing, as his arm came around his abdomen.

"Hurts, huh?"

"Only when I breathe."

Brit finished with the sheet, ripping it into four-inch strips. "Lift up your arms."

He held them out, and Brit knelt down on the bed. She wrapped one strip around his chest and knotted it. She took it several more times around him, tightening as she went. "How's that feel?"

"Like a suit of armor," he groused.

She shook her head. "Then you're in luck. Jousting is the state sport."

He gave her a half smile. "You're funny."

"And you're in pain." Brit eased off the bed and rummaged through her bag until she came up with her bottle of Advil. She grabbed the cup from the bathroom sink, filled it, and brought the pills to him. "Take them."

He eyed them and then her. "Four?"

"Yes, four. You probably tip the scales at . . ." She tried to size him up.

"Two thirty."

She handed him the pills.

"Thanks." He swallowed them.

Brit set the cup on the nightstand and busied herself with the bandage, trying to block out the smooth touch of his warm skin and the dusting of hair sprinkling his torso. "How many do you think are broken?"

Colt snorted. "Not sure I should be divulging that information."

He had a point. But there were other things she could determine. Brit placed her hand on his forehead. His skin radiated heat.

"I'm burning up." He wasn't talking about his internal settings, she didn't think, based on the lopsided smile he gave her.

Brit's heart sped up. "The Advil should help."

"Don't think so, doc."

"Let me take a look at your knee." Brit's butt dropped onto the ottoman at the corner of the bed. "Can you slide over for me?"

He angled his body, his thighs straddling hers. "Tried to dig it out in the shower."

Brit sucked air in through her teeth. More like he'd made a raw mess of his flesh. "It should be stitched."

"No hospital," he snapped.

She gave him one of her *you gotta be kidding* looks.

"Guess we've already been over that."

She patted his good knee. "Let's get some more light on it." She got up, unscrewed the lampshade, and brought the lightbulb above his knee. The wound sparkled back. "You didn't get all of it." She handed him the lamp. "Hold this up."

He took it from her, and Brit dug into her bag, grunting. She had so much crap inside. She pulled out the large bottle of Advil and her sewing kit until she finally found the tweezers.

"Ah . . . a needle and thread. You're not serious." Colt gave a nervous laugh.

"Not unless you want me to puke, buddy." She chuckled.

Even as a first responder, she didn't think she could stitch him up with her needle and thread. She only had it in case she lost a button. Besides, after her little episode in the kitchen, she was in no condition to attempt it.

Brit handed him the tweezers. "Hold this."

"Wha—"

"There's some whiskey under the bar."

He gave her a pained expression. "You thinking of toasting to my demise?"

Brit ignored him and dashed from the room. She grabbed the bottle of whiskey under the cabinet and flew back across the foyer into the bedroom. "Antiseptic."

Colt frowned at her. "You're crazy, Gentry."

"And you aren't as tough as you look." Brit took up her post on the ottoman again. She unscrewed the bottle, snatched the tweezers between his fingers, and dipped the metal inside the bronze-colored liquid. Recapping the bottle, she put it down for now and picked the glittering pieces of glass from the gaping, bloody tissue of his knee while Colt groaned through the procedure.

"That doesn't bother you?" His hand clenched the edge of the bed.

"What?" She continued to pick out tiny pieces of glass.

"The blood?"

Huh? Brit guessed she wasn't feeling threatened at the moment— threatened by him.

"I'm sorry for *earlier*." A groan escaped his lips.

"That was a deep one." Hands stilling on his knee, she gave him a curious look. "Earlier?"

"Making you have that panic attack."

"You could make up for it by telling me what you want."

He seemed to mull that over. "You have them a lot?"

Today she was deserving of one. Maybe tomorrow, too, if she didn't get some straight answers.

Brit took a heavy breath. "Look." She stared at him purposely. "You might have removed the gun from the equation, but I'm still a hostage. I'm only here because you've made it your business to stake out my house and then follow me up here. And, yes, *damn it*. Everything I own is free and clear."

"You don't know where the money came from, *do ya?*" he said with contempt.

Brit's mouth fell open. Totally done with him and a conversation she didn't want to have, she again uncapped the whiskey. Her eyes narrowed, and without giving him a heads-up, she poured a liberal amount into his wound.

"*Christ.*" His knee jerked.

"You don't want an infection, *do ya?*" She gave him a cheeky smile.

He leveled an accusing gaze her way. "You're a sadistic woman, Brit Gentry."

And he was a lot of things she couldn't say out loud.

"Just hold still," she snapped and took the roll of gauze out of her bag and began wrapping his wound. If he had it in his mind that she was going to level with him, he was wrong. He obviously didn't know she was a cop. Whoever he was, whatever his troubles were, that reality could change what she had going with him. She considered that for a moment. What exactly was going on between them? Whatever it was, it seemed they both held some part of a puzzle the other needed. She knew the piece she needed. Him? Not so much.

"Trouble in paradise?" Colt's voice was low and controlled, his thumb rubbing the pale line of her ring finger resting on his knee.

Brit pulled her hand away and stood. "It's none of your business." She turned to escape him and the memory of a beautiful gold band and matching diamond engagement ring.

He grabbed her hand. "I'm sorry. But judging from your reaction I guessed right."

Exactly. He didn't know everything there was to know about her, just the existence of a husband. Brit rubbed her bare finger. There was a time when she'd treasured the rings and their symbolism. *Rings.* She gritted her teeth. Seth had lost his wedding band for over a year, and he hadn't seemed the least bit upset about it. Not enough to search for it or buy a new one to replace it.

Brit cleared her head. She needed to let it go. She had more important things to worry about tonight than a ring that meant nothing now and Colt

Rivers snooping.

Brit shook his hand off. "Were you serious about our sleeping arrangements?"

Chapter Six

S O MUCH FOR A LITTLE GRATITUDE FOR PATCHING HIM UP. At least he'd used the leftover strips from the bedsheet to tie her wrists together instead of the thick extension cord.

Colt limped around the bed in a pair of blue flannel pajama bottoms and white T-shirt, compliments of Seth. "It's only while I sleep." He gave her an apologetic smile and climbed into bed, dark circles ringing his eyes. "I'm beat."

She wanted to snap out of it, this warm, cozy scene with him. It was ludicrous. No more than twelve hours ago, he'd taken her against her will, held a gun to her head more than once.

He rolled the covers down, took the last of the strips, and began tying her ankle to his.

"Is that really necessary?" Brit remained close to the edge of her side of the bed in a sitting position. The distance she'd created, a moot point now that he'd bound them together.

"Can you honestly tell me you won't run, given the chance?"

He had her there. Even the unexplained pull he had on her wasn't enough to keep her here. If she could find a way to escape him, she would— once she had her gun and he'd answered a few of *her* questions. Then she'd alert the barrack and have Pete arrest him. She wanted to stay as detached from the situation as possible. She grimaced. That was a joke. She was intricately involved in this one, too. Thanks to Colt.

"I can read your mind, beautiful." He finished with whatever crazy knot he was making and pulled the covers back up, smoothing them over her, and then fluffed her pillow.

Brit's blood pressure rose with every tweak of the down feathers. "Stop it!" She swung on him, hands up and bound by the wrists. "Tell me why."

"Tell me who Andi Hall is," he said pointedly.

Andi?

Shit. The call from earlier on her cell. Damn iPhones and their call and text reminders. It didn't matter if the phone was locked or not. You could still see the notifications once you tapped the phone. Good thing she was listed as just "Andi Hall" in her contacts. Otherwise, she'd have a lot more explaining to do. *Damn it.* She might be able to skirt this question. But there would be other calls coming in over the course of the week. Even with the lock on her screen, if he wanted to listen to her voice mail, his size dictated her full cooperation.

Although she believed him when he'd said he didn't want to hurt her. So how far could she push him before he did?

"It's a simple question."

Brit shrugged. "Just a friend."

"Uh huh." He shimmied toward his side of the bed, taking her leg with him.

The strain on her body made it impossible to remain in her safe zone, and she moved toward the middle on her butt.

He grunted and reached for the lamp on the nightstand, turning it off. "Honesty works both ways." He lay down.

Awesome. Brit let her head hit the pillow with a thud and went to punch it. She came up short, nailing her shoulder with both her fists. His laughter filled the dusky lit bedroom. She angled her head toward him, her eyes blazing. Not that he could tell. The moonlight from the sliding glass door— the storm had moved out hours ago—only cast them in a shadowy glow. But it was enough for her to make out his profile. His eyes were closed.

Nice he could settle down before bed. She'd helped him, too, with her Florence Nightingale act. Brit took a deep breath through her nose and concentrated on relaxing her muscles. She needed a few hours' sleep if she expected to function tomorrow. She shook her head. With this new drama, she'd all but forgotten the crises she'd left back on the eastern shore.

She didn't know how much more she could take before she really lost it.

Colt's breathing slowed, his chest moving in even waves. Brit wagged her fingers, trying to gain some dexterity. If she could reach the knot at her wrist, she might be able to work it free. Brit gritted her teeth. Whoever this guy was, he knew a thing or two about knots and, this was important, how to tie one's hands. No way was she going to be able to reach the knot. It was physically impossible. Now her ankle would be easy enough.

Brit eased up from her pillow to a sitting position. Keeping as little tension as she could on the blanket, she gave it some slack and pulled up on her side of the bed, easing it off. The cool air hit her feet, and she glanced back to see if Colt had stirred.

Nope. Like a hibernating bear, he snored soundly. Brit picked at the knot with her fingers, silently cursing her stubby nails.

Brit rolled her lips in and concentrated. Unlike a rope, the material from the cotton sheet was flimsy, making it easy to cinch down. She couldn't get the smallest amount of give or light to help her out. Brit's fingers slipped, landing on the top of his foot. She froze when he moved, but not before she noted the heat coming off his skin.

His fever was back.

Brit took her hand off one finger at a time and pulled the blanket up in increments. She lay back, taking her time, until her head touched her pillow. A chill raced across her skin. She wouldn't escape him tonight.

Okay. I'm stuck for the night next to sleeping Sasquatch.

Her lips quirked, and she angled her head toward him. Maybe he wasn't ugly. He had a nice profile—the hair thing notwithstanding. *Great.* She was actually attracted to him. How screwed up was that?

Go to sleep. I'm trying.

Brit settled her head into her pillow and closed her eyes, her mind picking up images of that night in September. This little retreat was to help her remember, give her perspective, and allow her to put a finger on the precise moment she pulled the trigger. Afraid she would fall asleep and wake up screaming—a scenario that had played out several times since the shooting—her eyes sprang open.

She should strategize on how she was going to retrieve her gun. But first she needed her damn keys. Brit tried to relax lying next to him, his even breaths more hypnotic than threatening She yawned, her eyelids becoming heavy.

She also needed to stop considering his needs.

Brit settled her head into the down pillow. Her eyes shut, and she floated toward sleep.

"Go, go, go, go, go!"

Brit jerked in her sleep, her eyes flying open. *What the hell?* She was snuggled up to a restless, clammy body. Chest hair tickled her nose, the weight of an arm curved around her back. But it was the warm fingers tucked inside the waistband of her pajama bottoms that made her heart race.

Sasquatch. Oh, God. She must have rolled into him during the night. Brit inched away, the heat of embarrassment warming her face.

Colt's arm tightened around her. "We need air support." His voice was clipped.

Shit.

What Colt Rivers wouldn't confess to her in the light of day rushed from his lips with undeniable clarity in the dark of night.

Brit's pulse thudded at her temples. She'd lived with PTSD since marrying Seth. It had been something she was unprepared for. He'd never warned her. She'd rode out many a fitful night, trying to comfort him. She hadn't been successful then and seriously doubted she could do any better for a man she didn't know.

"You fuckin' kidding me?" He thrashed. "No Hotel Echo."

"Colt." She nudged his shoulder with her bound hands. "Wake up."

Nothing.

"We're pinned down."

The light cascading in from the glass slider illuminated his contorted face with, was it anger . . . desperation . . . or fear? Fear for his men and himself.

She wanted to curse. She had veterans from the war on terror coming at her from all directions—Seth, Beau, and now Colt. Not that she could say definitively he was a vet or still active. Either way, he had definitely seen action, and for that she could muster up a little compassion.

This guy had problems.

"Gotta pull back, gotta pull back," he said on a labored breath. His body was hot and slick with sweat.

Brit frowned. It wasn't just a PTSD episode she was dealing with. His temperature had spiked.

"Goddamned war," he said through clenched teeth before his head jerked. "Sullivan's down! Gentry, did you hear me? Sullivan's hit!" He flew up to a sitting position, taking Brit along with him. His eyes popped open. "Brit?" he said, dazed.

"You had a nightmare." That was all she could manage, her mind still reeling on one word—Gentry.

"I'm thirsty."

"Your fever's back." Brit held up her bound hands. "I can't help you unless you untie me."

He remained quiet. She guessed weighing that one and only option.

"I won't leave you." She meant it. *God, please have my head examined.* She really did mean it. Must be her sixth sense. He could have done a lot of things to her by now. He hadn't. "Colt, untie my hands."

He nodded and took hold of her wrists. Digging at the knot, he then loosened it and unwrapped the strips of cloth.

"Our ankles."

Without a word, he pulled down the blankets and bent over. A moan rolled up his chest. She assumed the motion hurt his ribs. Undeterred, he gritted his teeth through the pain and untied their ankles.

Brit made a move to get up.

His warm hand grabbed her arm. "You're not dressed for the elements."

This guy really had trust issues. But it wasn't his distrustful nature that surprised her. She got the feeling he was worried she'd freeze out in the elements if she did take off. It had to be in the twenties. The mountains could be fifteen to twenty degrees colder than the eastern shore where she lived.

Brit put the back of her hand against his forehead. *Too warm.*

"Lay down. I'll get you some water." She climbed out, stepped into the bathroom, and turned on the light. Illumination extended out into the bedroom. He lay back down but remained fitful.

Strange. He'd been hot hours earlier. She hadn't thought too much about the timing before. But she didn't think he'd show symptoms of infection that soon after suffering lacerations to his body.

She filled the cup at the sink and grabbed her bottle of Advil from her bag on the floor in the bedroom, all the while wondering if something else was going on. Brit shook out five pills this time.

She neared the bed and sat down next to him. "Can you sit up and take this?"

His eyes opened. They were etched in discomfort and maybe confusion.

"It's okay." She handed him the pills, then the water.

He swallowed them and handed her back the half empty cup that shook slightly in his hand.

"All of it."

He downed it, sat the cup on the nightstand, giving her a wary look. "No cyanide?"

She shrugged. "I didn't think I'd need it this trip."

He eased off his elbows, dropping back into the bed. A half smile tugged at his mouth. "You're hilarious."

He wouldn't think so tomorrow. She'd connected a dot. Seth had been an Army Ranger, Second Battalion, Delta Company. Now that she thought about it, Colt Rivers could pass for a member of the elite special ops fighting force. She'd seen photos of Seth's comrades—not Colt specifically. But they were scruffy like him. What were the odds Colt knew another guy named Gentry?

Or that he'd kidnapped a woman with the same last name.

For now, she'd work on getting him coherent before she blasted him for terrorizing her. First, it started with getting him warm and dry. She'd noticed his chills earlier.

"The wraps need to go."

He stared down his nose at his chest.

"They're soaked." She touched the damp edge of his T-shirt. "This, too." Brit eased it over his chest and motioned with her chin. "Lift up, and I'll pull it over your head."

He complied with a groan and remained sitting but awkwardly like he was trying to take the weight off his right side. Brit unknotted the edge of the top strip and unwrapped it, doing the same for the next. The more of him she exposed, the more uncomfortable it became. He was hot and it wasn't only the temperature of his skin. He obviously worked out and had the muscles to show for it.

She held the damp bandages in both hands. "I'll have to rewrap you tomorrow."

He nodded, eyes heavy, and rolled over. But not before she got a nice shot of his ass where the pajama pants had slid down, exposing a pattern of nasty infected puncture wounds.

"Whoa." She grabbed his left hip and slipped down the pants farther. Definitely an older wound. "Where'd you get this?" She touched the red skin around it.

He grimaced. "Dog bite."

"When?"

"When I stole the car."

"The one you totaled?" She arched a speculative brow at him.

He looked over his shoulders, exhaustion and pain evident in his eyes. "Yeah." He swatted her hand away. "You done?"

Brit wished she was done with him. She was digging a bigger hole the longer she was in his felonious company. But if he knew something she didn't about her husband, it would be in her best interest to find out. She couldn't afford to have something else blow up on her.

Looked like Colt Rivers would now be her welcome houseguest and her obstinate patient for the foreseeable future.

Brit stood from the bed.

"Where you going?"

"You're in luck." She pulled the covers back up over his chest. "I packed amoxicillin." It was always *her* luck to get a sinus infection whenever she went away. It wasn't a whole course, but it might be enough to rid his body of infection.

Brit checked his forehead and frowned. The thought of giving him a sponge bath to help with his fever seemed way too intimate a task, considering he was a complete stranger. But the quicker she got him on his feet, found out exactly what he knew and wanted from her, the quicker she would be rid of him.

Chapter Seven

CURIOUSLY BRIT STOOD OVER COLT RIVERS'S SLEEPING form, tapping a finger to her lips. She'd given him a dose of amoxicillin, moved him over to her side of the bed where it was dry after helping him into a new T-shirt. She nixed the whole sponge bath. No way was she going to subject herself to touching him. He'd already jumped to a wild ass conclusion earlier in the bathroom. Well, maybe not in words. But his eyes told her all she needed to know.

Brit shook her head. She shouldn't have been checking him out before he'd hopped in the shower. She hadn't been. At least, not on purpose, anyway.

You keep telling yourself that.

This wasn't a case of Stockholm syndrome. She didn't identify with him. Yes, she'd done her best to make him think she had. But it was all an attempt at escape. Then why hadn't she left? Because Colt Rivers knew something about Seth that could help her explain a sailboat they could never afford and Memory Maker, a house she could only dream of owning.

Seth had told her it was his inheritance. Nice of him to check out and leave her front and center of a financial disclosure investigation with no answers as to where the money came from.

Colt's chest rose and fell under the thick comforter. Whether he knew it or not, she would never be his hostage again. Brit shoved Colt's handgun into the waistband of her jeans and tucked the extra key to the closet in her front pocket. Thank God she remembered the junk drawer in the kitchen. A smile touched her lips—patience, cool-headed thinking, and opportunity. The prospect could only have presented itself here at Memory Maker where he'd feel relatively safe.

He'd sleep for a few hours—enough time for her to do a little investigating about him. Brit slipped out of the bedroom and took the stairs to the basement. She entered the dark computer room that doubled as a bedroom with a pullout sofa bed and felt around for the desk chair. She swung it around and sat down. Good thing he hadn't followed through with his tour of her swank mountain home. Brit booted up the mini-computer. With all her digging into Seth's past, she never considered his military service. She'd met him during the tail end of his career. He'd been about to retire with military honors.

Seth had never mentioned anyone by the name of Rivers. But she had a sneaking suspicion Rivers knew him. If he'd come looking for her husband, he would have only found her. So what did Colt think she knew that he didn't?

The computer's light filled the small room with an eerie blue glow. Brit typed the words "Colt Rivers US Army Ranger."

She snorted and sat back, shaking her head as she read the list of search entries. The first one said it all.

SOLDIER ESCAPES US DISCIPLINARY BARRACKS FORT LEAVENWORTH, KANSAS, VIA GARBAGE TRUCK.

Brit calculated the current date and that of the article—almost three weeks ago—when the floorboards creaked above her. She unscrewed the monitor, throwing her into darkness, and then scrabbled for the plug under the desk, jerking it from the wall to the mini-tower. With the cord and tower, she bolted through the laundry room next door and into an adjoining utility room. She shut the door and flicked on the light. The room was filled with extra lamps, broken chairs, and a rollaway bed. Brit popped the strap to it and shoved the tower inside the thin mattress, and then muscled the strap closed.

Heart in her throat, she turned off the light, shut the door, and moved out into the living and recreation room. She rushed up the stairs, made a sharp turn on the landing, and took the last four steps until she reached the main level and the foyer. A toilet flushed. *Shit.* She should have known he'd have to pee after drinking all that water. Brit waited to the left of the bedroom doorway, hidden in shadows until the light went off in the bathroom. In only his pajama bottoms, Colt padded across the carpet, limping. Brit slipped in behind him, grabbing the throw at the end of the bed.

"Brit?" he whispered, then paused, tossing his head over his shoulder.

"I got cold." She took up a spot on the overstuffed chair and ottoman, making sure to cover her clothes in case he flipped on the light.

It was dark, he was still in pain, and it would seem he had a modicum of trust where she was concerned.

He lowered himself onto the bed. "You're still here."

"I made you a promise." His gun dug into her back, and she adjusted her hip.

The glint of the moon picked up the mass of unruly hair when he eased his head down onto the pillow. "Not too many keep them," he said with despondency.

Brit weighed his words. He was a fugitive. She couldn't afford to feel sorry for him. What she needed were answers. "We're in this together now. Will you tell me what all this is about tomorrow?"

Only deep, steady breaths responded back in the shadows.

Her head fell back. *Great.* What a waste of training that was. She checked the clock on the nightstand—4:37. Brit remained in the chair, doing her damnedest to stay awake while he sawed wood in the bed next to her. She wanted to have the advantage at daybreak. Her head nodded, lids drooping. She took a breath and opened her eyes wide.

Don't fall asleep.

Swaddled in blankets, Brit had the sensation of weightlessness. Something warm and substantial rested against her cheek, her fingers inexplicably exploring soft swirls of hair. Brit opened her eyes.

"Good morning, beautiful." Colt smiled down at her.

Brit stiffened. She'd been delving into his chest hairs while he held her to him. "Put me down."

"How about a few more hours' sleep?"

Oh, her body craved it in the worst way. But she was more interested in keeping the gun jabbing into her back a secret. "I'm fine. Put me down," she snapped.

He dumped her on the bed.

Brit kicked off the blanket, reached behind her, and jerked the gun out.

"Shit." Colt backed up.

"Shit is right, and I've had it with yours." She was so mad the gun shook in her hands.

"Whoa." He put his hands up. "Brit, a gun's nothing to play with."

Play with . . .

"Why don't you ease your finger off the trigger before you hurt someone?" His brows rose in unison.

Hilarious. He thought she was going to accidentally shoot him. "My finger's on the trigger guard."

"That's not the trigger guard," he said anxiously.

"It's not?" She gave him a look of surprise and then extended her arms out with the gun. "Then maybe you better sit down." She stood and waved the firearm at him. "And tell me what's going on before I . . ." She looked at the gun like she hadn't a clue and then at him. "Shoot you."

He sat down on the ottoman, and for the first time real fear filled those green eyes of his. "Seth Gentry is your husband." He looked at her like she would deny it.

"You already know that."

"I know you're the only Gentry living on Shore Drive."

Damn it. The black compact. She'd seen it before.

"What would a fugitive from Leavenworth want with my husband?"

He chuckled nervously. "You found me out."

She would have found out a lot more had he not woken up to take a piss.

"Answer the question."

"You have nice things, Brit."

"I'm the woman with the gun, remember." She kept it out in front and stepped around him, moving toward the door. "What's your rank, soldier?"

He shook his head with exasperation. "Sergeant Colt Rivers, Army Rangers, Second Battalion, Delta Company, ma'am."

She'd figured as much. "Who's Sullivan?"

"Sullivan?" His expression darkened. "Seth tell you about him?"

"No. You did last night."

"He was in our company."

"Did he make it?" Her foot caught the corner of the suitcase, and Brit tottered.

"Jesus!" Colt jumped up.

Brit jerked the gun up, pointing it at his chest. "Don't move."

"Then watch what the hell you're doing." He scrubbed the back of his neck. "You want answers, sweetheart. I'll give you them. Your husband killed Sullivan. He let him die while he and another in our fireteam ransacked a plane bound for Kabul."

"What are you talking about?"

"We did an airfield takedown on a small airport in Badakhshan Province. Must have missed a sniper on the roof."

"You couldn't call for a medevac?"

"Now that was a novel idea," he said dryly. "Only my job was to pick off the Taliban fighter on the roof." He shook his head. "You're missing the point, Brit."

She got the point. He was a sniper for one. Two, if Colt was telling the truth, Seth was not the charming, honorable Army Ranger he'd claimed. It had been one of the reasons she'd been attracted to him—honor like her dad—besides the obvious blond Adonis thing he had going. What a fool she'd been.

"But you went to prison."

"Because I was a threat. Not because I was guilty."

"I don't understand."

"Put the gun down, and I'll explain it to you."

She laughed, the sound mocking. "You jackass. Don't like looking down the end of a barrel?"

"I'm a trained marksman. If I had wanted you dead—"

"Cut the crap, Rivers."

"Four-man team. You with me?"

She nodded.

"One down. Two in the hangar. One picking off a lone sniper." He took a step toward her. "When I found Lt. Gentry—my buddy, the one who was supposed to have my back and everyone's on the team—he was pilfering a metal cargo container from Norway that was bound for Kabul and the Afghanistan National Museum."

"You're saying he stole what was in it?"

"It being filled with centuries old artifacts—gems worn by kings, goblets, stone tablets—worth millions."

Brit tried to process the information. They'd have to get it from this airport to what . . . their post? Then what? Stone tablets like the size of Moses's is all she could picture. Those suckers were big—at least in the movie. "How would you hide something like that?"

He shrugged. "He and Danner—the fourth team member—loaded up their packs."

"And you?"

"That wasn't what I signed up for." He looked around. "It takes most people years to pay off a third of what you have."

She knew what he was getting at. It made her sick to her stomach. The vacation home was free and clear—had always been since they built it two years ago—thanks to Seth's inheritance that just kept giving.

"Makes you think."

"Excuse me?"

"Your wealth."

She never thought of herself as wealthy. She'd worked hard for the money she had. This cabin—not that it even came close to a modest mountain chalet—had been Seth's. His money, his baby. Although, he had put her name on it, too. But Brit rarely came here after it had been built, until recently. As a financial advisor, Seth loved to lavish his clients with a weekend retreat at Memory Maker. Regale them with his war stories. Only she doubted this was one of them.

"Still doesn't explain why *you* went to prison."

"Over a lousy two by three metal box and a thing called a conscience."

"I'm confused."

"I gave them twenty-four hours to turn themselves in." He shook his head. "Seth turned me in instead."

Brit's mouth opened slightly. "But you said you didn't take part."

"Kind of hard to deny something like that when they find a missing emerald necklace worn by some Muslim prophet in your gear." He took a seat on the ottoman and put his head in his hands. "I got nine in Leavenworth. Your husband walked away with a fortune."

"What about this Dannon?"

"Danner." He gave her a sideways glance. "Never made it home."

The authorities had to be looking all over for these artifacts. It would be like stealing the *Mona Lisa* and looking for a buyer. "Who would risk buying stolen artifacts?"

"Black market."

There was that.

Brit's shoulders slumped. "I can't help you."

"Tell me where he is."

If only she could. Brit squared her shoulders. "I want my keys."

"I want my life back," he snapped. "Your husband is the only one who can do that for me." He took a step toward her.

The desperation in his eyes frightened her. She had a fair idea how he was feeling. Seth had screwed her, too. If what he was saying was true, she'd bet the whole Monopoly board that her house on the shore, the sailboat, and this over-the-top, eight-bedroom mountain mansion with its indoor pool, movie theater, sauna, and coveted view of the lake was built from the stolen spoils of war Seth had no business taking.

Just like Colt, she was going to be the one busted on this financial disclosure investigation—not Seth.

Brit nudged the gun forward. "Out the door."

"You're making a mistake, Brit. Just tell me where he is."

"Out!"

He put his hands up and moved past her and into the great room. She waved the gun at him. "Last time. Give me my keys."

"I can't do that." Sweat beaded his forehead.

"Then go, get dressed, and do what an Army Ranger does: survive without me."

He gave her a knowing look. "You're in this just as deep as me."

He didn't know the half of it. Colt Rivers could hurt her on so many levels. *Damn it.* She shouldn't feel the least bit responsible for what had happened to him. He was obstinate and sick and a freakin' fugitive who was probably telling the truth. *God.* She couldn't afford to get sucked into his tornadic life. If he wouldn't leave, she would.

Brit swung open the closet door she'd left unlocked. "Get in."

He stood his ground.

"Get in." She waved the gun at him erratically, giving him every indication she was an accidental shooting waiting to happen.

"You're making a mistake." Favoring his left side, where he'd been bit, he walked in.

Brit shut the door and locked it amidst his appeals to reconsider. She shoved the gun into the back waistband of her jeans and grabbed a coat from her suitcase in the bedroom. This was insane. She left out the sliding glass door in the dining room and down the deck steps and into the woods.

She dodged tree trunks, passing the decks and sharp-gabled rooflines of several homes. It wasn't just Colt and his screwed up life she needed to escape. It was her past, specifically the last night that she and Seth were together. She'd blocked it out for months. Simply telling Colt the truth wouldn't make him go away. At least she didn't think. She was his only link to Seth, his only hope of proving his innocence.

No, no, no, no, no!

He was *not* her only hope of proving hers when it came to the unexplained wealth. If they didn't believe him at his court-martial, why would they believe him now? No, his existence could only hurt her defense.

Brit jammed her hands into her pockets. Even with the sun streaming through spindly branches high above, it was cold. Something hard skimmed her knuckles, and Brit twined her fingers through the familiar chain of her

St. Christopher medal. She'd been searching for it for months. Her father wore it religiously until he retired. He'd given it to her when she'd graduated from the academy. It was supposed to keep her safe.

It wasn't doing a very good job of it.

Brit slowed her pace. She had enough of a head start to get to the main road. From there the plan was fuzzy; she just needed to get away from Colt Rivers. That dude was a major complication, one she didn't need right now. Getting the guys from the McHenry barrack involved didn't seem to be in her best interest either.

Her breaths came in waves, her mind full of indecision. She dodged fallen tree branches and stumps. Tripping could break her ankle.

A spring gurgled, cutting a serpentine path down the mountainside The lake shimmered to her right, and dead ahead a black bear and her two cubs drank from a spring running down the mountainside.

Holy shit!

Brit froze, her fingers a death grip on the medal.

Chapter Eight

*L*OSING HIS ONLY ACE IN THE HOLE WASN'T AN OPTION. Brit was a fool to think she could walk away from this thing. Colt continued to work the tiny screw of the doorknob with the screwdriver from the silver tool kit.

From what he gathered, someone, the IRS or maybe her employer, was looking into her and Seth's finances. She probably worked for some financial institution. He could see her sitting behind some fancy, ornate desk in some high rise in one of those dick teasing tight skirts and snug blouses that showed off her pert breasts.

Yeah, he was attracted to her. But it was a lot more than looks for him. He had been in no condition last night to keep her from leaving. Once he untied her, she didn't have to hang around and nurse him.

His ass cheek still throbbed. But it was bearable. And if he had a fever, he'd guess it was a mild one. He needed one good day where he could sit on his ass, preferably the right side, to be worth a damn.

It wouldn't happen today. By the time he located her and brought her back, he'd be starting at square one when it came to his health. The knob fell into his hands, and he pulled out the inner mechanism in the hole and opened it.

He rushed into the bedroom, jerked open the chest at the end of the bed, and slipped on a pair of, he guessed, Seth's jeans. After tying his boots, he retrieved the keys to the truck and her phone from a sooty shelf in the fireplace and headed out with a thick flannel shirt he'd grabbed off a hook in the hall closet. Colt sniffed and wrinkled his nose at the strong scent of cologne. Personally, he didn't wear the stuff. Soap and water did him just fine.

He came up on the front door and the combination pad that he still didn't have the code for and left the front door cracked before he hopped in the truck. He turned on the ignition, stomping on the gas. The truck lurched and something clunked next to him. Keeping his hand on the wheel, he headed up the drive and lifted the lid of the center console. He did a double take, then hit the brake.

"Son of a bitch." He hefted out a Glock semi-automatic sitting next to a roll of butter rum Life Savers and checked the magazine—fully loaded with jacketed hollow points. *Shit.* These weren't your average bullets. Made to expand upon impact for maximum damage, had she gotten a shot off, she would have killed him.

Colt stepped on the gas again. When he caught up with her, she had a lot of explaining to do.

He traveled Marsh Hill Road, looking for her and that familiar blond spiraling hair. He passed a few cars on the way down, his eyes banking from one side of the narrow mountain road to the other. Still no Brit. But he'd seen at least half a dozen metal trash containers. With the amount of traffic, he'd guess fall was low season until the slopes opened. Probably not too many people or too much garbage this time of year. A person could hunker down in one of those things. So the thought of her diving into a trash Dumpster if she spotted him wasn't out of the realm of possibilities. *Damn it.* He swung around, making a U-turn, and hopped out at the first one. Once he unlatched it, he peered in the dark abyss, gagging.

"Ah, excuse me."

Colt jerked his head up. A woman, he'd estimate in her fifties, stood in a pair of thick-soled slippers with a winter coat thrown on.

Her eyes darted from her trash can to the weapon in his hand he'd forgotten to secure in his haste. "You have a gun."

He eased the lid down. "I can ex—"

"Come quick," she said on a rush She motioned him down the macadam driveway. "I was having coffee, enjoying the view from my deck when a woman—I think she's my neighbor—came upon a black bear and her cubs."

"Blond?"

"I think so."

"Where!" He grabbed her arm.

Her eyes widened through a pair of oblong glasses. "In front of my house."

Colt released her and took off down the driveway, his destination the lake.

"I'll call DNR," she hollered after him.

DNR?

He'd learned long ago acronyms were never a good thing, and Colt stopped cold at the corner of her luxury home. He knew what DNRC stood for in Montana. "What's DNR?"

She ran up to him, hugging her coat around her. "Natural Resources Police."

Fuck!

"Ma'am, there's no time. I need you to grab a pot and the largest metal spoon you have and bang it as loud as you can on your deck."

"*Oh.*" Her hand flew to her mouth. "Of course." She ran toward her front door, then glanced back with one of those excited do-gooder expressions curling her lips. "I'll be right out."

He nodded and moved out down the side of her house and through the thicket of trees with the neighbor lady clanging away. He shook his head. Growing up near Glacier National Park, Colt knew from experience her efforts would amount to a big fat zero. But it would keep her engaged and off the phone.

Colt did a sweep of the area in front of him and recognized Brit on her butt several yards away. What the hell? She was inching herself backward while a black bear ambled toward her.

Damn it, woman, get up.

"Nice mama bear," she pleaded.

Although he wasn't a proponent of shooting a mother bear with her cubs, Brit had the gun. Why wasn't she using it?

Colt got himself into position and fired off a round into the ground. It rocked the air around him, and mama made an about-face along with her cubs and hightailed it in the opposite direction.

Brit dropped onto her back, laughing.

He pushed past pickers, thrashed through the leaves, and dropped down next to her. "What is so goddamned funny?"

"Oh, my God," she said breathlessly. "I almost died." She peered up at him, looking alien with her big brown eyes upside down. "You ever clean this damned thing?" She pulled herself up to a sitting position and handed his gun to him in pieces. "The guide rod's out of whack."

"Were you limp wristing it when you tried to shoot?" He juggled the gun in one hand.

Her brows snapped together. "*No*," she said somewhat indignant.

He pulled her up.

"Whoa, big, bad Army Ranger," she said, grimacing. "My ankle's killing me."

"You twist it?" He handed her back the gun she'd dismantled and bent down to examine the bones in her ankle. "Looks like a sprain."

"Hellooo!"

Brit squinted through the trees and giggled. "Who's that with the pot and spoon?" she whispered.

"Your neighbor." He motioned toward the gun with his chin. "Shove it into your coat pocket and let's get you up and walking before she decides you need an ambulance."

"Right." She took a few steps and faltered.

Colt came up beside her and put his arm around her. "Can you make it up the hill with my help?"

"Uh huh," she said through gritted teeth.

They passed by the crazy pot lady leaning over her deck. "The name's Maddie. Maddie Trusdale. You okay?"

"I'm fine." Brit waved up at her. "Just a twisted ankle."

"Good man you have there."

"I know." Brit smiled up at him through long lashes, her expression one of true sincerity.

They trudged up the incline to the driveway where Colt scooped her up in his arms. He groaned when a sharp pain shot through his chest. "Let's get the hell out of here."

"Good plan." Her hand came down on his pecs and lingered on the soft cotton of his T-shirt. "I'll wrap you up when we get back."

He angled his head down to get a good look at her. "What's going on with you? You're not like any woman I've ever met."

"You say it like it's a bad thing." She frowned up at him.

"Not bad—confusing."

"Facing imminent death puts everything in perspective." She leaned into him. "Thanks for not shooting her. Had I got a shot off, I would have done the same thing."

"Gotta respect nature."

She cocked her head. "Where are you from?"

"Montana."

"You always lived in Maryland?"

"Annapolis until . . ."

He set her down and opened the passenger door. "You married Seth."

"Yeah." She hobbled into the truck.

Colt shut her door and came around and got in. He put the key in the ignition and started the truck, never taking his eyes off her. Although tousled with dark circles under her eyes, she was beautiful and fearless. God knew he could be a menacing hulk of a man—more frightening when he didn't shave. But here she sat, calm and, it appeared, resigned if not content with her decision to remain with him.

He reached over and plucked a leaf from her mass of blond hair. "Can we start over?"

She pursed her lips. "I think we need each other if we're going to survive this thing."

He'd meant her full and unequivocal honesty. She'd skirted his question big-time. Something was up with Brit Gentry, and he didn't think it had anything to do with this bullshit with Seth.

He'd interrogated plenty of *hadji* during his tour in Afghanistan.

Deception he was used to. The thing of it was, he wanted this woman's honesty in the worst way.

It had nothing to do with saving his ass, either.

Chapter Nine

"**W**HAT?" Brit sat across from Colt at the dining room table, eating the last of the eggs and bacon he'd made them when they returned.

"How's the ankle?"

It sat propped up on the dining room chair next to her, bound with the leftover bedsheet strips after she rewrapped his ribs.

She wiggled her painted pink toes. "It'll be fine in a few days." She toyed with her food. "But that's not the only thing you want to know."

"Nope." He pulled her gun out of the back of his waistband and laid it on the table between them. "Jacketed hollow points."

"Not your everyday ammunition." She shrugged. "It was my dad's service weapon. He taught me to shoot when I was a kid."

His mouth fell open in disbelief. "You con artist!"

She laughed. "You assumed I didn't know how to handle a gun. I just went along with it."

"Seems you can troubleshoot them, too."

"They're just like anything else with moving parts."

He nodded. "You don't by chance have a gun cleaning kit?"

"Yeah." She repositioned her leg, grimacing. "I think there's one in the closet."

Colt sopped up the egg yolks on his plate with the other half of his muffin and took a bite. "When I put the knob back on the closet, I'll get it out."

"Better to have two working firearms."

Okay, so maybe her old man had taken her under his wing. It still bothered him the way her mind worked. "So . . . what, you work in banking, real estate? What?"

"Mortgages."

"Ah, mortgages." He stood with his plate and picked up hers, the second dose of antibiotics working its magic on his ass cheek. "So tell me again why, being in the business, you missed the whole settlement sheet and where the funds might have come from to buy Memory Maker."

"I didn't say I missed it. It was his inheritance. He owned the land before I met him and paid the subs cash." She got up and hobbled into the great room and stretched out on one of the sofas that formed an L. "I'm just saying that having met you, learning of what happened in Afghanistan, it makes sense that he lied about his inheritance and that the money might have come from the artifacts."

Colt entered the great room, grabbed the blanket from the top of the sofa, and covered her up. "Which sucks if he sold them all."

"I know. How do we prove it?"

"It starts with you leveling with me and telling me where he is." He narrowed in on her. "You still love him."

She shook her head, her eyes becoming glassy with emotion. "He changed."

"How?"

Brit shrugged. "I guess war changes you." Although, she'd never met Seth before the conflict. For all she knew, he'd been diabolical at birth.

"That's a cop-out. I'm the same Montana boy I was before I enlisted. You grow up. See things that are sobering. But you deal with it. Death is part of life, part of war."

"Then you're lucky to have remained untouched." It came off flip.

"You think differently." He sat down in the armchair next to her.

"I know firsthand what war does. It makes a man angry twenty-four seven. It invades your sleep, torturing you until you wake up screaming."

"You're talking about last night. I must have been talking in my sleep."

"Screaming. And I'm not just talking about you. Seth had PTSD."

"There you go."

"Excuse me?"

"Had. You say 'had' whenever you mention his name. You separated? Divorced?" Knowing she was unattached would be liberating. Since he'd met her, he'd wanted to press his mouth to hers and taste those pouty lips.

Her fingers tightened on the edge of the blanket. "I meant it when I said I couldn't help you with Seth." She pulled out the roll of butter rum Life Savers she'd taken from the truck's console and popped one in her mouth.

Colt fell back against the cushy chair and pinched the bridge of his nose. "Brit, help me out here. You either do or don't know where he is."

"I know where he is. Not the exact spot, not precisely. Maybe he's closer to one beacon than another. But he's definitely submer—"

"Brit." He leaned over. His hand came down on hers twisting the edge of the blanket like she was ringing out a wet T-shirt. "What is it?"

Her eyes widened like the *oh shit* look he used to get when he interrogated the hadji . . . right before they spilled their guts.

"Seth drowned seven months ago."

Colt's back went ramrod straight. The kind of fear that seized him when he thought too deeply about his own mortality rode up his chest in a white-hot panic.

Brit gave him her signature pout. "You're devastated."

Hell yeah, he was devastated and screwed. How would he ever trace the whereabouts of the artifacts? He stood, stabbing pain returning to his ass cheek—which told him he was under maximum stress.

Get it together, man.

He walked toward the sliding glass door. "He drowned in the lake?"

"No. Chesapeake Bay."

"The sailboat, then?"

"Yes." Brit came up next to him with the blanket wrapped around her. "I'm sorry."

He turned toward her. Small lines bracketed her full mouth, her eyes filled with what looked to be regret. He guessed for him, which reminded Colt that he wasn't the only victim in all this. It was all he could do not to pull her into his arms. "I'm sorry, Brit. This must have been hard on you. He was your husband."

"He hadn't been my husband for a long time," she said, her head falling to her chest. "He was a cold, abusive bastard."

He tipped her chin up, searching her pale, pretty face. "He hit you?"

She took a deep breath. "Can we talk about something else?"

"Okay." His hand fell away. "But can you tell me how it happened?"

Colt couldn't wrap his brain around Seth's death. *Drowning.* Maybe they weren't SEAL Team Six. But their training included combat water survival skills.

Brit took his hand and led him back to the couch, favoring her ankle. She sat down and patted the cushion. Colt dropped down next to her, drained.

"We had talked about getting a small sailboat. There was one at an Annapolis boat dealer that caught our eye. But when we got there, Seth found a different boat. It was longer, sleeker, and French." She glanced back at him. "I almost choked when the salesman told us the price—125K."

Colt whistled through his teeth. "I'm guessing it's the one docked at the pier on Shore Drive."

She nodded. "Jeanneau Sun Odyssey 33i, to be exact, and paid in full with Seth's so-called inheritance."

Colt clenched his jaw. *Cha-ching.* One more artifact bites the dust. At this rate, he seriously doubted there was even a single one left to recover and link to Seth and the Badakhshan airport.

"They delivered it on a Saturday—March 15. It was overcast, the water choppy." She pulled the blanket up over her. "And cold. I wanted to wait until Sunday. But Seth insisted."

It must have been rough, if a woman like Brit had warned against taking a sail.

"We went out around five, after he'd signed the delivery papers." She shook her head. "He spent a small fortune on a sailing jacket like he was some jet-setter from Martha's Vineyard. What a pretentious ass."

Colt snorted. "No arguments here."

She turned toward him, folding her legs underneath her. "I grew up in Annapolis, lived on the water, and piloted small skiffs with my brother. Not a problem. Seth had the riggings crossed, I tried to help him. But Mr. You Don't Know What You're Doing, Brit had it all under control." She rubbed her cheek, her hand dropping into her lap. "Booms have a mean right hook."

Colt held her hand, lost in those troubled eyes of hers as she relived that night. "You're still beautiful."

But for all her soft curves, her hands were calloused. It bothered him last night, too. He'd been in pain then, and it wasn't worth pondering. But today he couldn't put the two together, unless she was a regular at the gun range or maybe gym.

Brit wet her lips. "After that I took a seat and silently cursed him while he made an even bigger tangle of the ropes." Her eyes met his. "I made a mistake."

Colt's brows furrowed. "I don't understand."

"A storm rolled in after that. I'd never seen swells that big. And the wind . . . All I can say is I kept my head down. I couldn't afford another smack from the boom he still hadn't secured."

"Where was Seth?"

"Screaming obscenities, crawling around the deck like an ant until the boom nailed him in the ass and threw him overboard."

"Shit." Colt rolled his lips in. He hated the son of a bitch, and the thought of his body being plunged into the sea was, well, hilarious. Then he remembered she'd been with him. His humor faded, and he tightened his grip on her hand. "What about you?"

"Threw him a life preserver and secured the boom. I lashed the wheel and heaved to windward, trying to find the boat's equilibrium." Her speech was fast and agitated.

Colt smooth down her hair. "Speak English, beautiful."

"Allowed the boat to sail on its own so I could help Seth."

He nodded. "Go on."

Her eyes were anxious and darting. "It was awful . . . the rain and the swells. One minute I saw him, the next he disappeared behind a wall of water." She frowned. "I had his hand at one point. The look of horror on his face will haunt me until I die."

"What happened?"

"His hand slipped away. It was the last I saw of him." She shook her head. "It was my fault. I should have told him to go to hell and took control. But Seth is . . . was . . ."

"An asshole." An asshole who'd fucked him over big-time.

Brit remained quiet, sitting across from Colt, holding on to his hand. She blinked, her lashes fluttering until her lids closed. "Sometimes I can still smell his cologne." Her eyes popped open, and they latched onto his. "I can smell it now. You think that's weird?"

Colt clenched his teeth and moved to the edge of the sofa. "I think it's the shirt." He glanced down at the flannel shirt he'd been wearing since leaving the house to find her.

She wrinkled her brow. "Maybe . . . But I've smelled it before."

He didn't doubt it. They shared the same house. If she'd kept his clothes, which it appeared she had, his cologne would linger. The shirt on his back was testament to that. It was familiar, but he couldn't place the scent.

"What was the name of his cologne?"

She grimaced. "Obsession."

Colt chuckled and moved off the sofa. *Figures.*

"Where you going?" Her fingers tightened on his.

"You need some sleep." He hooked his chin over his shoulder. "I have a doorknob and a gun in pieces."

She let go of his hand and lay down on the sofa. "Don't let me sleep too long."

"I'll wake you up for dinner."

She gave him a strange look. "We have no groceries."

"They deliver pizza?"

"I think so." She motioned to the large square coffee table. "There's a list of restaurants in the guidebook."

"Got it." Colt picked it up and grimaced. "I'd say I'd treat you, but I'm low on funds."

She waved a dismissive hand at him. "It's okay. I have some cash in my bag." She threw off her blanket and stood.

"Whoa. I'll get it."

She seemed to be mulling something over. "*Crap.* It's still in the truck, shoved under the backseat."

Colt pulled the keys out of his front pocket, shaking his head. How'd he miss that? "I'll be right back."

"Okay, but . . ."

He could tell she was having a problem speaking her mind.

"I won't go through your purse."

She became flushed. "It's not that I don't trust you."

"I get it. You don't have to explain." Still not feeling a hundred percent, Colt ambled out the door.

She was still holding back on him. Not that he expected her to embrace the idea of living with a fugitive. But they both were fighting the same enemy. Joining forces made sense.

They also needed a plan. The world would be closing in on them soon enough. The military and law enforcement was and would continue searching for him. It pissed him off that there were no working TVs. It was like maneuvering in the dark. Hell, for all he knew, they'd tracked him to Maryland.

And Brit—she had a life. One she would have to get back to. Obviously she had people who cared about her. A father, brother, and this Andi. She'd need to return calls and texts. Otherwise they'd become concerned. Maybe even drive up to the lake.

He'd have to give back her phone.

Dumbass. It's an iPhone.

Right. He could search the Internet for news of his escape. Colt whipped it out of his back pocket, brushed his thumb across the unlock button, and moaned at the damn keypad.

He took a deep breath through his nose. Okay, he'd have to ask her for the passcode. Hell, she could search for all he cared. It wasn't like he had anything to hide from her.

What he really wanted to know was more about Brit Gentry.

Chapter Ten

"**N**O!" Brit jerked up, sweat beading her forehead. The neck of her sweater was damp.

Stomping came from behind her on the steps.

Brit pulled herself up to a sitting position on the sofa, her heart thumping.

Colt skidded on his socks and tripped over the edge of the throw rug, cursing. "You okay?" A pair of concerned eyes narrowed in on her.

"*Oh, God.*" The words rushed off her lips. "I wasn't honest with you."

He sat down on the edge of the coffee table. "Slow down."

She shook her head. "I let go!" she cried out.

Colt scrubbed his face hard. "You need to speak in complete sentences, beautiful."

Tears ran down her cheeks. "I let go of Seth's hand. I killed him."

Colt took her hands in his. "A lot of things happen in an instant. You're second-guessing yourself, Brit. Seth was a big guy. I know how difficult it is to haul someone in, and I'm six three."

He could try to minimize what she'd done, but she knew differently. Her heart beat a frenetic pace that night, hanging over the bow. The rain stung her skin, pierced her eyes, making it a challenge to see. She wouldn't lie. She'd been beyond frightened. Colt wasn't telling her anything she hadn't already thought about. Seth was twice her size. There was a real chance he'd pull her in.

But she'd reached for him anyway and clasped onto his wet hands. She had every intention of saving him. His panicked eyes clung to hers. But his expression had changed when she'd gotten him to the edge of the bow. It was savage, his words venomous.

Stupid bitch, it should have been you.

It was like a bite from a rattlesnake, and she recoiled. Maybe, in that instant, she hadn't meant to let go. But it was fight or flight. If he'd made it back on the deck with that attitude, he'd have likely struck her. She honestly didn't think she'd have the strength to fight him.

Now looking back with more clarity, she'd come to the realization he must have meant, because of his military training—and let her not forget his superior attitude—the likely drowning victim in all this should have been her, except *she* had ridden out the storm using her seafaring skills.

"What are you thinking?" Colt dipped his chin, his eyes sweeping her face.

Brit's fingers tightened around his. "He was such an ass-asshole." Her voice hitched, sobs racking her chest. "I tried to be a good wife. He could be so belligerent."

Colt eased his hand from hers, his thumb wiping a tear from her cheek. His gaze deepened. She must look like crap—puffy eyes, no makeup, and crying like a baby.

"Did he hit you, Brit?" His jaw tightened.

Their eyes connected. His were a serious green that meant business.

She'd never told anyone what Seth had done to her. The Brit everyone knew was strong, confident. If anyone found out at work . . . If they were afraid it would affect her performance or the safety of those on the team, they might remove her.

Maybe minimizing it would be in her best interest. "He didn't know what he was doing."

"What the hell?" Colt's face stiffened. "Don't make excuses for him."

"You don't understand. He'd wake me from a deep sleep, screaming, thrashing. Once he grabbed my throat—choked me."

"Jesus." His body stiffened. "You should have kneed him in the balls."

"I jabbed him here." Brit took her two shaky fingers and pressed into

Colt's neck just below his scruffy dark beard.

"That's my girl." A smile curled his lips, his expression turning more sober. "I thought I knew Seth as well as anyone. I was wrong. The dick set me up, paid witnesses—American and Afghani—to lie under oath." He leveled a serious, yet compassionate gaze at her. "So you're telling me he's only put his hands on you during one of these PTSD nightmares?"

Brit bit the inside of her mouth, debating. She'd wanted to tell someone, anyone—but mostly the man who would understand and not judge.

She frowned at him. "I'm not a wuss."

He chuckled. "I didn't say you were."

She nodded up at him. "No. Not just then."

"Okay." He said it like that was all he was waiting for—her to be honest with him. He let go of her hand and stood.

"Where are you going?" Brit peered up into his unreadable expression.

"I'm hungry. Pizza's been here."

"Oh. I didn't see it."

His stomach growled, and he grimaced. "Extra-large and it's in the oven on warm."

Made sense. Otherwise she would have smelled its doughy goodness.

He helped her up, catching the blanket, and tossed it onto the back of the sofa.

"You think I'm weak."

"I think I would have let his hand go, too." He winked at her and headed into the kitchen, pulling out one of the stools at the bar.

Brit slid onto it, careful not to knock her ankle, and placed her feet on the footrest. Colt opened the oven and pulled out a box. He set it on the bar, flipping open the top.

A mix of pizza sauce, cheese, and spices made her mouth water. "It smells so good."

Colt handed her a glass of water. "We might want to think about going to the grocery store tomorrow."

Brit gave him a doubtful look. "You really think it's a good idea for you to be seen in public?"

He sat down next to her with his glass of water and two plates. "I don't know. Maybe you can tell me." Colt reached behind him and pulled out her phone. "Can you do an Internet search on me?"

Brit eyed the phone and then him. He was just as capable of doing a search. Of course, he'd need her passcode. She took the phone and punched in the code, ready to give it back to him when he scooped up a slice of pizza. He placed it on her plate, grabbed a piece for himself, and took a bite.

Okay then. Appeared she was gaining his trust. Brit typed in his name, like she'd done before. Strange. He hadn't asked her how she knew he was a fugitive in the first place.

"Where were you coming from? I mean before I woke up?"

"Downstairs." He took another bite. "Nice setup. Seth pick out the atomic shuffleboard table?"

Was he baiting her? She'd been asleep for at least two hours. He'd done more than check out the sports tables downstairs.

"It was suggested by the realty company," she said, drawing in a shallow breath. "I only started renting it recently."

"Why?"

Because she needed the money for her legal fund. Brit shrugged. "Didn't want to deal with the upkeep. Railey takes care of that. They set up the hot tub and pool guy, fix the appliances or replace them once they get my okay."

He nodded but seemed to be mulling over other things in his head.

Colt could ask away. She'd answer him as best she could, trying to throw him off the truth.

But there was always her iPhone. Maybe the existence of a computer was a moot point, even though she still couldn't see him giving back her phone. It would allow access to Internet searches if he wanted to glean more information about her. He'd still need the passcode. It would be hard to deny him access to it now if he asked for it again. What would be her reasoning for not giving it to him? As far as he knew she was a mortgage loan officer. *God.* If she was anyone else, he might find a Facebook page or a Twitter account. But she wasn't. Once he entered her name into the search bar, she'd be at square one with him again. No worse. He'd tie her back up.

"Lots of bedrooms." He turned on his stool, their knees bumping until he repositioned his thighs on either side of hers. He was moving into her personal space.

"One of its appeals with multi-family renters." Brit kept direct eye contact with him but couldn't hold it for long before she dipped her head.

Damn him for being who *he* was. Otherwise her occupation wouldn't matter.

Brit hit enter, sending his name into the search engine. She needed to shift his concerns. Not that she wanted to find "they"—she guessed the military, even law enforcement—were closing in on him. She believed in his innocence. Brit opened the first link, thinking it would be the most recent.

"You live in Whitefish?"

"Just outside it, why?" He cocked his head at the small screen of the phone, concern creasing his forehead.

"Department of Defense questioned your father." Brit pushed out the screen and made it bigger. She handed it to him, her anxiety building. Her own father had left her a voice mail.

Colt sat down the pizza, wiping his hands on a napkin before he took it from her. His thick dark brows knitted together, his lips thinning. "I put him and my mother in a tough place. He said they believed in my innocence." He shook his head. "Can't imagine what he's dealing with now."

"You haven't spoken to them since you escaped?"

"Him and no." He shoved the phone back into his hip pocket. "Thought it best he didn't know."

She understood. His father would have two choices—give him up or lie. Knowing what she knew of Colt, it was the lying he was concerned with. It could cost his parents' freedom, too. Only he'd made a point of leaving his mother out of it. Now she was afraid to ask.

"She died while I was in prison."

Shit. That was what she was afraid of. Brit squeezed his arm. "I'm sorry."

His eyes held hers. They were a mix of torment and sadness. "I can't go back, Brit. If I have to, I'll cross the border into Canada and make my way west to Saskatchewan."

Something inside her panicked. That was remote. But what was more disconcerting was that she cared. Colt Rivers deciding to hop the border—

any border—should put her at ease. *Face it.* She was harboring a fugitive. Maybe an innocent one. But the likelihood of him proving it was nil in her book. Unless *she* could prove it.

Brit grabbed his hand. "This is crazy. But what if the answers are locked up in my subconscious?"

He smiled at her. "I'm not a shrink or a hypnotist."

"No, but you interrogated prisoners, didn't you? Do you think you were able to tap into their subconsciouses?"

His expression darkened, and then he laughed. "For a minute there, I thought you were serious."

Brit lifted her brows at him.

"Hell no." He pulled his hand away. "That's not an option."

Brit's head fell back, and she groaned. What was his deal? She had just as much at stake and was willing to subject herself to whatever Army intelligence techniques it took to pull it out of her. *Ugh.* Guantanamo Bay came to mind. Well, maybe not water boarding.

Chapter Eleven

*D*AMN IT. COLT WAS GOING TO SEE HER WAY OF THINKING on this.

"You're not the only one who needs those artifacts." Brit gave him a stern look and took hold of both his hands, rough scabs running the length of his fingers. "I'm under a financial investigation, Colt. I could go to prison, too."

His fingers tightened around hers. "Had a feeling it was something like that."

Well, it was only one of her life-derailing dilemmas. Beau Crenshaw was the runaway train she couldn't stop and an aspect of her life she needed to keep under wraps, especially from Colt.

But if she could get them to back off on this financial disclosure investigation, she could concentrate on the shooting. It still remained a blur.

"For weeks I've reviewed my and Seth's income taxes with my lawyer. I got a court order to open his safe deposit box. It was empty. I can't explain the money. I can prove he owned this land free and clear prior to me ever meeting him. But I can't prove how he came by the money to have Memory Maker built or pay for a sailboat and any other extravagant purchases he made during our marriage."

"You didn't question him?"

"I tried. He blew up." That night swirled in her head. It was the first and last time Seth had hit her. His fist came out of nowhere. She'd been about to go toe to toe with him and pull out every jujitsu move she had until he began to cry. Alas, PTSD waved its white flag at her, and she'd done what every good wife would do—forgiven him. Now she wouldn't be surprised to find it had all been an act. She clenched Colt's hands. "I'm not going to allow him to screw with my life from the grave."

"Eat your dinner."

"We're not done discussing this."

"This conversation is over until you eat something."

Brit beaded in on him. He sat back on his stool with his arms crossed, staring her down.

"Fine," she growled and took a bite of her pizza, refusing to wilt under his intense gaze. "You know I'm right."

"Keep eating." He plopped another slice on her plate.

Brit washed it down with her water and ate two more pieces before she pushed the fifth slice away. "I'm done."

Colt lifted it from the plate and ate it in three bites. After shutting the box of leftovers, he got up and stored it on the empty shelf in the refrigerator. "I got the rest. Why don't you get ready for bed?"

She checked the time on the stove—8:22. After her little catnap, she was wide awake. Then there was the issue of their sleeping arrangements. They were no longer adversaries with two different agendas. The only reason to remain in his bedroom was if she wanted to.

Now that's just crazy talk.

Brit stood and marched—sort of marched with her bad ankle—into the bedroom and through the bathroom door. She gathered her soap, shampoo, and conditioner. Juggling them as she entered the bedroom, she ran straight into Colt.

"Whoa." His arm went around her waist to steady her. "Where you going?"

"To my room upstairs."

"Oh." He pressed a loose strand of hair behind her ear. "I guess it would be ballsy to ask you to stay with me for my last night."

Warning bells went off in her head, and it had nothing to do with his invitation. "You're going to Canada, then?"

"Listen. I heard everything you said back there. Even if there's some important detail lurking in that pretty little head of yours, I don't think the techniques I've learned could draw it out."

"But if there's a chance . . ."

"I've done a lot of things in the name of freedom. I've never regretted it. But you're not the Taliban, Brit. I could never hurt you." His eyes lingered on her face. "Besides, I'm dealing with some serious shit. Getting involved with a fugitive is probably the last thing you should do."

"If it's the interrogation idea, we'll figure something else out."

Colt let her go and reached into his back pocket. He handed her the iPhone and her keys.

"Seriously?" God he was really going to leave. Brit's shoulders slumped.

"Okay." He sat the phone and keys on the dresser and scrubbed his face, eyeing her. "You know you're a pain in my ass, right?"

Brit gave an innocent shrug.

"I'm not going."

"Then why would you—"

"Trust." He took the bottles and soap from her and sat them next to her belongings on the dresser.

Was he trying to make the point that now that he'd given Brit back her things *she* needed to offer up a sign of faith?

She could fix that right now. Proving she had nothing to hide was a step in the right direction.

"My dad called." Brit picked up the phone. "I should call him back." She began punching in numbers, waiting for him to yank it out of her hand. He didn't, and it started to ring. She put it on speaker—more trust.

Colt's brows rose, and he took a seat on the end of the bed.

"Honey, you okay? Pete called and said you were involved in that pileup."

Brit pursed her lips at her father's worried voice. "I'm fine, Daddy."

"I didn't know you were going up to the lake. You did tell them where you were going?"

Oh, crap. She'd told her lawyer—not internal affairs. But she still had her police powers and wasn't under suspension. It wasn't like she couldn't travel in her own state as long as she hadn't been charged, at least not yet. "They know and it's fine. How's Mom?"

"Packing."

"For?"

"To come see you."

"Dad, no!" She gave Colt an exasperated look. "I really need this time to myself."

"Here, you tell her." The phone clunked.

"Brit, you shouldn't be there all alone." Her mother's wispy voice filled her ears.

"Mom, listen." Brit paced the bedroom. "I'm perfectly fine. Alone is good."

"But..."

"I'm serious. I'll just come home then."

Silence. She must be mulling it over.

"Mom?"

"Yes, sweetheart. Will you at least call me if you change your mind?"

"Of course."

"I love you."

"We love you," her father chimed in.

Brit smiled at that. "I love you, too. Good night." She clicked off before any more could be said and grimaced. "Overprotective."

"I can understand that." He stood and walked toward her. "Who else knows you're here?"

"Shit." Brit's hand flew to her mouth. "Andi."

"You should call her back."

That would not be a good idea. She wouldn't be able to control that conversation as well as she had with her parents.

"Ya know, I'll just text her." Brit waved a dismissive hand. "She's a talker." Brit clicked on her name in her contact list and typed a quick message.

Let's talk when I get back.

She'd get the hint. Brit sat the phone on the dresser. If Colt wanted to look, he had about thirty seconds before the screen locked. Of course, if Andi responded it would be displayed regardless of a passcode. Brit gritted her teeth. Didn't matter. She'd be dealing with possible texts and phone calls until she returned. She'd have to hope she could delete any conversation threads and phone messages before Colt was aware of them.

That meant staying in her own room.

Brit took a step away from him, grabbed her suitcase off the floor, and put it on the bed. She hooked her chin over her shoulder. "So why the change about staying?"

Colt came up behind her, his arm slipping around her waist. He pulled her back against him, his movement more intimate than she'd anticipated. He pressed his lips against her ear. "I'm not out of the woods yet."

Brit ignored the sexy rasp of his voice and the way it made her stomach tumble with temptation and concentrated on his words instead. She turned in his arm and placed her hand against his forehead. "You're a little warm. I'll give you some Advil."

"My fever could spike in the middle of the night." Something flickered in the depths of his eyes. It seemed more carnal than concern.

Brit laughed it off and stepped out of his embrace. "You'll be just fine." She opened her small bag and handed him the bottle of Advil and amoxicillin. "Take two Advil and one of the antibiotic before bed."

"I thought you wanted to talk about me interrogating you." He said it like it was something naughty.

"You said no." She gave him a lift of her brow. "You change your mind about that, too?"

"No." He tapped his finger to his lip in contemplation. "Ever hear of subconscious rapport building?"

Brit shook her head.

"It starts with *conscious* rapport building." He caressed her cheek, his eyes holding hers.

Seriously? Okay. So he'd been locked up for years. He was probably horny as hell.

Brit laughed. "I'm not sleeping with you."

He grinned at her. "You think you have me all figured out."

Not even close.

Brit bent down and shoved her clothes inside her suitcase. She snagged her toiletries, dropping them inside her makeup bag. Maybe he wasn't going there. But he needed to know, if he was thinking he was going to get lucky, it wouldn't be with her. He'd need to shave his face for one and cut his hair.

Shut up. You did not just think that.

A smile touched her lips. She was attracted to him, and it certainly wasn't his looks. He might have come after her today to save his own ass. But he'd saved hers instead. She knew a thing or two about people. The relief in his voice and in his expression had been sincere.

He'd been worried about her—not him.

Brit zipped up her suitcase. "Let me get settled, and I'll come down in about an hour . . . after you get your shower, and I'll wrap your ribs."

"I can rewrap your ankle, too."

"Sounds like a plan." Brit grabbed her makeup bag and suitcase and pushed past him. She stopped at the dresser on the way out and took her phone, depositing it into her back jean pocket. Her keys glittered, and she scooped them up, too, feeling a tad uneasy.

He is an escaped convict, Brit, who stole your keys to begin with, remember?

"I'll help you." He took her suitcase from her. "Upstairs you said."

She couldn't tell if he was really being a gentleman, or if he wanted to see for himself exactly where she'd be sleeping. Maybe it was a little of both.

"Ah, yes, second level." She walked by him and up the stairs, skirting the pool table in the center of the loft. "It's the one on the right."

"Whoa. What's this?" Colt pointed to a trapdoor with a keyed lock as he climbed up the steps behind her.

Huh? She'd forgotten about it. "It's Seth's."

He gave her a look of disbelief. "Does your key work for it?"

Brit sat her makeup bag on the pool table and strode toward him, taking the steps down until she stood on the riser above him. She handed him her keys. "It would be the same for the closet."

Colt took them and slipped the key inside the lock. He grimaced when it wouldn't turn. "Here." Colt handed her the keys and sat her suitcase on the landing, taking the steps down. He disappeared around the corner into the kitchen. Metal clanged together, and he returned, carrying a butter knife.

Brit gave him a lift of her brow.

"I can hotwire a car, too." He winked at her and then slid it inside the crack of the door.

Great. "So you didn't need the keys to my truck."

"Makes it easier." He manipulated the knife.

"Something you learned in prison?"

"Ranger school." The latch popped, and he eased the door open with the edge of the knife.

Brit came up next to him on the above step and peered into the dark space. She could just make out a pile of life vests, extra paddles, ropes for tubing.

"I vaguely remember him mentioning a storage area for water sports."

"What's this?" Colt pulled out a rolled parchment.

Brit chuckled. "Treasure map?"

"What?" Colt swung on her with a hopeful gleam in his eyes.

Shit. She gave him a pout. "I was kidding. It's the plans to the house."

He tossed the plans and knife into the opening, his eyes narrowing. "Woman, do you not grasp the severity of our situation?"

"I do. I do. I'm tired and punchy and—" Brit's foot slipped off the step.

Colt caught her, his arm coming around her. He tipped her chin up and searched her eyes. "You forgot fearless."

"I'm not," she said on a whisper. She had real insecurities about her feelings for him. All she had to do was press her lips to his. She doubted he'd resist. Brit's stomach fluttered, and she pushed away from him. "It's getting late."

His hands fell away, and he picked up her suitcase. "Let me put this in your room." He motioned her up the steps.

Brit grabbed her bag from the pool table. She had more to worry about than stealing a kiss from Colt if she couldn't remember a thing like the trapdoor she'd been told about. How could she remember some benign incident, conversation, or slipup on Seth's part that might help them find what was left of the artifacts?

Maybe there was something to this subconscious or conscious rapport building. She chuckled to herself. Their conversations bordered on being downright alarming. She may have been married to an Army Ranger, but picking locks and hotwiring cars had never come up with Seth.

Of course, her relationship with Colt was, well, unconventional.

That was what made him and what they had going here so perfect. There were no hard and fast rules. Special Forces, special ops—whatever they were called—were highly trained and intelligent. Colt was—had been one of them. All she had to do was find what she needed on the Internet. She'd use her phone to surf the net now that she had it back.

She would teach him how to hypnotize her.

Chapter Twelve

"**B**RIT!"

She jumped in her sleep, eyes flying open. Light from the loft cut a swath over her. She squinted at the lumbering giant marching past her bed, hair sticking up, bare-chested—except for his wraps—wearing the pajama bottoms she gave him. He whipped open her curtains to the sliding glass doors.

"Are you insane?" Brit rolled over and put the pillow over her head.

"It's snowing."

"They don't have snow where you live?" she mumbled into the mattress.

"There're footprints out by the hot tub."

Brit jumped out of bed and charged the sliding glass doors. "Oh." The hot tub sat two stories down. He must have seen the prints from his own slider when he woke up.

"Oh? What do you mean, oh?" His eyes blazed at her.

She waved him off, yawning. "Hot tub guy." She tiptoed back to bed and crawled under her covers.

"What the hell?" The mattress gave next to her when he sat down. "You're sure it's this hot tub guy?"

"Pretty sure." She shooed him with her fingers. "Now can you shut my drapes and my door when you leave?"

He scratched his chest. "You think you might have made these a little too tight last night?"

"No," she growled and threw the covers over her head. *Damn*. For an Army Ranger he was being a baby.

The mattress sprung back when he stood. His footsteps moved around her bed, the drapes slapping closed. More footsteps and then the door shut. Brit opened one eye to check the clock. Seven. Considering she hadn't gone to bed until two—caught up with her Internet search—she could use a few more hours' sleep.

"Brit!" Colt's voice shook with uncertainty. And was it fear?

Shit. She kicked off her covers, jumped out of bed, taking the steps two at a time. She was sure it was the hot tub guy. It wasn't like she was around full-time to keep the chemicals up. Brit crept into his bedroom and caught the light from the bathroom. She rushed in.

"What's the mat—" Brit froze. *Holy shit!*

Colt stood in the bathroom wearing only a pair of gray boxer briefs. He stared down his bare muscled chest with just the right amount of hair to leave a woman breathless with appreciation.

"You took off your wraps."

"Look at me!"

Brit rolled her lips in. "I am." She moved into the bathroom, her hands hovering around his sexy—although spotted—body. "You ever have chicken pox?"

"When I was *four*." He gave her a disagreeable look.

She nodded, moving around him. Little raised red bumps dotted his thighs and arms, but most were concentrated around his abdomen. "You said they itched?"

"Yeah, they itch." He scratched his chest.

"Don't do that." She quelled his hand with hers. "You allergic to any foods?"

"No."

What else had he ingested that would . . . Brit cupped her mouth, her eyes widening. "Oh, Colt. I think you're allergic to amoxicillin."

His mouth fell open in horror. "What the f—"

Brit pressed her fingers to his lips and gave him a pout. "I'm so sorry, baby." Her arms went around him. "You've been through so much." It was like he was cursed.

Ah . . . did she need to be reminded that she was hugging a half-naked man she was attracted to. And where the *hell* did "baby" come from?

Get it together.

Brit inched away from him. "I've got some Benadryl in my bag."

"Not so fast, crazy pill lady." He looped his arm around her and pulled her toward him. He peered down his nose at her. "What about my ass cheek?"

She squinted at him. *Ass cheek?* Not the response she expected.

"Dog bite?" He arched a brow at her.

"Ah, right." She put her hands on his chest, her fingers sinking into the soft swirls of dark hair. "I'd have to take a look."

He released her and gave her his backside.

Brit gripped onto the waistband of his underwear and began tugging it down, mindful of his wounds. Her heart raced—the downward movement of his underwear an erotic striptease. God, she loved his tight ass. Brit grimaced. She'd never make it as a nurse.

"How does it look?" Colt tried to angle his head back.

"Good." She patted his upper back. "The redness is gone, and the bites have scabbed over." She gently pulled his underwear back up. "I think we can stop the antibiotic, give you some Benadryl, and while I'm at the store I'll pick up some cornstarch and baking powder."

He gave her a strange look. "I'm not following you."

"You soak in it." Brit pointed toward the rose-colored double jetted tub. "It helps with the itching."

His lips quirked. "Seems to me since you caused all this, you should have to take a bath with me."

"Nice try." Brit laughed and motioned him toward the shower. "Lukewarm water for now. The heat will only exacerbate it." She turned for the door.

"Brit."

"Yeah?" She glanced over her shoulder.

"Ever think of having kids?"

Where the hell did that come from? She hoped he didn't mean with him.

"Excuse me?"

Colt turned on the water and scratched his stomach. "You're very nurturing."

"Or I'm a sucker for an unjustly accused man who's had his share of setbacks." She smiled at him. "I'll leave the Benadryl on the dresser for you." She eased the door shut.

I'm a sucker for you.

Brit leaned against the bathroom door, hugging herself. Her arms brushed against her nipples, and she winced. *Great.* No bra. Maybe he hadn't noticed. *Idiot.* The man noticed everything. Okay. Let it go. This was a new day. She'd get his Benadryl, make him a pot of coffee, and then get her shower.

Ugh. She probably had morning breath. Whatever. Brit cleared his bedroom and took the steps all the while making her grocery list in her head. Prison food must suck. She could go for a nice pot of beef stew. She passed the windows that looked out onto the parking pad from the loft. Snow. In October. It had been known to happen in these parts. She wouldn't be surprised to find tomorrow bright and sunny and inching toward fifty degrees.

Huh? How about that? She manipulated her foot. Her ankle didn't hurt. She passed the pool table, flipped on the light in her room, and went rummaging through her makeup bag for the Benadryl when she caught her reflection in the mirror over the oak dresser. *Yikes.* She moved closer.

"He must think I'm hideous." Dark circles under her eyes, pale skin, and a blond rat's nest.

Oh, this was bad. She shouldn't care about her appearance. He still looked like Sasquatch—a nice one, though, now that she'd gotten to know him.

She'd be lying if she said she wasn't curious about what he looked like under all that hair. A smile tugged at the corners of her mouth.

There was only one way to find out.

Colt stood in the great room with a hot mug of coffee, showered and dressed. He was sleepy thanks to Brit's Benadryl but relatively itch-free. He chuckled.

Between the pharmacy in her bag, this little financial disclosure investigation, and harboring a fugitive who was falling fast for her, the woman was a beautiful walking disaster. He wondered if she'd make it back from the grocery store unscathed.

Snow blew sideways, piling up on the deck and sticking to the heavy crowns of trees still sporting fire engine–colored leaves. He gnawed the inside of his mouth, his stomach growling. But there was always that fifty-fifty chance she'd played him and it would be the cops slipping down the serpentine driveway.

Nah. They had a connection. Yeah, Seth had been the driving force. But it was more than that. He liked her, respected her.

He'd meant what he'd said. She had a gentle touch and way about her. And he hadn't missed an opportunity to put his arms around her and pull her close. Itchy or not. He was drawn to her. If he didn't watch it, he'd walk away from this thing with an even bigger loss—his heart.

Maybe it wasn't one-sided. She seemed to like touching him, too. Even contemplated kissing him on the steps last night. Not that she'd admitted as much, but he could tell the way she'd leaned into him. He should have taken the initiative and kissed her on those tempestuous lips of hers.

Headlights veered across the great room. Colt's adrenaline spiked. With stealth, he maneuvered into the foyer, his shoulders relaxing when he recognized her Pathfinder backing up toward the portico.

He set down his mug on the foyer table and opened the door. Brit hopped out, her head hidden inside the furry hood of her parka.

"You remember my beef jerky?" He'd been salivating for it since she left.

"It's in the bag with the cashews."

"No problems?" Colt unlatched the tailgate.

She came up beside him, stomping her boots on the porch. "Usual craziness during a blizzard."

"Yeah, about that." Colt looped several bags through his hands. "You normally get snow this time of year?"

"Three feet on Halloween last year." Brit grabbed the two remaining bags and scurried into the main house. "But, no, it's not the norm," she called over her shoulder.

Colt shut the tailgate and followed in behind her. He rounded the steps to the loft and met her in the kitchen.

She peered around the refrigerator door. "I hope you like beef stew."

"Your own special recipe?" Colt's stomach rumbled at the thought, and he set the bags on the center island and began unpacking them.

"My mom's." Brit shut the refrigerator and handed him a deli-style wrapped sub. "You eat and I'll finish up."

Colt gripped some kind of can in the bag. *Damn.* If this was life with Brit, he never wanted to leave. "What about you?"

"Got it right here." She picked up the sub hiding behind a grocery bag, giving him a questioning look. "You are hungry?"

"Starved."

"What's wrong?"

He let go of what he was holding in the bag, irritated. This wasn't real. She wasn't real. And to think that son of a bitch Gentry treated her like shit. He strode past her. "Seth was an asshole," he grumbled and pulled out the bar stool. He dug at the tape and opened the paper covering the sub, his mouth salivating.

Damn, cold cuts with onions. How'd she know?

"What's wrong with you?" Her brows snapped together. "I'm here. I'm feeding you. Harboring you. Keeping you safe." She gave him her back and tore through what was left of the grocery bags, tossing items onto the island. "You're the one being an asshole."

That's it.

Colt stood and pushed back his stool. It clattered to the tile floor. Brit spun around, her brown eyes growing wider the closer he got. She backed up against the counter, holding some type of can in her hand. Didn't matter. He was going to do it to her first, and if she wanted to clobber him over the head, it'd be worth it.

He looped his arm around her waist and jerked her to him.

A silky feminine sound rolled up her throat, her coat slipping down her shoulders. "Let go of me," she whispered.

He couldn't. She was soft and pretty in her pink sweater and tight jeans. His hand came down on her ass. "You don't mean it." Colt dipped his head, his lips hovering over hers. Her lashes fluttered, her eyes closing. He kissed her, teased her with his tongue until she opened her mouth to him.

She tasted faintly of butter rum, and Colt remembered the roll of Life Savers in her center console. God, he needed to let her go. He slipped his hand up her sweater, his fingers roaming over her rib cage. Her arm snaked around his shoulders, and something cold and hard grazed the back of his neck.

Shit. Colt broke the kiss and jumped back.

Brit moaned, her eyes springing open with confusion.

Colt grabbed for her hand and ripped the can from her fingers. "I'll take that."

Her forehead creased. "I bought it for you."

Colt examined the can that looked like a candy cane—Barbasol. *Shaving cream?* He grimaced. "Shit. I thought . . ."

Brit rubbed her swollen mouth.

Colt chuckled. "You don't like my beard."

"It's scratchy, and you're a jerk who has a real problem with trust issues." She turned and opened up the refrigerator.

"Whoa." Colt laid the can down. He came around and shut the refrigerator. "I'm sorry. And, yeah, I figured I was taking a chance here. But you said scratchy." Was that her only complaint about his impromptu kiss?

"It is."

"So you bought the shaving cream so I'd shave and you could kiss me."

Her lips sputtered with laughter. "Don't flatter yourself, Rivers." She gave him a pointed look and took hold of the refrigerator door handle. "Let go so I can get us water."

He released the door. "Then why did you buy it?"

She grabbed two bottles of water, handing him one. "Because I can't trust someone I can't see." She pushed past him, hung her coat on the back of a dining room chair, and sat down.

Colt picked up his food and took a seat next to her. "If you have forgotten, I am hiding."

"Not looking like that you're not." Brit dug inside her coat pocket and pulled out her phone. She started scrolling and then laid the phone down between them. "I did a search on you this morning. These are the only photos they're releasing so far."

Colt craned his head. One photo came from Basic Combat Training. He'd been eighteen and didn't resemble the young close-shaven teen who had fire in his eyes. The other was a photo from Afghanistan while on a mountain ridge. Dressed for battle, he recognized the firm jut of his chin. They were taking the fight to al Qaeda. He had that same resolve in his eyes now, along with the beard and long hair.

Brit nudged his knee. "You need to shave and cut your hair."

Colt raised his chin to her.

"If you can't handle it." She gave him a lift of her brow.

He'd learned barbering in prison. But if she was offering, he'd take her up on it. Somehow the suggestion of Brit Gentry fussing with his hair made his gut coil with arousal.

"Ever cut hair before?" Colt took a bite of his sub, the Italian spices filling his mouth.

"No, but . . ." She cocked her head. "I can see you with short hair, tight around the ears."

"What about the beard?"

"You want me to shave you, too?"

Now that could be risky. His lips curled into a smile. "As long as you don't cut my throat."

Chapter Thirteen

"DON'T MOVE." BRIT HELD COLT'S HEAD FIRM BETWEEN her fingers. "Unless you want your hair to be crooked."

"Not too short," he grumped.

"I got it." She dipped her head and couldn't help but be drawn to him the moment his wary eyes locked onto hers. "Short on the sides and a little longer on top."

He nodded, gnawing his bottom lip.

Brit held back a smile and straightened. He was taking a huge risk, considering she'd never cut anyone's hair before. She sunk her hand into his dark curls. But she knew what she liked on a man, and she tingled at the prospect of cleaning this one up.

She slipped her fingers through the scissors sitting on the vanity in the bathroom. Colt sat on a small wooden stool, bare-chested in his jeans with a towel draped around his shoulders. The top of his head came to about her shoulder. She took a snip of his hair, the soft raven lock falling to the floor. When he didn't protest, she took a few more, maneuvering in front of him.

His hands came down on her hips. He held her in place. "That's a lot of hair," he said with concern.

Brit stopped and lifted the scissors. "Do you want to do it yourself?"

"No." His fingers moved up and under her sweater until they hovered at the waistband of her low-rise jeans. "I want to apologize for earlier."

"For kissing me."

"*No*," he said, like she was crazy for even questioning it. "I've been thinking about doing that for a while."

"Oh." Brit's stomach flittered. The only thing she regretted about his kiss was that it had ended. She didn't even mind his coarse whiskers. But if they were going to do it again, and she hoped they would, her tender skin was going to be chaffed. He kissed like it was his last. Intensity was good. She only hoped this wasn't more about availability. She'd read up on Leavenworth last night, too. If he'd had a girlfriend—jeez, wife, she should ask—Leavenworth didn't allow conjugal visits. That said a lot.

He was probably looking to get laid.

"I should have trusted you." His eyes held hers.

Brit regretted her last thought and couldn't stop the pout forming on her lips.

Oh, baby. Don't look at me that way.

There was a part of her he could never know about. But he had to know that she didn't regret her decision to remain with him. "I'm here because I want to be."

He pulled her down on his lap, her legs straddling him. "Can you see a future in all this?"

Brit rested her hands on his shoulders, angling the sharp point of the scissors away from him. That was a loaded question. Did he mean that they would prove his innocence and clear up this financial crisis of hers?

"I can't answer that."

He nodded. "If I'm recaptured, it could be years before I get out."

She knew that and refused to think that far ahead. "Then we can't let it happen."

His lips hovered over hers like a spell. They were rugged and shrouded in a beard that would be on every cop's radar as a distinguishing feature of fugitive Colt Rivers.

Brit eased off his lap, the warmth of his hands falling away. "You deserve to be exonerated. That's what we're going for here." Her stern words hung in the air. "It starts with this mop." She began hacking at his curls until there was a manageable amount she could style. She trimmed it around his ears, then snipped the top. She tousled it with her fingers and snipped some more.

She stood back, grabbed hair on either side of his head, and pulled it straight out to see if it was even. She smiled. "Not bad."

"Let me see." Colt made a move to get up.

"Oh, no." She pushed him back down on the stool. "I'm not finished." Brit eyed the scruffy beard.

"You're going to have to cut it back with the scissors first."

"Got it." Brit clipped at it, wiry hair falling on his thighs and the floor until she was close enough to use the razor. She reached for the can of Barbasol and sprayed the foam into her hand. She massaged it into his beard and mustache and wiped it away from his lips. Brit placed her hand on her hip, contemplating.

Colt's mouth quirked, his eyes filling with amusement. "You ever shave a man before?"

No. But she wanted to shave him and the thought tantalized her. "Maybe you could give me some pointers." She gave him a sweet smile.

Colt stood.

"Wait." Brit jumped in front of the sink and the mirror. "You can't look."

He took a step toward Brit. She wet her lips, wondering if he was positioning himself for another kiss. His arm reached around her, his eyes holding hers. "Heat up the razor," he said, his voice more intimate than what was necessary. With that, he turned on the hot water. "You'll get a closer shave."

Damn him. He was messing with her, and she could tell he was enjoying her awkwardness. Damn herself for being so attracted to him.

He pulled his stool over to the sink and sat down, taking her with him.

"What the hell?" She threw her arms around his neck for support, her legs straddling him. He seemed to like this position a lot. She should get up. But she was like a willy-nilly paper clip attracted to a magnet. She was drawn to him.

"I'm going to teach you." He gave her a lift of his brow. "It's what you wanted, right?"

Actually, it was killing her—his unveiling. Only the innuendo in his voice unnerved her. Now would be a good time to knock him off kilter and tell him what she had in mind.

"You teach me, and I'll teach you." Brit turned and picked up the razor. She stuck it under the hot running water and then turned back.

He cupped her butt with his hands. "And what are you going to teach me, Ms. Gentry?"

"Hypnosis." Brit cocked her head, deciding where to start, and lifted the razor.

"Hold up." His body tensed. "Hypnosis? I don't believe in that shit."

"No. You said you're not trained. Meaning . . ." Brit placed the razor about where she thought his sideburn should end and lightly shaved the hair a few times until she could see his skin. "You did believe, at least during our last conversation, that there are trained hypnotists." Brit positioned the razor on his cheek.

"Pull the skin taut," he instructed with a gleam in his eyes. "Does that mean I can make you do anything I want?"

Brit's pulse quickened, a flash of warmth spreading through her. His voice was teasing and deep, his words titillating. He liked to flirt, and he was good at it. Brit's shoulders sagged. He wasn't taking her seriously and, this was a biggie, if they succeeded with this hypnosis thing, she'd be under his control. She lifted the razor from his face. "This isn't going to work if I can't trust you."

His hand rode up the small of her back, his expression thoughtful. "I want you to trust me."

The sincerity in his voice should have alleviated her concerns. Maybe it was her. She needed to stop reading into everything he said. Like last night. She just assumed he was trying to coax her into sleeping with him.

Brit held the skin above his cheek with one hand and made downward light strokes. She then ran the razor under the hot water to remove the hair and heat up the blade. "I thought it was a line."

He laughed. "Which one?"

Brit gave him an exasperated look. "The one about subconscious rapport building." She finished with his cheek, moving on to his chin.

"It starts with conscious rapport building." He pulled her closer.

She didn't think she could be more conscious of him right now, sitting the way she was on his muscular thighs with her legs almost wrapped around him.

"And trust." She held the razor for emphasis and tipped his chin up.

He watched her intently while she shaved the thick whiskers along his throat. "Do you trust me, Brit?"

He obviously trusted her. She rinsed the razor, setting her sights on the left side of his face. "Yes."

"Where do you propose we do this hypnosis?"

"There's a solarium in the pool house complex. It's temperature controlled, and there's a nice chaise I could lay on."

He gave her a doubtful look and clucked his tongue. "The blind leading the blind."

"You don't think it will work." She stopped mid stroke.

"I'm not a smooth talker with a calming voice."

"How are you at sex?"

A smile played on his lips. "Excuse me?"

"How do you talk to a woman when you're"—Brit's cheeks warmed and she cleared her throat—"seducing her?"

He nodded. "I see your point."

Brit finished her last stroke above those well-defined lips of his. She sat it down and grabbed the wet washcloth, blotting the excess shaving cream from his face and neck.

Her breath caught.

"You nick me?" Colt's fingers shot up to his chin.

"No." It came out on a whisper. It was nothing like that. "It's a little red. I have some Sea Breeze in my bag." Brit hopped off his lap with the washcloth. She was more rattled than when they'd initially met. "I-I'll be right back." She tossed the rag in the sink and slipped out into his bedroom.

Her pulse quickened.

What the hell am I thinking? He may actually succeed in seducing me.

Brit cleared the bedroom, the stool scuffing the tile floor behind her. She guessed he was up checking her handiwork.

Well, she'd cleaned him up a little too well—clean-shaven, sharp angles, defined chin.

He wasn't handsome—he was flippin' gorgeous. Brit climbed the steps, all the while their conversation playing back in her head. It had been suggestive and provocative. Yet she said she trusted him.

But could she trust herself?

Chapter Fourteen

"**I**S THAT A BIKINI?" COLT'S HEAD TILTED, HIS BROWS rising suggestively.

Brit straightened from extending the back of the chaise in the downward position and pulled her zipper up higher on her sweatshirt. "It's a workout suit."

She'd let him believe that. In her haste, she'd only packed the black bikini. It wasn't like she could do flip turns. The pool was only three feet deep. But she could get a few laps in after this little hypnosis session. The motion would help to alleviate the pain in her upper back since the accident.

"Did you want to do this thing in the pool?" He peered through the glass door from the solarium. "Weightlessness might help."

"You don't have a suit."

He turned and grinned at her. "Didn't plan on wearing one."

"Exactly." Brit pointed her finger at him. "No suit, no pool."

Colt snorted. "Hypnotic suggestion perhaps."

She hoped he was kidding. Her body couldn't stop from trembling. This was it. If he couldn't pull something out of her subconscious, they were doomed.

"Hey." He grabbed her hand. "I was teasing. You can trust me."

She shook her head. "It's not that. I have no clue what I might have seen or heard that would help us. Maybe there's nothing."

He pulled her into his arms. "No more jokes on my end. We both knew your husband. Between the two of us we should be able to come up with a lead."

Brit leaned into him. He was solid and warm, his words reassuring. "Eventually they will connect you to me." She sighed.

He held her out from him. "You're talking about the car."

She nodded. "You stole it while in Kansas, I'm assuming."

"Not far from the prison." He slid an ottoman over, placing it behind the reclined chaise. He sat down, patting the long cushion in front of him. "Hadn't planned on wrecking it."

Brit sat down on the chaise, frowning. "They've run the VIN, I'm sure. They just haven't linked it to a particular escapee."

"Scoot back and lay your head down."

She eased back, folding her arms over her chest. "You're not worried?"

"Not a whole hell of a lot I can do at this point."

She guessed he was right—except hop the border. He had stayed because of her and her damned financial disclosure. She was concerned about it, but not enough to risk his freedom. Brit tipped her head back. "If this doesn't work I'm absolving you from any obligation toward me."

"Close your eyes."

Brit settled down, the contrast of green palms strategically placed in the tropical oasis inside the solarium and the snowflakes hitting the skylight overhead, barely making a sound, surreal. "Okay if I watch the snow instead?"

"Is it calming?"

"Yes."

"Maybe we should have had the Seth discussion beforehand."

"I'm good." Her anger had faded to indifference where Seth was concerned. Brit reached her hand back, searching for Colt's. "Ask me anything you think might jog my memory."

Colt's fingers intertwined with hers. "Questions, huh?"

"Yeah, like we need to figure out a timeline." She tipped her head back, a smile touching her lips. He was gorgeous—even from that angle. "Like how you and I fit into Seth's life chronologically."

"Gotcha." Colt loosened his grip on her. "Look at the snow."

Brit reluctantly let go of his hand and gazed skyward. She'd never been hypnotized before. What if that part of her life he couldn't know about sprang from her lips? She took a deep breath. *It is what it is.* Brit concentrated on the snow high above. "Did he ever mention me?"

Colt chuckled. "No. I'd remember."

"I met him just before he retired; he was all but out of the military. When did this thing happen in Afghanistan?"

Colt massaged her neck. "Six months before that."

"Then I hadn't come on the scene yet."

"How long have you been married?"

"It would have been three years this January."

"Did you bring your phone?"

Brit's heart sped up. If he was trying to keep her calm, this line of questioning wasn't helping.

Brit sat up. "It's in my bag. Why?" It came out a little defensive.

"Jeez. Relax." Something flitted in those eyes of his. Frustration, maybe. Frustrated that she still couldn't one hundred percent trust him. "You have a problem if we record this?"

Brit's shoulders relaxed. He had a point—a good point. They would have something to refer back to, something they could pick apart until they had a solid lead on the artifacts.

"No. I think it's a good idea." She gave him a conciliatory smile. "I'm trying. But trust got me into this predicament." She reached for her bag on the tiled floor. After punching in the code and accessing the video icon, she handed it to him. "Just hit play when you're ready."

He took it from her, his expression dubious. "This isn't going to work if you can't settle down. Is there anything else that could be upsetting to you that I need to know before we start?"

Oh, she could think of several things. But he wasn't her shrink. Brit searched her mind for what she thought may help their cause. "Maybe you need to ask me about our life together—our marriage, his extravagant spending." Her eyes widened. "What about an offshore bank account?"

"Wouldn't you know if you found a bank statement?"

"I don't know what I might have run across. At the time, I had no reason to question him. I believed him. So getting a peek at a bank statement in passing wouldn't raise my suspicions. I probably couldn't tell you how much was in an offshore account if he had one. But you might be able to jog the name of the bank out of my subconscious if you can first determine if it even exists."

He shook his head. "This is way beyond my expertise. You got a video—maybe from YouTube—so I can get a sense of how this works?"

"You mean hypnosis?"

"Yeah." He scrubbed the back of his neck, giving her a sideways glance. "I kind of like you the way you are."

How funny. He was afraid he could alter her personality. "So you like me."

He laughed. "In a pain-in-the-ass kind of way."

She should have known a man like Colt Rivers would find it difficult to express himself in a kinder, gentler way. After all, he'd been a member of an elite commando force as an Army Ranger. Witnessed and experienced things that would send most running for the hills. Problem was she was growing closer to him and getting to know the many facets of the man—not just the hardened career soldier who'd been dealt a bad hand.

His concern for her and willingness to see this through, knowing he could simply pack it in and be in Canada before the sun rose tomorrow, proved he was a man deserving of her trust—all of it—and her respect. But it was much more than that when you peeled back the layers. She liked him, too. This house had always been a hollow shell the few times she'd stayed with Seth here. Too many bedrooms, too many buildings, too many amenities. Funny thing was she wanted to share everything this house had to offer with Colt. Even the pool.

"Hey." Colt dipped his head. "You put yourself in a trance?"

Crap. Had she? She'd been lost in her thoughts, transported to a place of reflection. This was beyond her expectations. Brit grabbed his hand. "It's going to work." Her voice rose with a giddy excitement.

Colt frowned at her. "Glad you're so confident."

"No, I mean it." She took the phone from him and accessed the video. Handing it back, she smiled at him. "I watched this one last night. It's easy."

Amazingly so, she was finding.

Colt played it, his brows meeting over his nose. "You need to be facing me." He got up, gave her the phone, and repositioned the back of the chaise to a sitting position. "Sit back."

Brit followed his instructions, bringing her legs up to make room for him on the end.

"You need to stretch out." He slid the ottoman to the end of the chaise and straddled it.

Wow. He was taking this more seriously than she'd hoped. Asking him to try something that was out of their realm seemed crazy at best. But he'd agreed.

A smile touched her lips. He may be wearing Seth's clothes, but there was no comparison.

"What?"

She waved him off. "It's nothing."

"Tell me." He straightened her legs, his fingers massaging the arch of her feet.

Brit curled her toes and shrugged. "You're a nice guy."

He laughed. "A desperate guy."

Faded jeans molded his tight thighs. His fingers continued their hypnotic ministrations. He pushed her sweatpants past her calves and worked her muscles. They were tight, too.

Brit concentrated on Colt. He was bulkier than Seth, the white T-shirt stretching taut across his chest. He'd shed the flannel shirt on a nearby chair, complaining about the heat. He probably wouldn't like Maryland's humid summers.

Strange thought to have.

It wasn't like they would ever have a long-lasting relationship. It was immediate and fleeting. She sunk into the cushion. They had, maybe, a few more days.

It all depended on a little thing called an indictment.

Brit barely heard Colt's voice asking her to close her eyes. Her lids flickered shut—her last coherent thought troubling.

My indictment.

Colt lifted Brit's arm, letting it go. It dropped like dead weight.

"Son of a bitch." She was out. He hadn't even gotten a chance to tell her to go to that happy place. Or that she would clearly remember everything that happened. And this was a biggie—he couldn't make her do anything that she didn't want to do.

Shit. He could think of a few things he'd like to see her do with him. Only he wanted her wide awake and aware.

He sat back a little unsure. Now what?

He pressed Rewind on the video. Where the hell was he? What step? He hit play. *Damn.* He couldn't say for sure, but it appeared she'd put herself under. He guessed his little massage had relaxed her.

Hell, he'd enjoyed it.

He was a little concerned, though. She was frowning. That couldn't be good. Colt hit fast forward and then play again. The soothing voice of the hypnotist sounded, well, not like him, that was for damn sure. *Ah, hell.* This was going to be awkward. Then he remembered something Brit had shared with him earlier. Seduction.

Now that he could do. His mouth twisted—still awkward. Usually the women were awake and responsive. He shook his head. He'd promised to record it, too. Something told him this would be a one-way conversation.

Brit stirred and Colt went on alert. She'd be pissed with him if he screwed this up.

Talk to her, man.

Colt accessed the video icon and hit record, sitting it down next to her on the chaise. He leaned forward. "You're in that happy place where anything is possible." He closed his eyes, shaking his head at his singsong voice.

Lame.

Colt cleared his mind of embarrassment and concentrated on what was important here. He opened his eyes. Brit's expression was . . . serene. Okay. This was working.

"You will look back on this experience as a game changer in your life. As a result of these suggestions, you will feel as if you are headed for a certain and predetermined success."

He stroked her open palm. His thumb lingered over her callouses. He still didn't have an answer for that. Her fingers relaxed. Suggesting that she trust him would be his lead-in. He'd get to Seth in a minute.

"Trust your instincts. Level with the man you're with now. He needs your honesty. He's given you his." Colt held her hand, hoping it would give her reassurance.

Her breathing came in even waves, and Colt would do his level best to time his words to the rhythm of her breaths. "You're relaxed and focused and aware of the smallest of details in your life—your relationship with your husband and his behavior. You'll be able to clear your mind and pick up only on those moments that seem suspicious or deceptive where he is concerned."

He needed to be clear on this point. "You will share them with the man you're with now. Your lives are intertwined, your destinies are one. You will concentrate on unexplained cash, bank accounts you're not aware of, hiding places where artifacts lay hidden."

Colt couldn't help but feel his suggestions were focused primarily on his needs. Sure, the disclosure of said artifacts would assist her with this financial disclosure investigation. But what the woman really needed was absolution.

A thought curled his lips. Maybe he was overstepping his bounds—and she'd know it, too, once she reviewed the audio—but he'd risk it.

"You're not to blame for your husband's death."

It was a jackass move on Seth's part to take her out in the first place. Seth had done the same thing while in Afghanistan—leveraging his platoon recklessly to achieve his own goals. He'd done it with Colt's freedom that day in the hangar. He wasn't about to let Brit beat herself up any more over something she had no control over. If there was one thing he could give her before their time together ended, it would be peace of mind.

"When you awake you will no longer blame yourself for your husband's death."

Colt sat back. Sleeping Beauty had nothing on Brit Gentry. Dark lashes dusted her pretty face. Smooth blond hair draped her shoulders. And it was all he could do not to make his own fairy tale come true by kissing the sensual curve of her mouth.

He snorted. She'd probably slap him upside the head for breaching her trust. He'd deserve it, too. Good thing the recorder didn't pick up on his internal thoughts.

He did regret one, though. His objective had been to clear his name. He hadn't counted on Brit, and his reaction was mixed. She was a huge complication—more so after he commandeered her vehicle.

But now he couldn't imagine his life without her, which was a crazy-ass thing to be concerned with, considering he was probably on the Ten Most Wanted List.

Yet he couldn't get her out of his mind. She was soft, feminine . . . courageous—everything he ever wanted in a woman.

Now all he wanted to do was stop time.

He couldn't, and it pissed him off.

Chapter Fifteen

*P*EACEFUL DIDN'T COME CLOSE TO DESCRIBING THE restfulness that seemed to flow through Brit's body. Her eyes fluttered open. Colt sat next to her on the chaise, hand clasped around her hand, brow furrowed with lines bracketing his mouth.

"What's wrong?" The weightlessness evaporated, and she was left with only heavy reality. "It didn't work."

"I didn't say that."

"What did *I* say, then?"

"Nothing."

Her shoulders sagged. "Then it was a waste."

"Look." He shook her hand in his. "I only gave you suggestions. I think the idea here is that your subconscious mind will pick up on them and that your conscious mind will act."

Brit mulled that over. "You taped it?"

"It's all right here." He handed her the phone.

Maybe she didn't want to know his suggestions. "It might sway me."

He shrugged. "I don't know."

If that was the way it worked, she shouldn't chance it. "Then I won't listen to it."

He released her hand and stood. "I don't know," he grumped, then scratched his head. "It's your call."

Brit's temples throbbed along with her back. She'd been sitting too long.

"I'm going to work out in the pool."

"I think I'll run in the gym."

That was a good idea. The exercise would release some of those endorphins. Seemed he needed it more than she.

"Check the chest. There should be some running shorts in there."

He gave her a sideways glance. "Maybe I'll find a pair of trunks."

"Maybe." She gave him a lift of her brow and motioned him out the door that opened into the bedrooms and the second level of the pool house complex. "You remember where the gym is?"

"Down the stairs and on the left." He gripped the knob. "What time's dinner?"

Brit couldn't help but smile. When they left the main house, the stew had just begun to permeate the kitchen with its beefy goodness. But it was more than that. They were becoming this couple, working together on one common goal, living as though they'd taken that vow to be true to one another, which in a sense they had. She was the only holdout—with the honesty part.

A sadness came over her.

"What is it?" Colt gave her a curious look.

She waved it off and grabbed her bag off the floor. "Nothing. But do you think you could check the stew while you're over there? I should be done in forty-five minutes."

"Sure." He rubbed his stomach. "I saw that bread you bought. You want me to preheat the oven?"

"That'd be great." Brit turned toward the pool that lay beyond the glass windows of the solarium, the click of a door shutting behind her. *Crap*. She hoped he remembered the combo to the main house. She'd given it to him again when they opened the combo to the pool house complex. It was the same.

Oh well, she'd know soon enough if he couldn't get in. Brit opened the door to the pool and scooted in, closing it before the damn child safety alarm went off. It could wake the dead—a devilish thought came over her— or scare the bejesus out of a fugitive who wasn't aware the device existed, especially since one of the alarms was located on the staircase he would be descending. She made a mental note to tell him and set her bag down on a nearby chair, flustered.

I like him—a lot.

She shouldn't if she rewound their first several hours together. But knowing what she knew now—the stress and uncertainty he was under and remained under—she could see *herself* using the gun as an equalizer to get him to follow her directives, knowing full well she would never have used it. He'd admitted as much to her earlier when he confessed his true identity.

Brit slipped out of her sweatsuit and grabbed her cap and goggles. Still. What the hell were they doing? Grocery shopping, cooking meals, eating together. All her life she dreamed of having what her parents shared—dependence on one another but in a good way as they created a sound and loving environment for her and her brother.

Now in their twilight years, they were inseparable.

She needed to understand something right now. She *would* be separated from Colt. There were only two ways this was going down—he'd escape to Canada or be captured. Brit shoved her hair up in her cap and grimaced when her fingers slipped and the thick rubber slapped her forehead. *Great.* Like her head didn't hurt enough already.

Brit dipped her toe in the water and shivered. It was heated but still a shock compared to the South American jungle going on inside the pool house. Brit frowned. She wished she could teleport them to the Amazon. It would be a hell of a lot safer than the future awaiting them here.

She had to face facts. She felt no different since being hypnotized. There would be no miracle recollection that would save their asses.

What a crackpot idea.

Tonight after dinner, she'd help him pack up some supplies and clothes. She didn't like it, didn't want to say goodbye. But giving him a chance at escape and a new life, although devastating for her in many ways, would keep him alive.

Brit glided her goggles onto her head, positioned them over her eyes, and waded down the steps. The immediate chill reminded her of that night on the Chesapeake, but unlike her usual memories, there was no remorse or guilt.

That bastard had done it to himself. He should have never forced her to go out with an impending storm.

She came up for air and began her workout.

A smile tugged at the corner of Colt's mouth. Wine. *Damn.* He'd prefer a nice, cold Big Sky Ivan the Terrible Imperial Stout—best beer brewed in Montana.

The humor left him. Sounded more like how he'd treated Brit on their first day. Well, he couldn't take it back, but he could make up for it. He shut the lower cabinet of the wet bar and rummaged for a corkscrew in the drawer above it. After popping the cork, he filled two wineglasses and set one down at each plate. Then he checked the oven and shoved the cookie sheet with the bread inside to bake for twelve minutes. He tasted the stew again. Of course that was a lie. He'd had a bowl already because, well, it smelled good, but tasted even better—the woman could cook.

He'd helped. Not that tossing a salad with the fixings she'd already bought came close to her culinary skill. Hell, he could get used to this. Maybe not the extravagance, but the woman—definitely.

The question was could a woman like Brit get used to living a simple life? He snorted. "You're getting way ahead of yourself, man."

Before the war he'd lived in a modest log rancher with a green tin roof. But what his home lacked in size, his land made up for—horse pastures, private stream, all surrounded by national forest.

His father kept it up for him. It wasn't a piece of real estate he wanted to lose, if for no other reason than he'd buried his dog Beau there, on a knoll under the aspen behind his home.

It had been paid in full before Operation Enduring Freedom even had a name or a mission. But there was upkeep and taxes, which his father had been saddled with after his incarceration.

Looked like he might never return.

He didn't put much stock in their little voodoo session in the solarium.

For all he knew she'd fallen asleep. Still didn't explain why she hadn't stirred or woke up after he dropped her arm down to her side.

Didn't matter. He was running out of time. He'd have to make a decision here soon. He also needed to think and act like a fugitive. It started with the gun he'd cleaned. It should be with him when he left the house—even if that was the simple walk between buildings.

He'd really be in a world of shit if they ambushed him without a weapon. Colt strode over to the closet that had been left unlocked and picked his gun off the shelf. He shoved it into the waistband of his jeans.

He'd tell her his reasoning for carrying when he saw her. She wouldn't like it, but she needed to understand he wasn't going to be taken alive. All the more reason to walk out that door and keep going. He was beginning to care for her too much.

The oven beeped. *Shit*. Colt hightailed it into the kitchen, amazed at his agility. She'd patched him up, and for that he would be forever grateful. It was high time he returned the favor.

It started with saying goodbye.

Chapter Sixteen

*A*N EAR-PIERCING SIREN SHATTERED THE CALM WATER OF the pool. Brit covered her ears, her heart thumping. She splashed up the steps and darted across the deck, stubbing her toe on the concrete.

"Shit, shit, shit, shit, *shit!*" She stopped, gnashed her teeth, and then yanked at her ankle, trying to get a look at her big toe. She froze when Colt rounded the corner with a gun, an unmistakable dread lining his pale face.

"Shut the door!" Brit motioned behind him and then slapped her hands over her ears.

Colt aimed his gun to the right then the left before hunkering down below the window ledge that looked out onto the driveway, leading up to Marsh Hill Road.

Oh, God, he wasn't getting it. Dripping wet, Brit rushed to the door he'd left ajar, hitting the button on the wall and slamming the door shut at the same time. The inescapable blare of the alarm ceased, and she was met with blessed silence, if she didn't count her manic heartbeat thundering in her ears.

"God damn." He swung on Brit, his eyes still filled with terror. "It sounded like a fucking air raid."

"It's a safety alarm for God's sake. Do you see any flashing lights? Police cars? Get a grip."

He was kidding himself if he thought he'd made it unscathed through the war.

A suggestive smile formed on his lips. Not the response she expected. He shoved the gun into the waistband of his jeans. "What are you, the creature from the black lagoon?"

She jerked her head back, astounded with his comparison.

He took measured steps toward her and then tapped on the outside plastic of her goggles. "I'd say you're the sexiest monster I've ever seen."

Oh, hell. She was still in her cap and goggles. *I must look like a reptile.* Brit ripped off her tinted goggles, the fluorescent lights more intense. Or was it his stare?

His eyes swept over her. "I found those trunks."

Brit's arm flew across the swells of her breasts, barely covered by the scantily cut bikini top. She snatched her towel from the top of the hot tub near the door and held it to her chest, shivering. "Wh-what are you doing with the gun?"

"You're cold."

"I'm not." Her teeth chattered. "Answer my question."

"You're making me soft, Brit. Home cooked meals, a warm bed, amenities out the ass."

Her mouth fell open with an irritated breath. "You didn't give me a choice."

"I am now." He pulled her into his arms. "I can't stay. You and I both know it. That crazy voodoo magic we tried back there, even if it works, won't come soon enough. It could take months, if not years, for something to shake loose in that pretty head of yours."

Head? Jeez. She still hadn't removed her cap. Brit reached up and casually tugged it off, grimacing when it pulled her hair. But the pain wasn't as acute as her racing heart. He wasn't saying anything she hadn't already agonized over. "Will you stay the night?"

He rubbed her arms, the warmth of his hands sinking into her cold skin. "Only if you promise to relax and eat dinner with me like a normal couple."

"Couple?" She cocked her head.

He chuckled. "We're not normal."

It wasn't the word "normal" she'd clung to. "I need to pop in those rolls."

"It's done. I'm only waiting on you." Colt grabbed her sweats and handed them to her. "Not that I'm not digging the string bikini, but it's near freezing."

"Ah . . . right." She was tongue-tied and nervous and scared. More so for him. She wrapped the towel around her. "I'll change in the powder room."

"The one off the solarium?"

"Yeah," she said a little breathless and grabbed her bag, shoving her cap and goggles inside. "You go first, and I'll handle the door." She gave him a knowing smile.

"I'm not a mental case."

It was called denial. PTSD didn't make him any less of a man. If anything, it only proved his bravery. In this day and age, the military wasn't your average American male's vocation. She knew a thing or two about the unknown lurking behind a door. It had to be similar, if not more frightening, in a foreign land.

"I didn't say you were." She tightened her grip on the towel and opened the door. "Gotta be quick."

Colt leapt over the threshold. Brit was on his heels and slammed the door shut. Holding open the other one, Colt motioned her through, into the hallway that led to a sitting area and the two bedrooms off the solarium.

Brit entered the powder room off to the side and turned on the light. "I'll meet you in the foyer below." She shut the door, ripped off her wet suit, and stared at her reflection.

What am I thinking?

She wanted him. He was leaving. She'd never see him again. All the wrong reasons to have sex with him. The heat crept into her face, and she threw on her clothes, slipped on her clogs, and tried with desperation to get him out of her head.

Stupid. He's right down the stairs.

She opened the door and growled.

"You okay?" Colt called from below.

"Fine," she snapped and took the steps, meeting him in the foyer.

"Nice movie theater." He hooked his chin toward the open door on the right. "Don't suppose you have cable in there."

"*No.*" It came out clipped. "I mean it's only set up to show DVDs."

Holy shit! She'd forgotten about the theater. Relax. He couldn't tell from looking at the setup it was equipped with working cable.

"I haven't been to a movie since . . ." He chuckled. "This is embarrassing. I don't remember."

She took his arm and led him to the front door, facing the main house. "Then we can watch one tonight."

He opened it and ushered her out. "What movies do you like?"

She laughed. "War movies."

"No kidding." He shut the door and leaned into her with his shoulder like she was his buddy or something. "I think I'd rather enjoy that hot tub facing the lake for my last night. If you'll join me."

"No commando."

"For me or you?"

She ran in front of him on the parking pad to the house, the chilly, wet snow slipping into her clogs. "Both," she called back, giggling as she opened the door.

"I'll chance it." Colt eased his legs into the hot tub from where he sat on the edge.

"No you won't." Brit glided over from her sitting position inside the hot tub, grabbing him just below his injured knee. "I wasn't thinking earlier about your wound. You want the scab to stay on. The heat of the water will soften it."

He didn't care. What he did care about was splashing around in the hot tub with her in that bikini. "It's been three days."

"If it was anywhere other than the bend of your knee, I wouldn't be concerned."

That thought caught and held, and an inexplicable warmth filled him. Odd, considering he was bare chested, wearing only Seth's trunks. Colt gave her a curious lift of his brow. "You saying you care about me, Brit Gentry?"

She gave him an exasperated look. "I shouldn't. Not after our initial encounter."

Colt cupped her face. "It wasn't my intention to frighten you. I thought I had a few more days to figure things out but then you hightailed it out of Dodge."

"Left for the lake."

He nodded. "Even then I'd planned to approach you in a public setting—explain my circumstances and ask for your help."

"Would you have told me about the fugitive thing?"

Not likely. The wind picked up, ruffling his hair, and Colt trembled against the cold. "How do you think you would have reacted to that?"

A frown formed on her pretty mouth. "You're shivering. Let's go inside." Brit let go of him and slid out of the hot tub, grabbing the white terry-cloth robe from the hook on the outside wall of the house.

She slipped into it. But not before he got a good long look at her tight rump.

"Come on." She held out a matching robe to him. "We can light a fire downstairs *and*"—she eyed the bottle of wine sitting on the corner of the hot tub—"finish the merlot."

They'd already polished off the red wine he'd popped for dinner. She'd drunk more than he had. If he didn't know any better, he'd guess Brit Gentry was summoning up the courage for something. That was both good and bad.

Colt put on the robe and opened the glass slider to the basement level. "I'll go up and get some wood from the front porch."

"There's some already stacked on the hearth." She passed him on her way in with two empty wineglasses and the bottle. "I'll get a lighter."

He shut the door and then busied himself with building up the wood in the fireplace while Brit flitted from room to room.

"Found it." She stood next to him, barefoot with pink painted toes, sexy ankles, and shapely calves that disappeared beneath the heavy robe.

Colt took the lighter from her and broke off a piece from the starter log he'd found on the mantel. He lit it and laid it inside the wooden teepee he created. "You should start to feel the heat soon." He turned.

Brit sat on the carpet, propped up on pillows she'd taken from the sofa, her long legs bent at the knees. She patted the pillows next to her. "Come sit down."

Damn. Was she trying to turn him on?

She poured a glass of wine, then reached for his glass, refilling it. "Seth has a wine cellar. I thought it was pretentious."

"Where?" He sat down next to her and took the full glass of wine from her trembling fingers.

"Under the pool house complex."

"You've seen it?"

"No." She laughed. "By then I'd tuned out him and his Memory Maker masterpiece."

Must be the wine. He was having trouble believing this small revelation, if it meant anything at all, came from her subconscious.

"Can you show it to me?"

"Now that's a dilemma." She took a sip. "I don't know where it is."

Colt took her glass.

Her eyes widened. "I wasn't done."

"I think you've had enough."

"You have no idea," she mumbled and covered her legs with the robe.

"This could be important, Brit." His eyes held hers. "Wine cellars are temperature controlled. Artifacts would need a dry climate to preserve them."

"We could look at the plans." She made a move to get up and swayed.

Colt rose and caught her, sitting her down on the chair next to the sofa. "Stay. I'll get them."

He skirted the gaming table and took the steps two at a time. This had to be it. He rounded the banister to the stairs leading to the loft and opened the unlocked door. He grabbed the plans and returned to find Brit sipping her wine again.

Jesus. What was with her tonight?

"Hey." He sat down on the coffee table in front of her, laying the plans next to him. "What's wrong?"

"Nothing."

"What's with the wine then?"

Her head jerked back, offended. "What are you saying?"

He took it from her and set it down on an end table. "I need you sober."

Brit's expression changed from indignant to apologetic to one of discomfort. "God, this is embarrassing."

"Embarrassing? How?"

She folded her arms in front of her. "I was thinking about sleeping with you." Her head dipped, making it impossible for him to see her face. "Before you left."

Colt's brows rose. *Really?* He could think of nothing he'd want more than to have Brit Gentry writhing beneath him. He tipped her chin up, completely lost in those sensitive eyes of hers. "I'm flattered. But I don't want your mind clouded with wine when I make love to you."

"But you're leaving."

"Was." He lifted up the plans. "The voodoo is working, beautiful." He unfurled the plans and laid them out on the table. He'd built his rambler and knew a thing or two about schematics. It might take him a few hours to pore over the twenty- to twenty-five pages of Memory Maker. But if there was a wine cellar or any other unidentified room, he'd find it.

Chapter Seventeen

"**A**NY LUCK?" B<small>RIT SET A CUP OF COFFEE, THE WAY HE</small> liked it, next to his elbow on the dining room table.

"Thanks." With tired eyes, he took a sip of it. "Can you take a look at this?" He patted the chair next to him.

Brit gathered her robe while balancing her cup of tea, the caffeine doing little to keep her eyes open at two in the morning, and sat down with a twinge of guilt. She should have offered to look at the plans, but at the time her wine-fogged brain wouldn't have been able to pick out the great room, much less some wine cellar she couldn't say for sure existed.

"He'd been arguing about the temperature controls with the general contractor that day on the phone. I thought it was the cellar." She held her aching head with her hand and gave him a questioning look. "Maybe I had it wrong. It could have been the steam shower room he was talking about?"

"The one in the gym."

Brit nodded. "Maybe he nixed the whole idea of stuffy rows of priceless bottles he wouldn't break a seal on."

"What's this right here?" Colt smoothed out the eighteen by twenty-four inch curling page.

"Looks to be empty space." She pointed to the area in question. "HVAC's missing—no ducts."

"Heating, ventilation, and air-conditioning?" He gave her a curious look.

"Yeah?" She swung the plans over and took a closer look. Nope. She had it right. "They don't exist."

"Are there any other skills you have you'd like to share with me?"

Panic rode up her chest. *Shit.* She was giving away her training.

"Ah, no." She gave him a sweet smile. "I took drafting in college."

"Uh huh." He rolled up the plans. "Let's go next door and check out the exact location of this space."

"I'll just change." She made a move to get up when his hand caught her arm.

"Let's not make a big production out of this." His voice was terse and tired and . . . "I'm sorry." He stood up, taking her with him, his arms slipping around her. "I didn't mean to snap."

"It's okay. We're both tired. My boots are by the bench in the foyer." She freed herself from his embrace, each going in opposite directions—him to his room and she to the foyer. She gathered her boots and sat down on the bench to put them on, wondering where she'd lost her sense of style since meeting Colt.

He emerged from his room looking, well, hilarious in his boots and bare legs. Brit swallowed her laughter. They were a pair, and she was getting to know him under the most severe of circumstances. At first she'd been ready to blast him for his sharp tongue. But he'd realized his error. She'd commend him for that, especially considering what he—they—were up against.

Brit stood and scooped up the plans off the bench. "Let's go." She was out the door before him and making tracks across the parking area when she noticed the door was opened to the pool house complex. She swung around, her head missing Colt's shoulder by degrees. "Did you leave the door open?"

"I closed it." He made an about-face and ducked back in the main house, reemerging with his gun. "Go back in and wait for me."

This was stupid. She'd already proven she could handle a gun. Two were better than one. Fine. She'd let him think he was protecting her and go back. Only she'd retrieve her gun instead and head over. But, honestly, she thought he was making something out of nothing. If she remembered correctly, Seth told her that door had issues with the bolt catching. Strange how minute exchanges with Seth seemed to percolate from her brain since Colt had hypnotized her.

Brit cleared the door to the main house, reached for her gun from the hall closet, and ran across the parking pad with the plans. In all likelihood this would be nothing, and they'd need them. She slipped in through the door and tossed the plans onto the leather couch inside the theater room.

Colt peered down the stairs from the second level. "I thought I told you to stay put."

"I have my own theories about the door." She grabbed it and slammed it shut and tried to open it without turning the knob. It didn't budge. She tried it a second time. The bolt remained lodged in the hole of the jamb.

"What the hell are you—?"

Brit opened the door and slammed it a third time.

"Jesus." He thundered down the stairs. "Are you deaf?" He reached for the knob.

Brit smacked his hand away. "Don't turn it." Making sure to follow her own directives, she yanked straight back. It opened. "I knew it." She turned on him. "It's the lock. Sometimes it doesn't latch."

His shoulders visibly relaxed. "I didn't see anything upstairs."

She wasn't surprised. "Was the door leading in from the solarium locked?"

"Yeah." He motioned her back down a hall to the rear of the staircase. "Found another locked door, though."

Brit shook her head. She wasn't surprised about that, either. Truth was she'd been here very little and had hated Memory Maker and all it stood for. Seth all but abandoned her with his obsession at the lake. This was her second time back since he died.

She stood in front of the six-panel pine door. "We're going to need a key."

"Screw that." Colt pointed his gun at the lock.

"Whoa." She pulled on his arm. "What'd I tell you about destroying this house?"

He grunted and put the gun down. "Fine. Where are your keys?"

Brit pursed her lips. "In my room on the dresser."

He threw his head back and groaned. "I'll get them." Colt strode down the hall and out the door, slamming it behind him.

Be a brat.

Had he waited for her to think on it a little longer, she would have directed him back upstairs to the wet bar in the sitting room. Knives were in a drawer in the cabinet. For all they knew the key might not work for this lock, either. Brit made her way upstairs. She rummaged through the silverware drawer, someone had left it in a jumbled heap.

The door downstairs opened just as she located one of the butter knives. "I'll be right down!"

She'd bring it with her, just in case. Brit passed by the bedroom door on her right off the sitting room. Something drew her in, and she flicked on the light. King bed, nightstands, dresser—no TV—bathroom.

What? What is it you want me to see?

As if in a trance, Brit walked past the bed to the far wall, consumed with the image of Swallow Falls. The image was framed in a distressed wooden frame. Seth had taken her there once. He'd been on a mission that day on the path along the river. She could barely keep up with him. Odd that he'd chosen to go at sunset right before the park closed. Most visitors were going the opposite direction.

"Brit, get your ass down here!"

Okay, Colt's abrasive nature was getting on her nerves tonight. She got it. He was on edge—desperate. She was, too. But now she'd lost whatever train of thought she'd been on.

"Coming!" She skirted the bed, turned off the light, and took the steps to the first level, hanging a right down the hall. "What is it?" she said with heat.

"You tell me." He held open the door.

Chapter Eighteen

A STONE WALL RAN THE LENGTH OF THE OPENING OF THE door in the small alcove behind the stairs. Brit placed her hand against the irregular-sized rocks. She remembered the samples sitting on Seth's desk at their home in Chesapeake Beach.

"It's moss rock. Seth had been trying to decide between this and Pocono sandstone. He chose this one because it's native to Western Maryland. The other is indigenous to Ohio." She shrugged. "Just another factoid he could throw at his guests."

"Doesn't explain why he covered it up."

"No. But it was crunch time. The house needed to be ready for his mother of all client retreats."

"You saying it accidentally got covered up?"

Brit turned, walking toward the theater room. She reached inside the doorway and flipped on the wall sconces. Colt was behind her.

"The wall begins in here." She pointed toward the screen on the wall in front. Behind it beautiful stone ran floor to ceiling, which was about two-stories high to accommodate for the stadium-style seating. But unlike the chairs in a movie theater the levels held leather couches with throw pillows, blankets, and tables in between for food and drinks.

Where the couches ended, there was about twelve feet—plenty of space for Seth to set up a podium below and do his financial PowerPoint presentations. He could hook his computer into a port in the wall connected to the projector. Below the screen a built-in housed the electronics.

"Maybe the designer decided on drywall for the small space on the back wall of the hallway," Brit mused.

"Why a door? A locked door?" Colt took the steps leading down.

She didn't know. Seth was weird when it came to solutions. PTSD might have been a contributing factor.

"He was known for his fits of anger." Brit grabbed hold of the rail. "Even with the GC and the subs." She took the wide steps down, careful not to trip. "Pete told me once, if you aren't up here twenty-four seven while your house is built, shit happens." Brit shrugged. "Shit happened, and knowing Seth, he put a door and a lock on it so everyone would think it was something it's not."

"A fuckup." Colt pressed his hands against the stone.

She was going to say closet. But it was more than that. It was how Seth lived his life—pretending to be something he was not. Like a loyal comrade, a decorated officer, and a loving husband.

"What are you—?"

A stone door popped open, and Colt slipped inside, searching the wall. Brit shivered. She had no idea there was a hidden door. A switch clicked and the lights came on.

Brit's heart slowed. "Pumps for the pool."

"And AV equipment." Colt pointed toward the wall where the back of the cable box, DVD player, and stereo with all its cables ran from one component to another.

Brit stepped out and examined the door. It was thick with stone affixed to the front. They'd toothed the stones so that when it shut it was like a puzzle, the pieces fitting together with no straight seams to give away a location of a door.

"How'd you know?"

"Saw it a lot in the Middle East. They're big on false doors." He turned off the light and shut the door. "Only they didn't use them to create an aesthetically pleasing stone wall. They believe a false door allows the deceased a link between the living and the dead so the deceased could receive sustenance from the land of the living."

"That's creepy."

"Creepy, maybe . . ." Colt rushed up the stairs. "But where there's one there's more," he called back and disappeared through the doorway of the theater.

Brit ran up the stairs of the theater and made the sharp left down the hall of the foyer toward the back of the stairs. Colt pressed in on the stone from every corner. Nothing budged.

Brit leaned into the wall, yawning. It had to be close to three or later. "I think it's just a wall."

Colt's jaw tensed, and he hit the wall with his fist. "Bastard's screwing with me."

"Hey." Brit put her arm around him. "It's not the wall. There's something else. It's upstairs."

He lifted his brows.

"I'll show you." Brit took the stairs and entered the sitting area with Colt on her heels. "It's in here." She flicked on the light inside the bedroom and went over to the far wall.

"A picture," he said, his tone deflated.

Brit placed her hands on either side of it and lifted it off the wall.

"Whoa. I got it." Colt took it from her, his eyes narrowing. "What are you planning on doing with this?"

She took a deep breath through her nose. "I'm going to stare at it until it comes to me."

He gave her a look that effectively said she'd lost it.

"It's the voodoo." She walked past him and out the door, pausing. "You coming?"

He nodded his head, adjusted the picture so he could hold it with one hand. Skirting the bed, he checked out the other pictures hanging on the walls. "Why this one?"

"Because he took me to Swallow Falls where this photo was taken. He was acting odd that day—arriving when the park was closing. I think he was up to something."

"You can't remember?"

Brit reached in the bedroom and turned off the light. "I was that close before you told me to get my ass downstairs." She gave him her back and headed for the steps.

He followed her, grabbing her arm as she hit the tile floor of the main level. She turned.

His expression was contrite. "I was pissed."

Brit gave him a pointed look.

"Not at you. Seth."

Right. The stone wall. "Did it ever occur to you that space might be for the pool?" Brit took two strides, grabbed the plans from the couch, and turned off the light in the theater room. She covered up a yawn. "I'm talking about the depth."

Colt frowned. "Not sure what you mean."

"The space. Could it have been the pool we were looking at and the space needed below grade for the shell?"

"No. The space is to the right of it."

Brit contemplated that. "Then it's nothing but a crawl space."

"Maybe." Colt leaned the frame against the wall in the hallway and opened the front door leading to the parking area.

The cold air hit Brit's bare legs, and she shivered. "Where are you going?"

"Check around the foundation." He headed out and down the ramp, leaving her to stare at an open doorway.

She should shut the door and stay warm. But if there was something to find, she wanted to see it for herself. Brit closed the door and huddled into her robe. She took the ramp with the plans still clenched between her fingers, slipping when she made a sharp turn up the driveway. She climbed the slight grade and rounded the front of the glass enclosed pool area, the steam on the windows taunting her with its tropical climate. The snow had stopped hours ago, but it was high enough that the powdery crystals slipped inside her boot. It sent a chill up her legs.

Colt strode toward her. "I didn't see any entryways. Doesn't mean one doesn't exist."

"We can check it again in the morning." Brit cupped her mouth with her hand, breathing into her palm.

"Come on. You're freezing." Colt's arm went around her.

They traveled the way she came, retrieved the picture, double-checking the door after he shut it. It remained locked. They entered the main house, the door slamming behind them.

Brit jumped.

"Relax. It was the wind." He sat the frame down on the table in the foyer.

Relax. She'd been on edge and creeped out since finding the secret door. But it made sense—the door in the theater room—especially since Seth wanted the latest in innovations for his mountain retreat.

But there was more to Memory Maker than stone walls and hidden doors.

This place held secrets.

Chapter Nineteen

RIT WAITED ON THE TOP STEP OF THE LOFT FOR COLT TO shut his bedroom door. He'd already marched her up the stairs and ordered her to bed. Well, if he thought she was a subordinate on one of his Ranger fireteams, then he'd underestimated her.

She frowned at her bravado.

I'm hiding out on the steps.

Okay. So it wasn't the same as confronting him and standing her ground. Thing was he'd done it for her own good. She was fading fast in the pool house, her lids heavier than a trapdoor wanting to snap shut from sheer gravity.

That was it—the doors in and around the theater room. Something was nagging at her. Was it the door or the stone? She couldn't decide. But she was wide awake now, and she wanted the picture that remained downstairs on the table.

If she'd told him she wanted to stay up and look at it some more, he'd have objected. She would have done it anyway. Only his point was valid. At four in the morning she was running on adrenaline. She was going to poop out and be no good to either one of them tomorrow during the light of day. They still needed to check both house foundations for any hidden entrances. They hadn't found a wine cellar or a humidity-controlled room. They'd have to have ducts. At least she believed they would. Otherwise how could it be controlled? So maybe the plans had been dummied up, and there was a real set somewhere else. She didn't know. But she did know the framed picture of Swallow Falls was calling her name.

The door to Colt's bedroom clicked shut. Brit waited a moment and then made her way down on tiptoes. She grabbed the eighteen by twenty-four inch frame and crept toward the steps. She took the first riser. It creaked.

Shit.

She waited, which was stupid. That was a surefire way of getting caught. Brit flew up the steps, rounded the pool table, and slipped into her room. She sat the frame down on the comforter of her bed and shut the door with her heart in her throat.

Talk about cat and mouse.

She'd felt like this ever since Seth's death. She was hiding from the guilt which, inexplicably, had somehow vanished. Then there were her colleagues. She'd avoided them since the shooting. And the media . . . she'd dodged them by coming up here. Eventually, they'd find her. Even Andi's old boyfriend from CNN had hounded her for an interview. What a jerk. Even if she wanted to give a big media outlet an interview, she wouldn't give it to him. He'd caused her friend a lot of pain during their breakup.

Brit climbed into bed in her robe and sat Indian style. She positioned the frame in front of her. What was it about the photo? Where had her mind been going earlier?

Seth was ahead of her that day on the path. He'd been angry. *That's it.* It wasn't that he took her there willingly. She'd asked to come. They'd been cooped up in the architect's office all day in McHenry. They hadn't even broken ground on Memory Maker yet. They—Seth and his architect—were still poring over the plans. She'd witnessed a few escalating arguments. She'd tuned them out and went into the sitting area of the office to get a drink of water.

Seth had come out flustered and red-faced, saying he needed a break. He was going to Swallow Falls—without her. The architect, who seemed ready to pitch the project and tell Seth to go to hell, was not someone she wanted to make small talk with for who knew how long it would take Seth to get it together.

She'd followed behind him out of the building and opened the passenger door before he could lock it. She jumped in. He only growled and tore out of the parking lot, refusing to talk to her.

He'd done the same at the park—the not talking part—and was out and on the path before she could get her seat belt off. That was fine. She didn't want to be with him anyway. She took her time, checked out the natural resources signs, learning about the native trees. She'd been awestruck at the falls and the rush of water. She'd passed people heading out with her going deeper into the park.

Although breathtaking with outcroppings of rock ledges, trees, and small rapids, the exhilaration of being one with nature ceased the moment she caught up with him.

He'd been bent over checking a small footbridge. Screened by trees and rushing rapids on one side and a sheer rock wall on the other, it was damp and murky in that particular area. Brit shivered. The look he gave her when she came up on him had been malicious and full of hate. She'd backed up, her heart pounding in her chest. This was her husband. The man who was supposed to love her. All he had was contempt for her, and she'd done nothing to him but try to love him. There was no weapon she could think of that could combat that kind of malevolence.

Knuckles wrapped on her door. Brit jerked and flew off the bed. Spying the picture out of the corner of her eye, she reached back and threw the comforter over the frame, the decorative pillows landing on the floor. Brit skirted the four-poster bed and reached for the doorknob.

She cracked the door. "Hey. I thought you went to bed."

A dubious Colt Rivers, barefoot and wearing a T-shirt and pajama bottoms, stood on the other side, drinking from a bottled water. "I got thirsty."

"Oh. Do you need something?" Brit kept her body hidden. She was still in her bathing suit and robe.

"Only if you're the art smuggler who heisted one Swallow Falls original from the table downstairs."

Brit's shoulders slumped, and she opened the door. "This is all your fault."

"Mine?" He strolled in and cocked his head to the side, eyeing the tip of the frame sticking out from the floral comforter.

"Your voodoo."

"It was your idea as I recall." He flipped back the bedding. "Did it come to you?"

"We need to go there tomorrow. I think I know where he might have hidden the artifacts."

"*Really.*" His brows rose, and he set the water on the antique dresser. "All from a photo." He picked it up from the bed and held it in his hands.

"It's a long story." Brit plopped down on the bed. "Bottom line, I caught him on this bridge fooling with something underneath. It's a state park. There shouldn't be anything in a forest other than the wonders of nature. Why would he be so interested in what's under a bridge?"

Colt leaned the frame against the wall. "Unless he's a troll."

Brit laughed. "Well, there's that."

"And there's this." Colt pulled her up from the bed, his arms going around her waist. "Tell me why you thought you needed to get plastered in order to make love with me?"

Heat crept into Brit's cheeks. The wine had worn off hours ago, but her embarrassment was still in full bloom. "I've only been with one man. I wasn't sure if you were going to make a move. If you didn't, it would have been up to me."

"Ah." He pressed back a spiral of her hair behind her ear. "That was your first mistake."

Brit's brows furrowed. "I don't understand."

"You were intoxicated."

She couldn't say, having been on the inside looking out. She certainly was feeling no pain.

His gaze was intense yet gentle as he searched her eyes. The wooziness returned, and it wasn't from alcohol.

"I'm not now." A yawn came over her, and she tried to hide it when her nostrils fared. *Damn.* He was seeing her at her worst.

"No?" A smile touched his rugged lips. He cupped her face, tilting it up. "You're sleepy."

He was right. This wasn't quite what she had in mind. "Will you still be here when I wake up?" She wet her lips. "I mean . . . you're still in?"

His eyes held hers. "It's not about the artifacts anymore." He bent his head, his eyes closing before he pressed his lips to hers.

Brit's stomach tumbled sweetly, her legs weak. So much so, she thought they'd give out and she'd find herself in a heap on the floor. But his arms were around her, holding her hard against him.

She kissed him back, her lips greedy for his. They were firm and in charge like she imagined he was on the battlefield. Her hands rode over his chest and looped around his neck. Her fingers shifted through his crisp raven hair she'd trimmed earlier. Tall, dark, and handsome. He epitomized the saying. But it was his selflessness and strength she clung to. He should be making tracks for Canada. Not hanging out to see this thing through with her. Their troubles were connected, she felt sure, because of the artifacts. But there was no guarantee they'd prove any of their assumptions. If he left now, he could have that chance at freedom. Unless they tracked him down, but that could be years.

His kiss deepened, his tongue exploring until he reluctantly pulled away. Brit's lids flickered open. He was flushed and breathing heavy. Her arms remained looped around his neck. She couldn't imagine life without him now. If he hadn't agreed to stay, she would have been waging war with herself on whether or not to go with him.

She caressed the strong angle of his jaw rough with stubble. "You're sure you should stay?"

"You're a calculated risk. One I'm willing to take." He smoothed down her hair, his eyes lingering on her face. "Get some sleep. We have an early day tomorrow."

Chapter Twenty

UNDLED UP IN HER PARKA, BRIT TOOK HOLD OF COLT'S hand. With Seth's ski jacket, skull cap, and scarf—thank God she hadn't gotten around to emptying the chest they used for winter clothes—he blended in with the visitors at the park and could easily conceal his face.

Brit threw on her hood. She could just as easily be recognized.

Innocent until proven guilty.

She'd cling to that mantra for now. But it didn't mean someone might not level an accusation her way. She'd be hard-pressed to explain herself to Colt then. Although folks around here—even visitors—were a friendly group and not so caught up in the headlines.

She'd reiterated that same thought to Colt when he wanted to arrive at dawn before the park opened. Not that it was a bad idea. It had been her first instinct as well after they'd awoken early to search the foundations of both buildings and found nothing to suggest there was a hidden entrance. They still had time to make it before it opened. But then it hit her. DNR patrolled the park. Being stopped for trespassing was a real risk. One they couldn't afford. They'd take their chances under a bright autumn sun with temperatures close to freezing at eleven in the morning.

Brit led them across the parking lot, a parking lot filled with cars. Even the cold couldn't keep those looking to venture out from exploring the frosty white forest. She and Colt slipped into the tree line of tall hemlocks, its evergreen branches caked in snowfall. Like that "normal" couple they were supposed to be, they headed down the path toward the falls into a winter wonderland right out of a Currier & Ives Christmas card.

They passed a group coming up as they gathered for a photo.

"Excuse me." A woman with a bright smile held out an iPhone. "Would you mind taking our photo?"

Colt's hand tensed on hers.

Brit released his hand and reached for the phone. "Sure."

They appeared to be a family of three generations, the children jockeying for positions next to Grandma and Grandpa.

"Let me know when you're ready." Brit held up the phone.

"Ready," they chimed.

Brit snapped off several photos, handing it back to the woman. "You're a good-looking family—very photogenic."

"And crazy." The woman chuckled. "You two have kids?"

"No," it came out shrill, like, *Perish the thought.* She loved children—wanted some of her own someday. No. It had been the inference of marriage that threw her. Brit still hadn't gotten around to asking Colt that all-important question about whether he was married. She'd left it and her good sense on the table last night when she picked up that bottle of wine.

"We're working on it," Colt said on a laugh and took Brit's hand. "Enjoy your day." He waved them off and pulled her with him as he made his way down to the rush of water coming from the falls.

Once they were out of earshot and range of sight, Brit whacked him across his chest. "They had kids with them."

He laughed out loud. "I think it went over their heads."

"Not their mother's."

"She asked." He pulled Brit behind the wide trunk of a tree and kissed her. "What polite answer did she hope to get if we had none?" He stared into her eyes unabashed.

God, he was gorgeous, sure of himself without being smug, and just the type of guy she could fall for and hard.

"Are you married?" It was out before she knew what to do with it. "I-I just thought I should know."

He snuffled like he was catching a cold or just plain cold, judging from the redness in his cheeks. "Divorced." Vapor rushed from his mouth, and he moved closer, placing his elbows on the tree on either side of her.

"How long?" Her heart pounded, her own breath filling the space between them. She trembled. It wasn't from the chill in the air.

"Years, before I even went to prison." A smile played on his lips. "No kids."

Relief washed over her, which was silly. There was no future here. But somehow the thought of having his children—his only children—made her feel inexplicably territorial where he was concerned.

Get a grip, Brit.

She wheedled her way out from under him. She needed to stop thinking like that. The falls beckoned with its powerful roar. "Come see," she called to him and trudged over the bridge through the snow until she came to a flat outcropping of rock. Water lapped the smooth bronzed surface, disappearing over the edge. She took a step, the rushing water of the river cresting the tip of her hiking boots.

A firm hand latched onto her arm. "That's close enough." Colt's voice was rough with demand.

Usually she'd ignore a command like that. She'd been in riskier situations than standing five feet from the edge of a thirty-foot vertical drop of tumbling white water.

Five feet. I'm not even close.

But he thought so and that was what mattered.

"Okay." She backed off. "Let's take the stairs."

Wide wooden steps, built into the earth, led down from the falls. They passed people on the way down admiring the falls and taking pictures. She hoped the herd would thin out when they got to the bridge.

"Lot of people," Colt mumbled under his breath and grabbed for her hand to help her over several rocks at the bottom.

"Got any ideas?"

"Always have those."

They hiked the path with the river to their left and trees and rock outcropping to their right. The sun's rays, catching prisms of light, filtered through the towering trees. The fresh scent of pine and crisp, clean water surrounded them.

Colt led them off the path toward the water, helping her over irregular rock formations until they stood at the water's edge, the rapids rushing by. They remained silent on the smooth plateau, the river buffeting hewn rock on its way downstream.

"What are you thinking?"

"How much I miss home," he said wistfully and shrugged. "Don't know if I'll ever get back there."

"You will." She shook his hand in hers. "I've always wanted to live out West."

"There's nothing like it, Brit." He gave her a half smile. "Come on. Let's go find what we came for." He covered the same ground, only in reverse, treating her like a piece of fine china as they maneuvered over the rocks.

She'd never considered herself a girly girl. Well, she did like to wear nice things, but she could get down and dirty. She liked four-wheeling, fishing, camping, even archery. It kind of went with the whole gun thing and the rush of hitting that bull's-eye.

Once they were back onto the path, Brit continued to guide him on a circuitous route of mangled roots hidden below the snow until they came to the small wooden bridge suspended about a foot over a thin stream. A couple walked over it on their way back toward the falls. Voices, a mix of young and old, carried on the wind from either direction.

Brit pulled on Colt's hand. "I don't know about this."

"Sit." He patted the bridge. "Pretend you're tying your boot."

She stepped onto the bridge and then down, the water barely covering the tip of her boots and took a seat.

Colt bent next to her, his hands coming down on the tops of her knees. Their eyes connected. "Normal couple, right? Just out for a hike." He began clearing the snow, which wasn't much with the running stream. "You said he was reaching underneath?"

Brit nodded, her hand coming down on his shoulder. "People."

He gripped her boot and then her calf. "Does it hurt, baby?"

Her breath hitched at the sincerity in his voice. Maybe it was an act. But had she truly sprained her ankle, she didn't believe he'd act any differently.

"Only when I turn it a certain way."

He manipulated her ankle while a group passed by. Brit grimaced, keeping them accounted for in the corner of her eye.

She rapped him on his shoulder. "They're gone."

Colt dug like a dog looking to bury a bone. He angled his body and bent his head, reaching under.

A dark form swayed above them, a radio crackling. "Can I help you folks?"

Panic spread through Brit's chest. She'd been so preoccupied with the group before, and now Colt, she'd missed the man behind her. Brit glanced over her shoulder. Clean-shaven and wearing a black skull cap with a patch denoting him as a Department of Natural Resources police officer, he stood peering down at them in his olive green parka—his expression a little too curious.

A shiver came over her, and Brit shoved her hands inside her coat pockets, the gold chain from her St. Christopher medal twined around her fingers.

Colt remained bent, his head down. "It's—"

"My necklace." It came out louder than she hoped. Brit frowned up at the officer and covertly pulled her hand out of her pocket with the necklace tucked inside her palm and fingers. "It was a gift from my dad." Brit nudged Colt's arm and then inconspicuously dropped the necklace next to his knee into the snow.

The officer stepped off the bridge. "You saying you lost it in this area?"

"I'm not sure. I felt something slip from my neck." Brit's hand hovered around the furry front collar of her red parka.

The officer leaned over near the area where Colt had cleaned out the snow under the bridge. He grabbed a flashlight off his hip and shined it underneath. "What kind of . . ."

Brit's heart thundered. He was too close.

Gold shimmered under the beam of the policeman's light. "Is this it?" He brought the light closer.

"I got it." Colt lifted the chain from the snow.

"Thanks." Brit smiled up at the officer.

He hooked his flashlight onto his belt. "Glad I could help. You two enjoy the rest of your day." He stepped up onto the bridge and continued down the path, talking into the radio at his shoulder.

They waited until he turned the corner of the rock wall, taller than a two-story house, that ran along the bank of the river.

"Quick thinking." Colt manipulated the chain in his one hand until he held only the medal between his fingers. "St. Christopher the protector?"

"Yeah."

"Who do you need protecting from?" A pair of concerned eyes held hers.

She wanted to say him—her heart. But she had the medal way before now. With all he did know about her, she hoped her answer made sense. It was the truth, anyway—just not all of it.

She shrugged. "It was my dad's when he worked the road."

He handed it back to her, giving her a doubtful look. "It was an act, right? It falling off, I mean."

"It got caught on one of my sweaters last spring. I took it off to untangle it and shoved it into my coat pocket."

"If there's any truth to the legend, maybe you should wear it for both our sakes." He got up, dusted his jeans off, and put his hand out. "Let's go."

Brit stood, a little shaky. "What about the bridge?"

He hoisted her up onto it. "Do we go back or does this loop around?"

"It loops."

Colt hurried her over the snow-covered path and up the incline around the rock wall.

"Wait." Brit jerked her hand from his. "What's wrong with you?"

He beaded in on her. "Too many cops, for one."

"Did you even do a thorough search?" Brit placed her hands on her hips.

"Whatever was under that bridge is gone now."

"So we're screwed."

"Depends on how you look at it." He started to move out, following the signs that would eventually take them out of the park.

What the hell? It pissed her off when he talked in riddles. Brit caught up with him and grabbed his arm. "I hate when you do that."

"What?"

"Act so mysterious."

He pulled her into a stand of blue spruce. "Look. It was there, judging by the size of the hole I found." He eyed their surroundings. "But this is the last place we should be talking about it."

Okay. That she could understand. But it was more than that. He was angry. Maybe disappointed. She was, too. They were running out of time. And she was forgetting the real reason she'd come to the lake in the first place.

"Let's go. We can talk in the truck." Brit gave him her back and trekked up the path with Colt coming up beside her. The forest opened up to the parking lot. "I need to use the bathroom."

"Meet you in the truck."

Brit nodded and entered the ladies restroom. She did her business, then remained inside the stall and checked her messages—nothing from Andi and several from her lawyer.

She clicked on his number and waited.

"Dahlgren and Tate, may I help you?"

"Jay Dahlgren. It's Brit Gentry."

"Just a moment please." The phone clicked.

Brit leaned into the stall door.

"You don't return messages, Brit." Jay Dahlgren's acerbic voice echoed in her ear.

"You know where I am. Any news?"

"Haven't you been watching it?"

"No. It's mostly PA news up here."

"Damn it, Brit. This is getting national attention."

She shut her eyes, shaking her head. "Are they close to making a decision?"

"They're talking in the next thirty-six hours. I want you back in town before it's announced. And avoid another pileup, *please.*"

"I will." She bit down on her lip. "My father fill you in on the accident?"

"Someone had to." He huffed in the phone. "This isn't a game, Brit, they're looking to hang another cop out to dry. They also found—"

"I'll see you soon." Brit clicked off amidst his protest.

She shook her head. More evidence against her, she was sure. Brit sighed. Nothing was going her way. So a day and a half until a possible decision. She'd been hoping for a week. When she got back to the house, she'd catch up on all the news she'd missed on her phone. Then she was going to live the next thirty-six hours as if they were her last because, in a sense, they were.

At least on the outside of a jail cell.

Chapter Twenty-One

"**S**OMETHING WRONG?" COLT DIPPED HIS HEAD TO GET A good look at Brit. Since jumping inside the SUV after her pit stop to the john, she'd been quiet.

"You hungry?" She lifted her chin to him, her dove-white skin rosy from the cold.

Colt checked the clock in the dash—1:21 p.m. "What'd you have in mind, leftover stew?"

She smiled at him and warmed her hands by the heater vent. "No. Cream of crab soup and a table for two near the fireplace at Unos on the lake."

"You think that's wise?"

She tapped her finger to her lip. "It's off-season."

He'd like nothing better than to share a cozy lunch with Brit and talk about trivial things. Like how much powder was on the slopes in, of all months, October, which didn't mean a hell of a lot since the ski resort wasn't even open. *Damn.* It'd been years since he had skied. He'd more than likely fall on his ass.

Colt took the left onto 219. He'd seen the restaurant on their way to the park. "Let's scope it out."

She reached over with concern in her eyes. "Forget it. It's too risky. I was just feeling reckless."

And he was feeling fed up. "Do they have ribs?"

"Baby back."

Colt's mouth watered. Last time he'd had barbequed ribs had been while he was stateside after one of his deployments. Whitefish Lake Restaurant, located in his hometown, had the best Cajun rub and apple butter sauce.

"Then we're there." He was a risk taker, had always been. He'd chance it today to spend quality time with the beautiful blonde sitting next to him who wanted a hot bowl of cream of crab soup. Colt turned into the parking lot. Not too many cars. He took a space facing the highway in case he needed a quick getaway. Colt unclicked his seat belt. "Come on."

Brit hesitated with her hand on her belt. "I should check the Internet first."

Oh, he *knew* they were still looking for him. But after nearly four weeks of being on the lam, he felt sure all the hubbub about convicted ex-Army Ranger Colt Rivers would be at the bottom of CNN's newsworthy stories. There had to be some other poor schmuck they were feeding on like piranhas.

"Go ahead." Colt remained in the driver's seat while Brit's fingers ran across the glossy screen of her iPhone.

"Nothing new." She gave him a quick smile before it morphed into a pout.

Okay so she was worried now and maybe feeling like she'd started something she was not prepared to finish.

Colt hooked his chin toward the entrance of the restaurant. "Let's go, beautiful. Those baby back ribs are waiting." He opened the door and got out, meeting her at the tailgate of her SUV. He took her hand in his. "Relax. Maryland is miles away from Kansas."

"Until they connect you to me."

Colt slipped his arm around her waist and led her to the double wooden doors. With his hand on the brass doorknob, he looked straight into those gorgeous brown eyes of hers. "No more talk of prisons, escaped convicts, or missing artifacts, deal?" He raised a brow at her.

She nodded, and Colt opened the door.

Brit slipped through. "Just you and me and nothing else," she whispered as they entered the dark wooden foyer and met the hostess coming in from the dining room.

"Good afternoon, can I seat you by the lake?"

"Table in the corner," Brit countered.

"We'll take one by the fireplace, if it's available." Colt squeezed her hand.

"I have a nice quiet location." The hostess smiled and grabbed two menus. "Please follow me."

They rounded the corner, dark knotty-pine floors and wooden tables giving it a rustic feel. He liked the place already. Windows opened up onto the lake with several piers. The few boats at the dock were covered in a blanket of snow. The hostess led them up a step and onto the level with a massive stone fireplace and a roaring fire, the warmth immediate against his skin. Colt pulled out Brit's chair and slid the one across next to her before taking his seat.

The hostess handed them menus. "Can I get you something to drink?"

Brit opened her menu. "Water's fine."

"Make that two."

"I'll be right back with your drinks." The hostess left them and headed toward the bar.

"I take it you've been here before."

"Yeah." Her lips quirked. "But you're much better company."

Right. She was with him now, and that was all that mattered. He needed to take his own advice and relax. The photos that were circulating looked nothing like him now. His shoulders leveled off.

Still didn't mean he didn't feel like this was the last supper. He wanted to indulge her. "Whatever you want"—he flipped open the menu—"that soup you like, steak, desser—"

Shit. His brows bunched and he wanted to punch the table.

"Hey." Brit patted his fist. "When this is all over, I want you to take me to Montana and treat me to dinner at *your* favorite restaurant."

Colt wrapped his fingers around her hand and winked. "I know just the place."

"Where you get your ribs."

He laughed. "It's upscale, if you can believe that."

Brit leaned in. "Even if it weren't, I wouldn't care."

Lost in those sincere eyes of hers, he fidgeted with his silverware. "Has a stone fireplace and built from the best Montana pine."

"It's a lodge, then?"

"One of the oldest log structures in use."

A server brought them their drinks and set the glasses down, greeting them. "Would you like to order?"

Colt looked to Brit. "You ready?"

"Yes." She tipped her chin up toward the server. "I'll take a bowl of your cream of crab soup, side salad, and the baked chicken spinoccoli."

"And for you, sir?"

"Cream of crab soup and the baby rack ribs." He guessed that was their play on words.

The server jotted down the order. "I'll bring your soups first." She stepped away, checked on another table, and headed into the kitchen.

"So you grew up on the water."

Brit laughed. "You don't have to make small talk with me."

"I'm not." He leaned in and smiled. "You're an intriguing woman."

She got that worried look again. "There's nothing to tell. I grew up in Annapolis, one of two children—my brother's a surgeon at MedStar, a trauma center in D.C. My dad . . . well, you know about my dad." She toyed with the napkin in her lap. "My mom stayed at home." She smoothed down the napkin on her thighs. "How about you?"

"I grew up on a ranch—hunting."

"The kind people pay to stay and hunt?"

He nodded. "Fair chase, fully guided hunts. None of that penned in crap where the animal doesn't have a chance."

"What kind of game?"

"Antelope, elk, and bighorn sheep."

The server brought their soup, sitting the steamy bowls in front of them. "Your entrees will be out shortly."

"Thanks." Colt waited until the server moved on. "You shoot. Do you hunt?"

"Near the water it's fowl." Brit stirred her soup and took a taste. "God, that's good."

Colt took a spoonful, the creamy goodness and chunks of crabmeat the best he'd ever had. "You'll have to take me there someday."

She shook her head, soft blond waves dusting her shoulders. "What are we doing here, Rivers?"

"What was our deal?"

"You didn't say anything about fantasies."

He didn't have to. His fantasy was sitting across the table. "You think too much."

"So you're saying I'm no fun."

He took several more spoonfuls of soup and couldn't stop from smiling. "I didn't say that."

"How are you with heights? Fast moving . . ."

"Cars?"

"No. Rides."

"Rides? You mean of the amusement park variety?"

"The mountain variety." The dauntless look in her eyes made her all the more endearing to him.

"Care to expla—"

"Here's your order." The server opened a stand and then placed a tray of food on top.

They made room for their meals with Colt waiting patiently for the server to set down their food and leave so he could get back to their intriguing conversation.

"Is there anything else I can get you?"

"We're good." Brit slid her empty crab bowl to the end of the table for the server.

"Enjoy." She took the bowl and excused herself.

"Mountain variety, huh?"

"Mountain Coaster to be exact." She took a bite of her salad.

"Where is it?"

"Here."

"No shit." He dug into the ribs, trying not to make too big of a mess. "They open this time of year?"

"Every day." She took a bite of her chicken and swallowed, wiping her mouth. "Even in snow."

"Let's go."

A smile curled her lips. "You're on."

Damn. The woman could hunt, sail, and had a zest for life he'd lost a long time ago. He wanted his life back.

He wanted to share it with Brit.

He gritted his teeth. There were a lot of reasons that would never happen.

Chapter Twenty-Two

*J*UST LIKE BRIT THOUGHT, THE MOUNTAIN COASTER WAS deserted. It was only the two of them and the attendant from Wisp Resort.

"Tandem or single?" The attendant pointed toward the board with the prices—twenty-eight dollars for two singles or nineteen for the tandem.

Brit looked to Colt.

He stood next to her sizing up the twisting metal rails that ran up the mountainside through spindly tree branches. "Tandem."

She pulled him aside. "If it's about the money, I can afford it."

His arms went around her waist, pulling her close. He pressed his lips against her ear. "I want to experience it with you," he whispered roughly.

Brit tingled. She did, too. Only she didn't think it mattered to him. Brit reluctantly pulled away from his embrace and paid for their ride. They followed the heavyset attendant who reminded Brit of her uncle Stew with his silver comb-over.

"All right, haus, you're in the back." He motioned to Colt to take the rear with the high backseat. "You're in charge of the brakes." He eyed Brit. "And why don't you, little lady, take a seat in front."

They obliged him by taking their assigned places and buckling up.

"So relax and take in the views while the pulley gets you to the top." The attendant made his way to the controls and turned back. "There's no one but you two. You have the green light all the way."

Brit nodded and settled in against Colt's solid chest. Her stomach fluttered with awareness. She sat in between his muscular thighs, his legs pressed up against hers in the tight space of the cart.

"What'd he mean 'green light all the way'?"

The cart slowly made its way up the rail system to the top of the mountain. "There are lights, red to stop, yellow to slow down, and green to go. It's a type of warning system when you come up on another cart and its riders who are concerned with the speed."

He laughed, his arms coming around her, and leaned in against the side of her face. "I have a need for speed. How about you?"

Actually, she wanted to take it slow—not the Mountain Coaster, but with him. Ever since leaving the park, a sense of heightened urgency had plagued her. Brit had no one else to blame. She'd done it. Promised herself she was going to have that whirlwind romance with the man of her dreams—too bad he was a fugitive.

That was saying a lot, considering a woman in her position had no business being within miles of a man like Colt, much less snuggled up against his chest and relishing the strength of him that surrounded her, literally.

They passed through a sort of mesh tunnel on their climb. A dusting of snow remained caked to the rails on either side of them, the cloudless blue sky and crisp mountain air invigorating. She felt so alive and happy and whole.

"You ready?" she called back as they reached the top.

"Full speed ahead."

She laughed out loud. "Isn't that Navy talk?"

He squeezed her tight and kissed her neck. "How about some sweet talk tonight?" His deep voice rumbled with desire.

Brit held tight to his legs as they took the first corkscrew. Her stomach tumbled from the sheer height. She squealed when they picked up speed around a sharp turn. Branches and tree trunks flew past them in a blur. She loved the speed. Loved sharing this moment with him.

"Hang on, baby." Colt leaned into the next turn, his weight giving them an extra boost down the straightaway.

"Oh, my gosh!" The cart aimed for a large branch, coming straight toward them. Brit closed her eyes.

"Wasn't even close." Colt gave a deep-throated laugh. "You *are* a girly girl."

Brit grinned. She didn't mind being one around him. They came upon the last corkscrew, laughing as they spiraled downward.

They slowed, entering the last straightaway before the cart came to rest in its starting position at the bottom of the track. She turned for a brief second and their eyes met. His were smiling down at her. And for the first time in a long while she felt an overwhelming connection, like she'd known him all her life. Or was it *waited* for him all her life?

"That was so much fun."

"You're so much fun." He kissed her long and deep.

Brit kissed him back, and she didn't care about the spectacle she was making in front of the old man running the ride or the words he'd called out to them as they came to a complete stop—until something flashed.

She jerked away from Colt, her heart strumming in her chest from their passionate kiss and the old man's words she was trying to string together.

"Did he . . . ? *Oh, God.*" Brit's hand flew to her mouth. "He said cheese!"

"You got it." Colt's jaw tensed, and he ripped off his seat belt and hopped out.

"Wait!" Brit unbuckled hers and grabbed for him.

He pulled her up.

"What are you going to do?"

He raked his hand through his dark hair. "Take his camera."

"It's digital." She pointed up to the camera mounted on a pole. "It must be where we paid on some computer in the booth."

"Awesome." He marched across the parking lot from the Mountain Coaster and to the booth where the old man had taken a seat inside behind a Plexiglas window. "Hey, buddy."

"Ya interested in taking a look at your photo?"

"Yeah, want to see how photogenic we are."

"I'll bring it up here in just a minute." He fooled with the computer next to his elbow. "It's up on the screen."

Colt gave him a quizzical look.

"Out here on the screen," Brit whispered, pulling Colt away from the window. Attached to the eave of the small building was an LCD screen, encased in Plexiglas.

The photo almost took her breath away. It was fun, like him. They were nose to nose, and she was kissing him. She tingled just then, which was nothing new where Colt Rivers was concerned. His arms were around her, and she could just make out the tug of a smile on both their lips. It wasn't a photo that could help pick them out in a crowd or a lineup. It was honest and special and so how she felt about him.

She yanked on his arm. "No one can tell it's us," she said in a hushed voice.

"No. But if they're looking, they'll put it together."

Brit nodded. "Have any peaceable ways of getting into the booth?"

He shook his head. "Not a one."

Well, they couldn't very well storm the booth and rip the computer out without the attendant calling the cops. Who knew where else the photo might have gone? For all they knew—Brit glanced back at the ten story hotel—it was now on some main hard drive in an office of the Wisp Resort.

This wasn't good.

But before Colt went all Army Ranger, and bashed the computer or something, she wanted the picture—for herself. Brit pushed past Colt and leaned into the window. "I'll take two five-by-sevens."

"What are you doing?" Colt said through gritted teeth.

She pulled her wallet out to pay the twenty-four dollars for the color photos and matching Mountain Coaster cardboard frames. "Getting my keepsake before you do whatever it is you do when you're destroying computer files," she whispered harshly under her breath.

"Hurry the hell up." He shoved his hands in his coat pockets.

Brit paid and the attendant handed her the photos with two frames for her to place them in.

"Thanks." She took them and stepped aside.

Colt came up behind her and jerked his chin at a few people approaching from the parking lot. "When he leaves to take them over, I'll take care of it."

Brit nodded, glancing down at the photos. They looked good together. She had never considered the tall, dark, and handsome type until Colt. The contrast of her pale, soft features and his rugged, almost threatening characteristics were, well, tantalizing.

"Let's go."

Brit jerked. Completely mesmerized by the photo, she'd missed the attendant taking the group over. Colt strode past her, opened the door to the booth, and ducked inside. Brit bounced on the balls of her feet. Any minute someone was going to come—maybe a customer or someone from the resort. They'd be scrambling to explain Colt tinkering with their computer. This had all happened because she'd let her guard down. She knew better. The old Brit wouldn't have been caught kissing in public. Actually, acting like an enamored teenager had helped to conceal their faces. Still, the old Brit would never broadcast her feelings out in the open. She'd never had the urge or the need.

He was a need—like the air she breathed.

This was so unlike her. Even if she got up the nerve to sleep with him tonight—without the wine—she was only setting herself up for heartache. This thing wasn't going to end well. She also had to tell him the truth about herself. In two days, she'd have no choice but to return home. He could stay. *Shit.* She needed to check with the rental office. She'd blocked out ten days for herself. For all she knew there were renters already on the books after that.

"Mission accomplished." Colt came up behind her. He looped his arm around her waist and led her toward the truck.

"What'd you do?"

He motioned for her to get in. She opened the door, slid in, their doors shutting simultaneously.

"You get me in more shit, Gentry." He started the ignition and then reached inside the deep pocket of his coat and pulled out a piece of metal.

"The hard drive."

"Go big or go home." He tossed it behind him into the backseat and pulled out.

Oh, if he only knew.

Chapter Twenty-Three

"**W**HAT?" BRIT JUGGLED HER BOTTLED WATER AND several DVDs she'd been perusing on the large bookcase in the loft.

Holding his own bottled water and a large bowl of popcorn, Colt chuckled. "This is crazy."

Not to Brit. She was doing exactly what she'd set out to do since receiving that call from her lawyer earlier in the day.

Brit motioned him out the front door and into the frigid night air. "I want to do *normal* with you." Meaning she wanted to mosey on over to the theater room, watch one of the war movies she'd picked out, snuggle next to Colt on the couch, and share a bowl of freshly popped popcorn she'd cooked on the stove because, well, microwave popcorn sucked.

The door clicked behind them, and they trudged through the snow-covered parking pad in their boots, pajamas, and winter coats. Colt worked the combination on the front door of the pool house complex and opened it. He waved her into the warmly lit foyer, shutting the door behind them. Brit flicked on the light in the theater room and traveled down the wide carpeted steps using the handrail. She set her water and the DVDs on the floor and opened the entertainment center.

"Which one?" Brit angled back toward the row of couches staggered like stadium seating to allow guests optimal viewing.

Colt put the popcorn down on the table separating two leather couches and plopped down on one of them. "We going for world wars or recent conflicts?"

She considered that for a moment—recalled his nightmare and the pool incident with the alarm—and decided to steer clear of any dramatizations about the Middle East. Brit picked up one of her favorites of all time, flipped open the case, and slipped the disc into the Blue Ray player. She hit play and traveled up the steps with her water, shucking off her coat and dropping it on the couch closest to the door. She turned off the overhead in the foyer, shut the heavy six-panel door, and flipped off the switch at the wall. Draped in darkness, except for a swath of light coming under the door from a nightlight in the foyer and the staggered safety lights running down the steps, she scrambled down one level as the previews began to play and took a seat next to Colt on the couch.

"Do you like Lee Marvin?" She snatched a chenille throw off the back of the couch, tossing it over both of them.

The main title came up on the screen.

"Ah, *The Dirty Dozen*." His arm went around her shoulders. "Now, Bronson, he's a badass."

Brit snuggled against Colt. He was her badass. Only she was coming to know the softer side of the wrongly accused convict and disgraced Army Ranger.

Colt grabbed the bowl of popcorn, chuckling. "So . . . let me get this straight—convicts *turned* soldiers."

Brit's eyes widened. *Shit, shit, shit, shit.* "Oh, God." She turned in his arms, knocking the bowl from his lap. Popcorn scattered on the couch, the floor. She jumped to her feet, tried to scoop what she could into the bowl. "I'm sorry."

"Come here." Colt yanked her down on the couch.

She fell back, her head hitting a throw pillow in the corner. "I should have . . . I thought . . ."

Colt leaned over her, the jut of his strong chin catching the glow from the movie screen. "Stop thinking, Brit." His hand slipped under her lace cami.

Brit trembled. Looked like she was going to get what she wanted tonight and the sexy silk matching pajamas she'd opted for instead of her steel-caged exercise bra and flannels were going to make it easy for Colt to explore.

His fingers traveled up her rib cage. "You're soft." His voice was gruff, the weight of him more noticeable the farther he moved up her torso. His palm cupped her breast, his thumb brushing her nipple.

Brit moaned and bit down on her lip, her arms going around his neck. Colt lowered his head. His mouth hovered over hers, tempting.

"Don't tease me," she whispered, his hand stilling on her breast.

"Kiss me, Brit." His words were rough and demanding.

With shaky fingers, Brit shifted through his hair at the nape of his neck, drawing him closer. "Is this a test?"

"You know I want you."

Warmth spread through her. It wasn't desire—although her heart was ticking like a timer on an explosive device demanding she kiss him right here, right now. No, it was more than her attraction for him. It was the underlying meaning behind his words.

At least she hoped there was more to him than just availability and sex.

Her breaths became shallow, her heart slowed. For such an elite warrior, his vulnerabilities were splayed wide open like a wound that wouldn't heal. He'd been divorced. He hadn't said if it had been mutual. Had she hurt him?

Brit didn't want him to wonder any more about how he made her feel.

"I want you, too." She pressed her lips to his. They were firm and moving against hers, but tempered.

He was holding back.

Her hand moved down the front of his white T-shirt, his chest muscles flexing the moment the tips of her fingers brushed his nipple. His mouth started to move more urgently against hers. Brit parted her lips and touched her tongue to the sensual curve of his tough guy mouth. He groaned, and the hand cupping her breast traversed downward, past her belly button to the elastic waistband of her silky, thin pajama bottoms. He tugged, his fingers brushing her bare skin just above her lacey thong. She quivered, fully aroused and aware of his intentions.

Brit slid her hand under his T-shirt. His skin was warm, his muscles ripped beneath the swirls of hair. Colt held himself up on one elbow and yanked down her bottoms, Brit helping by lifting her butt. He stroked her sex through the sheer lacey pink triangle.

"I feel like an awkward teen," he said against her mouth, his voice rough and a little bothered. "Let's find a bed."

She found the whole thing erotic, with her bottoms around her knees, her bare ass against the leather, and him fighting for position.

"I'm good," she whispered and nipped his coarse chin with her teeth, then kissed him there, coaxing him to forget the idea of interrupting their lovemaking for a more comfortable location.

He hesitated.

It had been a long time since she played with a man's desires or wanted to. She wanted to with him and slid her hand inside his pajama pants. A smile curled her lips when he relaxed against her touch.

"You win." He kissed her hard, his finger looping through the slender strap of her panty.

Something clicked.

Colt froze, then pulled away. "Did you hear that?" he whispered.

"Yeah." Brit pushed up, trying to pull on her bottoms. "It sounded like—"

"A door." Colt jumped up, adjusted his crotch, and swung toward the door of the theater.

Brit hung over the back of the couch, her stomach in her throat when a shadow passed by, interrupting the swath of light at the bottom of the door. She grabbed Colt's arm. "Someone's here," she croaked.

"*Shit.*" He stumbled while he slipped on his boots.

"What?"

"My gun. It's in the main house." Colt yanked up the spindly wooden table between the couches and gripped a leg. The wood cracked, splintering right before he broke it off. "Wait here." He raced up the steps and opened the door.

Brit was right behind him. Her breath hitched. The front door sat wide open. The mountain air swirling inside the foyer and the faint scent of Obsession chilled her blood.

Fuck.

Colt flew out the door and down the ramp. This wasn't a coincidence, and he had the sinking feeling that someone else knew about the artifacts. It had been years since Afghanistan. Lost time for him. But Seth—Seth had four unaccounted years that Colt knew nothing about, except for Brit.

He knew for a fact Danner had died overseas. But someone else, very much alive, was interested in locating lost treasure same as he. That presented two problems—competition, which he could deal with, and a witness to his whereabouts. Now that concerned him. If they knew who he was, knew he was here and after the same thing, removing Colt from the equation made sense. He'd do the same thing.

Question was who was he dealing with? A disgruntled black market dealer who'd been double-crossed made sense. Or someone Seth had trusted and confided in who, now that he was dead, wanted the treasure for himself.

Either way, this was a huge complication. One that required his immediate attention.

Colt's jaw clenched. *Damn shame.* He and Brit had a good thing going here. He wasn't looking to disrupt it. That meant one thing—shock and capture.

Footsteps in the snow, smaller than he expected, traveled up the winding driveway. Colt followed them to the end and the set of tire tracks going north down Marsh Hill Road.

Damn it. He could speculate and wait it out rather than uproot them.

"You're shivering." Brit stood next to him in snow up to the ankles of her boots, the cold air blowing against her thin pajamas, and her winter coat snapped up to her neck. She handed him his coat. "Put it on."

"You know we can't stay here." He slipped his arms into the ski parka, struggling to zip it with the leg of the table still in his hand.

"I got it." Brit tugged on the bottom of his jacket and pulled the zipper up. "We need to pack."

"I was thinking more along the lines of you going back. Maybe stay with your parents until I hunt this bastard down."

She gave a hard laugh. "You thought wrong."

"This isn't wild game, Brit."

"I'm just as capable at tracking as you," she growled and shoved something black at him. "This isn't about Seth. It's about me." She eyed the tire tracks in the snow, the road, walking toward the green trash Dumpster that, now, upon closer examination, looked askew.

She bent over it and rubbed the dented, rusted corner, glancing back. "White paint transfer. Must have lost control when she sped out of here."

"She?" He gave her a curious look.

"The boot prints. Too small to be a man's, for one. And I recognize the tread—Ugg Adirondacks." She shook her head. "It's a woman's brand. Thought about buying a pair for myself." She made an about-face and marched down the driveway. "I'm going with you," she called back in a terse voice and then disappeared behind the pool house complex.

Great. Now they were going to fight about keeping her safe. He wasn't budging on this issue. She was going to take her pretty little ass back to that eastern shore she hailed from and stay with her father. The man obviously was trained to protect. Colt squinted down at the soft material in his hands. A skull cap. Fine. His ears were freezing. He shoved it on his head, maneuvered down the driveway, careful not to fall on *his* ass all the while wondering what had just happened back there with her uncanny ability to detect clues that had somehow escaped him.

Colt punched in the keypad combination, stomped his boots to remove the snow, and opened the door. He slipped into the house, the door shutting behind him.

Brit came from his bedroom, carrying a metal box.

"You want to tell me what that was all about back there?"

Her eyes darted toward him then back toward the top drawer she had opened to the entertainment center in the great room. She pulled out a cable and began screwing it onto the back of the. . .

Shit. Was that a cable box?

Chapter Twenty-Four

"**S**ON OF A BITCH!" COLT'S FACE TWISTED WITH ANGER, AS he marched over to Brit.

She placed the cable box down inside the fake drawer of the mahogany chest made for electronics, her heart racing, and seized the remote. "I'm not who you think I am."

"Thought you said this place had no service until the DirecTV changeover?"

"I didn't want you to have access to the news."

"For crissake." He raked his fingers through his hair. "Haven't you been checking the news on your phone for me?"

"A phone doesn't broadcast the news twenty-four seven the moment you turn it on."

"You make no sense." He grabbed the remote out of her hand and aimed it at the television. QVC popped on. "Does this thing change the channels?" he snapped.

"No. This one does." Brit picked up the cable remote and punched in a sequence of numbers until the channel moved to CNN. The anchors were talking about ISIS and some new terror plot. Brit checked the time on the wall clock—10:55 p.m. The top of the hour would start a new rehashing of the day's events and other noteworthy sagas. She'd be one of them, based on her conversation with her lawyer.

Colt threw off his coat and dropped down on the couch. With his elbows on his knees, he leaned over and tossed the remote onto the table. "I needed to trust in someone. I thought I could trust you." He sat dejected, somewhat confused in his pajamas, boots, and the stocking cap she gave him.

Brit's heart broke for Colt. She rushed to his side and sat down next to him. "You don't understand." She cupped his face in her hands and turned him toward her. "I wanted to tell you. But I was afraid of your reaction."

"Tell me what?"

She pulled off the stocking cap, smoothing down his hair. Holding the cap in her hands, she ran her fingers along the letters sewn with red stitching—CNN. "It's not news about you." She lifted her chin. "It's about me."

Colt took the cap from her. "Where did this come from?"

"I found it tonight stuck to a low-lying tree branch before you get to the road."

"The news agency?"

She nodded. "I'm pretty sure it was a reporter here tonight. Better yet, one of his minions he'd sent down to the house to investigate before he showed up with his crew." She knew of just such a reporter. Deke Vickers— Andi's ex-boyfriend—would have no problems enlisting the services of some starry-eyed young woman. Knowing him, he'd promised to launch her career if she'd do him a little favor. "She was a woman."

"You keep saying woman like you're dead sure."

"Among other things, I've been an accident reconstructionist."

"So insurance—not mortgage?" He gave her a doubtful look.

"Not quite."

The news at the top of the hour came on. Brit startled when a photo of her in her uniform and Stetson came up on the TV. She raised the volume and leaned back. Her photo spoke volumes. Colt turned his attention to the screen. The caption, *Breaking News* and *Awaiting MSP S.T.A.T.E. Team Maryland State's Attorney Announcement*, ran across the bottom.

Colt's jaw tensed.

She should have had the guts to explain it to him. But the reporter was efficient, albeit maybe a little one-sided in her reporting and not in Brit's favor.

Colt clicked off the TV and stared at her in disbelief. "You're a fuckin' sniper."

"Counter-sniper. There's a difference."

"Doesn't change who you are."

"I'm not a threat to you." She reached for him.

He jerked away from her and stood, then paced. "I can't believe this shit. I kidnapped a cop." He laughed, the sound mocking. Then he swung on her, pointing his finger. "Now I know why you knew that state trooper—you're one of them." He threw his hands up. "*Jesus.*"

Brit came to her feet, blocking him before he could pass by her. "One who cares for *you.*" She caressed the sharp planes of his face, rough with stubble. Their eyes met, his were . . . hurting. "All I wanted was to make the next thirty-six hours a lasting memory for both of us. One that would help me get through my time sitting behind bars for a shooting I can't even remember pulling the trigger on."

His brows furrowed, his head tilting slightly. "Come again?"

Her hands fell away, and she turned to fool with the stitching on the paisley wing-backed chair. "You need to go, Colt. CNN could be bringing the whole camera-crew, reporter-in-your-face deal to my doorstep." She picked up the remotes and took a step toward the mahogany chest.

"*Damn it.*" Colt's fingers laced her arm, his eyes clinging to hers. "You think it's that simple."

"Yes." Brit lowered her lashes.

"Well, it's not." He pulled her up against him, forcing her to make eye contact. "I'm angry with you. But leaving isn't an option."

She searched his eyes. "Why?" she said on a whisper.

His eyes swept over her face, his lips parted.

Brit waited. Her heartbeat, keeping time with the minute hand on the clock over the mantel, ticked away the seconds. All he had to do was say it, say he had feelings for her. And not some line to get her into bed, either.

"It's just not, *okay.*" His last word came out on a growl. Colt's hand fell away, and he raked his fingers through his tousled raven black hair. "Tell me what happened."

Oh, God. She was falling in love with him. And he . . . he was still with her to save his own ass. Of course he was having trouble admitting it because that would make him a self-serving bastard who was only using her for his own personal gain.

Brit swallowed hard and willed the tears burning the backs of her eyes to take a hike. He didn't have to love her. It was stupid to think that three days would be enough for a man like Colt Rivers to feel the same way.

Brit folded her arms over her chest and nodded toward the sofa. She walked past him and sat down.

His large frame dropped down next to her. "Let's have it."

Any hint of warmth in his voice was gone. Well, if he thought they could revert back to captor and captive, he was making a critical error. Her secret was out. They'd be like Brad Pitt and Angelina Jolie in the movie *Mr. and Mrs. Smith*, using their tactical skills to best the other until one of them was dead.

Brit groaned inwardly. Rehashing the events in her life that had led her to this moment were painful and, if she was being honest, a bit fuzzy. She wet her lips, trying to decide where to begin.

"Six weeks ago we got a call—"

"We?"

"Maryland State Police S.T.A.T.E. Team." She grabbed a nearby pillow and hugged it to her.

He lifted his brows.

"Similar to SWAT."

He nodded.

"Road troopers took the initial call—domestic violence. But it quickly turned into a hostage situation. When I learned the hostage taker was a vet who served in Iraq and had a history of PTSD, everything changed for me. He wasn't just some perp. I'd been through it with Seth. I was angry with our government for not recognizing these invisible wounds and letting our soldiers suffer."

"You felt he wasn't completely at fault for where he ended up." Colt pressed a wisp of her hair behind her ear.

The simple act made her stomach flutter. *Damn him*. He was sending her mixed messages. If Colt thought he could pick up where they left off and get laid at her expense, he was an even bigger jerk than she thought possible.

Brit stood and pinned him with her eyes. "We're done playing house."

He raised his hands, his expression offended. "My mistake."

She cocked her head, baffled. "Why are you still here?"

"Hell if I know." He leaned forward, placing his elbows on his knees.

"Then go." She pointed toward the door.

He hung his head, shaking it. "We're this close, Brit." He lifted his face to hers. "I won't touch you anymore. Not like that. Just tell me what happened."

Yeah, well, she'd done that once already—jumped at the chance to tell her side with internal affairs. She wasn't even worried about having a lawyer. She knew she hadn't pulled the trigger. But by the time internal affairs was finished with their interrogation—and that's exactly what the so-called interview had turned into—she had more questions than answers.

Colt didn't pose a threat. If anything, he'd be long gone once he knew the truth.

"Fine." She took a seat on the ottoman across from him. "The man I allegedly shot was a casualty of war. Only difference is he was killed stateside by me and his own government." She hung her head. "That night might not have even happened had he had access to dependable healthcare. We let Sergeant Beau Crenshaw down." Brit lifted her chin to him, her head throbbing.

"Beau?" Colt winced. "Ah, babe, I'm sorry." He stood.

"Whoa." Brit put out her hand. "I'm not your babe."

Colt grudgingly sat down. "Beau, my Beau, was my chocolate Lab." He shook his head. "Best hunting dog. It was the first name that popped into my head."

She nodded. "I thought maybe you knew something, at first. Then I thought you were just an asshole."

"And now?"

Now she didn't know what to think. She was so screwed up where he was concerned. And he was the king of mixed messages. Brit's lips thinned. "Do you want to hear this or not?"

"I think I need to know."

Well, gee. He made it sound like she'd put a big wrinkle in his plans.

Brit gripped the edge of the ottoman. Those days prior to the shooting came screeching back. "They'd put me on desk work. I was bored out of my mind and pushed them to put me back on call-outs. They granted my request." She sighed. "I was wrong. I shouldn't have come back to full-duty," she said, thinking out loud. "As soon as I looked through the scope, my hands shook."

"Who was the hostage?"

Brit sighed. "His wife. I was too close to that one. I should have got up from my position on that damned hill and waved Andi over."

"Andi? She's the one who called?"

"Yeah. We grew up together, went through the academy together. We made a pact during our training that when we were eligible we'd try out for the men-only club."

"This S.T.A.T.E. Team."

She laughed, the sound derisive. "Even my own father was against it." Brit glanced up at him, leery. "You'd probably like him. Don't know of any women in special ops, either." Well, there were the two females that just passed Army Ranger school. Even so, the Army hadn't agreed to let them fight in combat.

He threw his hands up in defense. "I don't make the rules."

"But you wouldn't want to fight side by side with a woman?"

He took a heavy breath. "Men are built different than women. I'm not knocking it." He gave her an appreciative smile. "You're soft, pretty, and a hell of a lot better company than a platoon of men."

Smooth. "You're sidestepping the question."

He chuckled. "On the grounds it may incriminate me."

Brit gave him a lift of her brow. "A woman may save your life someday."

"She already has." He gave her a lopsided grin.

Brit tried not to smile at that. *God, the man was incorrigible.* Not to mention he did inexplicable things to her insides, even when she was mad at him and hurt that he didn't share the same deep feelings she had for him.

Brit stood. She couldn't breathe. This thing wasn't going away with the state. They were going to indict her. "In case you're not aware, there's a public outcry for arresting cops these days."

He rose and strode toward her, his lips thinning. "Brit, I know how serious this is."

Brit crossed her arms in front of her chest, trying to create a wall between them. Something flickered in those green eyes of his. If it was real concern for her or himself, she couldn't say. But now that she had begun talking about that night, she didn't think she could stop until she finished.

"I had my sights on him. He was erratic, frightened, confused. But there was a moment of clarity in his eyes. Surrender. His wife was talking to him, trying to calm him down. She didn't want this for her husband." Brit raked her fingers through her hair, the pads of her fingertips pressing painfully into her skull. "That's when I saw it, a flash like the edge of a knife." Those feelings of disbelief and horror flooded Brit. "I can only describe it as slow motion between the time I saw it and when the bullet pierced his brain. He slumped against his wife." Brit fell back against the large-paned glass window and closed her eyes. Tears seeped past her lashes. "I still hear her screams."

Colt's arms went around her, and he pulled her into his embrace. She didn't fight it and lay her head against his chest.

"But he had a knife, Brit, you did your job."

Brit shook her head. She was never given the green light. But it was far worse than that.

"They never found a knife—it was only his military signet ring catching the light." Brit's heart pounded, the air around her thinning. She was in real fear of crumbling to the floor and dug her fingers into the soft flannel of Colt's pajama shirt. "I don't remember pulling the trigger. I was as surprised as anyone when he went down."

"How many counter-snipers?"

"Three."

"And your weapon was the only one that had been fired?"

Brit nodded against his chest. "Gunshot residue was all over my hands." Her voice hitched. "If it weren't for Andi, I would have lost it right there in front of my team, the brass."

"Sounds like she's a good friend."

"The best."

"Did they get back the ballistics test?"

"It was my gun, my fault."

"And now the Maryland state's attorney is deciding your fate."

"Yes."

"Okay. So we prove the evidence wrong." He pulled her away from him, holding her by the elbows, his eyes set and deliberate. They never wavered from hers. "Someone else shot Crenshaw."

"No they didn't. I did." She furrowed her brows at him.

"I don't care how fucked up you were that night. You'd remember pulling the trigger."

"This is crazy." Brit jerked from his grasp. "I'm going back. I spoke to my lawyer today. He expects an announcement soon."

"What if you didn't do it?"

She skirted him and the question and headed into the kitchen to get a drink of water. She opened a cabinet, grabbed a glass, and stood in front of the sink, eying the faucet. The water would more than likely turn to blood the moment she turned it on. She frowned when Colt's footfalls came up behind her.

"I'm a CADI, Colt." She took a heavy breath and stared out the window, shaking her head. "I've been reduced to an acronym."

"Woman, what the hell are you talking about?" He turned her toward him and none too gently. His eyes pierced hers. "Stop walking away from me and tell me what the shit you're talking about."

"I could have caused Crenshaw's death. I was a CADI before I ever knew what one was."

"What?" He jerked his head back.

"It's a label." She shrugged. "Like MIA or DUI. In my case, CADI is an acronym for a person who has caused an accidental death injury."

"That's bullshit." His hand tightened on her shoulders. "You hadn't killed anyone before the standoff, right?"

She turned away from his incisive stare. "I killed Seth."

He cupped her chin and brought her face even with his. The sharp planes of his cheeks flushed, his lips thinning. "*Jesus*, Brit, you didn't kill Seth. He killed himself."

"I realize that now. But when all this was going down—the hostage situation—I wasn't fit for duty."

He shook his head. "I'm not buying it. Something happened that night. I don't know what it was, but we're going to find out."

Her eyes widened. Why would he stay? "B-but . . . you need to go, Colt."

"You helped me. I'm repaying the favor." He stalked into the great room.

"No!" *No he wasn't.* She wasn't going to let him carry this honor thing to an early grave. She loved him. That wouldn't change.

Brit stopped short. Colt stood in front of the towering stone fireplace, hefting his gun. "Whoa." Her hands went up.

"Seriously?" He gave a disappointed look and bent down, grabbing her handgun from the coffee table. "Clean your gun. We need two working firearms."

"You're crazy. We're not doing this. I can't get into the evidence room. Besides"—she took the gun he held out almost like she was starting to believe his self-vindication crap—"if the state police can protect my ass, they will. They don't want to see me go down for manslaughter any more than I do. I'll get a fair shake."

"*Fuck* you will." His booming voice rose, echoing in the rafters above them.

Brit took a step backward.

His stance was combative, his expression savage, the way his eyes darkened—almost predatory. "I trusted the system. Put my faith in my innocence. I got nine years with no chance of parole."

A chill trickled down her spine. If she was convicted, she'd go to prison with a target on her back. More than likely she'd get her throat slit by some inmate looking to off a cop before her time was served.

Brit swallowed hard. She was a dead woman either way.

Chapter Twenty-Five

*T*HE FOYER, WITH ITS HONEY-COLORED WALLS, SEEMED TO close in on Colt while he paced the rustic wooden floors. He'd told Brit he owed her. What a crock. Oh, he owed her—owed her his life. Hell, he'd just about had to twist her arm to get her to agree to help herself.

Dumb.

He could have taken her truck—she'd have probably given it to him—and been well on his way to the Canadian border.

Face it, man. She's the best thing that's ever happened to you.

He gritted his teeth. All she wanted was a little reassurance, and he couldn't give it to her.

Commitment.

He'd gone that route and came home to an empty house and a Dear John letter. But it was more than that. He didn't deserve a woman like Brit. His mission was clear—prove her innocence. Easier said than done. What he needed was an inside man. Just so happened, Brit had one. Well, an inside woman.

Brit stood no more than twenty-five paces in front of him in the great room, her back turned, talking to her friend Andi on her cellphone. The fact that she was spilling her guts about the missing artifacts and him, a fugitive she'd been harboring for the last four days, to a Maryland state trooper trained to kill, had his chest tightening like a bad case of heartburn. If it weren't for his age, he'd swear he was having the big one.

He was taking a huge risk trusting a woman—no, a cop—he'd never met before. But this Andi Hall had helped Brit out during one of her darkest moments. If Brit trusted her, he'd have to as well.

Brit clicked off the phone. "She'll meet us at St. Michaels. I'll call her when we get close." She eyed the clock over the mantel—11:32 p.m. "If we can get on the road by midnight, we should get there before five."

"A church?" His words came out dubious, and he frowned.

Brit took a step closer, her brown eyes questioning. "You can walk at any time."

Knowing Brit, she'd put her faith back into the system. No, they were going to use this Andi Hall. "You said she's tight with the internal affairs captain."

Brit shrugged. "If you count an affair as being tight, then yes."

It was on the edge of his tongue to ask why she hadn't capitalized on this relationship of her friend's before. But then he remembered who he was dealing with. It was one of the reasons he was drawn to her. Integrity. Going through normal channels was not an option. And he damned well wasn't going to get all righteous now. He knew what that had gotten him.

Colt nodded. "What does this church have to do with it?"

"No. It's a town on the eastern shore."

"So what's the plan?" He took a step back, grabbed her gun off the end table and handed it to her. Then he took his, checked the chamber and shoved it in the waistband of his jeans.

Brit secured her weapon inside her chest holster, which she'd retrieved from the spare tire tool compartment located in the back of her Pathfinder. It also housed her police ID. Colt grimaced. It pissed him off he'd not done an entire sweep of her vehicle on day one. It only proved he wasn't the elite fighter he used to be during the war. And this was a biggie. He'd have figured out she was a cop a lot sooner.

"She has this old Victorian." She grimaced. "A fixer-upper in Fishing Creek. She's put some work into it, though. I wouldn't say it compares to Memory Maker, but . . ."

"It's a place to hide out." He couldn't mask the skepticism in his voice.

"No one would look for us there. Even if they find we've joined forces."

"She's your friend."

"Yeah, well, there are plenty of cops facing similar charges. I'm sure they have supporters. Cops stick together. So she's letting me stay at her place."

"With a fugitive."

Brit fell back a step. He guessed she'd forgotten that small little detail. Somehow he didn't think this Andi valued her job as much as Brit did. She was screwing the brass for one and didn't seem too concerned about the company her friend was keeping and would be keeping on her property.

The more he thought about it, the more uneasy he became.

Didn't matter. He was in too deep now. So deep he should just pull her into his arms like he wanted to and tell her he had feelings for her. But the hard ass that he was couldn't take the time to quantify what that all meant. Or wouldn't?

That would leave him exposed and vulnerable.

Idiot.

He was staying. That meant he was concerned about her, her safety. Damn it. Her future. That was another added complication. It wasn't just himself he had to worry about. She was highly trained. He knew she could handle herself in a gun battle or even survive in rough terrain. But bullets didn't discriminate. If he had a bulletproof vest, he'd be strapping it on her.

"You ready?" She stood with her hand on the doorknob, frowning at him.

He grabbed the backpack he'd taken from the closet and filled with extra clothes, bullets—to aid them in an ambush—and food like the beef jerky she'd bought for him and the cashews she'd had a craving for. If they were forced to survive in the elements, they'd have some supplies.

Brit snagged her keys off a ring next to the door and scooped her backpack off the floor. "Let's go."

Colt strode to the door, every ion in his body warning him that this was a bad move. Andi Hall better be all that and more. Hell, he knew better.

He wasn't one for miracles. They didn't exist. He'd lost his freedom, his mother, probably his father's trust by now, and in the not too distant future he felt sure the home and land he'd toiled over would be gone. The upkeep and expense was exhausting his father financially and physically.

What I wouldn't give to see my old man again. Only the reunion would be sweeter if he was vindicated.

Colt gave a hard laugh. He didn't see that happening. All his energy would be tied up saving the woman he was having a hard time saying goodbye to.

Brit stepped off the portico and turned around. "You okay?"

"No." He slammed the door, double-checking the lock. He took two strides and scooped the keys out of Brit's hand. "I'm driving. Get in."

She gave him a lift of her brow.

He took a deep breath. "Please, get in."

She pursed her lips, seemed to think about it for a minute, then handed off her pack before giving him her back and stomping around the front of the vehicle.

Colt hit the remote and unlocked the doors, stowing both their packs in the backseat before getting in. He shut the door. Brit's followed with a heavy thud.

"Why the attitude?" She swung around in her seat after securing her seat belt.

"You're the one slamming doors."

"Because you're acting like a jerk. This was your idea. I wanted to wait for the state's attorney."

"Dumb." He shook his head and started the truck.

"Did you just call me stupid?"

Colt pulled up the drive. "Yep."

"Stop the truck."

Noticing the flare to her nostrils, Colt ignored her and crested the top of the driveway, made the right onto Marsh Hill.

"Stop the truck, *Colt.*"

He shook his head, then out of the corner of his eye spotted her hand on the door handle. He went for the lock. Her door swung open, and he cursed, slamming on the brake.

"What the hell!" He grabbed her arm.

"Let go." She eyed his hand clenched onto her red parka, then him.

"So you can what? Take on the state yourself?" It came out smug, and he wanted to kick himself for being a dick. He removed his hand and placed it on the steering wheel, gripping it. "You got a lot of baggage, Brit." He turned in his seat. "Shooting an unarmed man, financial investigation, marrying an asshole."

She remained in the Pathfinder but with one foot out the door, her eyes blazing. "That asshole was your buddy first," she slung at him.

His head fell. "I take that part back."

"But not the rest." Her voice shook.

Colt lifted his chin from his chest.

The bravado in her eyes dwindled under the interior light. "You should have voiced your opinions way before now, Colt Rivers."

The pout tugging on her lips just about killed him. He didn't mean it. He was stressed to the max.

"You're right. But it—the financial investigation—was connected. Find the artifacts, prove my innocence, get you off the hook." Back then he believed she was a mortgage broker not . . .

"Just say it. It's because I'm law enforcement."

And, yeah, he was still trying to swallow the whole cop thing she'd dumped in his lap. Not to mention, he was leaving his ass wide open for capture trusting this Andi Hall.

He shook his head. *A fugitive and a cop.* What an unlikely pair.

He drew in a deep breath and exhaled. "For all I know this safe house is a trap."

"Andi?"

Now she was getting it. "Canada would be a smarter choice." Colt gave her a quick smile. "You can start a new life there, too."

"I'm not running for the rest of my life." She turned to gaze out into the dark night. "I'm surprised you're willing to let Seth dictate your life from the grave."

She was a shark, too. She knew just where to strike, and that bothered him. It was one of the reasons he headed east instead of north to the border.

"You're a giant pain in my ass, Gentry." He put his hands on the steering wheel. "We have five hours to kill. So you can start talking. We'll begin with this financial disclosure investigation, your life with Seth, and then the night of the shooting."

Somehow he believed the two were intertwined. At least Seth's death had played a major role in what happened that night.

Brit sighed, pulled her door shut, and folded her arms over her chest. "I'd rather be hypnotized."

He chuckled. He was even attracted to her obstinacy. Colt put the truck in drive and maneuvered the narrow mountain road to Route 219 until he got to the interstate. He drove a good fifteen minutes, then glanced over at Brit.

She'd been a little too quiet. Now was as good a time as any to get the conversation started. "This financial disclosure investigation . . . was it before or after Seth's death?"

"Before. Why?" She turned in her seat.

"What was he doing to help?"

"Nothing."

"Asshole," he hissed under his breath.

"I didn't tell him."

"Why not?" His brows snapped together.

She pressed back into her seat. "I had my own suspicions about the money. Knew it was only a matter of time before someone in the department became leery of the wealth we kept putting on show."

"You were looking into Seth's money before your agency made the investigation official."

"Uh huh."

"Then you should have known about the trial . . . my court martial."

"I was working backward. I hadn't gotten that far before he found out I was digging into his past."

"So he knew of your concerns before his death."

"Yep and he *was* ticked."

"How long before he died?"

"It was right around New Year's. He died in March."

Seven months.

Something had been bugging Colt. It pissed him off the bastard received an honorable discharge. "Did the son of a bitch end up in Arlington?"

She shook her head.

Good. He wasn't deserving of it.

"They never found his body."

A lead weight sunk to the bottom of Colt's stomach, and he veered across one lane of traffic to the shoulder, kicking up rocks as he skidded to a stop.

"What the hell, Brit?"

Chapter Twenty-Six

"ELAX!" BRIT COULDN'T HIDE THE AMUSEMENT IN HER voice at his absurdity. "He's not alive."

"How can you be sure?"

"I was there. The water was treacherous." She shrugged. "Besides that, he was in no condition to save himself, especially the second time he went under. He sank, and he never resurfaced."

"He was an Army Ranger, Brit." He said it like Seth was invincible. Maybe if Colt took a closer look at himself, he'd find that the label he shared with her husband didn't amount to much. His life was in shambles. Not his fault to a certain extent, but being an elite Army Ranger hadn't helped him one iota.

She waved a dismissive hand at him. "You haven't seen him in years. He drank too much, partied with his clients. He wasn't that lean warrior you remember."

"He got fat?" Colt said with disbelief and fell back into his seat, chuckling.

"No. He had been *drinking*. He'd drunk two of the three bottles of champagne on board. The first he'd smacked against the bow." She shook her head. "He christened her *Ariana*."

His laughter subsided, and he pinched the bridge of his nose, closing his eyes. "Arrogant son of a *bitch*."

"What are you talking about?" Brit's brows furrowed.

"Land of the Aryans," he said in a hollow voice before his lids opened.

"Aryans?"

"Aryans, Ariana. Doesn't matter. It's Persian and one in the same. Zadran, our Afghan interpreter, told Seth and me about it one night over beers. It was part of the Persian Empire back in the day." He angled his body toward her. "Northeastern Afghanistan, the area where he stole the artifacts, was part of that ancient land."

Unbelievable. Seth had been dropping clues right in front of her. He thought he was so slick, but he really *had* outsmarted them. Knowing her husband, he'd have rather died than gone to prison for what he had done.

He'd won after all.

Brit sat dejectedly in her seat, darkness surrounding them, except for the green dashboard clock. They'd been sitting too long. "We should get moving." Brit placed her hand on his seat back and peered over her shoulder at the roadway behind them. "We don't want a trooper coming up to check on us."

"Right." Colt sat up, checked for traffic, which was almost nonexistent at quarter to one in the morning, and started to pull out.

"Wait!" She grabbed his arm.

"Shit! What is it?" he snapped, his head twisting back at her.

"Sorry." She fiddled with the navigation system. "I thought I'd put it in the GPS."

"Can't you do it while I'm driving?"

"Some you can. But not this one." Brit punched up previous addresses and hit the one to her favorite restaurant in St. Michaels. She and Andi still needed to confirm a meeting spot. She'd figure that out once they got close. But the restaurant's location would give her an idea of the mileage and estimated time of arrival. "We're good."

He nodded and entered the highway.

They traveled the next hour in silence, passing the location of the accident and the jagged opening of Sideling Hill. Whether Colt was still fixated on a missing body, she couldn't say. But she was.

Even in death, Seth lingered.

He'd affected her decision making. An innocent man was dead because

Seth had been screwing with her head that night. She had the brass up her ass because of his extravagant lifestyle. If only she could be rid of him for good.

The faint, infuriating scent of Obsession filled the truck.

Damn it! I can still smell the bastard.

With the windows wound up, it was inescapable. She was beginning to resent Colt.

Brit turned sharp in her seat. "If Andi's got a washing machine, we're going to do those damn clothes you have on."

He gave her a sideways look, his dark brows meeting over the middle of his nose. "What's wrong with you? I just put them on. They're clean."

"No, they're not." Her voice cracked.

Colt gave her a sympathetic smile. "*Okay.* I'll wash them."

It wasn't just the damn cologne. She'd been rattled since Colt had asked about Arlington. For the first few days after the boating accident, she had real hope that Seth might survive. Not that she'd wanted to continue her life with him, but she hadn't wished him dead, either. There were small uninhabited islands in the Chesapeake that he could have washed up on. State police had utilized the helicopters, even after they'd officially ruled it a recovery operation. They protected their own. But as days turned into weeks, she'd felt relieved he hadn't surprised her by surviving his ordeal and crossing the threshold of their Chesapeake Beach home, ready to resume their life together. If he had, he'd have been in for a shock. She didn't want him back.

Brit gritted her teeth. The only thing she regretted was not being able to tell him that to his lying face. She never would, either. Contrary to what Colt seemed to think, Seth could cheat everyone else, but he couldn't cheat death.

Regardless he had screwed her in the end. That night still haunted her. Having a body would have given her closure. Tonight's conversation with Colt hadn't helped her on that score. He'd chipped away at her confidence, replacing it with a niggle of doubt.

Now she needed more reassurances—reassurances that he really was dead. Talking about it, going over that night frame by frame, would ease her concerns, although suggesting Colt help her work through that aspect seemed pointless. They were on opposite ends of the spectrum on that issue. He wanted Seth to be alive. It might solve all their problems—except for one.

She'd still be married to him.

Brit picked at the trim running along her leather seat. "The underwater recovery team warned, in all likelihood, there wouldn't be a body to bury."

"Yeah, well, they didn't know Seth like I did."

"He's not coming back, Colt. And I can't give you a body to prove it. It's science. The guys from the recovery team sat me down and explained it to me. The depth and frigid temperatures of the water could keep the body on the bottom indefinitely. It's been seven months."

"Nothing's definite without a body." Colt kept his eyes on the road, his profile under the highway lights, set and determined.

Great. Now they had a new debate to add to their growing list.

Err. Even if Seth was alive, it didn't mean he was going to reveal himself to them. If he was smart, he'd have hightailed it to Mexico with his artifacts. Still . . . she lived that night, witnessed the cold, angry seas. If she was guessing, to get to land he'd have at least a two-mile swim in either direction from where he fell in—if he hadn't succumbed to the rough water.

No, he was dead. She was sure of it.

"You stopped talking." Colt's voice was accusatory.

"You don't want to hear what I have to say."

"Difference of opinion."

"That's the point. It doesn't change anything. He's not going to *show* himself to us. We're screwed either way."

"Not if *we* locate him."

Brit threw her hands up. "This is insane! We can't prove our innocence, locate these artifacts, and find a dead man in twenty-four hours."

His hands tightened on the wheel. "Who said anything about you turning yourself in?"

"I thought it was implied."

"*God*, Brit." He reached for her, his voice pained.

Not falling for it. Brit turned away and stared out the window, tears filling her eyes. *Stop confusing me.*

He didn't mean any of it. He was using her, same as Seth. As much as she wanted to be consoled by him, she knew this wasn't real. *God.* Brit wiped her face. This wasn't how she imagined falling in love again. She was a hot commodity for a fugitive who hadn't gotten laid in four years. Nothing more. Even this Canada thing had been more along the lines of *I'll get you to Canada where you can start a new life, too.* Not *Let's start one together.*

Brit didn't want to start a new life. She liked her own, minus the drama of a police-involved shooting and a financial investigation. How would she even begin a new life? She couldn't be a cop. She probably couldn't be Brit. Changing her name, not ever seeing her family—no, disgracing her family—wasn't an option.

Not to mention, she'd always be on edge. She'd be a fugitive just like Colt. And if she managed to make a life for herself, she'd forever be in jeopardy of losing it. She herself had been responsible for ending a few fugitives' freedom during her law enforcement career—after they'd created a new life and, in most cases, a lawful one.

Of course they were guilty of their crimes. But Colt wasn't. That only left her, and she couldn't say for sure what had happened that night up on the hill with Andi and the other counter-sniper on her team, CJ. It all remained a fuzzy blur.

"I want to know the truth." She swallowed hard. "Even if that means I'm guilty."

"I know, ba—" He growled. "*Brit.*" It came out forceful, like he was making a conscious effort to correct the aforementioned word that he had been warned against using.

A smile touched her lips, and then she frowned. What was with him, anyway? Either he was or wasn't attracted to her. Okay, so maybe he was, but wouldn't he be attracted to any female at this point? The "babe" thing kept throwing her. It just rolled off his tongue so naturally. Only it was almost like it made him angry when it did. Like he was trying to suppress it and couldn't. *Weird.*

Of all the things she could and should be thinking and worrying about, this shouldn't be one of them. She was facing real jail time if she couldn't prove her innocence. And sitting around waiting for the state's attorney to make a decision—or God forbid, he turned it over to a grand jury—was both maddening and, well, the most helpless she'd ever felt. Then there were the doubts.

"What if I'm really guilty?" Her fears filled the dusky space between them, her voice shaky and uncertain.

His jaw tightened under the flash of a highway light, and then he cursed under his breath.

Whatever. She was done talking. Brit curled her legs up on the seat and gave Colt her back. "Wake me up when we get to the bay bridge."

Colt gripped the steering wheel. Self-doubt could eat a man alive on the battlefield. The woman needed answers. If she didn't have clarity and soon, she'd incriminate herself.

He scowled and hit the steering wheel. What he wouldn't give to find that son of a bitch alive. It wasn't even about the artifacts anymore. It was about Brit.

Seth had been screwing with her head for years. His death and the way it had come about—literally at her hands—had sent her into a tailspin. She was beating herself up over something she hadn't done. The only reason his butt ended up in the water was because he couldn't get off his high Army Ranger horse and let a woman, who was far more capable, captain the boat.

Colt, for one, recognized that quality—the capability—and many more. She was impressive.

But it was more than that. Something was gnawing at him. It all seemed too convenient to Colt.

Seth knew that Brit was investigating him. She was a cop with connections. If anyone could uncover what he had been involved in, it would be Brit. Too bad for her he'd died before she could nail his ass. Although, if anyone needed to walk away from his life and start over, it was his buddy Seth.

Only if he had staged his death, why would he walk away from his prized possessions? Brit's blond hair glowed under the moonlight and his fingers ached to sift through it. She was the treasure Seth should have been worried about losing.

She was as tenacious as she was soft.

Ah, hell.

Colt reached over and stroked the side of her pretty face. Dark lashes dusted her alabaster skin. As much as he appreciated her feminine side, he needed her to buck up. It tore him up to hear her quavering voice earlier. The woman was highly trained, had received an appointment to an elite tactical division in her department. They just didn't give those spots away, especially to a woman. She'd earned it.

Brit slept soundly next to him. The delicate curve of her shoulder bent inward like she was trying to ward off an impending assault. He hated seeing her that way. He liked the other woman who slammed the window in his face and tried to lock him out. Or the one who bent his hand backward and stole his gun.

Where was she?

If she thought she could check out of this thing without a fight, she was wrong. Colt jabbed her side with his index finger. She made a mewling sound and snuggled against the seat back.

Colt jabbed her again but harder. "Get up."

"What?" She swatted his hand away, then looked over her shoulder, scowling.

"You're a quitter."

Chapter Twenty-Seven

EALLY? BRIT STRAIGHTENED IN HER SEAT, WIPED A LAYER of dried slobber from her cheek, and glared at him. "Go . . . to . . . *hell.*" It came off her lips like she was possessed.

"I'm already there, babe."

Err. She damn sure hoped he wasn't talking about the company. This was all his idea. She was prepared to go back, wait for the decision, and turn herself in. Brit blinked at a passing road sign, catching the light of the headlights—Frederick—then the clock. They still had a good hour and a half before the bridge. "Why'd you wake me?"

"We need to talk."

Ugh. A total rehashing of the biggest mistake of her life—Seth.

Brit dropped her head back against the seat. "I'm not giving you every last detail."

He raked his fingers through his hair, a sly grin forming on his lips. "You can leave out the sex."

"*Eww!* You're disgusting."

He laughed out loud. "Just give me the lowdown on Seth. What he was involved with in the days leading up to the boating accident."

Brit shrugged. "His usual. Working." She turned in her seat so she faced him. "He stayed at the office late . . . a lot."

Colt snorted and nodded.

"What? What's with the head bob?"

"Nothing. He worked late. Go on."

She knew what he was getting at, and it infuriated her. She'd have known if Seth was having an affair. Wouldn't she? It didn't matter, the man was dead. But it did irk her that it *was* possible, and now Colt knew, on top of everything else her husband had done to her, she wasn't woman enough to keep Seth interested.

"This is stupid! I'd rather talk about the shooting." She folded her arms in front of her and stared out the windshield.

"I'm waiting."

So was she. Talking about that night was uncomfortable. No, having another panic attack scared the crap out of her, and this was just the kind of subject that could summon one like a specter from the great beyond. She took a deep breath, wishing she had that damn paper bag.

"I already told you about Crenshaw."

"Describe the scene before and after the shooting."

Brit nodded. "It was September 1." She smiled. "I was having a good day. It was Sunday, my day off. I worked in the garden, had crabs at my parents, and—"

"Crabs?"

"Chesapeake Bay blue crabs, steamed and spiced." The memory of that night at Mom and Dad's was so vivid she could almost taste the sweet crabmeat—which could only be found in the Chesapeake—and Old Bay seasoning melting in her mouth. "Have you ever had them?"

"It's on my bucket list."

Great. Now he had a bucket list. "Is this new . . . your bucket list?"

"I started it the day I broke out of prison." He snorted. "Already checked one off the list."

"Oh, yeah?"

"Kidnap a cop."

"Real funny." She squinched her face at him. She knew it was his way of ignoring his underlying fears, and that bothered her.

In the end, he hadn't planned on surviving long on the outside. A pang of regret filled Brit's chest. She'd be the reason for his death, too. But she'd already argued with him on that subject numerous times. He wasn't going to change his mind. But she could at least help him check off something on his list.

"Crabs are still in season, and there's a front porch that overlooks the bay at Andi's place with a small picnic table." *Shit!* The bay. She'd forgotten about that little hang-up.

"You looking to make a memory with me, Brit Gentry?" The boyish grin he gave Brit made her heart flutter.

She'd hoped lots of memories, but he'd made it clear the only reason he was still here was to clear his name and repay the favor. Part of his twisted honor code, she assumed.

"It's one very casual"—she smiled—"messy dinner."

"I love ribs, remember?"

How could she forget? It was the best first date she'd ever been on. Why did things have to be so complicated?

"Where do you see yourself five years from now?" *Wow.* Where did that come from? Brit rolled her lips in.

"Excuse me?" He eyed her speculatively.

"You heard me, Rivers. What is it you want out of life?"

"To survive."

"Let's say you do. We find the missing artifacts and prove your innocence, and you're exonerated."

"What about you?"

"I asked you first."

"I mean, in order for this scenario to work *for me*, you'd have to be cleared, too." He glanced her way, the little bit of light vanishing when he traveled under the overpass of Route 32.

When they reemerged into the bluish glow of the highway lights, there wasn't a hint of emotion lining his profile.

"They clear me of the shooting and the financial investigation."

"Right—the artifacts." He kept his eyes on the road, nodding like he was taking it all in.

"Well?" Brit sat up and tapped her finger to her lips. If he cared for her, thought there was a future in all this, she'd removed all the obstacles.

He sniffed and kept his face turned toward the road. "See my dad." His voice hitched.

Brit's chin dropped, and she frowned into her hands. She couldn't even be mad or hurt. He'd spoken from his heart, which just about tore hers in two. Regardless of how he felt about her, Brit's feelings had only deepened for him. He wasn't lofty like Seth. His needs were basic—family.

Whatever it took, she was going to do her damnedest to make that happen.

They rode in silence the next hour. Her agreement to relive a humid, airless night in September when she'd killed a man in cold blood only hung in the periphery of her subconscious. She'd gotten a reprieve for now.

Although, she had picked up on one thing. Every time they discussed the past, whether it be his or hers, they always ended up in the future together.

The bridge came up quickly, and Brit let that thought go. At four thirty in the morning, with lights aglow from the toll booths, she and Colt were the only souls on the road.

"Can you hide your face?" Brit dug out four one-dollar bills to pay the cashier.

"What? Why?" He sounded like she was asking him to do something ridiculous.

"Cameras." She didn't know exactly where or what angle they were located. They could be inside the booth, pointed toward cars and occupants in the toll lane as they paid.

When they came up to the attendant, Colt turned and reached behind him into the backseat, pretending to search for something. Brit lifted herself onto her haunches and reached over with the bills, keeping her chin up, her head high as it grazed the soft liner of the ceiling.

"Have a good evening." The attendant took the cash, the light turning green for them to go.

"You do the same." Colt lifted his arm and waved, more to block his face, and proceeded past the toll booth toward the bridge. The two parallel steel structures, lit at night, cut an impressive backdrop against a velvet sky. Brit trembled.

"So this is the infamous bay." Colt's gaze spanned the horizon from one side window to the other.

"Keep your eyes on the road!"

His body jerked along with the truck.

"*Shit.*" Brit's hands flew to the door and the dash, bracing herself.

Colt steered out of it and speared her with his eyes. "I *am* gonna end up in the water if you shout in my ear again."

"Sorry," she whispered. She hadn't been on the bay bridge since the boating accident. It was bad enough that her home overlooked the bay. She'd solved that problem by installing shutters. But it still couldn't block out the memory of that night.

Now she was surrounded by water on all sides. Her fears had kept her from enjoying the thing she loved most—the beach. She couldn't even get up enough courage to visit her parents' beach home in Ocean City, a place she loved as a child.

Or Andi's haunted Victorian across the bay.

Brit bit her lip. "Do you believe in ghosts?"

Colt chuckled. The woman loved to throw him a zinger. "Seth's either alive or dead. He's not haunting us."

"I'm not talking about Seth. I'm talking about Andi's house."

A laugh rolled up his chest. "You're serious?"

Brit shrugged. "That's what she *says.*"

"Have you seen this ghost for yourself?"

"Ghosts, and no." Her voice quavered.

"You're afraid."

She waved a dismissive hand. "For all I know Andi started that rumor to drum up business for when she finally opens."

"Sounds like she's a sharp businesswoman and close to opening, then."

"Ah . . . there's quite a bit of work still left."

"So we're sleeping on the floor." Like that had ever bothered him before. But he'd been spoiled the last three nights, sleeping in a king bed. The only thing missing was having Brit next to him the last two.

"I'll see what the accommodations are." Brit held up her cellphone and punched in numbers. "Besides, I need to find out our meeting spot."

Colt's body tensed. Either this Andi was in it to help, regardless of the consequences, or she'd sold them out. It was a toss-up. One Colt couldn't afford to lose.

"Hey, it's me," Brit said into the receiver. She nodded, glancing out the window at the last of the shimmering bay. "About thirty minutes."

Colt moved into the left lane now that he was off the bridge. "Where are we meeting—"

She held up her hand. "The docks in St. Michaels," she said for his benefit and then listened intently to her friend on the phone.

"What about a bed?"

Brit gave him an exasperated look.

Fine. He'd find out when he got there.

"Beds," she said with an emphasis on the plural before her brows rose, either in warning, or, in one of those *see it's not as bad as you thought* looks.

Kind of was. He was hoping for just one. Although she'd told him in no uncertain terms their days of playing house were over. It was just as well. Brit deserved a man who could give her tomorrow. He was not that guy. Hell, even if he were a free man, he was flat-out terrified of being rejected a second time. He laughed to himself. A dog seemed more practical.

Now that was loyalty.

Right. It was going to hurt like hell to walk away from her. A damn dog wasn't going to come close to making up for it. Even now he was breaking out into a cold sweat just thinking about it, and she was only an arm's length away.

Better to have loved and lost, than to never have loved at all.

Well, he'd laid his heart out there once, took the vow for better or worse. Dana had taken everything he believed in about the sanctimony of marriage and made a complete mockery of it.

Colt scrubbed his face. Even if he could chance it, he couldn't offer Brit the lifestyle she was accustomed to. She had bay front property, lake front property, a bigass boat.

Shit.

Reopening his ranch for hunting wouldn't come close to providing her the things his dirty, double-crossing buddy Seth had. He snorted. The guy was on the take. But she hadn't known that, now she was going to take the fall for it and lose everything in the process.

Brit seemed accepting of it, though.

He believed her when she said it was Seth who lived and loved the grandiose lifestyle. She enjoyed the simpler things like gardening, having Sunday dinners with her parents. Things that were important to him, too. Maybe not a flower garden. But vegetables . . . now that was living off the land and something they could both enjoy.

Hell. The only thing he was proving was that she was perfect for him.

Take her job. She had the same staunch work ethic he'd had when he had a career he could be proud of in the military. Her paramilitary job with the state police even paralleled his, well, before his court-martial.

That was another thing. She loved her job. Maybe not this bullshit, but he could tell she was good at it. She knew her guns, how to take them apart and put them back together again.

Now that bothered him. Why wouldn't she remember pulling the trigger? Those puppies had a mean kick. She didn't have much meat in her shoulder. She would have felt that, unless she was experiencing an episode like he witnessed that first day in the kitchen. Now he could see that. It still pissed him off that he'd been the cause of it.

"Turn right onto 322." Brit pointed with her finger. "What's wrong?"

"Nothing."

"You were preoccupied with something." Brit gave him a lift of her brow.

"You were on the phone."

"I've been off for the last ten minutes." She turned in her seat, head cocked, looking at him like he'd suffered a blackout.

"You should have said something if you wanted to talk."

"I was thinking."

"Me, too."

"You know I'd never turn you in, right?" Her hand came down on his forearm, her eyes black orbs in the dark on the quiet two-way highway void of lights.

"You're going to have a tough time explaining the company you keep, if they find you with me."

"You need to promise me if it gets to that point, you'll be long gone for your own sake." The tips of her fingers pressed deeper into his skin. "I mean it. That's something I can't bear to witness."

He pinched the bridge of his nose. It was pretty much how he saw it with her. Skipping out on Brit when she needed him the most was the last thing he could imagine doing, which certainly put a chink in his plans. Not that he wanted their affiliation to hurt her, either. He only hoped when the time came he wouldn't second-guess his final decision and get her hurt or even killed.

"You're still dead set on staying." If it sounded like an accusation, it was.

"I know you understand." Her hand fell away, and she slid down into her seat. "You didn't run from your court proceedings or your court-martial. You believed in the system. You're an honorable man."

He snorted. "And look where it got me."

"Make a right on North Talbot Street."

He took it sharp, the wheels squealing. "You need to reconsider proving your innocence. You need to let this go."

"Left on East Chew Avenue." She scooted up toward the dash. "Left on West Harbor Road."

He pulled into a hotel parking lot, facing a marina, his heart rate on overdrive. "You're not listening."

"I heard you," she snapped.

"What's wrong?"

"I don't see her car."

"What color?"

"White."

From his vantage point there were a ton of white cars in the parking lot. Granted, they were interspersed throughout the parked cars.

"What's the make?"

"I think a Honda."

Brit fumbled her phone and dialed, he assumed, her friend's number.

"Where are you? I don't see your car." Brit nodded. "Okay, we'll see you in a few." She clicked off.

"Which car?" Colt pulled into a space facing out, his flight-or-fight responses on high alert.

"She's driving a rental—hers is in the shop getting brakes."

Colt put the truck in park, his eyes constantly scanning his surroundings. "She coming to us?"

Brit undid her seat belt. "No, we're going to meet her." She opened the door, a cool October sea breeze ruffling the hair at his nape.

He'd never felt so exposed in his life.

Chapter Twenty-Eight

HE COLD, BRINY AIR FILLED COLT'S LUNGS, AND HE
shoved his hands inside the pockets of Seth's ski jacket. At quarter
to five in the morning, the hotel remained still. The entrance was
lit, and if there was a nighttime manager, he didn't see one behind the
counter as he peered through the sliding glass doors that appeared to open
on command once he stepped on the welcoming black carpet leading inside.

If he had known on the front end, he'd have demanded they choose a
more secluded spot. Not that there was anyone milling about. But there
would be soon. It was a harbor for crissake.

Brit rounded the corner of the building, taking a sidewalk leading to the
dock. The plan was to meet Andi Hall there. She'd give them a key to the
house and a refresher for Brit on how to find it.

With his head on a swivel, checking every well-manicured bush to his
left, balconies positioned a floor above them to his right, and his flank, he'd
let Brit get ahead of him. Colt jogged the ten yards or so and caught up with
her.

"Whoa, babe, you're moving a little too fast," he said, keeping his voice
low, and grabbed her hand.

Brit jumped. "Don't do that!" She pulled her clammy hand from his.

Colt frowned and held tight. He never noticed her hands being that
moist before. It was downright chilly with the sea air. "You okay?"

"Just want to get the key and get going." She continued down the sidewalk, her fingers twisting in his, trying to wriggle free.

Colt held tight. He couldn't discount her condition, this CADI thing. That's all he needed was her having an anxiety attack.

Something was up. She'd been out the door and moving at a high rate of speed the moment her boots hit the parking lot. He got it. Get in, get out. But it seemed more like she was trying to beat the clock before she self-destructed.

Colt's grip tightened. "Hold up." He stopped and pulled her back against the wall of the hotel, checking the balcony above. The drapes were shut. Didn't mean there wasn't a guest behind the thick room-darkening shade.

Her body trembled, and he moved in closer. "You're that cold?" If he had to guess, the temperature hovered close to fifty or slightly below. He pressed back a wave of her blond hair, fixated on the perspiration dotting her forehead.

"Brit? What's going on?" He placed his hands on her shoulders.

She opened her mouth slightly, breathed in a shaky breath and then exhaled through her mouth. She gulped in another breath, then another, like she was fighting for air.

"*Shit.* You're having an attack." Colt scrubbed his face hard. He should have had enough sense to grab one of the hundred or so paper lunch bags back at Memory Maker. "Stop breathing through your mouth. You're going to hyperventilate."

She nodded, her eyes wide and glassy. "I'm feeling tingly. My fingers." Her voice shook, and she lifted up a pair of pale, unsteady hands.

Colt took her two hands—still clammy—into his and began massaging them. "Come on, sweetheart, don't freak out on me." His own voice was strained. What was it about the carbon monoxide? She was losing too much because of her rapid mouth breathing.

"Brit." He cupped her face. "Listen to me. You need to close that pretty mouth of yours and breathe through your nose."

"I-I'm trying." Her lips closed, then opened, warm vapor filling the space between them.

Damn it. No! She needed something to occupy those pouty lips, like sucking on a straw or breathing into a paper bag, which he didn't have. Or . . .

Hell, she'd either snap out of it and smack him across the face or thank him for his ingenuity. Colt dipped his head and pressed his lips to her open mouth. What he got in return was a mouth full of hot air that made his cheeks puff out and beautiful wide brown eyes that clung to his. Brit inhaled and exhaled into his mouth again. Colt moved his lips against hers, coaxing her to kiss him back.

Come on, baby, just kiss me like you did last night.

His arm slipped around her, pulling her close. The feel of her against him made his body shudder with awareness. She was soft and feminine and frightened. That was what he concentrated on, and he stroked her back, hoping to relax her. Brit's lashes fluttered, eyes slowly closing, and she began breathing from her nose.

That's my girl.

Colt closed his eyes and applied more pressure, hoping to elicit a response. Her lips were pliant and trembling beneath his. He kissed her again more urgently. Any other time, he'd welcome the slow ache of desire that came from kissing Brit. Not tonight. He had her pressed up against the concrete wall of the hotel, the rustling crown of leaves overhead casting shadows across them and a brightening sky threatening to flip a lightswitch from night to day if she didn't get it together and soon.

Her lips parted, still trembling, and Colt deepened the kiss, giving her a little tongue. She accepted him warmly, the suction of their lips telling him all he needed to know. Finally, she was kissing him back, breathing harder, but still through her nose. *God* she tasted good. His fingers sifted through the heavy fall of her blond hair, and he gave her a rough tug against him.

Her arms looped around his neck, and she mewled into his mouth like a gentle kitten waking from a nap. His blood pounded through his body, his core awakening to her touch when he reluctantly ended the kiss and dropped a quick one on her forehead.

Brit's fingers came to her lips. She frowned up at him. "You shouldn't have done that," she said, her voice little more than a wisp of air.

"Next best thing to a paper bag." He chuckled softly. "What happened?"

"The water." She pressed a strand of hair behind her ears. "I don't think

I can meet her on the dock."

"This a reoccurring phenomenon?"

She let her head fall back along the wall. "Since the accident."

Water? When he'd found her along the lake, which was visible through the trees, it hadn't bothered her then. "What about the lake?"

"I think it has more to do with the bay, the salt air." A seagull flew by above and called out. Brit's body tensed. "Even the gulls."

He gave her a stern look. "You had a feeling this wasn't going to go well."

"I thought I was stronger than that." Her forehead crinkled. "Andi's place is on the water."

"Andi know about this CADI thing?"

"Yeah."

"Okay." He reached into Brit's coat pocket and pulled out her phone. "Call her and tell her where we are." He sure as hell wasn't searching the docks, looking for this Andi. It was clear Brit wasn't going anywhere in her condition. And the whole thing smelled of fish bait. Andi Hall knew of her weakness. Suggesting they meet on a dock facing the bay seemed suspicious.

A trap seemed more likely, now that he thought about it. For all he knew they had already connected him to Brit through the stolen car left at the accident scene. He reached back and yanked the gun from the waistband of his jeans.

Brit's eyes followed his movements, growing larger when Andi answered. "Ran into a snag. Can you meet us down the sidewalk against the hotel?" She clicked off. "What are you doing?"

"Protecting our assets."

"She's on our side."

He looked down his nose at her. "Yet she asked to meet on a dock." Either Andi Hall was an insensitive bitch or she was setting them up.

A dark form turned the corner of the hotel and headed in their direction. Colt's grip tightened on the gun. With his finger on the trigger, he held the gun down to his side, his gaze on the swaying movements of Andi's arms and hands. The closer she got, the more distinct she became, and it was clear there was no weapon. Colt kept her in his sights, glancing past her, making sure she was alone.

"*God, Brit.*" Andi's arms stretched out, and she folded Brit into her embrace. "I wasn't thinking, honey. *God* I'm so stupid." She peered over at Colt, her dark shoulder-length hair sticking out from under a black CNN skull cap.

What the fuck!

Colt whipped out his gun, pointing it toward her head. "Get on the ground." His voice boomed.

"No!" Brit pushed Andi aside, ready to take the bullet.

"*Jesus.* I could have shot you!" His heart thundered in his chest, his hands damp with sweat. "She's got the same hat on." His bewildered voice echoed in his ears.

"Wh-what's he talking about?" Andi jumped back with her hands in the air. "Control your bitch," Andi growled.

"Colt, put the gun down. She dated a CNN reporter." Brit glanced back at Andi.

"Yeah." Andi beaded in on him. "This is about all I got out of the deal— the bastard was cheap."

He guessed he'd jumped the gun, literally. He was jittery as hell. Last place he'd seen that cap was up at the lake. Judging by the scowl plastered across Brit's face, he'd fucked up.

He lowered his gun, shoving it into his waistband. "Sorry."

Andi put her hands down. "You need to relax. I'm doing you the favor, man."

He nodded. "My mistake."

"It's okay. It was an honest one." Brit's shoulders relaxed and she grabbed Andi's hand. "Maybe we should figure something else out."

"No, no. I want to help." She peered over Brit's head. "There's no reason why you can't stay there, except for him. You can always say I didn't know." Andi reached into her coat and eyed Colt. "Just getting the keys."

Colt scrubbed the back of his neck. He'd really screwed up. "It's okay."

Andi handed Brit a jangling silver ring. "You know how to get there, right? Just take the left on Goldenhill Road. The post office is on the left and then right on Hoopers Island Road. Go about seven miles and the house is on the right."

"Got it." Brit gave her a quick hug.

Andi smiled, her lips thinning at Colt. "When this is all over, let's celebrate at the Crab Claw Restaurant."

Brit nodded against Andi's dark head. "I was telling Colt about blue crabs."

Andi pulled away. "Ya know it's probably not a good idea for you guys to travel around town. There's a refrigerator and a cooktop but no stove. I just got off and need a good eight hours of sleep. But I could swing by and grab a bushel of those crabs and bring them over for dinner around five."

"No, you're not. That's too expensive." Brit reached into the parka of her ski jacket and pulled out a wad of cash. "Let me pay." She handed the bills to Andi.

Andi took them, counted it out, and handed her back some. "Hundred's enough."

So he was wrong about Andi, and he was going to hear about it once he got back in the truck.

"Can we give you a lift?" It was the least he could do, and it would delay the ass chewing he was going to get.

"No. I live right across the way." She pointed to a condo on the other side of the harbor. "Can't beat the view. Unit 602 on the end."

Colt hooked his chin toward Brit. "We need to go."

"Ah, right." Brit hugged Andi one last time. "You're the best. I love you."

"Me, too." Andi released her and shooed her with her hand. "Go. The sun will be up soon."

Brit waved Colt on, and they walked toward the front of the hotel.

"Oh, jeez." Andi ran up behind them. "I forgot to tell you. They found a body in the water near Tilghman a few days ago."

Brit swung around first. "Seth?"

Andi shrugged. "I don't know. They couldn't identify it. But the medical examiner should know once the dental records come back."

Brit nodded. "I'll see you tomorrow."

"Bye." Andi turned and headed back toward the dock.

Brit strung her fingers with Colt's. "I told you he was dead," she whispered.

Chapter Twenty-Nine

RIT GRABBED HER KEYS FROM COLT'S FINGERS. SHE rounded her vehicle, opened the automatic door locks, and got in. He plopped down beside her in the passenger seat, shutting the door.

She slammed hers. "You need to get your shit together!" She jammed her truck key into the ignition and started the engine.

"It was an honest mistake," he grumbled.

"Yeah, right." Brit pulled out, her head aching and her stomach growling.

Colt stared out the window. "Why would she suggest you meet her on a pier looking over a body of water that makes you physically ill?"

"Because she lives there, and it's five freaking o'clock in the morning and she's doing me—us—a huge favor that could cost her job. Not to mention, her freedom for harboring a fugitive."

He only nodded.

He was wrong, and he knew it. He'd embarrassed her big-time. Andi was the sister she'd never had. They'd grown up together, went through those horrible, awkward teenage years. Brit hopped back on Route 50 going east. They still had a solid hour before they reached the house. She could barely keep her eyelids open. She should have let him drive. But she needed to feel in control after her episode at the hotel.

She owed him a lot for tonight. She was surprised by his methods, but it had worked amazingly well. Her stomach fluttered. His kisses were ardent and sensual and so not what she should be thinking about. And totally not okay. She couldn't go back to their little bubble of bliss.

Tomorrow, if she was lucky, Andi might have some information about the investigation. She'd already calmed her fears about Seth. They had a body, and in a few days—a week tops—they'd have an identity.

"You going to let the Seth thing go?" Brit peered over at him.

"Whatever."

Men. She guessed he was still sulking for making an ass out of himself.

"Everybody loves Andi. What's your hang-up?"

"She called me your bitch for one."

Brit laughed out loud. "First, you deserved it, and, second, that's Andi."

"She's nothing like you."

Brit's brows furrowed. "What do you mean?"

He shrugged. "She's abrasive."

"Comes with the job."

"You're not like that."

Brit caught the sign for a small market up ahead. There were probably other stores closer in to town, but it was still early. She couldn't guarantee they would be open. Route 50 was a desolate, flat state highway, and patrolled heavily by troopers. The last thing she needed was to run into one with Colt. The store came up, and its lights were on. She made a quick right into the parking lot and pulled in.

Colt reached for the dash. "What the hell are you doing?" His eyes darted to their surroundings. One vehicle other than theirs, probably the cashier's, and a single gas pump.

"I'm hungry. I can't wait until tonight to eat crabs." Brit unbuckled her seat belt and reached for the door.

Colt latched onto her arm. "What if someone sees you?"

"Sees you, you mean."

His face twisted with confusion.

"I'm not a fugitive, yet." She threw his hand off, opened the door, and got out.

"Can you grab me some coffee, oh, and cream, and if they have any donuts?" He dipped his head, looking embarrassed. "I'll pay you back."

"It's not a problem." She waved him off and started to shut the door.

"And a map."

"Map?" She ducked inside the truck. "What for?"

"I want to get my bearings."

"So a map of Maryland, then."

"Yeah. I'll pay you—"

Brit shut the door. If anything, she owed him. She'd buy him his map and whatever else he wanted. It had to be hard for a man like Colt to be so dependent on someone.

She entered the store and kept her head down. She selected a box of honey buns and then a package of eggs, milk, cream, coffee, tea, cereal, and bananas. Then she thought about how long they would be there and snagged a pack of chicken breasts, frozen veggies, and olive oil. She passed by another aisle and tossed a frying pan in and gasped at the price—seventeen bucks. Well, if she didn't buy it, she'd be kicking herself later. She tossed a spatula in and a pack of plastic silverware.

Entering the checkout line, she flipped through the maps and grabbed Maryland and a *Washington Post*.

"Good morning." The cashier began ringing up her groceries.

"Hi." Brit scratched the back of her neck and craned her head slightly while the old man totaled and bagged her groceries. Then thinking better of it she turned. "Can you give me sixty worth of gas?"

"Sure can."

She paid and scooped up the bags. "Thanks." Brit strode to the door and swung it open.

"Have a good day," the cashier called.

The door shut behind her, and she opened the back door and dropped the bags in, hopping in front.

"Any problems?"

"None." Brit put the truck in reverse and backed out, then maneuvered toward the pump before getting out and shutting the door on Colt's queries.

Colt rolled down the window, scowling. "I would have done that."

"I got it." She waved him away. "Troopers patrol this stretch hard."

He punched the window up, and she finished filling the tank before sliding back into the front seat and closing the door. "Your donuts are behind your seat."

"How about the map?"

She headed east on 50 again. "In one of the bags."

He reached back and rummaged through them until he came up with it. He settled back down into his seat and opened it.

Brit eyed him and the map. "Doing some recon?"

A smile curled his lips. "Doesn't hurt to have some direction. God knows I need some."

"Are you religious?"

"I wasn't a regular churchgoer." He laughed and lay his head back against the headrest. "But I witnessed God's grace on the battlefield, and knew that when I finally made it home I'd give Him the time and respect He deserved as my savior."

He'd been angry that night during his nightmare. She was glad to see he didn't resent God. He had all the reason in the world to question things, especially after his comrade Sullivan's death. Of course, it wasn't God who killed him. That burden lay squarely on the shoulders of her husband.

"How about you?" Colt turned his head toward her and smiled. It was a tired smile, lit by the early morning sun. But one she could imagine him giving her after a hard day's work on his ranch in Montana. It melted her heart. She reached over, hesitating.

He followed her hand with his eyes.

She gripped the knob for the heat instead and adjusted it. She needed to remind herself that there was no future here. He may not have said it in so many words. Actually, it was the lack of words that rang clear.

"Every Sunday." She sat back, putting her hand on the steering wheel.

"Oh, yeah."

She nodded. "Methodist."

"Good Christian woman," he said under his breath and turned to stare out the window.

Well, she'd have to leave that up to God. She'd killed an unarmed man. She didn't know how favorably God would look down on her now. And if she was being honest, at least to herself, she hadn't been to church since the shooting.

Brit took the right turn on Route 16. Ten more miles. She needed to prepare herself. From what she remembered of Andi's place, it had water views on at least two sides, facing both the Tar and Chesapeake bays. She took a left on Golden Hill and passed the post office Andi had mentioned. They'd be there in less than ten minutes.

Jeez, it was warm in here. She unzipped her parka. Her body had turned into an instant oven. She placed her clammy hand on her leg, rubbing it back and forth.

Colt grabbed her hand. "Keep breathing through your nose."

She gave him a nervous smile. "It's not that easy."

"It is." He sat up. "Take my first tour. My heart was beating like a jackhammer."

"So you have had panic attacks?"

"Panic, not PTSD." He winked at her and grinned.

Somehow she got the feeling he knew he was kidding himself about the latter.

Brit kept up the steady breaths. *In out, in out.* She pulled her hand back and took the right onto Hoopers Island Road, traveled a few more miles, passed a Methodist church on the right, and counted the driveways until she came to a fat white pine tree and the second gravel entrance with a mailbox and the numbers 263. The driveway was circular and made of gravel. The Victorian, a yellow clapboard house with all its signature looks—tall, steeply shaped roof, welcoming porch, with gingerbread—stood against an ethereal autumn sky with its pink and blue hues, the morning sun peeking over a glinting bay filled with whitecaps.

"The water's a little rough this morning." She pulled around the driveway and parked in front of the wraparound porch. "She's done a lot with the place."

"I'll get the bags in back." Colt got out and opened the rear door grabbing the plastic bags by their handles.

Brit did the same but looped one of the backpacks over her shoulder, the other tight in her hand. She shut the door and followed behind Colt, keeping her face averted, trying to avoid a direct shot of the bay.

The waves lapped the bulkhead, the slosh of water making her queasy the closer she got to the house. She was a good ten paces behind Colt when the ground started to spin, and she tottered.

"Whoa." The rustle of bags came from in front. A strong arm slipped around her waist. "You okay?"

Brit shook her head and bit down on her lip. "I don't think I can do this."

"Yes, you can." He set down the grocery bags, then took the load off her shoulder and from her hand. He held her by her shoulders like he'd done before. "Look at me, Brit."

She lifted her chin. A pair of serious green eyes held hers. "It's nothing more than a panic attack. Take slow deep complete breaths through your nose."

Brit nodded and concentrated on her airflow.

"Good girl." He dipped his head. "Stop whatever negative thoughts are running through your head by yelling stop."

"Stop," it came out on a whisper.

"In your head. Scream it as loud as you can."

Stop! She yelled to the far recesses of her brain, trying to rid herself of her thoughts. It was dark, raining, the wind buffeting her face. Seth was yelling at her. *Stupid bitch. It should have been you.* Stop! Stop! Stop!

"Replace the thought with something calming." Colt's hand rested on her hip, the other stroking her cheek.

She peered into his face. Strong jawline, tough-guy lips, pronounced nose but perfectly proportioned with sensitive green eyes and dark brows that were currently furrowed.

Brit moaned inwardly. She shouldn't be thinking of him. The rugged, unjustly accused soldier would remain a bittersweet memory into her twilight years. Only it was becoming clearer that she didn't want a day to pass without him. She wanted time to stop. It wouldn't. But he was here with her now, helping her through one of the most debilitating moments of her life when he had so much to lose.

"You had every right to feel helpless and afraid that night on the bay."

He stroked her hair.

She nodded. "I wish you could have met the woman I was before the accident."

"I see her even if you can't." His eyes swept over her like he was seeing her for the first time.

Her cheeks warmed, and Brit turned away to view the water. It sparkled from the sun's rays. For the first time in a long while, it was soothing. Colt had done that for her. "I'm feeling better. We should get the groceries in."

"Good idea. I'm starving."

Brit laughed. "It's a common theme with you."

"Aw." He wagged a finger at her. "Now don't tell me you're not hungry."

Brit's stomach growled, and she grimaced. "I'll open the door." She dug into her front jean pocket and trapped the warm metal between her fingers, pulling it out.

"The key to our castle, me lord." She snorted, stepped over the backpacks, and climbed the stairs of a newly built Trex deck then stopped cold at the intricate design of the pretty lead glass door. She'd seen it before, only she couldn't place where. An icy finger ran up her spine.

Colt came up behind her. "Wrong key?"

"Ah, no." She glanced back. "I was just admiring the door."

"Expensive."

"Yeah, looks it." Brit shook her sense of foreboding, slipped in the key, and opened the door. Drywall mud and fresh paint filtered past her. She stepped into the foyer, her breath catching. Alabaster marble tiles spread across the entryway, with a showy but elegant design done in coppery browns and olive greens.

"She has good taste." Colt peered over her shoulder. "Where's the kitchen?"

"I-I don't know. I'm guessing left or right."

Colt squeezed past her with one hand gripping the grocery bags, the other the two shoulder straps of their backpacks.

"Here, I got these." She took the packs from his hands and stepped in, closing the door.

Stained-oak stairs ran to the left, widening at the base, with an elaborate-carved banister and coordinating spindles. Detailed wainscoting, stained to match the stairs, ran halfway up the walls, including the one leading up the stairs to the second level.

"You coming?" Colt popped his head around the archway from a room to the right.

"Yeah." Brit followed him into an empty living room with arched windows looking out onto the bay.

"You okay?"

"Of course." She gave him a quick smile. "I didn't know Andi had such a flare for re-creating the past."

"All I care about is the fireplace. I hope it works."

The chill that had arrived the moment she stepped onto the front porch remained. "Yeah, I'm kind of chilly." Brit turned away from the fireplace's detailed marble façade.

A Victorian had been her dream home. Seth liked modern lines. She ended up with a cold concrete box with no character.

Brit placed the backpacks down on the wooden floor of the living room and followed him into the kitchen. She wasn't disappointed. Wooden planked floors continued with moss green cabinets and white marble counters. White dishes were stacked neatly behind the cabinet's glass doors above the back kitchen counter that housed the sink. The cooktop was located in the center island with a wide open space below—probably for the stove and maybe a dishwasher.

Colt set down the bags and rummaged through them, putting the cold things into a stainless steel refrigerator. "This place is classy. She expecting a high-dollar clientele?" He frowned over his shoulder at her. "You sure you're okay?"

She waved him off. "Tired."

He stopped and came around the island and pulled out a wooden stool. There was no kitchen table. "Here. How about a glass of milk and a donut?"

Brit took a seat. If he wanted to wait on her, she'd let him. She'd even indulge herself with a donut and the whole milk she'd grabbed by mistake. "Sure."

He located two glasses and two small plates. He filled her cup, then his, and came around with two glazed donuts. He put one on her plate, licked his fingers, and sat down next to her. He took a bite and groaned, his expression anything but pained.

He motioned to her. "Eat."

Brit took a bite. It was soft and sweet and a lot like the man sitting next to her. She remembered that day at the lake when he was covered in itchy hives. "Ya know, Rivers, you're very nurturing, too."

His brows rose, and he looked down his nose at her.

"I'm serious." Brit took another bite. "You'd make a great dad."

Shit. I did not just say that.

Heat flooded her cheeks, and she took a long sip of her milk, lowering her eyes.

"And as your doting parent"—he glanced up at the ceiling—"you need some sleep."

"What about you?"

"I think we should sleep in shifts."

It made sense. And she was grateful he suggested she take the first one. Brit polished off her donut, hoping the sleeping accommodations were just as comfortable as the rest of the house.

Colt stood and took her empty glass and plate. "I got this."

Brit slid off the stool.

"Oh, before you go." Colt set the dishes in the sink and reached behind to his back jean pocket. He pulled out the map and spread it across the counter. He grabbed at his flannel breast pocket, then looked up under a pair of dark furrowed brows. "You have a pen?"

"In my backpack." Brit scooted under the archway of the kitchen, snagged a pen from the outside pocket, and returned.

"What do you need a pen for?" She handed it to him.

"Bearings, remember." He uncapped it and placed his hands down on the map he'd opened. "Can you show me where your house is in relationship to where Seth went in?"

Brit's heart sped up. "Ah, sure." She cocked her head and studied the outline of the bay and placed her finger on the town of Chesapeake Beach.

"Here."

Colt peered down, made a circle, and filled it in. "The boat."

"Right." She took a deep breath through her nose, tried to judge the distance, and placed her finger where she believed he'd gone in. "Your circle goes here." Brit caught a glimpse of the bay through the kitchen window. Drawn to the water, she walked toward the window. "You can see it from here." She waved Colt over. "I'll show you."

He took a step back, looking skeptical. "You're sure?"

For once she could inexplicably say yes. She nodded and grabbed the handle of the back door and stepped out onto a small porch. She took a deep breath, the salty sea air more comforting than it had been in months. She walked the flat grassy land, heading toward the stone bulkhead.

Colt came up behind her. "What do you see, babe?"

Brit smiled. She wasn't going to be able to break him of that. She frowned. She wouldn't have to worry about it too much longer.

He slipped his arm around her, his hand resting on her hip. Brit leaned into him. He was solid and warm.

"Just the bay." She breathed deeply.

"If you find you can't catch your breath, you let me know."

He was the only one who could steal it—and her heart. And she got his joke. That incident only confused her more. She took a step forward, his hand falling away. She wrapped her arms around her waist. No good would come of letting him touch her the way he had last night.

Brit squinted against the sun and pointed out in front of her. "The spot's not that far from here. I could see Hoopers Island Lighthouse that night."

"Isn't this Hoopers Island we're on?" He turned her toward him, pressing a wisp of her hair behind her ear, his eyes intent on her face.

"What?"

"You're stronger than you think."

Brit's shoulders sagged. "Not strong enough to push you away."

"Do you want to?" He pulled her against him.

God, he was making this so hard. "What I want is something you can't give." Brit eased herself from his embrace and covered up a yawn. "I'm going to lie down." She hurried toward the house. If she didn't, she'd be tempted to ask him to join her.

Chapter Thirty

ITH THE KNOB TO THE FRONT DOOR FIRMLY IN Colt's grasp, he swung the door open and crossed the threshold. He shut it behind him and turned the inside lock. Another door, leading upstairs to the bedrooms, clicked closed. Brit was right to run away from him. He'd only hurt her.

Colt entered the living room and bent down to examine the gas fireplace. He found the switch and gave it a full turn. It puffed, flames shooting out through the ceramic log set. It wasn't one of those forced air jobs that threw much heat, but it would take the chill off. Somewhere there had to be a thermostat for the house.

He entered the kitchen, cleaned up the dishes, and dried them with a dishtowel he found in a drawer. Something had spooked Brit the moment she stood at the front door. Honestly, he didn't think she even understood why.

All he knew, taking in the updated kitchen, was that Andi Hall had fine taste that could rack up quite a bill. Probably why this house was a work in progress. Seemed a hell of a lot of effort for a bed-and-breakfast she was going to hand off to some manager to operate. From what he remembered, she was Brit's age. Nowhere near retirement or ready to take on running it full-time.

Colt took a seat at the center island and leaned over the map. He double-checked the mark he'd made in the bay with Brit's help. She'd been right.

Seth would have had a good two-mile swim toward land. He guessed today's news sealed the deal.

Seth was dead. He was back at square one. Colt stared at the map, located western Maryland and the water denoting Deep Creek Lake, and made another bull's-eye.

If he thought some overlooked theory would come to him, it didn't. If he thought he'd have access to a TV, he shouldn't have. He did have Brit's phone, but as she pointed out while she was re-hooking the cable box, you had to search for it on the phone whereas the TV broadcast it twenty-four seven.

Who the hell knew if they'd already linked him to the pileup through the stolen car? Not knowing was driving him bat shit crazy. Colt reached back, his fingers skimmed the metal barrel of his gun, and he relaxed. From now on, his weapon remained on him at all times. His anxiety levels had spiked since leaving Memory Maker. He couldn't relax. Waiting around didn't help, nor the inactivity. They needed to get a look at the internal affairs report. Once he read it, he'd have a fair idea which way the state's attorney would side. His conscience was bothering him, too. He should level with Brit about his ex-wife, explain why he'd sworn off commitment.

The wounded look she'd given him earlier tore at his soul. He was the cause of it—not this CADI thing or the shooting. Colt scrubbed the back of his neck. He missed her now, and she was only one flight above him.

He stood and gazed out the kitchen window. This house with all its windows—the flat topography—wasn't ideal. Memory Maker was nestled down the mountain and protected in the forest. Here it felt like every eye was on him, almost like someone was watching. A chill rode up his spine, and he shook it off. Paranoia. He'd let it get the best of him at the hotel with Hall.

Colt folded up the map. Wouldn't be a bad idea to familiarize himself with the layout of the house and find that thermostat. He swung into a door off the foyer and hit the lightswitch. Nothing. He took a step in. Wires hung from the wall with a pedestal sink below. Feeling the urge, he took a piss, flushed the toilet, and went to investigate some more.

He found a door that led to the basement and hit the switch at the top of the stairs. He took the steps two at a time. Cans of paint and extra floor tiles sat against the wall. A set of concrete steps ran up to a cellar door. If he had to guess, the house would have been built at the turn of the nineteenth century.

Colt took the steps up to the first floor and peered into the room across the foyer—another fireplace and a chandelier with windows overlooking the bay. Must be the dining room with—he reached for the small box on the wall—the thermostat. He clicked it on and moved it to seventy-two. The bay was hypnotic, the way the waves lapped at the bulkhead, and he stood there for some time before sauntering over to the window. He wasn't afraid of the water, but he could well imagine what Brit had been dealing with that night. It was choppy now. He took a tired breath through his nose. The cozy warmth that came from the first use of the heat had his lids drooping.

God, I'm beat. He really needed to lie down before he fell down.

Colt climbed the stairs. Wooden floors ran the length of the hall with the same wooden wainscoting as the first floor. Six panel doors with crystal knobs were open, except for the one at the end.

They were still playing house, whether she wanted to admit it or not. He was still touching her in ways he shouldn't. He wanted to touch her now— to feel her beneath him. He groaned and straightened his crotch. He had a hard-on just thinking about her.

He eyed her door and cursed. "What I need is a cold shower," he mumbled under his breath. Feet dragging, he shuffled down the hall, ducked into the hall bathroom, and flipped on the light. Great, no towels or mirror. He flipped the shower curtain aside. No soap. This sucked.

Giving up, Colt entered the bedroom across the hall—one queen mattress on top of a box spring sat in the middle of the room with the frame and matching headboard and footboard against the wall. Colt dropped down on the mattress, swinging his legs up. All he needed was a little rest. With all the traveling they'd done and the lack of sleep, his knee was aching like a son of a bitch. He should count himself lucky his ribs had been only bruised not broken, the pain had already subsided to a dull ache.

He moaned but more from the thought of having dinner with Hall. He got the distinct impression she didn't care for him. He guessed waving his gun in her face hadn't earned him any brownie points, either. Like it or not, he was stuck with kissing her ass. Or Brit would kick his.

Colt nodded off, woke, and nodded off again. He rolled over and opened his eyes. *Shit.* Falling asleep could cost him his freedom—his life. Eventually, he'd get some rest while Brit took the next shift. The house remained quiet. A more muted light filtered in from the window, letting him know the sun was going down. It had to be close to four. Colt scrubbed his face and got up. He entered the hall. Brit's door was still shut.

Well, Sleeping Beauty was going to have to get up. He wasn't entertaining Hall by himself. He strode past the stairs leading to the first level and stopped at the closed door. He grabbed the crystal knob and hesitated.

Hell. A gentleman would knock.

Colt rapped his knuckles against the door and waited. Nothing. He knocked harder and still a good thirty seconds later—no movement. His chest tightened, and he gripped the knob, swinging the door open.

Damn it, man! Get a grip.

Brit lay no more than a few steps away on crisp white sheets in a four-poster queen bed, her body facing a partially opened window onto the bay. Wispy curtains floated in the sea breeze. A smile tugged at Colt's lips. They were making huge progress based on the view she had chosen before she fell off to sleep, except the temperatures had dropped.

Colt stepped in and shut the window. Her blond hair swept the pillows. Her breaths were deep, even, and peaceful. But it was her bare skin, the tantalizing curve of her lower back where the sheet dipped, that held him mesmerized. He crossed the wooden floor, debating, then eased his butt down on the edge of the bed. He stroked her smooth, warm skin, forgetting that promise he was having trouble keeping.

The thought of hanging around and getting to know every nuance about Brit Gentry, especially in bed, was tempting.

"Brit," he whispered, caressing the slope of her bare shoulder.

"Mmm."

"It's time to get up."

She rolled over on her back, her hair mussed from sleep and looking soft and feminine. "What time is it?" Her eyes darted from him to the sheet and the swells of her breasts before her arm secured the thin material over her chest.

Colt noted the time on a digital clock on the nightstand. "Four fifteen."

"Andi will be coming soon."

"All the more reason for you to get up."

She closed her eyes and took a deep breath, snuggling into the mattress. "What did you do while I was asleep?"

Think of you.

"Checked the house out. Thought of taking a shower but forgot this isn't Memory Maker."

She nodded, eyes still closed. "There are towels in the hall closet." Her eyes flickered open, and she scooted up on her bottom, keeping the sheet swaddled around her. "Andi said there are toiletries in there, too."

"She spends time here, then."

"Sometimes, if she's working on the house."

He was making small talk. Colt didn't give a damn about what Andi did or didn't do. He only cared about prolonging this quiet, uninterrupted moment with Brit and seeing what she had on underneath that sheet.

"What is it?"

Colt raked his fingers through his hair. "I'm just trying to figure out if I'm in heaven or hell."

She gave him a lift of her brow.

Did he have to spell it out? She was the most desirable women he'd ever met. But more than that. He plain loved being around her.

"I'm having a problem keeping my word." He stroked her arm, then twined his fingers through hers.

Brit's tightened, her big brown eyes searching his. "What is it that you want?"

"You." The word tore from his throat, and he cupped her face, his thumb brushing the sweet curve of her bottom lip. "All of you."

Brit's lips parted, and her eyes closed. He leaned in, his mouth hovering over hers. "For however long I can have you." He kissed her, slowly at first, then more urgently.

She kissed him back, inching closer, the sheets rustling when the crunch of gravel outside the window had her drawing away.

"It's Andi," she murmured. She scooted away from him, wrapped the sheet around her body, looking like a modern-day goddess of love with her shimmering blond hair, the slopes of her pale full breasts plumped against the sheet.

"Should I tell her to go away?" Colt raised his brows at her.

"No!" Her eyes widened.

Colt chuckled. "Fine. I'll go down and entertain Cat Woman while you get dressed."

"Don't call her *that*." She pointed a slender finger at him. "Not even jokingly."

Which meant he nailed it. Andi Hall had claws.

Colt took a step toward the door, then stopped and made an about-face. He scooped Brit into his arms amidst her shrieks. "Love the goddess look." He kissed her hard on the mouth and slipped out the door, grinning.

Screw the past.

Chapter Thirty-One

CRAP. BRIT HOOKED HER BRA AND THREW ON HER SHIRT, taking glances out the bedroom window with a direct shot of the driveway. She'd forgotten to remind Colt to be nice. *Damn it.* She'd been lost in those conflicted green eyes of his.

Brit slipped on her jeans and hobbled on one foot and then the other while putting on her socks and then her boots. Andi had her car back and was hefting out a half bushel of crabs when Colt intercepted her and—good man—took it from her.

She just assumed the two would get along. Granted, their initial introduction was anything but ordinary. Consumed with guilt, Brit sighed and headed for the steps. She should have never gotten Andi involved or accepted her offer to harbor them. Brit took the stairs. The front door opened, and their amicable voices floated to the second level.

Okay, so they hadn't drawn down on each other yet.

Brit hit the landing and rounded the banister, following their chatter into the kitchen and the aroma of crabs and Old Bay spice. "*God,* they smell so good."

Colt set the weathered bushel basket on the center island, orange claws poking out the slats.

Andi spun around, her shoulder-length brunette hair shimmering under the recessed lighting. "You look rested." Her hand came down on Colt's arm. "Colt said you took a nap."

"Yeah." Brit walked over and gave Andi a hug. "I was beat."

Colt unlatched the top to the basket and pulled out a crab by its claw, his brows furrowing. "This crustacean come with an owner's manual?"

"*No.*" Brit took the crab and dropped it back in the basket. "We use a mallet and a knife."

Colt fell back a step. "You're serious."

"Yes." Brit pushed past him. "Andi, did you grab a couple of mallets?"

"I've got a set in the drawer." Andi sidestepped Colt and reached for the brushed nickel pull to open the top drawer of the center island. "Knives are in the one next to the fridge."

"Got it." Brit grabbed three butter knives, catching Colt out of the corner of her eye checking Andi out. His gaze ran down her backside and the hip-hugging jeans she'd poured herself into, then hovered around her shapely ankles, disappearing into the furry gray top of her boots.

You gotta be kidding.

No more than fifteen minutes ago he had been seducing her upstairs, and she had bought it. Brit gritted her teeth. What did she expect from a man who had been locked up for four years? Now that he had two women to choose from, he must have figured his odds of getting laid had doubled.

Andi slid her coat down her shoulders. Brit frowned at the plunging neckline of her sweater. *Come on, Andi.* She was runway-model tall, seductive, and, it would appear, she was using it to get a little attention. Or, and this really ticked Brit off, tempting a man who hadn't had a woman in years.

Andi liked to screw with people's heads, men especially. Brit gripped Andi's arm. "Can I see you in the other room?"

"Ah." Andi eyed Brit's fingers digging into the soft cream angora of her sweater and then Colt who was preoccupied with something outside the kitchen window.

Now that concerned her, too.

"Colt." The words left Brit's lips with urgency. "What are you looking at?"

He turned and shrugged. "Nothing."

"Andi and I are going to get the table set up outside. How about you get the newspaper I left upstairs in the bedroom?" There had been nothing in it that was noteworthy about her or Colt.

"Sure." He strode toward the entryway leading into the living room. "I'm guessing the paper is for the table outside."

"Yeah, that's where we'll be." She turned and then swung back. "It's chilly, so bring your coat."

He nodded, walked past Andi, who had her best *check me out* pose going. Only this time, he barely gave her a nod and continued into the living room, disappearing to the right. Brit waited until his boot hit the first step and he continued up.

"He's hot." Andi grabbed paper towels off the back counter for the table. "Bet he's a handful in bed."

"Can you not?" Brit snapped and, with a death grip on the knives, reached for the mallets on the counter. If there was one trait she didn't like about Andi, it was her forwardness. It was like being back in high school. She never liked competing against Andi for a man's attention. She certainly wasn't going to do it now at twenty-nine years old. Brit gave Andi her back and walked out.

"Wait." Andi came up behind her. "I'm sorry. I didn't know you liked him."

"I don't. Not like that."

Andi laughed. "Yes, you do. I can see it now."

"We're just helping each other." Brit opened the front door and stepped onto the porch, admiring the beveled glass in the door.

"Oh, okay," Andi said with a patronizing tone.

"We are," Brit said with force and pulled out one of the benches to the square picnic table.

Andi ducked back in and came out carrying a portable heater; she plugged it in by the table. "Doesn't mean you can't screw like bunnies."

"Shh." Brit's shoulders rose. "He'll hear you."

"Well, have you slept with him?"

She gasped. "No!"

"You should."

"Should what?" Colt with his tall frame and newly combed jet-black hair—had he done that while he was upstairs?—cleared the front door, carrying the bushel of crabs and the newspaper on top.

"Put the paper down first." Brit motioned toward the table.

It niggled at Brit that the man had combed his hair. They'd been together for a good few days, and she hadn't seen him put that much effort into his appearance. Of course, he was drop-dead gorgeous no matter if his hair was unkempt or not. And he wasn't listening because he was looking at Andi. *Err.* Brit ripped the paper off the basket and opened it up on the table. "You can sit the basket in the middle."

He set it down, frowning. "What are we drinking?"

"Oh." Andi spun around. "I have Corona in my car." She patted her jean pockets.

Brit wanted to bust out laughing. Andi couldn't fit a stick of gum in her pockets, much less a ring of keys.

"I think I saw you put it in the pocket of your coat." Colt hooked his chin toward the front door.

"Oh, shit." Andi laughed. "I think you're right." She squeezed by Colt, running her hands along his back, and winked at Brit. "I'll be right back."

Brit shook her head. Andi loved messing with her. Although, and Brit believed this was no exception, this time she thought she was helping by goading *her* into making a move on Colt.

Jealousy was a great motivator.

Colt angled his head as Andi stepped over the threshold and entered the house. "I want to get a look inside her—"

Brit smacked him hard on his back. "You're an asshole."

"Ow." Colt arched his back and scowled at her. "What the hell was that for?"

"You like her."

"What?" His brows met in the middle of his nose, and he speared her with unsmiling eyes. "She's a fuckin' whore."

Brit's eyes widened. "Shut up. She'll hear you."

"You see her boo—"

Andi sashayed out the door with her keys in hand.

Oh, my God. Now he wanted to discuss how big Andi's breasts were, probably compared to hers.

Colt grabbed the dangling keys from Andi's hand. "I'll get it."

Andi's brows rose, a pretty shaped O forming on her glossy pink lips. "It's in the footwell of the passenger side."

Colt took the steps and strode toward her white Honda CRV.

"Didn't know they taught manners in prison." Andi kept her gaze on Colt, then turned and took a seat on the bench. "The sunset is especially pretty tonight." She placed her hand under her chin, admiring the autumn fireball dipping below the bay's shimmering horizon.

Brit sat next to her, staring her down. "What's wrong with you?"

"What?" She jerked her head back with mock surprise. "I was just kidding."

"I told you he's innocent. And you of all people should believe it. You always said Seth was sneaky." Brit fell back against the house. "You hated Seth."

She swung on Brit. "And I was right."

Brit shook—more from anger. "Why are you being so nasty?"

"Because I think the last thing you should be doing is hanging out with a convicted felon who's on the lam."

"Then we'll leave." Brit pushed up from the table.

"I'm sorry." Andi grabbed her arm, holding her in place. "I want you to stay. I just don't want to see you make things more complicated than they already are."

She wasn't walking away from Colt. Seth had ruined *his* life, too.

"Three Coronas coming up." Colt set down the twelve pack of glass bottled beers and took the bench across from them. He twisted off the cap of one and handed it to Andi. "How's the car ride?"

Andi cocked her head, her expression one of momentary confusion. "Oh, you mean the new brakes." She laughed. "Fine."

"Beer?" He gave Brit a lift of his brow.

"Yeah." Only one wouldn't be enough to get her through dinner.

He opened another and handed the slick bottle to her. "Weather's a lot warmer on the eastern shore."

Brit took a long draft of her beer. And he was going to talk about the weather. She wasn't buying it.

"Ever eaten crabs before?" Andi took a medium-sized one from the basket. "Feels heavy. I can always count on Jake to pick out the best." She chuckled, her attention drawn to her meal.

Colt gave Brit a knowing look.

Brit shook her head at him and frowned. Andi's love life was none of her or Colt's business. She dug into the basket of steamed, spiced crabs and felt around until she came up with a large one for Colt. Brit handed it to him. "Rip off its legs, but slowly."

Colt wrinkled his nose at her. "I never took you for a sadist."

Andi laughed next to her.

Brit snagged his crab from him. "Look, like this." She pulled the large leg and grinned with satisfaction at the chunk of meat hanging off the end. She held it out to Colt. "Taste it."

He leaned over and took a bite, a hint of naughtiness flitting in his eyes.

Brit's nether region tumbled. Why did everything the man did elicit a sensual response from her?

"Mmm. That's actually good."

Brit handed it back to him. "You work on the legs, and I'll show you how to open the body." Brit took another from the basket and began removing its legs, glancing over at Colt.

He was ripping the last leg off and getting ready to open the main part of his crab.

"See, you're getting it." That was progress.

"I think I'm going to starve in the process," he grumbled.

Andi reached across the table with a chunk of crabmeat in her hand. "Here. Try this."

Colt took it from her, gave her a wary look, and then ate it. He slapped his lips together. "Wow, that's spicy."

"But good." Brit handed Colt a butter knife. "Turn your crab over. And see that little thing there?" She pointed with the end of her knife. "Stick the knife under it like you're opening a can of Coke and pop it up, then pull the shell apart."

Colt followed her instructions and opened the shell. "What the—" He gagged. "I can't eat that. It looks like green intestines."

Brit and Andi laughed.

"You're not supposed to eat that. *God.*" Andi gave him her crab she'd cleaned. "Break it in half and pull out the meat."

His face twisted with disgust, but he broke it in half and started picking and eating.

"I should have asked you to grab some corn." Brit nudged Andi's side.

"I thought about it, but it's not really in season, and I was stuck on the phone with CJ before I left about tomorrow's training."

Brit's shoulders sagged. She missed the team, missed workouts. "How's he doing?"

"Good. He asked about you."

Brit nodded. He'd been with her on the hill that night, too. The three of them, highly trained counter-snipers. She'd let them down, especially Andi. It would be that much harder for another woman to make it on S.T.A.T.E. in the future.

Colt picked up another crab and started picking.

"You getting the hang of it?" Brit leaned forward and plucked a piece of seaweed grass off his crab.

"Yeah. I like a challenge."

Andi grabbed some paper towels and cleaned her hands. "I've got some vinegar in the pantry. I'll go grab it."

"Vinegar?" Colt didn't sound too sure.

"It's good." Andi climbed out from the picnic table. She turned and walked toward the door, glancing up momentarily at the porch ceiling before ducking inside.

Colt's gaze swung toward Andi, his attention on her line of sight and then her backside. He stood. "Did you see her boo—"

"What the hell is wrong with you?" Brit beaded in on him. "No. I don't make a habit of staring at her *breasts*," she hissed.

Colt's jaw tightened. "Her boots, damn it." He waved an irritated hand in her face. "She's not my type. It's her boots. And another thing. I dug through her glove box and I found—" He sat down, lifted his chin, looking beyond Brit, and smiled. "You find it?"

"Yeah. Wow, it's getting dark." Andi flipped on the lights in the ceiling of the porch.

"Looks like one's not working." Colt pointed to the two recessed lights over the door, but in particular, the dark one.

"It's burnt out. I need to change the bulb." Andi came over. "There's not much left, but there's enough for you to try it." She sat down with the bottle of apple cider vinegar and a small glass dish and poured it in. "Just dip a little of the crab in." She smiled at Colt. "It's delicious."

Brit's head was spinning. Colt was acting psycho. Who cared about her boots? And he shouldn't have been snooping in her car. What was up with him? Tonight he was the biggest piece of excess baggage she'd ever carried. Before long, Andi was going to kick them out on their asses. Brit couldn't take him to her place. Reporters were probably camped outside her house.

Colt shot Brit an agitated look. Not good.

"Ah, Andi, I think I have a piece of spice in my eye." Brit batted her lashes and jerked her head toward the house, hoping Colt had gotten the message to follow.

His eyes, filled with desperation, widened. "You were the one at the lake last night," Colt slung across the table.

Andi looked from Colt to Brit with confusion. "Were you talking to me?"

"That's right. You were at the lake last night. You and your CNN hat that you obviously have two of."

"Hey." Brit's heart rattled in her chest. "What's wrong with you?" She gave him a look that said *cool it.*

Andi's face stiffened. "What's his deal?"

"I-I don't know." Brit speared him with her eyes.

"You going to deny it?" Colt's voice rose, his cheeks becoming flushed.

"I think you have a lot of nerve, asshole." Andi pushed up from her seat.

Colt stood, the bench toppling over.

Brit's stomach lurched. "Don't!" The sound of her voice seemed distorted and slow.

Colt reached behind his back and whipped out his gun. "What's going on, Andi?"

"Colt!" Brit jumped to her feet. "Put it down!"

"Not until she tells us why her boots match the ones in the snow."

"You kidding me?" Andi narrowed in on him. "Do you know anything about women's footwear? This brand is sold in the millions."

"Then you're one in a million, Andi Hall." He sneered and threw a quartered piece of paper at her. It landed in the Old Bay. "Open it, Andi, and tell Brit what it says."

Andi eyed Brit, her eyes darting from the paper to Colt.

"Read it!"

Brit's heart raced. "Stop it!" She implored with her eyes.

Colt used the gun like an extension of his arm and pointed it erratically at Andi, same as he'd done with Brit that day on the highway. "Pick it up," he snapped.

Brit's stomach knotted when Andi's trembling fingers snatched up the paper. Colt was making a huge mistake. Andi was nowhere near the house in Deep Creek. She had no reason to be.

"Colt, just relax, baby." Brit eased a little toward the railing of the porch, trying to get closer to him where he stood on the other side of the table. He'd told Brit that day when *she'd* held the gun on him that if he had wanted her dead he would have shot her. But tonight he really did seem unstable.

Andi was still alive, and she needed to keep her that way.

Damn it. It never occurred to her that Colt could flip out. He was highly trained—granted, years ago, and then four years in prison after that. She should have seen this coming. Actually, she thought she'd be the first to crack.

Although the man *had been* unjustly accused, tried, and convicted. Prison could eat at you, if you were guilty. She couldn't imagine if you were innocent. Not to mention Colt had suffered setback after setback—the accident, Seth's death, her identity. Now he was going to self-destruct and shoot her best friend if she didn't equalize the situation.

"Give me the gun." She motioned with her hand.

He raked his fingers through his dark hair. "Read . . . the . . . invoice." His voice was razor sharp.

Andi's throat bobbed, and she wet her lips, opening the folded sheet of paper. "Right, front end fender damage six hundred and sixty-two dollars." She sighed.

Brit's forehead creased with consternation. "So what? She hit somethi—" *White transfer paint, the green Dumpster.* Brit's head throbbed at her temples, and she gave Andi a bewildered look. "It *was* you?"

Andi pinned Colt with a long stare. "Damn it, Colt, you're a high-strung bitch." She shook her head and lifted her chin to Brit, her expression contrite. "I wasn't there by choice."

"You make no sense." Brit stared at her friend in shock.

"Your mom asked me to go up and check on you. I figured I'd stay with you for a few days. I knocked on the main house and got no answer. I tried the door and it was locked. Then I checked the pool complex. It was dark but the door was wide open, which made me a little concerned. So I went in, got as far as the steps, and heard voices." She turned toward Colt, still holding the gun on her. "Yours and his. Didn't sound like a conversation I wanted to interrupt."

"Why park your car up at the top?" Colt shot back.

"Because I've gotten stuck before on that steep driveway in the snow."

"Put the gun down, Colt." Brit rubbed her temples. "Now!"

Colt's expression seemed dubious. "Why didn't you just admit it from the get-go?"

"I should have."

"Why wear that damned CNN cap?" His shoulders visibly caved inward.

"To throw you off." Andi touched Brit's shoulder. "I'm sorry. I should have told you. But I figured you didn't need to know."

"*Oh, God.*" Brit squeezed her eyes closed in mortification. "You didn't tell my mother I was with a man, I hope."

"You know what? I'm done." Colt's voice rang hollow, and he shoved his gun into the back of his waistband. "This has been a cluster fuck since we left the lake." He pushed past Brit, took the steps, and stomped toward the bulkhead, his body a silhouette against a darkening sky.

Brit stared after him. "He's dealing with a lot."

Andi took Brit's hand in hers, jiggling it. "I'm sorry." She tugged until

Brit turned toward her. Brit didn't miss the sparkle of mischief in her eyes. "You guys were really going at it that night."

Brit groaned and threw her head back. "Don't *say* any more." The thought of Andi dissecting every sigh and moan would be complete and utter torture.

The woman even analyzed Brad Pitt's love scenes. One of the reasons Brit had stopped watching chick flicks with her.

Andi peeked over Brit's shoulders at Colt. "He's falling for you."

"Colt? No, he's running out of options."

"He has no options, and he knows it. He's only staying because of you."

"Bah." Brit waved a dismissive hand.

"Then why doesn't he head for the border?"

"I told you. He wants to clear his name."

"That's bullshit and you know it." She leaned into Brit. "You, on the other hand, could make this whole Crenshaw thing go away if you'd just listen to me and let me help you reenact what happened that night."

"What about the IAU's report?"

Andi shook her head. "I don't know, Brit. I thought maybe I could get a copy, but Dan and I are . . ."

"No, no. I totally understand. You can't risk it."

"But if we could trigger something—something to help you remember—we could figure this out."

Brit mulled it over. Like that night hadn't played in her head with horrific clarity—at least the bullet-piercing-Crenshaw's-forehead part. She knew there were bits and pieces missing from her memory that night. She'd been afraid re-creating it could send her over the edge. There was the real possibility she'd be staring at four padded walls for the foreseeable future. But without the report, she was clueless as to which way this thing was headed.

"I have my rifle in the back of my car. It's still too early, but I could meet you and Colt on that hill overlooking the farm."

"It hasn't sold yet?"

"Not in this market. Plus, Crenshaw's widow wants a fortune."

"She'll get one soon," Brit grumbled.

"You think about it." Andi let go of her hand and glanced up at the eaves of the porch, her forehead creasing before she turned back. "How about I sit the bushel in a garbage bag and put it in the fridge for you guys? I'm thinking everyone's lost their appetites."

Brit kept sight of Colt still standing at the water's edge. "Right. I'll help you."

Together they cleaned up the porch and put the crabs and what was left of the beer in the fridge.

Brit walked Andi out. "I guess he's going to sulk the rest of the night."

Andi squeezed her hand. "You can't help him, sweetie. No one can. Seth's dead. After everything you've told me, it makes sense that he's the only one who could tell us where the artifacts are."

"Yeah, well, it's tied together. I still have that damned financial disclosure investigation hanging over my head. I'm positive Seth bought our house, the boat, and the lake house with those artifacts."

"Maybe. But people get off all the time for white-collar crime. I wouldn't worry too much about it."

"But it was all Seth. I had nothing to do with it."

"Either way, I think this shooting will be more devastating if they convict you. You're a cop, Brit. Cops don't survive in prison."

Brit gripped the bench hard. Andi wasn't telling her anything she hadn't already considered.

Andi nudged her shoulder. "Think about what I said." She tapped the face of her watch. "It's only eight. I go in at three in the afternoon tomorrow. I could meet you guys tonight at around ten. I'll bring my rifle since you don't have one, and together we can map out what happened that night."

Brit gnawed the inside of her mouth.

What choice did she really have?

She wrapped her arm around her waist. Question was, would Colt go along with it? For all she knew, he'd really meant it when he said he was done.

Brit shivered. She couldn't imagine doing this—all of this—without him.

Chapter Thirty-Two

*W*ITH A STEAMING CUP OF COFFEE IN HER HANDS, THE way Colt liked it with cream and sugar, Brit picked her way through the grassy expanse of land facing the bay. Even with the plump moon overhead, she was careful to watch her step. The last thing she needed was to fall in a hole or twist an ankle.

She was seriously thinking about Canada. Brit would need both her legs for that.

It was becoming more apparent that the only way she'd find out what was in the internal affairs report would be during the discovery phase of her trial. IAU would do a thorough investigation. If they could exonerate her, they would. But the longer this thing dragged out, the less likely that scenario had become.

Andi's offer made sense. *Try and prove your own innocence.* Or, at the very least, Brit wanted to know the truth. If she had an epiphany, one way or the other, no matter how painful, it would be worth it. If it was guilt, she'd turn herself in. But if she had clear evidence she hadn't pulled the trigger, hopping the border might be in her best interest.

Innocent people went to jail. One of those statistics was in her midst. Well, he still remained standing in the dark overlooking the bay, thinking God knew what after his meltdown. Witnessing his frustration and despair left her with one conclusion. As much as she wanted him to stay and help her through this, she didn't know how much more he could take before he snapped.

She wanted him safe and over the border more.

Colt's back was toward her while he stared out over the water, a shimmering path of moonlight illuminating small whitecaps. She'd hoped he would have come in when Andi left. Instead, he remained brooding by the bulkhead. After about thirty minutes she'd made him a hot cup of coffee and decided some tough decisions needed to be made.

Her eyes slid from his broad shoulders to his tight ass.

God, he is good-looking.

Brit sidled up next to him. His arms were folded in front of his chest, his profile set. She held out the mug. He clasped it in both his hands but said nothing. He put the mug to his lips and took a long sip.

More confident and secure than she'd ever been this close to the estuary she'd grown up on, Brit smiled out over the bay, then to the man who was ignoring her. "Did anyone ever tell you, you have a nice ass?"

He choked, coffee spewing from his mouth. "Damn it, Gentry." He gave her a sideways glance as he wiped his wet hands down his jeans, trying not to crack a smile.

"Well you do." Brit fidgeted with the zipper to her parka. "I really don't want to see anything happen to it."

"Where's *this* going?" He turned toward her.

"Andi can't get her hands on the internal affairs report. The evidence room is more fortified than Fort Knox." Brit gazed out over the bay.

God, I'm going to miss him.

She'd text Andi about the change in plans. It would only be her tonight, and Brit would need a ride.

"We're done here." Brit pulled the keys to her Pathfinder from the pocket of her coat the same time her phone alerted her to a text. "Andi's picking me up in about twenty minutes."

She handed them off.

"Whoa." He juggled his coffee and took the keys from her. "What's going on here?"

"Andi and I are going to reenact that night at Crenshaw's farm. It's not that far from here." Brit pulled out her phone, touched the screen, and read the text from Andi.

Just found out MSP linked Colt to the stolen car from the accident. They know he's in Maryland. But not traveling with you, yet.

"*Shit!*"

"What is it?" His deep voice was edged with alarm.

She whipped her head up. "You gotta go." Her voice was frantic and breathless. "They know you're here."

"I'm not going."

"Oh, *yes* you are." Brit pulled out the cash she'd set aside for him. She had almost exhausted the five hundred she'd brought to the lake. With groceries, lunch at Unos, the Mountain Coaster, crabs, and, now, the money to get him over the border, she had about a hundred and twenty. Didn't matter. After this little reenactment with Andi, she was going home to do some serious soul-searching. There were only two outcomes: turn herself in or flee over the border in Seth's car.

"It's about six hundred miles to Montreal from here." She held out the folded bills. "There's a hundred and fifty. Enough to get you there and a little for food."

"Put your money away, Brit."

She placed one hand on her hip, the other still holding out the cash. "This isn't a debate, Colt."

"You're right. So don't make it one." He turned and walked toward the house.

What the hell?

Brit shoved the bills in her pocket and darted after him. Her foot hit a high patch, and her ankle twisted.

"*Damn it,*" Brit hissed on her way down before she landed on the ground hard on her hip.

"*Jesus.*" Colt charged toward her and dropped to his knees. "You okay?" His arms went around her, and he helped her to her feet.

With her hip throbbing, Brit put weight on her left ankle immediately to test it out.

Please, God, don't let it be broken. Don't let it be broken.

"How is it?" She didn't miss the concern in his voice.

"It hurts, *okay*." She speared him with her eyes, spitting mad. "And if it's fractured it's all your fault." Her voice hitched. "I can't do this anymore with you. You need to go." And if he was going to make a huge stink, she'd make it easy on him. "I don't want you here."

He pulled her roughly to him. "You're lying." He searched her eyes. "We've both been lying to each other." He bent his head and kissed her hard, his tongue sweeping across her parted lips.

Brit moaned into his mouth, her body trembling with a yearning she hadn't felt for a man in a very long time. He broke the kiss and scooped her into his arms and carried her up the steps and into the house. He set her down in the hall under the gleaming chandelier, leaving her exposed and vulnerable.

"How's the ankle?" His face was flushed, his words somewhat breathless.

She put weight on it and took a few steps. There was a little pain, but she could work through it. "I think it's okay."

"Good." He raked his hands through his hair. "Do you want to know about my marriage?"

Brit fell back a step. "If you want to talk about it."

"No." He gave a half laugh. "But I will with you."

He said it like she needed to know, like this was the point when everything would change between them, and, it would seem, he wouldn't be leaving. "Does this mean you're going to ignore your good sense and my kind offer of transportation?"

"What it means, Brit Gentry"—he took a step toward her and pressed back a wisp of blond hair from her face—"is that I can't live without you. Not for one day, one hour, or even a minute. And I'm sure as hell not going to let you leave tonight with Andi and relive that night without me."

Brit focused on his words. Even though the words "I love you" were missing, it was the most profound statement of devotion she'd ever witnessed. Her eyes filled with tears, and she blinked them back. Never in her three years of marriage had she ever felt so cherished.

She did with Colt.

"You're going to make me cry." She snuffled.

"Don't, babe." He whisked away a stray tear on her cheek with his thumb, his gaze intense and glassy with emotion, too. "I want that future with you."

She nodded. "We need to meet Andi at ten at the Crenshaw farm."

"I don't like it." He shook his head. "You really think this is going to help you remember?"

"I don't know." She shrugged under his intense scrutiny. "Nothing else has."

"Okay." He took her hand in his. "Let's do this thing."

She always considered her hands to be steady and sure. Recently, they'd been anything but. Only tonight the warmth of his fingers radiated strength.

Brit squeezed his hand, tipping her chin up to see his handsome face. She loved him. She could wait to hear those words from Colt. They were only words. Brit had heard them many times from Seth, but they had been empty.

She knew that now.

The treetops rustled under a moonlit sky on the knoll overlooking the Crenshaw's twenty-acre farm. Andi handed off her state agency–issued rifle with the scope to Brit, the metal cold and unyielding against her palms and fingers. Patches of clouds floated by. The moon vanished behind a wispy cloud, and Brit trembled.

Colt's hand came down on her shoulder. "You okay?" he whispered.

"Yeah." She swallowed her anxiety. "I haven't handled a rifle since the shooting."

"Gotcha." He rubbed her back. "You're stronger than your fears, babe."

She hoped.

"Come on, Brit." Andi waved her over. "Take your position on the hill."

Brit hustled over to the stand of trees, the earthy scent of pine bringing her back to that night. She got down on her knees and set up the bipod attached to the rifle. Something landed on her head, crooked, and she reached for it.

"Your cap. You left it in my cruiser that night." Andi's words were terse and totally unexpected.

"You okay?" Brit grabbed the hat and peered at the familiar MSP patch. She turned the cap around and placed it on her head with the bill facing backward.

"Yeah. Why?"

"Nothing." Brit hooked her chin toward a clump of bushes where Andi had been positioned to her right. "Can you take your place?"

"Wasn't really planning on getting dirty."

Brit pulled her head back, astonished by her lack of cooperation. "This was your idea."

Andi remained standing and not making a move one way or the other.

"Whatever," Brit muttered under her breath. Andi could be such a diva. This wasn't going to be perfectly choreographed. CJ wasn't here to play his part. He'd been to the left of her, several feet away.

With the stock against her shoulder, Brit took a deep breath and put a level eye through the scope, lining up her sights. Without Crenshaw she'd have to rely on her memory, which was something she was having trouble with. Brit took another breath. She tried to block out Colt standing off to the left and Andi who was fooling with her phone.

Are you freakin' kidding me?

Brit rolled on her side, squinting up, her brows knotting into one pissed off unibrow. "What the hell are you doing, Andi?"

"Uh." The light of her iPhone shone bright against her face. Mouth open, looking totally busted, she shoved it into her coat pocket. "I'm sorry."

Yeah, you better be.

Brit shook it off and repositioned herself. She gazed through the scope and blocked everything out, except for the gentle breeze tugging at her hair. The dirt road in front of the farmhouse where Crenshaw stood with his wife cut a wide path through the cornfield, and that night began to play out in horrific detail.

His body was at an angle, his arm a noose around his frightened wife's neck.

Come on, man. Just loosen up.

Brit waited, sweat pooling between her shoulder blades. The last thing she wanted was to pull the trigger. He didn't appear to have a weapon, but his arm flexed with sinewy muscles around Jessy Crenshaw's slender neck.

Thank God it wasn't up to her to make the decision to take him out. Brit remained in position and adjusted her earpiece. What in the hell had sent Crenshaw over the edge tonight? All she knew was they were married. Jessy had called because her husband was acting erratic. He'd threatened to kill himself with his gun.

There was no gun now.

"He's a vet—served in Iraq. We may be dealing with PTSD." The negotiator's grim voice filtered through Brit's earpiece.

Her head dropped. *Damn it.* Not what she wanted to hear. Okay, keep cool. She took a breath. They'd talk Crenshaw through this.

"Beau, this is Lieutenant Wallace of the Maryland State Police."

"Get the fuck away," he yelled.

"I want to help you, Beau. Let your wife go, and we can talk."

Crenshaw's arm tightened, and he cinched her closer, whispering something under his breath. Jessy started to gag with the added pressure of his arm.

Don't go there, Crenshaw. Please, dear God, don't let him go there.

Brit's body began to sway. Her struggle with Seth that night on the bay invaded her thoughts. She shook, tried to keep her hands steady, and pressed her eye to the scope.

"I don't want to hurt her," Crenshaw shouted. "Just go away."

"Not until you release your wife."

Crenshaw held Jessy's gaze, tears running down his face. He spoke to her, the words "I love you" discernible through her scope. His grip loosened, and he lifted his hand to wipe a tear from her face when something glinted.

The air exploded, the ground shaking beneath her, and a grisly hole the size of a dime appeared on Crenshaw's forehead.

Brit gasped. *What the ... ?*

She jumped to her feet, her head reeling until her mind slammed the door shut on those haunting images, except for one. She hadn't pulled the trigger. She was positive.

Andi rushed over and jerked the weapon from Brit's trembling fingers. "Did you remember anything?" Her abrasive words prickled.

Still breathless, Brit worked to control her airflow and her anger. Andi had acted in the same exact manner that night. If she was trying to re-create the mood, she was doing a damn good job of it.

Colt marched over, reaching for her.

"Leave her alone," Andi shouted at him.

He froze and then scowled at her.

"She needs to work through this." Andi placed the rifle on the ground and took Brit's hands in hers. "Breathe, Brit. Steady breaths, honey."

Brit concentrated. *In out, in out.*

Andi patted her hands. "It's okay. I'm here."

Same stroking of my hands.

Only this time it struck Brit as totally bizarre. Even her last words seemed contradictory. Was Andi here for her tonight? Or was she here for herself? She'd been stubborn and preoccupied since they'd arrived.

Brit nodded, slowly catching her breath. She didn't like the way Andi peered into her eyes. It was like she half expected Brit to self-destruct.

She wouldn't.

If anything, she was annoyed—annoyed with herself. There was something nagging at her, but just like earlier tonight it remained elusive.

Colt cocked his head, his brows furrowing. "Are you okay?" His voice was stern yet wary.

Brit made eye contact with Colt and nodded. "Yeah. I'm fine." Keeping a steady bead on him, she pried her fingers from Andi's clammy grasp. "Will you take me back to the house?"

"Of course." Colt's arms went around her. He turned her hat so the bill faced forward and directed her down the hill before glancing back. "You coming, Andi?"

"I'm right behind you. You take her." She gave Brit a sympathetic smile. "I'll talk to you tomorrow."

"Okay." Brit's unsteady voice seemed to float on the crisp, dry air. She had remembered one thing. She was highly trained. She might have forgotten that in recent months, but she remembered it now.

Something wasn't quite right, and Brit's sixth sense told her Andi was the last person she wanted to talk with tonight.

If only she knew why.

Chapter Thirty-Three

"**W**HAT HAPPENED BACK THERE?" KEEPING HIS hands on the steering wheel, Colt glanced over at Brit in the passenger seat.

Brit gnawed her bottom lip and stared out the windshield. "I didn't pull the trigger."

He snorted. "I could have told you that."

Brit shook her head. "Explain the gun."

"If you're talking about the ballistics report, you're going to have to do a lot better at remembering."

Brit blew out an agitated breath. "I'm trying here."

Colt turned into the gravel drive of the Victorian. "You got something to write with and paper?"

"I have a pen in my pack. I'll need to work on the paper part." Brit turned in her seat to face him. "Why?"

"Because that exercise tonight didn't amount to shit." He tapped his head. "I got the layout up here. But what I don't have are all the players. It's kind of like a football playbook. I need to see the formation. There had to have been a tactical command center. Like this guy you mentioned, I think you said CJ? Where was he positioned? And Andi. Hell if I could tell where her location was in relation to yours. What about other police vehicles, officers from other jurisdictions? We're mapping it out."

It still didn't explain her gun—the only one that fired the fatal shot.

Colt put the truck in park, his attention drawn to the front porch.

"What is it?" Brit leaned forward, trying to see what he was looking at.

"The porch." He turned toward her. "Your friend's bat shit crazy. See the way she was checking out the porch ceiling tonight?"

Yeah, she'd noticed it. But Andi was a perfectionist. "Maybe she found something askew with the workmanship."

"Not buying it." Colt got out and strode toward the front steps.

Brit scrambled out of the truck, favoring her ankle. Soon as she corralled Colt, she was hobbling up those damn stairs and soaking in that vintage pedestal tub off the master bedroom.

Colt moved the picnic table bench toward the front door and stood on it.

"What are you doing?"

He pressed in along the soffit, ran his fingers inside both recessed light fixtures.

"Get down! You're going to burn your fingers."

Colt hopped off and moved the bench back. "I get why she'd help you— although tonight she was a total bitch." Colt scratched his head. "But why would she risk harboring a fugitive?"

"Because she's my—"

"BFF?" He scowled at her. "Give me a break. Her show of support was laughable, and you know it. She was on her fuckin' cellphone for God's sake. And what was with all that touchy-feely bullshit?"

Brit's brows snapped together. That was it. The way Andi had patted her hand, like she was rewarding a dog for good behavior.

"You think of something?" Colt eyed her intently.

She didn't want to give credence to Colt's suspicions of Andi. He didn't know her like she did. Besides, she couldn't validate her own uneasiness about tonight. Brit's temples pounded.

Let me remember.

It was there right in front of her. She just couldn't put a finger on it.

"No," she snapped and adjusted her weight onto her good ankle. "I need to soak my foot, and then I'm having a cup of hot tea and one of your damned thousand-calorie glazed donuts and going to bed." Brit jammed the key into the lock and swung open the door. She shuffled across the floor and grabbed for the banister.

"Hurts, huh?"

"It'll be fine." Brit frowned at the flight of stairs winding its way up to the second level—that would be a challenge.

"Let's go." Colt scooped her up.

Brit shrieked, her arms looping around his neck for support.

"Put me down." She was laughing up at him, completely captivated by the strong contours of his face and his glittering green eyes full of mischief. She relaxed in his arms.

"A bath sounds good."

Brit's heartbeat sped up. "Ah . . . you meant separately."

He took the steps, a smile tugging at the corners of his mouth. "I thought I could wash your back for you."

Brit snuffled. "You're so lame, Rivers."

He set her down in front of her bedroom door. "So that's a no."

She squinted up at him. "I'm not one of those bare it all kind of girls."

Colt placed his hand on the doorjamb. "So I'm relegated to the hall bathroom, then?"

Brit bit the inside of her mouth. She'd never taken a bath with a man. Oh, sure, she'd seen some racy movies with couples spooned together enjoying a hot bath with the guy's hands . . .

Whoa. Heat pooled between Brit's thighs, and she blushed. Just the thought of Colt's hands exploring every dip and curve of her body made her wet and warm with wanting him.

It wasn't going to happen. At least not tonight, not until they finished that conversation about his ex-wife.

"I'll get you a towel." Brit ducked under his arm and hobbled down the hall. She opened the linen closet, grabbed him one of the fluffy white towels on the shelf, and one of those mini sets of soap, shampoo, and conditioner like hotels provided. Andi really had a supply closet. Brit guessed for her impending guests. "Didn't you pack a toothbrush and paste in your—"

"It's in the backpack." He came up behind her, his hand coming to rest in the small of her back.

God he was so tall, so male, and so close that she tingled with indecision.

She wet her lips, trying to formulate her all-important words. "Will you tell me about your ex-wife later?"

"Sure." His hand fell away. "I'll go down and grab our gear."

"Thanks." Brit couldn't help but roll her eyes. *Still reluctant.* "I'll put this in your bathroom."

Colt took the steps and then turned. "His and hers." He winked and disappeared down the stairs.

Brit smashed the towel and toiletries to her chest and leaned against the wall. *You're so mean.* The guy hadn't had sex in four years. And that was the problem. She didn't want it to be just about that. She pushed off and entered the hall bathroom. She set down his supplies on the vanity, took note of the missing mirror, and hung his towel, then entered the hall.

Colt crested the second level and handed off her pack. "I'll see you downstairs for donuts, and we'll create a diagram of that night."

"Yeah, before bed."

"His and hers, right?" He gave her a boyish grin that almost melted her resolve. Brit grabbed her pack, avoided eye contact, and made a beeline to her room. She shut the door.

Oh my God, what's wrong with me? I love him. I want to be with him.

But he'd avoided the whole ex-wife thing, again. No. It was more than that. She was afraid. Once she became intimate with him, he would change.

Dumb. Intimacy was supposed to bring a couple closer together.

It hadn't with Seth. To him it was only a means to an end—his own gratification.

Brit shut the door to her bedroom and dropped her pack on the floor next to the bed. She dug out her small tube of toothpaste and toothbrush, a comb, her body cream, shampoo, and conditioner. She dug further until her fingers skimmed the box of her Oil of Olay soap. She got undressed and folded her clothes, leaving them on the bed. Padding across the tiled bathroom floor with her supplies, she peeked around the ivory silk-paneled room divider. Her eyes lingered on the white Victorian tub.

Could a man like Colt even fit in a tub that size?

Will you stop!

Brit bent over and started the tap. She brushed her teeth and then peered around the divider at the water level. It was high enough that she could get in. With her soap, shampoo, and conditioner, she dipped her toe in. It was luxuriantly hot. Brit stepped in, lowering her chilly body into the water, setting her stuff in a silver wired tray hanging over the edge of the tub. She sighed and leaned back against the porcelain and sucked air through her teeth. Now that was still cold. Cupping her hands, she scooped the hot water and splashed her arms, chest, and back, willing the tub to fill up faster. When it covered her shoulders, she turned off the water and slid down under to her neck.

"Mmm." The heat of the water seeped into her muscles, her bones, and she closed her eyes. The donuts could wait. Brit dipped her head back, wetting her hair. She washed it, then rinsed, pressing the heavy shafts of hair away from her face. A pink puff ball for bathing hung from the chrome faucet, and Brit snagged it. She took her time, running the nylon puff she sudsed up with the soap down her arms, legs, abdomen, and shoulders, grimacing when she tried to reach her back.

The doorknob to the bedroom clicked, and Brit froze. "Colt?"

Colt chuckled. Her voice shook with uncertainty. "It's me. I'm looking for my shaving cream and razor," he called from the bedroom.

"Ah . . . it's in the front pocket of my backpack. Yours was full."

In his towel, he bent down next to the bed and the crumpled sheets she'd slept in earlier and unzipped the front pocket. He dug around until he found what he needed. "Can I use the mirror in your bathroom?"

She splashed around no more than ten paces away. "Now?" Her voice rose.

Colt smiled at her discomfort. He wasn't about to push himself on her. He took three easy steps toward the open doorway, frowning. *Damn partition.*

"When you're done."

More splashing, then a *thunk*, and a bar of soap slipped out from under the silk panel. He stepped onto the white-tiled floor with small black diamond accents and picked up the slippery bar.

"Lose something?"

"N-no, it's okay."

He shook his head. The woman was cute as hell. "I'm not going to look at you." Not that he wasn't horny thinking about Brit naked and wet only an arm's length away.

More splashing. "Can you hand me my towel? It's on the towel rack."

"Yeah." Colt strode over, grabbed the towel, and caught the reflection of her long, shapely legs in the mirror.

Ah, Brit, baby, you're killing me.

He hadn't had a woman in years. Even if he had, the ache he felt for this woman was something he'd never experienced before—his ex-wife included. He owed Brit that explanation. Colt hung the towel over the wall of the partition.

"You're nothing like her," he called over the sheer fabric that, now, after she'd climbed out of the tub, revealed every soft curve of her body.

Brit snagged the towel, the rustle of terry cloth against her smooth dove-white skin erotic. Colt's pulse quickened, his balls tightening. *Great.* He had a hard-on. He groaned and adjusted his dick. Didn't do him a bit a good until he leveled with Brit and gave her a full disclosure about his marriage.

She rounded the corner, her skin soft and pink, hair wet and clinging to her shoulders. Brit tipped her chin up. "Your wife?"

Colt scrubbed the back of his neck. "Yeah."

Her eyes glided over him, her attention drawn to his towel and, he guessed, the bulge that was his erection. She lifted her eyes to him, her cheeks more flushed than before. "I'm sorry for staring." She sidestepped him.

He reached for her arm—gently—like she'd break into a million pieces. "You could make up for it by not leaving."

Brit's gaze held his. "If I stay I won't be able to deny you anything."

"Then don't." Colt bent his head and tasted her.

She moaned into his mouth, then pulled away, her eyelids fluttering open. "Tell me you're over her," she whispered.

"I am." Colt pulled her into his arms and kissed her.

Brit's arms looped his neck, her fingers slipping through his hair at his nape. Her sweet lips moved against his, and he scooped her up in his arms, flipped off the light in the bathroom, carrying her into the bedroom.

Heart beating like a jackhammer, he laid her down in the crumple of smooth, cool sheets. "Let me show you." His voice was hoarse with desire, and Colt reached for the bedside lamp and turned it off.

She was the most desirable women he'd ever laid eyes on—and it wasn't only her smokin' hot body.

Brit Gentry got him. No other woman had. He wanted that future to have and to hold.

For now he'd have to settle for tonight. Because he couldn't be guaranteed tomorrow.

Chapter Thirty-Four

RIT'S FINGERS SIFTED THROUGH COLT'S THICK RAVEN hair, and he reached for her towel.

"W-wait." She held fast to the thick terry cloth, her heart thudding. "I want to know about her first."

Colt moaned and rolled on his side. "Her name was Dana. We were married for two years."

"Did you love her?"

He took a deep breath through his nose. "Yes."

Brit wriggled away from him and sat up against the headboard, still clutching her towel. So he had loved, and, it would seem, professed those words she'd yearned to hear. Which meant he was capable of saying them—just not to her.

"What?" He frowned at her.

"Nothing." She motioned with her hand. "You loved her."

Colt groaned. "I know where this is going."

Nowhere unless he filled her in.

With his hand supporting his head, he slipped his arm under her and slid her down. Brit gasped, trying to keep her butt covered.

Colt pressed back her hair. "You're cute when you're jealous."

Damn but he could read her. Denying it was pointless. "You're stalling."

"Maybe I am because . . . it's not something I like to talk about."

"I'm not here to judge," she whispered, her hand coming down on his flexing biceps.

He nodded. "I was on tour. Couldn't wait to get home to see . . ." His voice faltered.

"Dana," Brit said.

"Right." It came out hushed, his Adam's apple bobbing in the thick column of his neck. "I got a letter instead." His eyes held hers, searching. She guessed waiting for her to reach her own conclusion.

A moan rolled up her chest, and she clasped his whiskery face between her hands. "She was a fool." Brit kissed him long and deep until he sighed into her mouth and began kissing her back. Here she thought he had a problem with commitment. God, what an idiot she'd been.

His strong hands rode up her thighs, and he broke the kiss. "It gets worse."

Brit gave him a pout. "I don't want to hear any more."

"She married our dentist." A smile, or was it a grimace, tugged at his lips.

"*No.*" Brit's hand flew to her mouth.

"No lie." He shook his head and chuckled. "Pencil-necked dentist smiled in my face the few times I needed his services, *knowing* he was banging my wife." He scrubbed his face hard. "I should have killed him."

Brit caressed his rough cheek and frowned at him. "She wasn't worth it."

Colt rolled away from her and sat up at the end of the bed. "You hungry?" He peered over his shoulder.

It was hard to make out his expression. But his despondent tone, now that she could gauge.

Good job, Brit. She shook her head. She'd been so persistent. Of course he didn't want to talk about it. But if he thought he was any less of a man because some cheating wife hooked up with the local dentist, she'd prove to him he wasn't.

Colt pushed up off the mattress. "I'll meet you downstairs in the kitchen."

Brit's shoulders sagged. Well, maybe not tonight.

Shit. Talk about dousing the mood with cold water.

It was just as well. There was no salvaging this. Brit gathered her towel, more confident than ever what her feelings were toward Colt. Seth would have ripped off her towel and punished her with angry sex.

Colt, on the other hand, was sensitive and, it would appear, vulnerable, which was refreshing for a man who could turn any woman's head with his good looks.

He was the total package.

Brit scooted off the bed and slipped into her pajamas. She combed her wet hair, grimacing at the knots she'd made by washing her hair in the tub, and then padded downstairs.

Colt was bent over a paper towel on the center island with a glazed donut on a plate by his elbow. He lifted his chin. "Got you a donut right here and your tea's in the microwave."

She passed by him, popped open the microwave door, and balanced the teacup, trying not to spill it. She added sugar and then cream from the fridge, stirring it with a spoon. She sidled up next to him. "Aren't you eating?"

"I already had one with milk." He motioned for her to sit down.

She did and peered over. "What are you writing on?"

He gave her a quick smile more in keeping with the Colt Rivers she'd come to know. "A paper towel."

Brit shook her head and smiled back. "This is crazy."

"Not so crazy." He took a step in her direction and slid the towel over. "I've drawn out the landscape. Tell me if I'm missing something."

She tilted her head, amazed at the detail. He had the stand of trees, the hillside, and the farm out in front with the dirt road. He'd even drawn her on the ground and the Crenshaws with boxes and an X drawn through each one.

X marked the spot, all right. Brit held tight to the warm mug. "Andi was here." She pointed to the right of her figure. "And CJ was here." She pointed to the left. "And there was some type of berm he was using for cover."

Colt drew them in. "What about the command bus?"

Brit chewed the inside of her mouth. "They were down the road. My commander, the one negotiating with him, was at the entrance to the farm. Then a cruiser was parked behind us." She put her finger down on the paper towel. "Cruiser, here."

"Was this cruiser a state police vehicle?"

"No. Dorchester Sheriff."

"Did he have an in-car camera?"

Brit rolled her lips in. "I don't know, but CJ had told him to deactivate his emergency lights so they wouldn't give up our location. So if he had one, it would not have been on without the lights."

"Gotcha." He fell back a step.

She patted his arm. "It was a good thought, though."

He leaned over and kissed the top of her head. "What else are we missing?"

Brit took a deep breath. "I don't know. It all happened split-second." She pushed up from her stool. "But I know I didn't pull that trigger."

"If you didn't, who did?"

Sitting her mug down, she stared at her hands. "They bagged them."

"Come again?" Colt gave a lift of his dark brow.

"My hands. They bagged them, and CJ's and Andi's." She pursed her lips. "And the sheriff's deputy who was up there with us, too."

"No GSR on anyone else's hands but yours."

"You got it."

"Is it normal for someone on your team to take a weapon recently fired during a shooting?"

Brit shook her head. "Nope. The evidence should have been preserved for internal affairs. But I was shaking, and I think everyone, including Andi, was afraid I'd accidentally fire off another round."

"But you didn't fire the first one."

"No." She gave him a pointed look. "I know that now."

"Who would have?"

She threw her hands up in frustration. "I don't know."

"Anyone on the team have anything against you?"

Brit shrugged. "Nothing personal that I know, except the obvious."

"And what's that?"

"Andi and I were the first women to make the team. And it wasn't easy. There were some who resented our existence."

Some that might have thought once they got rid of Andi and her, the likelihood of other women coming behind them would be small or next to none.

But they wouldn't have resorted to cold-blooded murder to achieve their objective. They were cops, for God's sake, and in the last two years, most, if not all, had come to accept them and were their friends.

She clucked her tongue. "No. No one on the team would have killed Crenshaw to rid them of one female." She dropped down on the stool. "That would still have left Andi."

Colt pulled at his bottom lip. "Right, Andi."

"You don't like her."

He laughed out loud. "I don't trust her."

"Come on. She told you why she was at the lake." Brit would have thought, considering the circumstances, he'd have understood why Andi had been less than truthful. It was embarrassing.

He wagged a finger at her. "Maybe in the morning you should follow up her story with your mother."

Brit's head fell back. "Please don't ask me to call my mother. I never asked Andi what, specifically, she told her when she returned."

"Fine." He walked around the kitchen, staring up at the ceiling. "I don't know about you, but this place gives me the creeps."

"She said it was haunted."

He turned. "Maybe. But not by the dead."

Chapter Thirty-Five

*I*T HAD BEEN QUARTER PAST TWO BY THE TIME COLT talked Brit into going to bed. He would have liked nothing better than to snuggle up next to her and fall asleep with her in his arms.

But it was more important that he take a closer look at this house, which he'd done before the sun had risen. There was no sense discussing it with Brit. She trusted Andi, had known her, from what she'd said, most of her life.

Well, he'd believed the same of Seth. Maybe he hadn't known him a lifetime, but in war, bonds were formed quickly. He always believed Seth had his back. Fast-forward four years at Leavenworth with time for reflection, and Colt recognized, now, the telltale signs of bitterness festering in his pal Gentry back in Afghanistan. Whether he resented the war, the military, or Colt himself, he couldn't say.

But what he could say with certainty was that Andi exhibited the same signals. He'd witnessed it firsthand in the kitchen when she'd tried to seduce him in front of Brit—jealousy. Or when she refused, after suggesting they re-create the shooting, to lie down in position to help Brit remember— selfishness. Oh, sure, she'd offered the use of her home. And that bothered him most. *Call me paranoid.* But he still felt he—they—were being watched.

Colt checked the clock on the microwave—11:12 a.m. He should wake Brit up. She'd had about nine hours of sleep—him only four after he'd crashed next to her early this morning. His ass was dragging. Colt took a sip of coffee—black this time. No, he'd let her wake up on her own. As he recalled her BFF was supposed to call and check on her. Colt lifted Brit's cellphone from the counter in the kitchen. He might not have the passcode, but he could see if Andi had called. The only message was from a guy named Jay and her mother, which reminded him. He still needed her to make that call, regardless of how uncomfortable it might be for Brit.

He sighed and set down his coffee on the center island, admiring the sun cresting a clear autumn sky. How many more sunrises would he get to see? The last few weeks had been hell. He smiled. Well, not the last five days. He'd treasure them for as long as he lived.

Colt's body tensed. He wasn't going back alive. That was for damn sure. They'd tracked him to Maryland. It was only a matter of time before they caught up with him. But it didn't matter. He wasn't leaving Brit, regardless of what he'd promised.

He loved her, and he would die trying to clear her name. His chest tightened. Even if they caught him alive, he'd die a little every day in prison, knowing she was behind bars.

A familiar pinch hit the backs of his eyes, and he sniffed. The last time he cried had been when Beau died. Dana could go to hell. That dog had seen him through his divorce. A damn tear ran down his cheek. Colt rubbed his face against his shoulder, Obsession filling his nose.

He gritted his teeth. Brit was right. He needed to wash every piece of clothing he'd gotten out of that damned chest. It was like the bastard was still alive, laughing at him.

Fuck it.

Colt strode out the front door, jerked the bench to the picnic table, and stood on top. He studied the two recessed lights.

Burnt out my ass.

It was here. He slipped his finger under the soffit and ripped the yellow piece of aluminum down and didn't give a shit that he'd bent it. He ripped another piece closer to the electric can of the burnt-out recessed light and growled with triumph when he exposed a black video wire running into, what he believed to be, one of those high-res spy cameras made to look like a ceiling light.

Son of a bitch.

Tempted to rip it from the stud, he inched back from the camera instead. Okay, so if she was watching in real time, Andi'd know he fucked up her ceiling, which was the least of her worries.

Although it wasn't a good idea to tip his hand just yet, Colt reinserted the soffit, careful to stay away from the lens of the camera. Damn his anger, and his haste. Colt eyed the lens, his shoulders leveling off. It was one of those lenses with angling adjustment. Andi had it angled away from the house facing forward. She could catch anyone coming toward the house or leaving. But the view behind the lens and the location in which he stood on the bench couldn't be seen. That didn't mean the aluminum he'd tossed to the ground hadn't crossed the lens of the camera.

That was a concern. But he had an even bigger one. Where there was one camera, there had to be more. He also hadn't noticed an audio cable. Didn't mean their conversations weren't being taped. Colt stepped off the bench and put it back. He crossed under the porch ceiling in front of the door and grimaced at the crease in the soffit. As Brit pointed out, Andi was particular. She'd eventually notice the dent in the aluminum.

Colt crossed over the threshold to the open front door, shutting it behind him. Before he went up to wake Brit and let her in on his find, he'd check each room for a hidden camera.

He entered the living room and flipped all the switches. Three recessed lights were positioned over the fireplace. Only two came on, the left and the right. The middle remained dark. Bingo. He did the same in the dining room and found a similar set in the middle of the ceiling. Then the foyer— those lights came on and he sighed with relief. If a camera had been there, it would have picked up him on the bench with the door open. Next he strode into the kitchen. Two sea glass pendant lights hung over the center island with one lone recessed light between them. He flipped on every switch until the kitchen glowed with light, except the recessed bulb between the pendants.

Huh? She had one in every room. He shook his head with disgust. He wouldn't be surprised if they were in the bedrooms, too.

Sick bitch.

Colt pocketed Brit's phone and climbed the stairs. He wasn't going to let his anger boil over. Not on Brit. But she needed to face facts. This wasn't normal. For all he knew, this was a setup, and the video was going straight to the state police. That had him taking the steps two at a time. Of course, if they were aware of his location and his every movement, they were taking their sweet time.

Nah. He didn't believe this had anything to do with a police sting. Colt opened the door. The bed was made. The bathroom door was closed, with the water running in the sink.

He scanned the ceiling and zeroed in on a lone recessed light over the dresser. Had to be it. He tried all the wall switches. The light in question popped on. Okay maybe she wasn't a deviant.

The bathroom door opened.

"Hey." Brit stepped out of the bathroom, dressed in a pair of comfy jeans, T-shirt, her draping black sweater, and boots. "You shouldn't have let me sleep so long."

"You needed it." Colt took a step toward her and gave her a quick kiss, pulling her to him. He leaned in, his lips grazing her ear. "Don't say anything. Just follow me downstairs and out the front door."

A cold dread filled her chest. Brit clasped onto his hand, and he led her from the bedroom, his head on a swivel. He was killing her. Her brows furrowed, and she pinned him with her eyes.

Ignoring her, he guided her down the steps and opened the front door. She went first, glancing back. He followed, pulling the door closed.

"Wha—"

Colt shook his head a definite no and directed her down the front steps and to the right of the porch. He turned toward the house, seemed to weigh his options, and then steered her toward the right and the stone bulkhead near the water.

Brit pulled her hand away from his and crossed her arms over her chest, shivering. "Tell me what's wrong."

He handed Brit her phone. "Who's Jay?"

"He called?" Her voice sounded panicked, and she hit a number, placing the phone to her ear. "Mr. Dahlgren. It's Brit Gentry." She shook her head. "No, I'll wait."

"Who is he?" Colt beaded in on her.

"My law—hey, you called?"

Lawyer, he assumed.

"A check written out to H & R Builders in Cambridge?" She shook her head. "I have no clue. I know. I'll see you in a few days." Brit clicked off.

"No decision?"

"Nope."

"What's up with this builder?"

"I told you my lawyer's been helping me investigate Seth and his money trail, which I'm not giving up on even though everyone thinks I'm wasting my money, including my BFF."

"So what'd he say?"

"The bastard wrote a check to a builder for ten grand."

Colt whistled through his teeth. "For what?"

"Like I told *him,* I have no clue." She reached back to pocket her phone.

"Not so fast. Call your mother and confirm she sent Andi to the lake to check on you."

Ugh. She didn't want to. This was embarrassing, but judging by his stiff expression this was non-negotiable. He needed the peace of mind, and because she loved him, she would give him that, regardless of her mother's scrutiny.

"Fine." She hit the speed dial number to her parents' phone. Only thing was, she had no idea what Andi had said to her mother. "Hey, Mom. No, I'm fine. Yeah, she did come visit me at the lake." Brit nodded to Colt. "You asked her to." She shook her head. "No, I'm not mad." How could she be? If she had a daughter in the exact same situation—perish the thought—it would have been a tactic she would have employed if she were concerned. "Right, she spent one night. No, I'm fine. I'll see you soon. I love you, too."

Brit clicked off and took a deep breath. "Now will you relax? Andi was telling the truth."

"But she's still keeping secrets."

Brit pocketed her phone and put her hands on her hips. "What has she done now?"

"The recessed light that she claimed was burnt out is a camera."

Her eyes widened. "As in surveillance?"

"*Yeah*," he said it like, *What else would it be?*

She considered that for a moment. Andi's beloved Victorian hadn't been much to look at when she'd bought it, but now that it was almost completely refurbished, there was value here. "I'm sure it's for security, Colt. She's not here much. She's only protecting her home against vandals."

"I'm not buying it. She's up to something—hiding something." He turned to walk away.

"Seriously." Brit grabbed his arm. "You honestly think she had time to install a surveillance system in a few hours so she could watch us? What would be her motive?"

Fear filled his eyes. "She could have sold us out. That feed could be going to some computer within the state police."

She shook her head. "You'd be sitting behind bars, waiting for extradition if that were true."

He shrugged. "Either way, your friend's actions seem suspicious to me, and I'm going to get to the bottom of it." He jerked his arm away and stalked toward the house.

Great. He was mad. She got his uneasiness. If she believed for one moment he was in imminent danger of being captured, he'd be taking her truck and making tracks across the border. She turned her back on the house and breathed in the sea air, trying to relax. He'd cool off soon and realize what she said made sense. Andi must have a security system, and, yes, she could review the tapes whenever she wanted. But they—she and Colt—weren't doing anything that Andi wouldn't expect them to do after she'd offered to harbor them.

Brit wrapped her sweater around her waist. With a good fifty yards from the bulkhead to the rear of the house, she walked as swiftly as she could toward it, careful to avoid a repeat with her ankle. She climbed the steps to the porch of the kitchen and cleared the back door. "Colt?"

She passed by the center island, a square piece of paper towel fluttering when she walked by. In Sharpie were the words, *I've gone to search Andi's condo.*

Brit gripped the note, fear blazing up her chest. No, no, no, no, no! She ran to the front door. *Damn it.* Her truck was gone. Her head fell into her hands. It was only one in the afternoon. He could be recognized. And what about Andi? She said she worked at three. Brit calculated the time. With any luck, she would be gone by the time he arrived.

She threw her head back. "Please, dear God, protect him." Brit's eyes narrowed at the ceiling, and she scowled. *Shit.* Andi would notice the bend in the soffit where she guessed Colt had ripped it down. Again, he was making it impossible for them to remain here.

Now all she could do was wait and wonder about his well-being. A chill rode up her spine.

I may never see him again.

Chapter Thirty-Six

WITH BRIT'S MSP BALL CAP ON HIS HEAD, THE BILL pulled down, Colt sat behind the wheel of her Pathfinder. He kept a steady bead on Andi Hall's condo building and her white CRV that was parked several rows over.

Colt played back that morning on the docks—the conversation about her apartment. He knew he had the right building. What the hell had been her apartment number? She said end unit. The dash clock flipped to 2:56. She should be leaving soon. Brit had told him last night her shift started at three in the afternoon.

A group coming from the dock passed by his vehicle. *Shit.* He turned his head like the fugitive he was, trying to avoid detection.

Shouldn't be sitting out in broad daylight, asshole.

Like he had a choice. Brit—they—needed to know what was going on with the woman who was hiding them.

God. Colt's shoulders slumped remembering last night. Brit Gentry meant everything to him. He couldn't believe how bad he'd screwed things up last night. He told her he'd loved Dana. He hadn't missed the disappointment in Brit's eyes when he didn't take it a step further and profess his love for her, too.

Thing of it was, telling Brit he loved her in the same breath would have only cheapened how he felt about her. He couldn't even sum it up into words. The usual "I love you" didn't come close to all the thoughts and feelings running through his head, and, he chuckled, his body.

What he shared with Brit in the past five days would last him a lifetime, if his life ended today. But the next time he saw her he'd make it clear—she was the only one that made all this shit worth fighting for. He wasn't fighting for his freedom or to be exonerated. He was fighting to stay with her. That was all he cared about. She'd be pissed when he got back. But as she had pointed out about the Crenshaw shooting—she'd been too close to that one.

Well, she was too close to Andi to see things objectively. He didn't know what was going on in that crazy brunette's head, but he was going to find out. It started with her apartment.

Colt squinted up at the building with entry doors facing out toward the parking lot. A door opened on the sixth floor at the end—602. That was what she'd said. He was sure. He waited, keeping track of the individual hitting the stairs. Hall was in tiptop shape, same as Brit. She'd utilize the steps. Colt leaned into the dash. It was Hall, dressed in olive pants and matching T-shirt, carrying a long black duffel bag. He'd guess her rifle. Colt craned his head to get a better view and relaxed when she slipped into an unmarked cruiser and drove away.

He remained in the truck for a good five minutes, making sure she didn't return to retrieve something she'd forgotten. Getting out, he then made a beeline for the stairs to her building and took them two at a time. He rounded the corner, checked the apartment number, and pulled out his makeshift lock picking set he'd put together from the kitchen. The thin tined fork was crude, but . . . He gritted his teeth and waited for the familiar sound that let him know he'd popped the lock. *Click.* His lips curled with victory, and he swung open the door, slipping inside. Colt entered a hallway with beachy wall decorations. He took a few steps and peered into a doorway on the right—powder room. A few more steps and it opened up into a combo kitchen–living room with a balcony overlooking the harbor. Another door to the left revealed the master bedroom and bath. A set of vertical blinds were shut. He guessed another slider leading to the balcony.

The bedroom seemed the likely place. Colt started with a small walk-in closet. High heels, tennis shoes, and some tactical gear sat on the floor. He picked up her Uggs, which had started the whole fiasco at dinner last night, then set them down in the same spot. Digging through pockets, while he scanned the top shelf, he came up empty. What the hell was he looking for? He'd know it if he found it.

Colt opened boxes on the top shelf, more shoes. Another smaller floral box sat on the shelf in the back. The top had one of those openings for a photo, and Colt opened the box. Photos. He flipped through them and hesitated on a photo of Brit. Wearing a summer dress that hugged her sexy curves, her skin kissed by the sun, she was smiling at him. At least that was the way it made him feel. *Screw Andi.* He shoved it in the pocket of his flannel shirt. It might be the only thing he'd have to remember Brit by, and he was taking it.

Putting the top back, he eyed the two nightstands next to the king bed from where he stood in the closet. He strode over, ripped through the first one and came up empty, then he put his sights on the second nightstand and opened it. *Sex toys.* His jaw tightened, and he slammed the drawer.

He went through her dresser, looked under the cushions in the living room, checked the kitchen cabinets, the freezer, refrigerator, bathroom cabinets, and even the lids of the toilets.

Nothing.

Shit. He placed his hands on his hips and surveyed the room as a whole. A framed painting of a lighthouse sat over the couch. He lifted it off the wall, laying it facedown on the couch. The back was enclosed with brown paper. He grabbed a knife from the butcher block on the bar and made an *X* with the sharp point and flipped the paper back. There was only the back of the painting.

Damn it. Colt scrubbed his face, his eyes darting from one corner of the room to the other.

Shit. He threw his hands up in the air. He'd forgotten the bed.

He charged into the bedroom, checked the mattress and box spring, ran his hand inside the pillow cases, then dropped to his knees and peered underneath. An oddball tennis shoe and a sock—it was still too dark to see underneath. Colt stood and opened the blinds to the balcony and bent down again. His eyes did a crisscross of the carpet when something glinted along the back wall where the headboard rested.

On his belly, he reached, stretching his hand until his finger slipped inside something cold and cylinder-shaped. He curled his finger around it and shimmied out from under the bed.

He lifted his finger and studied the ring, then he caught the fine etching inside the band.

All my love, Brit.

Brit gnawed her cuticle and sat on the picnic bench of the Victorian's front porch with her eye on the road. Colt had been gone for over four hours. She had no way to go after him. Her phone was useless since he didn't have one. There was no one she could call, especially not Andi.

She scooted the bench back against the house. If Andi was monitoring their movements, Brit didn't want her BFF to see her fidgeting at the picnic table, clasping onto the only photo she had of Colt.

Brit held up the photo from that day on the Mountain Coaster. It sat in the colorful cardboard frame she'd slipped the photo in when she'd gotten back to the lake house.

A tear slid down her cheek.

I wish I could see your face.

With her stomach in aching knots, Brit sat immobile. She wouldn't even be mad at him. *God, just bring him back.* What a jerk she'd been last night, forcing him to relive his past with his ex-wife.

She wouldn't push anymore. If only he'd turn the corner of that white pine and come back to her.

Colt was right, and all she could do was make excuses for her friend. Brit pulled her legs up, hugging them to her. This wasn't the first time Andi had been hot and cold to her like she'd been last night—one minute Andi was being difficult, the next consoling. It had been like that after Seth's accident, too, especially the first couple of days.

If Brit didn't know any better, she'd think she was bipolar. But it wasn't that. She wouldn't have remained on the S.T.A.T.E. Team.

So what was it?

Brit stood, clasping the photo tight in her hand, her heart heavier and more frightened than it had been since the boating accident or the shooting. The not knowing was killing her. Her heart pounding, her breathing shallow, fearing the next car to drive around the bend would be a state police cruiser informing her, among other things, that fugitive Colt Rivers had been cornered and killed during a gun battle with police. She wouldn't have even cared if they arrested her on the spot for aiding and abetting.

Damn Seth.

Colt Rivers was innocent and had been protecting her since she found out the truth about him.

Brit chewed her cuticle some more, staring blankly at the front door. What was it about this freakin' door? She placed her hands along the lead design and ornate glass. It looked so familiar. Brit's breath caught. She'd seen a brochure of it on Seth's desk with a paid invoice stapled to it, probably last year. He'd said he was replacing the front door of Memory Maker.

Only why hadn't he installed it?

A motor rumbled in the distance, and Brit froze. Out of the corner of her eye a sedan drove by. Her shoulders relaxed when a gold and black shield didn't gleam back under a twilight sky.

Brit reached for the doorknob when the crunch of gravel brought her around. The familiar grill of her Pathfinder, with the headlights on, pulled forward.

Oh, God.

Brit leaped off the porch and tore across the parking lot. The door swung open and Colt stepped out. His eyes locked onto hers. They were wary.

Well, he should have figured she'd be angry with him. But she couldn't muster up one sharp word. Relief flowed through her, and she wrapped her arms around him. "I'm not mad."

He pulled her away from him, his eyes darting from the house to her and then back at the house. "We need to talk and not in *that* house." He eyed it like it was possessed.

"What is it?"

He hooked his chin toward the road that led to the church and several properties overlooking the bay. Dusk had settled in like a heavy blanket of purple hues with just a touch of pink where the sun had set over the shimmering water.

Colt took her hand in his. His fingers were warm and steady, unlike hers that were shaking, and he led her away from the white gingerbread peaks of the Victorian.

Brit glanced up at him. The sharp angles of his face were rough with stubble—he'd never gotten to shave last night.

She held tight to his hand. "You're scaring me."

"I'd never do anything to hurt you." He pulled her into a stand of trees. "Brit," he said, his voice pained.

"What is it?" She kept a steady gaze on him, white-hot panic riding up her chest.

He shook his head and cursed under his breath. "There's no easy way to say this."

Brit swallowed. "You're leaving," she whispered.

"What? No." He scrubbed his face. "Damn your husband," he mumbled under his breath.

"Seth?" She gave him a questioning look.

"I found this under Andi's bed. Do you recognize it?" He held out a gold band between his calloused fingers.

Brit's breath caught, her hand with the photo of them pressing in on her chest. "I don't understand."

"Brit." His voice was stern. "Is this Seth's wedding band?"

She shook her head. "No."

Colt shoved it closer. "Look at it. There's an inscription."

"No!" She pulled away, wrapping her arms around her waist. "I'm cold. I'm going in." Brit took a step to the right and dodged Colt's arm.

"Brit," he called after her.

She ran down the narrow road toward the house, tears flowing down her cheeks.

This cannot be happening.

She reached the door and smacked it with her open palm. Brit lowered her head, her forehead coming to rest on the cold glass. A check for ten grand to a builder in the same county as this house, an invoice for a door she couldn't account for that matched this one, and a remodel that screamed extravagant.

He'd bought her a house, too.

What a fool she'd been.

He never loved her. She choked back tears. How long had Andi been lying to her? Pretending to be her friend. Brit grunted and yanked open the door.

I'm leaving. Screw my innocence.

And if Colt thought she'd drive to Canada smelling Seth for eight hours . . .

Think again.

Brit bolted up the stairs, swung into the room Colt had been occupying, and grabbed the backpack off the floor. She'd seen the laundry room off the kitchen.

That bitch better have laundry detergent.

She flew down the stairs and marched toward the kitchen. Throwing on the light in the laundry room, she scanned the room, snagging the detergent from a shelf on the wall, and set down the photo of her and Colt on the dryer.

She ripped through the backpack on the floor, yanking out a T-shirt, underwear, flannel shirt, and a pair of jeans.

Boots stomped into the foyer. "Brit?"

"Laundry room!" She stood with the clothes in her arms, wanting to gag.

Heavy footsteps entered the kitchen, and he stood in the doorway. A pair of sensitive green eyes swept her face. "I'm sorry."

"He's a bastard, and sh-she's . . . dead to me." Her voice cracked, and she wiped her face hard on her sleeve. "Take off your clothes."

"Excuse me?" He eyed her speculatively, a smile playing on his tough-guy lips.

"Jesus." She shook her head, throwing in the clothes she'd already dug out. "To *wash.* I'm taking you up on your offer. I'm going to Canada with you, and I'm not smelling that bastard another day."

"The cologne." He unbuttoned his shirt, kicked off his boots, and seized his gun before he slid his jeans off.

She waved a dismissive hand at him while she turned the dials on the washer. "And don't worry. The last thing I'm looking for is commitment. I tried that." Her voice broke, and she placed her hands on the washer, her head falling to her chest. Throat burning with emotion, she wanted to throw herself on the bed and cry like a baby.

"Hey." Colt placed his clothes on the dryer and bent his head, his hand coming to rest on her shoulder. "Look at me, Brit."

She shook her head, grabbed his clothes, and jerked away. Something fluttered to the ground. Sniffing, she got on her haunches and scooped up a four by six photo and turned it over.

Her breath caught. It was a photo of her taken at the Crab Claw Restaurant in St. Michaels, on their deck overlooking the bay. She had been with her family celebrating her brother's engagement.

Brit lifted her chin to him. "Where did you get it?"

He took it from her and set it on the dryer next to the one from the lake and chuckled. "You didn't think you'd see me again."

Brit threw his clothes into the running washer. "You're like a bad penny."

"You don't mean that." He pulled her into his arms. Their gazes locked. "You know where I got it and you know why."

Brit snuffled. "Then tell me."

"I know this. If you think I'm taking you to Canada and letting you walk out of my life, you're sadly mistaken, Brit Gentry." He pressed a wisp of her hair behind her ear. "I'm in love with you."

Chapter Thirty-Seven

RIT SHOVED HER HANDS HARD AGAINST COLT'S CHEST. "I'm not a charity case, Rivers." Something flitted in her brown eyes—not quite defiance, more like *how dare you patronize me.*

His mouth fell open. "Where the hell did that come from?"

She slipped out from under his arms, grabbed the framed photo of them from the lake, and walked out of the laundry room with her gun wedged inside her waistband.

"Hey, where are you going?" He laughed because he was in shock, mostly, and even a little embarrassed. *Hell.* She'd left him standing there bare-chested, bare-footed, and in his underwear for crissake, holding his firearm. It wasn't like he could shove it in his underwear, either. He took after her, grabbing the banister, leading to the second level. "Brit, you get your ass back here!"

"No." She turned on the steps, gazing down at him from the top of the staircase, her blond hair loose and flowing past her shoulders. "You know I love you. I don't have to say the words. All this time I've waited for you to say them to me. The only reason why you are saying them *now* is because you feel sorry for me." She sniffed. "Obviously I wasn't interesting enough, smart enough, pretty enough." She threw her hands up in the air. "Whatever enough to keep Seth from Andi's bed."

"You're whatever enough for me."

"*Enough?*" She gave him the evil eye. "I don't want to be enough. I want to be all. All you think about, all you want. I'm not." Her voice cracked, and she fled down the hall.

You gotta be kidding me.

"I'm a simple guy, Brit," he called after her. "I like simple things." He took the steps two at a time. Cresting the second level, he marched down the hall. He caught the swoosh of her blond hair before she slammed the bedroom door. He shook his head, and within two steps he stood at her door. "I'd like to make this all go away, especially for you. But I can't. All I can do is promise to love you all the days of my life. And if it sounds like a damned wedding vow, it is, until I can legally call you my wife."

She wasn't listening. *Damn it.* Did she honestly think he didn't understand? If anyone knew what that was like, it would be him. So Seth cheated on her. Dana did the same to him. Yeah, he was pissed. But he got over it. He wouldn't be over Brit any time soon. And he didn't have time to play games, proving to her she was everything to him.

Out of the corner of his eyes, he checked out the dark recessed light above him. The quicker they got on the road the better he'd feel. But since Little Miss Smell Freak tossed all his clothes in the washing machine, they'd be spending one more night in this creepy-ass house.

Maybe it was just a security system. So why not tell them? It didn't make sense and it was a huge concern.

But he had an even bigger one tonight, and she was about five foot six and causing him a mess of trouble.

Colt gripped the crystal doorknob.

Screw being a gentleman.

He turned the knob. It didn't budge. *Awesome.*

She'd locked him out.

Fine. *Screw the goddamned door.*

Colt put his shoulder against the wood and threw his weight into it. Something cracked, probably the frame, and he didn't give a shit. He pushed open the door and slammed it behind him.

She gasped and turned around. But not before he got a nice shot of her shapely little ass. Colt took a step toward her, mesmerized by her matching black bra and thong, the sheer triangle covering her sex, leaving nothing to his imagination. His balls tightened and he hadn't touched her, yet.

"Get out."

"Not on your life." He set his gun on a tall dresser by the door and flicked off the overhead, bathing her alabaster skin in moonlight. He strode toward her, cupped the back of her neck, his other hand sliding to the small of her back. He jerked her against him.

A soft feminine moan escaped her lips.

"God, you know I want you, Brit. Stop fighting it."

He'd never had to force a woman to share his bed. As much as he loved her, wanted to be with her on the most intimate level a man and woman could share, she needed to come to him. Colt released her.

"Wh-where are you going?" She looped her arms around his neck. Colt cupped her curvaceous bottom and lifted her off the ground. Her legs went around him.

"Where do you want to go?" His gaze swept her face.

Her brows creased—he believed with indecision. Then something flickered in those brown eyes of hers. "The bed," she said breathlessly.

He kissed her hard, took two strides, and deposited her in the middle. She scooted up, her long sexy legs angled to one side, and reached back to the clasp of her lacey bra and unsnapped it. The thin straps slid down her slender shoulders. He liked her initiative. They weren't teenagers who hadn't a clue.

The bra slipped down the tantalizing slopes of her breasts, and she tossed the silky lingerie to the floor. Colt's erection bulged uncomfortably in his briefs and he shed them. He knelt down on the bed. "You're beautiful." His voice was low and rough.

"So are you." Her eyes swept over him, lingering on his penis.

She reached for the lacey triangle between her thighs.

He came down next to her. "Not yet." He took a pert, pink nipple into his mouth and teased it with his tongue. She arched her back, lips parting.

He dropped kisses up her neck and then sought her lips. He kissed her long and deep, and then brought her hand to his erection. "Stroke me."

Her fingers curved around him, taking a tight grip. Brit began to move her fist up and down his hard length, then, she bent her head and took him in her mouth. Colt moaned and slid his arm around her, cupping her ass. "God, woman, that feels so good."

Colt squeezed her round white rump, nudging her body closer until he could slip his finger inside her. She was warm and wet and convulsing. As much as he wanted to come in her mouth, he wanted to be inside her more.

Colt stroked the back of her hair. "You're going to make me come."

She flicked him a sultry look without breaking her rhythm.

"No, you don't." He pulled her up and kissed her. "I want to taste you now."

"Ah, I've never . . . no one's ever given me oral sex." Her voice was tremulous.

He caressed her warm cheek, the thought of making her climax in a way she'd never before experienced made his blood strum through his veins. Here was something she'd only share with him. "Then let me show you how enjoyable it can be."

She nodded and grabbed her panties. He quelled her shaking hands with his. "Let me." He patted the pillow. "Lay down, baby."

Brit placed her head on the down pillow, her thighs shaking. She'd always told Seth no—not that he'd insisted. As nervous as she was, she wanted Colt to know her in her most intimate spot. Mostly she wanted to make him happy.

And it seemed, this was as much for him as it was for her.

He looped his finger through her thong and slid her panties down like a striptease, tossing them on the floor. His rough fingers glided over her stomach, and then lower. "Sexy."

She guessed he liked the barely there look.

He moved down to the end of the bed and positioned his hulking body between her thighs, his hands cupped her bottom and he slid her down. He kissed her folds, his lips warm and sensual. His tongue darted inside her.

She stiffened.

He glanced up at her, his eyes impassioned. "Relax." His warm breath caressed her skin.

Brit willed her body to go limp.

Colt stroked her, his tongue awakening a pulsing, pooling heat between her thighs. She gripped the sheets, her hips lifting off the mattress. She thrashed her head. "Oh my God." She panted. "What are you doing to me," she moaned.

He continued to stroke her labia with his tongue, suckling and darting. Her heart raced, her body glistening with sweat.

"Come on, baby," he said, breathing heavy. "You're almost there." His hand brushed her stomach.

She quivered.

He took her extended nipple between his fingers and rolled it. She cried out, bucking against him, riding the crest. She licked her fingers and began rolling her other nipple between her fingers.

She caught him watching her, his eyes dark with desire. "It feels good. Doesn't it, baby?"

Brit couldn't think. She reached for him, raking her fingers through his hair as he resumed exploring her, his clever tongue drawing her ever closer to the giddy heights of desire, until she reached her peak and tumbled sweetly over the edge.

She sunk into the mattress. He moved up, kissing her. She could taste a musky sexiness created from the two of them. He nudged her knee with his and thrust himself inside her.

He kissed her lips, her neck, her breasts. The wave again began to grow inside of her over and over, rising. He continued to seek his own release, plunging and pulling back, plunging and pulling back. He moaned and pulled out, spilling his semen onto her stomach. The warm wetness sent her spiraling into another heady orgasm.

Colt took the sheet and cleaned her off, then himself before he pulled up the duvet at the end of the bed, covering them both.

He kissed her cheek. "So no more misunderstandings?"

She gave him a sleepy smile. "No," she whispered.

"I love you."

She grabbed his hand resting across her stomach. "I love you, too."

"Let's get an early start tomorrow." He yawned.

Suddenly Brit felt wide awake and focused—they needed to get away before Andi showed up to check on them.

Brit jiggled his hand in hers. "Why do you think she brought us here?"

"I don't know. But we're not waiting around to find out."

"Your clothes." Brit jerked to get up.

"Just lay with me for a few minutes. I'll throw them in the dryer."

She snuggled up against him, content to be in his arms. A man like Colt Rivers was a rare find.

Whatever it took, she wasn't going to lose him. It was about time she stopped playing the victim and started acting like the highly trained cop Colt would need by his side.

If they survived until they crossed the border.

Chapter Thirty-Eight

*T*HE WATER FROM THE SHOWER RAN THROUGH THE pipes above the ceiling in the laundry room. Brit had gotten up early to wash and dress first. She pulled Colt's clothes out of the dryer, a smile touching her lips. She'd never been so content, at least with her relationship with Colt.

She was in love.

Climbing out of bed had taken a Herculean effort. She wanted to stay snuggled next to the strength of his warm chest, her fingers tangled in the soft matting of his dark chest hairs.

It didn't take her long to decide that luxuriating in bed and making love one last time before they got on the road could be a catastrophic error, especially in light of what they'd learned about Andi.

More importantly, if she'd been having an affair with Seth, it would stand to reason Brit would be the last person she'd want to help. Unless she had real remorse for what she'd done and felt, then, in her mind, this might be a way of making up for an affair that would end their twenty-four-year friendship if Brit had ever found out.

Brit's mouth twisted with indecision. She wanted to believe that Andi didn't have any other ulterior motives for inviting them here to stay. But Brit couldn't deny the overwhelming feeling that Andi had brought them here to spy on them and keep them accounted for.

That spelled surveillance with a capital *S*. But for who? If it was her own agency, what more did they need to know? She had been harboring a fugitive. If they'd positively ID'd Colt, they knew who he was and probably his connection to her husband. They would have arrested them. Same for the Army.

An icy finger ran up Brit's spine. It wasn't the police or the military.

Fold the laundry, pack your shit, and get out of here.

Brit resumed her task with urgency; she grabbed an armful of clothes, straightened suddenly, and sneezed. She ripped off a paper towel positioned in a holder under the cabinet above the washer, dropping some clothes on the floor. She blew her nose, stuck the wet, crumpled towel in her front jean pocket, and bent to retrieve a T-shirt and pair of underwear. She noticed something dark and rectangular on the floor. Brit picked it up and ran her finger along the raised insignia shaped like a sail. It must have come from inside the dryer.

Strange.

None of the clothes she'd laundered had a zipper pull. It must belong to one of Andi's jackets. But it looked familiar. Only Brit couldn't place where she'd seen it.

Brit slipped it inside her front jean pocket with her tissue. She'd ask Colt about it when he came down. Refocusing on the clothes, Brit sniffed the flannel shirt.

Yes! Outdoor fresh.

At least that was the fragrance name on the package of dryer sheets. Honestly, it could have been eau de skunk and she would have delighted in the scent. Carrying the clothes into the kitchen, Brit couldn't help but be drawn to the window and the water beyond. She'd hoped to witness her last sunrise over the bay. This morning at quarter to seven, under a crowded sky of dark storm clouds, it was a sailor's nightmare with frothy whitecaps and vomit-inducing swells.

Brit shivered. It had been the same that day on the sailboat.

Although eerie, she wasn't going to have a panic attack. She now recognized the symptoms and could work through them, thanks to Colt.

No, it wasn't the bay that bothered her. More like it was trying to tell her something. Brit pulled out the blue object, her thumb pressing into the triangular shape. Colt's map of the bay took shape in her mind with his two coordinates—her home in Chesapeake Beach and Seth's point of entry into the water. Something was missing, just out of reach. Maybe if she drew the coordinates . . .

Brit grabbed for the map Colt had left on the far end of the counter. She snagged a pen out of the outer pocket of her backpack, identified the marks for her house and the accident, then on impulse plunked down a small circle where she estimated the Victorian sat on the coast of Hoopers Island.

Huh?

What did this house Seth had a financial interest in have to do with the other coordinates? Brit drew a line from each point and studied it. A perfect triangle—no—her very own Devil's Triangle.

Brit frowned.

I don't know what it is I'm supposed to remember.

Folding the clothes, Brit continued to ruminate. She grabbed the jeans and shook out the wrinkles before folding them in half. Something caught the light, hit the counter, and rolled. Brit trapped the ring with her fingers and read the inscription: *All my love, Brit.*

Her cheeks warmed. Last night she'd wanted to explain it away—the ring. She couldn't. There had been only one explanation, and she wasn't ready to admit to Colt she was that undesirable and stupid.

Maybe it wasn't the coordinates on the map at all. *Err.* There was the lovers' triangle, too. Not that she had been aware it ever existed until Colt found the ring.

She should have known about Seth and Andi, though. But they had been too covert. After Seth's death, and even before it, Brit noticed subtle changes in their friendship—a coldness or a little obstinacy here or there. But nothing she could put a finger on, until now.

Andi had lost a lover and, it would appear based on the work stoppage on the Victorian, her financier.

Well, too damn bad.

Andi wasn't facing manslaughter charges for a murder she didn't commit. She wasn't forced to leave her family, either. It would be a long time before Brit's parents could live down the shame. The media would be relentless.

Once she was safe, Brit would contact her parents and explain. Tears filled her eyes. A conversation by phone was a poor substitute for doing it in person. She'd miss them and her brother. Brit would never forget them. But she'd have to forget she was ever Brit Gentry.

Well, the Gentry part was easy. It was more of who she was as a person, her job in law enforcement, which she'd never have again. Her brows furrowed. She'd have to change her first name, too. Brit rubbed her temples. She'd never done anything illegal in her life. How in the hell were they going to survive?

She snorted and shook her head. Colt had been an Army Ranger. If anyone knew how to survive, it was him. It would help if they had cash to live on, and her hundred and twenty bucks wouldn't get them far. They needed capital, which meant they'd be visiting her bank on their way out. She was withdrawing every dollar. She sure as hell couldn't start using her debit and credit cards. Although eleven thousand wasn't a fortune, it would be enough to live off until they could figure their Canadian citizenship. She wouldn't delude herself into thinking that would be a legal transaction.

Footsteps shuffled, the front door swinging open. "Brit?"

Shit! Brit's heart leapt in her throat.

Relax. Colt would have seen Andi pull up. Brit hoped he had enough sense to stay upstairs. They couldn't risk an altercation with her. For all she could tell, Brit was doing laundry. It was a normal chore. Andi wouldn't know they were planning to leave. She hadn't even packed their food. Brit eyed the pack on the floor and slid it under the opening of the center island that faced away.

"Hey, how was work?" Brit tried to sound cheerful.

"Fine." Andi marched into the kitchen, wearing her olive-colored training uniform and agency-issued Glock on her hip. She glared at the ceiling and the sound of Colt's footsteps overhead. "I have to be back this morning at nine."

"Have you heard any more about the manhunt for Colt?"

"No." Andi swung around and scowled. "Noticed a nice big ding in my porch ceiling, though."

"Guess you should be calling out your GC on that." *Or admit you've been watching us.*

Andi huffed. "*My* G. . ." Her mouth fell open, and then she snapped it shut.

Go ahead. Give yourself up.

Andi knew Colt had done it. She also knew he cracked the frame of her bedroom door if she'd reviewed the tape from last night.

Andi tapped the counter with an agitated finger and dropped her head. "I should have told you about the security cameras."

"*Oh*, you want to be transparent now." Brit gave her a lift of her brow.

Andi leaned over the counter. "I don't know what type of kinky games you were playing last night, but he can't go around busting my house up."

"Jealous someone other than you is having sex?" Brit slung back, her fingers tightening on the gold band.

"What'd you say?" Andi nailed her with a pair of steel-blue eyes.

Brit chewed the inside of her mouth. If Andi wanted a cat fight, she was going to get one. "How are your reflexes?" Brit tossed the band at her.

"Wh-what's this?" Andi bobbled it before catching it in her hand.

"Colt found it under your bed."

Andi gazed at it, her eyes widening and filling with alarm. "Ah . . . he . . . you both have been here before. You helped put the bedframe together."

Nice try.

The woman had been spying on them for the last twenty-four hours and made no apologies for it other than to say, "I should have told you." Damn straight she should have told them and turned it off while they were living here. The woman was sick. Thank God Colt had slammed the bedroom door shut last night. Otherwise Miss Voyeur would have been sitting back with a bowl of popcorn, watching them like some love scene in a movie.

Screw it.

Brit didn't care how pissed off or violated Andi felt. "Colt found it under your bed in your St. Michaels condo."

Confusion lit her face. "He was in *my home*?" Her dark brows snapped together.

"Don't you dare get an attitude with me, Andi. You were sleeping with *my* husband."

Andi gnawed her lip. "Because he was unhappy."

"Oh my *God*. That makes it right?" Brit snatched up a pair of underwear and folded it, placing it on top of the jeans, tears filling her eyes. "You are supposed to be my friend. Friends." She pointed an accusing finger at her. "*No*. Best friends don't sleep with other best friends' husbands." Brit's shoulders began to shake. *Damn it*. She was going to cry.

"I'm sorry." Andi came around the counter. "I never planned for it to happen." She put her arms around Brit.

Brit jerked away. "I hated him. Now I hate you." Tears streamed down her face, and she grabbed at her front pockets for the Kleenex she'd used earlier to blow her nose. She pulled it out, the navy blue thing falling to the floor.

Andi scooped it up. "What's this?"

Brit snatched it back. "I found it in your dyer." Her fingers rubbed the raised little sail design. She'd touched the same imprint before. Where and when had that been? Like a rewind button, she concentrated until that switch flipped in her brain. Her life began to play back frame by frame: the last few days with Colt, the pileup in the fog, her interrogation, the shooting, the boating accident.

That was where it stopped, and Brit began to relive that night with a newfound sense of clarity.

Seth cursed and stomped his foot on the deck, ignoring the wind change and the shift of the boat. "You'd think a thousand dollar jacket would fuckin' zip," he groused and jerked at the zipper.

Brit's heart thrummed in her chest, wind swirling her hair and the splash of fat raindrops hitting her face and hands. Any second he was going to explode. There wouldn't be anywhere for her to hide if he did. "I got it." She came around the boom and grabbed one side of his jacket and the zipper, trying to slip it into the other end. Her wet fingers trembled. Just go in, *please*. She focused on that stupid little zipper pull with its pretentious little sail taunting her. The metal locked in. She sighed and pulled up the zipper.

Brit's breath caught, cold terror spreading through her chest. Something rocked Brit's shoulder.

"What's wrong with you?" Andi's lips thinned. "I have no clue where it came from."

Brit gulped. She did and her mind raced. "I-I'm sorry. I just need some time to work through everything." Like the kitchen—granite counters, the Viking cooktop. "He bought this. Didn't he?"

She shook her head. "Just the renovations."

Right. The check to the builder—correction, remodeler—in Cambridge. She guessed the department had no idea what was really going on inside this clapboard turn-of-the-century home that, as she recalled, had gone for a modest two hundred and fifty K.

Andi was just as screwed as Brit if they ever found out.

"You're not going to make trouble for me with the brass." She set Seth's wedding band on the counter, placing her hand on her service weapon.

Brit backed up.

Andi took a step closer. "You messed everything up."

"I *did*?" Brit fisted her hands. "You're crazy." She eyed the gun, under Andi's palm, that remained in its holster and regretted her last words.

Now would be a really good time for Colt to come down with *his* gun. She should have remembered her promise to be that highly trained cop Colt and, it would appear, she needed right about now. She should have tucked her firearm into her waistband, instead of leaving it on the nightstand upstairs. She should have avoided a confrontation when she was unarmed. But this was her best friend who had an affair with her husband. She expected harsh words, anger, resentment, and going their separate ways because as much as Brit wanted to wear her big girl panties and forgive her, she couldn't.

"You were never adventurous." Andi laughed, the sound mocking. "In *bed*."

Brit took another step backward, trying to put more space between them, shocked and revolted that Andi would bring up something so personal. "This is not a conversation we need to have."

"Yes, it is!" Tears filled Andi's eyes. "You were always the one people gravitated toward."

"That's not true." Andi was striking with her tall, voluptuous figure and glossy hair. "You're beautiful and smart."

"He loved me, wanted to be with me."

"I would have given him a divorce."

"But you wouldn't stop digging."

Brit beaded in on her. "What are you talking about?"

"The money, Brit. Your financial disclosure investigation. It was only a matter of time before you found out about the artifacts."

"You knew?"

"Yeah," she said with a smile, like she was proud of what Seth had done.

"A soldier died because of what Seth did, *Andi.* Colt went to prison. He was innocent."

She shrugged. "Maybe he shouldn't have threatened Seth in Afghanistan."

Brit jerked her head back in disgust. "I don't even know who you are anymore."

Andi whipped her gun out of her holster.

"Whoa." Brit's hands went up, her chest tightening. "Seriously? You're going to draw down on me?"

"It should have been you that night."

Brit's mind reeled. Seth had said the same thing when she had him within inches of the boat.

Oh my God. Brit's legs shook. "He was trying to kill *me.*" Her voice was little more than a whisper.

"*We* were trying to kill you." She leveled her gun at Brit's head with a sick, sadistic smile. Andi almost reminded her of a female Joker the way her lips stretched. "Colt would have been better off in prison and never knowing Brit Gentry."

Real fear trickled to every part of Brit's body.

Andi was going to kill them both.

Chapter Thirty-Nine

VERY NERVE ENDING IN COLT'S BODY TINGLED WITH apprehension. He should have gone straight down, but at the time, he assumed it wasn't his place to intervene. It was Brit's deal if she wanted to have one final showdown and let Andi know she'd done her wrong.

He'd had his with the two-faced, lying dentist Dr. Steven Dooley—chucked a few chairs around in his office and messed up his desk. Dana wasn't worth him getting slapped with assault if he'd slugged the son of a bitch.

Judging from the non-conversational tones filtering upstairs, it was heated. But it was Andi's last volley, her quivering, desperate voice filling the foyer while he descended the stairs—*we were trying to kill you*—that had him going into full-on assault mode.

Although who would take him seriously in his tighty-whities and tube socks—the rest of his clothes were still in the dryer. He grimaced and shook his head. Only for Brit would he be going commando, literally.

Colt edged his way down the wall leading from the stairs, his footfalls undetectable. A smile curled his lips. He was still cursing the underwear, but it turned out socks were a good tactical move. Andi was a trained assassin, which meant she had the advantage of an acute ear.

He already knew she was armed when she'd gotten out of an unmarked cruiser, wearing the same tactical training uniform from the other day with her Glock holstered at her side.

Judging by the inflection in her voice, she was unstable at best. At worst, minutes, if not seconds, from pulling the trigger.

With his semiautomatic out in front, he peeked around the abutment of the wall leading into the kitchen, then swung back.

Shit. She was locked and loaded with Brit trapped against the back counter.

Ah, hell, that's not good.

He should just take the shot.

Sweat pooled between Colt's shoulder blades. He wiped his brow with his upper arm, keeping his eye on Hall. Colt's gaze veered toward Brit, and his gut clenched. Her beautiful brown eyes were fixated on Andi's gun, very deadly, and pointed at her center mass.

Damn it. She should have had her weapon on her. Not left on the nightstand and now shoved in his backpack that sat on the bottom of the stairs.

Brit glanced toward the ceiling, probably wondering where the hell he was, and then narrowed in on Hall. "So what was the plan? I think if you are going to end my life, you owe me that much." Brit's voice cracked.

Colt came around the corner and drew down.

Brit's eyes widened. "*Tell me.*"

Come on, Brit, let me take the shot. He jerked his head, his meaning clear—*move left or right. But get out of the line of fire.* He was a marksman, but it had been years since he'd shot a gun. If he missed, he could hit Brit. She wasn't making a move in either direction because—he'd hazard a guess here—she wanted to know why the two people who were supposed to love her most would plot to kill her.

He wanted to know, too. But not enough to risk her life.

Colt pinned her with a steely gaze that could shake the resolve of a hardened Taliban fighter. She wouldn't budge. He shook his head and moved back to his position behind the wall where he could still keep them in his sights.

Brit took a step closer. "We've known each other since we were kids. You were the sister I never had. I told you how I felt about Seth. You knew I hadn't loved him in a long time. You could have come to me. Told me. I would have given him a divorce."

Andi's shoulders sagged. "You wouldn't let it go." The despondency in her voice told Colt that Andi really wanted no part of killing her childhood friend.

"So, what, I was to be your fall guy? I had no choice but to keep investigating him. It was either that or lose my job and my freedom."

"I didn't want to do it." Andi began to sob, her arms shaking. She pulled them in against her sides, the gun pointed in a downward position. "He made me." She wiped her face on her shoulder. "Like he's making me now." Her words came out on a jagged cry, and she jerked her arms forward.

Colt aimed for her heart and squeezed off a round. The air around him exploded, reverberating off the walls. Hall's body arched. Her knees hit first, the gun clattering to the floor before her head smacked the hardwood.

Brit groaned and reached for her. Colt was on her in seconds. "We gotta go." He seized her arm, dragging her past Hall's body, and scooped up her backpack next to the center island.

"I can't leave her." Brit tried to pull away.

Colt's grip tightened. "It was either her or you."

Her face crumpled, tears streaming down her face, and she nodded. "I need her keys."

He released her and kept his gun trained on Hall. He'd missed his mark. She wasn't moving. Didn't mean she still wasn't alive.

Brit checked Hall's pockets and came up with a ring of keys. "Got it."

"Take this." He handed her the backpack he'd snagged under the counter and his gun and grabbed his jeans and a flannel shirt off the center island and slipped them on. He took the gun back. "Get the clothes." Colt motioned Brit past the stairs where he stepped into his boots, lacing them while she jammed an undershirt and extra pair of socks in her pack. He then lifted his off the floor. "You have *your* keys?"

Brit reached into a side pocket of her pack, pulling them out. They cleared the front door and flew down the stairs, his shirt open and flapping against his chest.

"Take the keys." Brit tossed them to him. "Start it up. I'm right behind you." She tore across the driveway and swung open the door to Andi's cruiser. Brit looked inside and then popped the trunk. She took a small box that looked to be ammo and slung a black bulletproof vest over her shoulder before snatching a small duffel and . . . *Shit*. Andi's rifle that looked locked and loaded.

Colt jumped in and threw the packs in the back, starting the truck. Brit got in weighted down, breathing hard, her head dropping against the seat back.

He peeled wheels. "We need to stop for gas. *Shit*." He banged the steering wheel. "I forgot the map."

"We don't need one. We're going back to the lake." She set the ammo in the footwell, tossing the vest and duffel in the back, then checked the slide to the rifle.

"*No way in hell*." He hit the brake.

"*Go*," she shouted. "I'll explain on the way."

Colt hit the gas and headed toward Route 50. "What, what do you need from *that* house?" He jerked his head toward her. "I just killed a cop, Brit."

"She had a pulse. But it was faint."

"Great. If she lives, she can ID me." He took a sharp right. "What's going on?"

Brit placed the butt of the rifle down into the footwell, leaning the barrel against the seat cushion. She then pushed back and lifted her bottom from the seat, digging into her front jean pocket. She held out a small navy blue object.

"It's a zipper pull to a pricey Musto sailing jacket. I found it in Andi's dryer before she got there."

"Let me see it." Colt held out his hand.

She dropped it into his palm. "I hadn't put it together until Andi showed up." She turned in her seat. "Seth bought one of those jackets. He wore it that day on the bay. If he drowned with it on, how did a zipper pull identical to the one he was wearing end up in Andi's dryer?"

Colt held out his hand, his eyes widening on the raised logo of a sail. "Son of a *bitch*." It had to be a good two miles in rough seas. Not that it wasn't possible, and Andi's B&B would be the logical place after his plan went afoul.

"Ah, see, you're following." Brit plucked the zipper pull out of his palm and held it up, eyeballing it. "He's alive, and I'll bet you he's been living inside the pool complex behind that freakin' door with the stone."

Colt thought back on Andi's last words. *Like he's making me now.*

"We were getting too close." A determined smile curled Brit's lips. "She was in love with him. So she says. I wouldn't be surprised to find he put her up to offering us sanctuary to get us out of that house. She could keep an eye on us with her security cameras, and he could continue to do what he's done for the past seven months until he figured out his next move. Or I got indicted, and you fled to Canada."

"I wasn't leaving without you." Colt gave her a knowing look and exited onto Route 50. "You think he had a direct feed?" Meaning they'd be fighting the clock to catch him with the five-hour drive they had ahead of them, if he'd been watching in real time. It all depended upon the angle of the camera, too. He hadn't found an audio cable. Seth wouldn't have heard shit.

"No, I don't think so. It sounded like it was all on her computer at home. Either way, they were keeping in close contact." Brit pursed her lips and sat back in her seat. "I didn't ask. But I'm thinking Andi initiated that call to my mom. Probably at Seth's request. She said the door was open to the pool house."

Which wasn't out of the realm of possibility since the damn door didn't always catch.

Colt tapped the steering wheel as he worked through the sequence of events. "She'd left it open when she ran out."

Brit turned in her seat. "But I heard a door click." She raised her brows at him. "That cologne . . . it was way too strong to have been coming from your clothes. He was in the foyer with her."

"It's gotta be fake. We just couldn't find the button."

Brit shook her head and frowned. "He really did a number on her. Highly trained and yet she walks into a building at night with an open door. It could have been a trap."

"Like she said, he was making her do it. She was in deep."

"Which means he would have told her to report back to him once she'd killed us. I don't know what the timetable would have been. But we're going to be close."

Colt hit the gas.

"*No.*" Brit patted his thigh. "They're not taking you away from me for a stinking traffic citation. Five to ten over. That's it. Anything more than that and they *will* pull you over."

He snorted. "You would know."

"Yes, I would." She chuckled while putting her hair in a ponytail and then reached for something in the backseat. She stuck her MSP cap on her head, pulling her blond ponytail through the back. "If he's onto us, he's probably on foot, unless he's stashed a car somewhere." She winked at him and smiled.

It was bright and confident and on a woman he could never live without. He reached out and grabbed her hand. "I love you."

"I love you, too." She gave his fingers a squeeze. "This is our chance to clear you and me. We have to go back."

Problem was it had nothing to do with the Crenshaw shooting. If they went back, and he still wasn't convinced they should, it would only solve part of their problems.

"I can't do it." He was going to Canada, and she was coming with him. He pointed toward the GPS in the dash. Hell if he knew how to work it, and from what she'd said, they had to be in park. Colt pulled over to the side of the road.

"The hell you can't." Her pretty face twisted in confusion. "What are you doing?"

"I can't do it." He gave her a pointed look. "You're still facing possible manslaughter charges."

Brit blew through her nose like a little bull getting ready to charge. "You deserve to be exonerated."

"No. Now put in the directions for Montreal."

She hung her arm back along the seat, and her eyes darted behind them. "Damn it. You're a pain in my ass," she grumbled under her breath.

More than she knew. If he recalled, this was that state trooper route. Colt turned off the ignition and pocketed the keys. "Then I guess we're at an impasse."

Chapter Forty

SERIOUSLY. TEARS WELLED UP IN BRIT'S EYES. HE WAS going to make her cry.

Colt bent his head. "What are you doing?"

"Nothing, *okay*." Brit wiped at her eyes, emotion welling up in her chest. "Andi's dead. Seth's alive. If it weren't for the artifacts, I'd give anything to reverse the order."

"*Shit.*" Colt scrubbed his face and leaned over, his arm coming around her shoulders. "Don't cry. I know this sucks. If I could have avoided shooting her—as much as I don't like her," he groused, "I would have. You know that."

Brit nodded and lifted her tearstained face to him. "We're both highly trained. We can do this and not raise suspicion. He doesn't want to be caught by police, either." She wept, her breath catching. "If we fail, we're still heading north."

"Northwest." He wiped away a tear from her cheek with his thumb. "So what's the plan? We go up there, find him, capture him, and find the artifacts, if they're even left. Then what?"

She hadn't planned that far ahead. She shrugged.

"Come on, Brit, think this through. As much as I want to be vindicated, I can't risk your freedom."

"I haven't been indicted yet." Brit sniffed. "I'm willing to risk it. It should be my choice, not yours."

Colt removed his arm, placing his hands on the steering wheel. He stared out the windshield. "You're all that matters to me."

"Then do this for me."

He shook his head. "If we corner him, find the artifacts, it doesn't do a bit a good *unless* law enforcement is there to witness the takedown, him in possession of the goods, and any incriminating statements he might make. Otherwise it's my word against his."

"He faked his death, though—built a house with a panic room."

He gave her a dubious sideways glance. "The death part I'll give you, but the rest is unproven."

"You know it exists."

Colt pinched the bridge of his nose, taking a deep breath.

"Come on." Brit grabbed his arm. "No one fakes their own death unless they have a really good reason."

"The bastard tried to kill you, Brit. Dumbass fell out instead." He laughed and shook his head. "You put a huge wrinkle in their plans. By now he'd be the sole owner of two luxurious homes, a sailboat, and an investor in some popular upscale bed-and-breakfast on the shore."

"He still would have had the financial disclosure to deal with."

"It was yours, initiated by your agency. They might have alerted the feds, but he would have paid someone to make it all go away. Or, at the very least, had time to procure phony documentation of his so-called inheritance and no one would have been the wiser. Instead his life has been reduced to four walls."

"Meaning he's desperate."

"That's what I'm afraid of."

"We're wasting time."

He tapped the steering wheel, then pulled the keys from his pocket. "I'll head that way." He turned on the ignition. "But you're going to call your lawyer and find out what's going on with this indictment. He told you thirty-six hours. It's been almost forty-eight. Something's up." He pulled out onto Route 50, heading west.

Brit snuffled and wiped her face on her shirt, then reached for her backpack in the rear seat. Colt was right. She couldn't help but feel the state's attorney was delaying his decision. That could be either good or bad. But if it gave her a few more days, they could accomplish this mission first. She was still free to move about the state, granted, not with a fugitive. But if they could prove his innocence, then they were making headway.

As much as she wanted to have a life with Colt and have his babies, she didn't want to have to look over her shoulder. If they discovered their true identities, she'd lose more than Colt—she'd lose her children, too.

Brit hit her speed-dial for Jay and placed it on speaker. "Mr. Dahlgren, please. It's Brit Gentry." She rolled her lips in. She'd been kind of short with him the last few times they spoke.

"Ah, you must want something." His irritated voice filled the interior of the truck.

Brit gnawed her bottom lip. He knew her well. "Any news on the indictment?"

"Funny you should call. Now it's not until next week. My sources tell me they have new evidence."

Brit's shoulders sagged. "To nail their case shut."

"Now, I didn't say that." He shuffled some papers. "You know anything about this fugitive from Leavenworth, Colt Rivers? They linked a car he stole to that pileup you were in."

Brit gave Colt a knowing look. "If he was the one from the compact, I couldn't locate him."

"Gotcha." The tapping of—she guessed his pen—filtered through her phone. "I guess you can remain at the lake for a few more days. That's where you are, right?" He sounded skeptical.

"Yeah." She grimaced. But in five hours she wouldn't be lying. She smiled at Colt. "It's been what I've needed."

"All right then. I've got another call and, Brit?"

"Yes."

"Nothing's going on that as your lawyer I should know about, right?"

Brit bit down on her lip. "Nope. Just call me when you know something."

"You bet." He clicked off.

Brit dropped the phone in her lap and leaned into the seat back, her eyes closing. "Please say you'll agree to try this first."

A warm, strong hand clasped hers. "My heart tells me I should say no. But my gut's telling me different. I don't ever want to be separated from you. I don't want to lose you in the end, especially after building a life together."

She nodded, her eyes fluttering open. "We won't alert the police until we have him and the artifacts." Brit sat up. "Take the far right lane onto the bay bridge."

Colt changed lanes. "And if he doesn't have the goods on him, we walk away from this thing."

Brit smiled with relief and squeezed his hand. "Deal."

Colt drove by the McHenry State Police Barrack. The same twinge of uncertainty twitching his ass cheek like the first time he'd driven by five days ago. Injured and traveling with a woman he'd never met before, he'd felt the most alone in his thirty-eight years. He smiled at Brit's sleeping form next to him. She probably had every intention—now that he knew who she really was—of killing him in those first few hours.

He chuckled. *Make love not war.*

He'd give anything to change course, get them over the Canadian border, find some way to legally marry her, and make those babies. He always wanted a family.

And she was the only woman for him. She was beautiful and fierce and, it would seem, a strategist. Must come from being in law enforcement and the elite tactical team she belonged to.

During the drive up, they'd discussed "the storming of Memory Maker" as she dubbed it.

He was all for making light of their circumstances, but when it came down to it, this little operation could mean the end of this bit of freedom and a love he'd only experience once in his lifetime. He didn't want to give either one of them up. He'd said it before, and he meant it. She was it for him. No matter where they ended up—him back in prison serving out five more plus whatever else they threw at him for escape, stealing a car, taking Brit hostage. Although knowing her, she'd tell them they'd joined forces from day one.

Oh, shit.

Colt's shoulders dropped. He'd forgotten about Hall. He'd get life for killing a state trooper, maybe death if Maryland still upheld the death penalty. He'd have to hope, in the end, they could connect Andi to Seth.

Didn't matter. He was in.

He made the left on to Marsh Hill Road. He should wake her. The house was about three miles away. Colt reached over and caressed her cheek. She slept serenely next to him with long dark lashes dusting her ivory complexion and the most kissable lips he'd ever encountered. He loved her.

Shit.

Colt slowed the truck down, squinting through the windshield. Was that the neighbor—what was her name—Melanie? No, Maddie Trusdale flagging him down?

"Brit." He shook her shoulder. "Wake up."

She stretched and did that mewling thing that totally turned him on.

"Hey." He shook her again but harder. "Wake up."

"What?" Her eyes fluttered open, and she sat up, blinked, sucking in air. "Is that the neighbor lady?"

"Yeah." Colt gripped the steering wheel. "What do you think she wants?"

Brit rolled her eyes at him. "Hell if I know."

"Should I stop?"

She shrugged. "Kind of rude not to."

Right. He guessed that would be the neighborly thing to do and not raise any suspicions where Maddie Trusdale was concerned.

Colt did a double take. "Is that a phone in her hand?"

Brit leaned into the dash. "Looks like it."

"Great," he mumbled under his breath.

Brit placed her hand on his shoulder. "Just stop. I'll talk to her."

Colt pulled over and rolled down his window.

Brit leaned over. "Hi, what's up?"

"*Oh, my, God.* You're Brit Gentry. I didn't put it together before. I just called the police."

Holy fuck.

Colt hit the gas and rolled up the window.

"Whoa, whoa, whoa, *whoa.*" Brit gripped the dash. "What are you *doing?*"

He jerked his head at her. "You kidding me? She called the cops."

Brit angled back. "Look, she's still waving. Back up."

"Hell no!"

She breathed through her nose, looking like that little bull ready to put up a fight. "Back up the damn truck, Colt." Brit glanced behind her. "If she called the cops about us, I don't think she'd still be waving and running toward us."

"You're serious." Colt checked the rearview. Damn if she wasn't. "Okay, so maybe I overreacted."

She gave him a look that said he needed to get a grip. "Ya think?"

Colt let off the accelerator and braked, putting the truck in reverse. He stopped when he got close enough and let Trusdale walk up to the window.

"Hey, what happened?" she said breathlessly.

Colt clucked his tongue and gave her one of his best smiles. "Damnedest thing. The accelerator got stuck."

"Oh." Her brows furrowed. "I've heard of that happening."

"Let me do the talking," Brit whispered under her breath and leaned over. "So *why* did you call the police?"

"Okay, so don't freak out or anything." Her expression changed like she just remembered something. "Oh, and I'm sorry about your husband, Seth. Arnold and I met him several times, even had drinks one night around your pool. But that was last summer before the accident."

"Thank you. I appreciate that."

She waved a dismissive hand. "We're safe, though. I called the barrack."

"Safe? Safe from what, Maddie?"

"Oh, right, I was walking Brutus. He's my little pug, and I saw a man coming from your pool house. I didn't think much of it until he turned toward us." Her phone rang, and she checked the caller and put up a finger. "I have to take this, one sec."

Colt dropped back in the seat and stared at Brit, his heart jackhammering in his chest. "We gotta go. The cops will be here any minute."

She patted the air. "I know. Just give me one minute." Brit leaned over right as Trusdale hung up

Trusdale grimaced and then gave a nervous laugh when she saw Colt glaring at her. "Sorry. Anyway, I think someone has been impersonating Seth. The guy looked just like him."

Colt threw open the door and got out. "Where'd he go?"

Maddie backed up, her hand pressing against her chest. "Oh, my. He-he . . ."

Shit. Now he was scaring her.

Brit jerked open her door and came around the front of the truck. "Maddie. It's okay. We know about the man. That's why we're here." Brit put her arm around Trusdale's shoulders. "If you know who I am, you know I'm also a state trooper."

She looked from Colt to Brit. "I never believed for one minute you shot that man in cold blood."

Brit nodded. "I appreciate that. I didn't. I'm only hoping the state's attorney sees it that way." Brit then turned Trusdale toward the mountaintop. "Now this man. Which way did he go?"

"Up Overlook Pass."

"What was he wearing?"

"All black with some sort of pack on his back."

"How long ago did you see him?"

Good thing Brit was interviewing her. She would have run screaming up the mountainside if Colt was asking the questions—he was so jacked up.

Trusdale tapped her finger to her lips. "I'd say about fifteen minutes ago."

"Okay." Brit slipped her hand in Trusdale's and gave it a friendly shake. "You did a good job, but I want you to go inside. I don't know what this guy's intentions are. We don't want him doubling back if he's up to no good with you here by yourself."

"But I told the troopers I'd meet them here."

"They'd want to ensure your safety first. If they need you, they'll knock on your door."

Colt eyed Trusdale's phone. If they got separated, they had no way to communicate. He pulled Brit aside. "Ask her for her phone."

Brit gave him a questioning look.

"To talk," he whispered.

Brit faced her. "Maddie, can we borrow your phone?"

"Ahh . . ." Her fingers tightened on it.

"It will only be used for police business."

"Ah, sure." She handed the phone to Brit and waved down her driveway. "I'll be inside if you need me."

Brit gave her a sweet smile. "You've been great. Go on. I'll watch to make sure you get in safely, and lock your door."

"I will." She turned, then swung back. "Oh, my, I forgot I tied Brutus to a tree by the house." She scurried down the hill.

"Make sure you bring him in, too," Brit called down to her, craning her neck until Trusdale slipped inside with the pug and shut her front door. Brit ran around the front of the truck. "Get in."

Colt jumped in with her, both slamming their doors. "Where to?"

She angled her head back the way they'd come. "We have to turn around. The road's down and on your left. It takes you through a development and into the Fork Run recreational area."

"What's that?"

"The turn's coming up." She leaned forward. "Here, make the left. They've got a man-made white-water rafting course and trails."

"You think that's where he's headed?"

"If he's started up the mountain, it's the only thing. He knows the area well. He's done a lot of that team building with his clients. Ya know, rock climbing, obstacle courses." She sighed and fell back in her seat. "Yeah, he knows it like the back of his hand."

"How about you?" Colt hit the gas.

"Not so much. But we've got the truck, and I can stop and grab a map of Fork Run. We'll make up some time there. And"—she grabbed his arm—

"I'm counting on your Army Ranger skills to track him."

Colt snorted. "I wish it were that simple."

"Make it simple." She nailed him with a pair of serious brown eyes. "No more jokes about Operation Memory Maker. He's here and, it appears, he has the artifacts on him. There's no leeway. Once we flush him out, I can hit him from a hundred yards, depending on my line of sight."

"You can't *kill* him." Shit, he needed the son of a bitch alive.

"I'm not. I only want to stop him from giving us the slip. Eventually, he'll find his way out and over the mountain. Then we've lost him, maybe for good."

Chapter Forty-One

*A*BULLET WHISTLED PAST BRIT'S HEAD.

Shit.

She ducked down behind an outcropping of rocks that led off one of the hiking trails in Fork Run. They'd driven as far as they could before going on foot. Brit tightened the sling to her rifle and placed the stock into her shoulder, raising the barrel. Deciding to split up made sense. They could cover more ground.

Using the scope, Brit scanned the area in front. The snow had melted while they'd been gone. Lots of tree trunks, wide enough for a man to hide behind, fanned out in front. Brit rocked forward on her right foot, trying to get a good plant. Standing was the worst position for a sniper. It was hard to get a steady shot off.

Her phone rumbled in her back jean pocket. Brit shook her head. She didn't need to view the screen to know who was calling. She repositioned her rifle and reached behind, pulling her phone out. The name Maddie Trusdale was backlit on her phone. It vibrated again, and she took the call.

"You okay?" Colt's rattled voice blared into her ear.

Brit pulled the phone away, giving him—or rather the phone—an exasperated look before putting it up to her ear. "Yes. Relax. It came from the"—she peered down at the compass she'd pulled out of Andi's gear, sitting on a cool matting of leaves—"northwest."

"What are the chances?"

"It's him." Brit checked her watch—3:17 p.m. They had a few hours of daylight left. "Any ideas on how to flush him out?"

"We pin him. Keep moving in the direction of the fire and engage him."

"Until he runs out of bullets."

"Or makes a mistake."

Brit stiffened. A lot of flying lead, all within close proximity, was never a good thing. "Watch for friendly fire."

"Roger that. And keep your line open," he snapped.

Brit smiled. He was worried about her. She'd warned him before they got out of the truck that they were splitting up. He argued the dangers of a woman in combat until she reminded him she was probably better trained than he was, considering his little four year hiatus.

"Roger that." She ended the call and shoved the phone in her jean pocket. He didn't have to worry about her having a panic attack, either. Brit was beyond that now. She knew she hadn't pulled the trigger that night. That was enough for her.

The only concern she had was for the hikers and those on four-wheelers. Just because she hadn't seen one didn't mean they weren't relatively close. That was the other thing that bothered her. Maddie had called the state police. They would have interviewed her by now. They knew about the man in black with the backpack and Brit and Colt who were actively searching for him.

If nothing else, Maddie Trusdale loved drama. She'd give them every detail.

They'd be here soon. Her only fear was for Colt. He was still considered a fugitive. That's why she wanted to make damn sure they had Seth with the goods. That wasn't the case, at least not yet. The presence of the MSP could also complicate things. Troopers entering the woods with a gun battle in full swing could cause confusion and an accidental death. Something she didn't want on her conscience.

She should call-out the S.T.A.T.E. Team herself. She had all their personal cells in her phone. Brit dropped her head. Deep Creek was five hours away. Besides that, she didn't have their training schedule. They could be anywhere in the state of Maryland. Knowing her luck, it wouldn't be anywhere close to western Maryland.

A bullet ricocheted off the top of the boulder she was behind. Judging by the sound and the accuracy of the shot, the bastard had a high-powered rifle and a scope.

Seth knew where she was. She needed to even the odds. Brit scooped up the compass, the edge of Andi's bulletproof vest digging into her stomach, and cursed. It was the one thing Colt wouldn't budge on—not that she didn't believe in the practicality and safety of body army. But this one had been measured to fit Andi's voluptuous body. It was too big.

With her compass in one hand and the barrel of her rifle in the other, she skirted the giant rock and used the trunks of trees for cover while she moved in the direction of the last shot. Brit kept a steady eye on the needle of the compass and the ground. Last thing she needed was to trip and fall. She'd already done that this week. Her ankle didn't bother her. But a re-injury could slow her down or get her killed.

That was what she struggled with. She was going against everything she'd been trained to do. She needed a perimeter—two highly trained assassins weren't enough. There was a good probability that Seth would slip through them. What they needed was a heavy law enforcement presence to keep Seth accounted for and to protect those innocent bystanders by keeping them out of the line of fire.

Ugh! Even if she came upon a hiker, the only thing she was wearing that identified her as a Maryland state trooper was her badge she had attached to her belt. But from a distance they'd only be narrowing in on the rifle. Brit stepped around a wide stump in her boots, jeans, and long sleeve shirt, snagging several briars. She pushed forward until the clinging barbs released their angry grip.

A tree branch clipped her cap. Brit grabbed it, smashing it back on her head. Okay, well, she did have her sniper cap with the MSP patch stitched to it. Most people would get that she was a trooper—she hoped.

Several more shots rang out, and Brit scooted behind a large trunk, keeping her body tucked tight, her rifle at the ready. The *whip whap* of bullets hit several trees to her left and right.

Son of a bitch.

He was close. Quiet and close. That bothered her, too. He was never at a lack for words. He was messing with her. Brit clenched her jaw. It was like he was the grim reaper—no words—just a dark presence of death.

Brit chewed the inside of her mouth. There was a lot she had on her mind and on the edge of her tongue. Her head fell back against the tree and she growled. Yelling at him, because that's exactly what she wanted to do, would only give up her position.

She took a deep breath. She hadn't received one phone call from Colt or heard any volleys coming from the southeast quadrant they'd mapped out as the direction he should have been heading. Juggling her rifle, Brit slipped the phone out of her pocket. She hit the new speed-dial for Maddie's phone and put it up to her ear. It rang then clicked into the singsong voice of Maddie's recorded greeting. Brit clicked off, her chest tightening. *Damn it.* He should have answered. She'd give him a few minutes to respond before she jumped to conclusions.

She needed to get to higher ground—eye level wasn't cutting it. She'd heard Seth talking to ASCI, the adventure sports folks here at Fork Run about some team building rappelling weekend a while back. There had to be some high ground here somewhere. She needed to beat Seth to it.

Shoving the compass in her front pocket, she then placed her rifle out in front and zigzagged through the woods. To the left the ground shifted upward, and she followed the rise of the land until she came to a cave. Easing her way around the opening, she swung the barrel in, keeping her body away from the entrance. Something scurried inside. She hoped a chipmunk and not a bat. She shivered. They gave her the creeps.

Brit passed the cave and trudged through fresh fallen leaves, the scent of pine all around her. She turned in a three sixty, a heavy weight on her chest, trying to get her bearings. Everything looked the same, except for a towering gray rock formation jutting skyward about seventy-five feet away. Brit picked up the pace, her head on a swivel. A shot rang out behind her, and she ducked, still running until she stood in the shadow of the cliff, and hunkered down below it.

On her haunches, with her elbows resting on her knees—bone to bone—giving her maximum support, Brit leveled her rifle and looked through the scope, banking right then left.

Nothing.

She couldn't tell the trajectory of the bullet, but it came from out in front. Above was a sheer thirty-foot drop. A bitch to climb but a sniper's dream if she could reach the top.

A barrage of gunfire erupted, ricocheting overhead and kicking up dirt clods several yards out in front. He had her pinned.

Wherever Seth was, he knew her exact location. He'd missed her on purpose. One after another, bullets zinged past her. Brit kept her head down. If he was hoping she'd unload on him, he'd miscalculated. Unless she had a clear shot, she wasn't taking it.

Brit gnawed her bottom lip. She knew where she was—sorta. It was Colt's location that had her baffled. She'd joked about him being a rusty shot. She couldn't understand why she hadn't heard return fire coming from his location.

More bullets whizzed by, and then Brit's breath caught. Colt and Seth had fought together. They were like a pair of identical twins that could read each other's thoughts and movements—at least on the battlefield. What was Colt reading into Seth's?

Oh God, he wouldn't.

The dread of understanding sunk in, and it turned Brit's blood to ice.

Brit jerked her phone from her back pocket—no calls or texts from Maddie's phone. With shaking fingers, she hit redial. Brit waited. Her neighbor's voice came on, and Brit disconnected, her stomach churning.

She needed that high ground and now. She jammed the phone back into her pocket and took off running. She had a fair idea of what Colt was up to.

God, Colt, don't do me any favors. Don't do me any favors.

Valor was one thing, stupidity quite another.

Brit rushed up the steep incline, climbing over boulders. Her foot slid, her boot slipping into a crevice between two rocks. She gasped and placed her hands out in front to brace herself. Her palms hit first, then the rifle smacked hard, and she fell to her knees. The crunch of rock and bone colliding sent shock waves down her leg.

I can't be hurt. Oh, God. I can't be hurt.

With her ankle at an odd position, she turned her body, trying to free herself. The gunfire had stopped, and Brit worked like mad until her boot dislodged. Pulling herself up to a standing position, she put weight on her foot. *No pain.* She gripped the rifle and climbed like a cat, leaping from one rock to the other, higher and higher, the land below opening and expanding until she crested the top.

Brit got down on her belly, a layer of moss cushioning her. She set up her bipod. Something told her Seth had her exactly where he wanted her. Even with her rifle and the thick fiery treetops as cover, she felt wide open and exposed. More disconcerting were the bullets. He'd stopped shooting.

With the stock firm against her shoulder, Brit peered through her scope.

Everything stopped, except the pounding of her heart.

Chapter Forty-Two

"**L**OOKIE HERE, BABY GIRL, I'VE GOT LOVERBOY."
Gentry's taunting voice filtered through the trees, echoing.
Colt remained out in front with his hands clasped behind his head, his old buddy Seth—a few pounds heavier and looking rung out—using him as a shield and leveling a Ruger semiautomatic at the back of his skull.

Colt gritted his teeth. It wasn't like the son of a bitch caught him. He'd walked up to him with his hands high and tossed his gun at Gentry's feet to give Brit a fighting chance. He had a world of trust in her abilities as a sniper. She'd get to high ground and pick the bastard off.

Problem was Gentry knew it, and Colt would be his body armor unless he could outmaneuver him. The catch—Brit had to be above them looking down through her scope to know his intentions and react split second.

All Colt could do now was stall until she was in position. "Andi Hall tip you off?"

"About you screwing my wife?" He jabbed the gun into Colt's head.

Colt groaned. "Did you even give a shit about Hall, man? She's dead. You idiot, I had to put a bullet in her back thanks to you." He hocked up some mucous and spat, missing Gentry's expensive tactical black boot by millimeters. "You always were an asshole."

"And you always were a dick. All you had to do was shut your goddamned mouth and go along, and none of this would have happened.

You'd have been partying it up for the last four years as a rich man." Gentry cinched Colt's collar up, his breath hot against his face. "Nice of you to join my party, though."

"Didn't really have a choice." Colt jerked his head and gave Gentry a sideways glance. Dressed in black military fatigues with the same flashy smile and blond surfer dude hair, Colt wanted to bust him in his pretty boy mouth. "You look good for a corpse."

"Didn't plan on dying."

"Yeah, I heard. Brit outperformed you *and* outsmarted you."

Gentry clucked his tongue. "Shit happens. You just gotta know when to adjust and regroup. I'm a strategist."

"Oh, you're a real tactician all right. You killed your own man."

"Sullivan."

"Guess that doesn't bother you."

"Collateral damage."

"You *fucking* asshole." Colt pulled his hands apart, his fist making an upper cut when Gentry's gun clicked.

"Go ahead. I'll end this thing right now. Put your hands back on your head."

Colt's blood simmered, his chest tightening. "*You* killed him." He laced his fingers behind his head again, heat flooding his face. He'd never felt so powerless.

"Like I'm going to kill you once she gets us in her scope."

That was the plan, huh? Send Brit spiraling into a panic attack. One she might never recover from after seeing her lover shot in the head. It would be easy for Gentry to track her down in the woods and kill her then.

Well, the dumbass wouldn't know when Brit had him in her sights unless she engaged him. Brit was savvy. She wouldn't be goaded into talking to him. She'd take the shot and be done.

God, he hoped he was right for both their sakes.

"Brit!" Gentry called out in an agitated voice. "I don't have all day."

"She's not going to answer you, man. But she might shoot you between the eyes."

A laugh rolled up Gentry's chest. "You're fuckin' funny. The dumb bitch doesn't even know when she pulls the trigger these days. Doubt she's going to take the kill shot. She might hit the wrong target."

"Been keeping up on the news in your little climate controlled room in the pool house?"

"Keeping up on you mostly, pal. You remember old Zadran?"

"I remember what he said."

"Thought you'd find the whole thing poetic—the door between the living and the dead."

"Spooky, man—not poetic." If Gentry wanted to talk, he'd let him talk. In his sick mind, he was walking away from this thing. "Hall help you?"

"The woman was in love. She'd do anything for me."

"Even kill."

"Oh." He angled his head so Colt could see him better, a self-satisfied smirk on his face. "She already did that for me."

Already?

"But then you're here for the artifacts."

Those timeless pieces had landed him nine years' hard time. They were the reason he was here. He needed to remember that fact and not concern himself with the mutterings of a deranged man. But he did want to know about the artifacts, and Gentry's mind seemed crystal clear on that subject.

"Where are they?"

"You were hoping I still had them."

"Do you?"

"You see them?"

No. That bothered him. By Trusdale's account, Gentry had a black backpack. Colt assumed the spoils of war that were left would be inside. Seth must have stashed it here on the mountain. That sucked. Without them he'd be hard-pressed to prove his side of the story.

A twig snapped behind them. Gentry grabbed Colt's neck. "You're dead either way."

Great. No artifacts, a suicidal gunman surrounded by cops—at least he hoped they were hidden among the trees, listening to the smug bastard incriminate himself—and a counter-sniper he loved with all his heart, missing in action.

"Guess you're screwed, pal." Gentry gave a hard laugh. "Let me tell you how this is ending. I'm going to count backward from ten. At three I'm blowing a hole in your brain, and Brit, she's either gonna end up in a padded cell after witnessing your murder through the same scope she watched Crenshaw's, or she's gonna go to a prison cell for a murder she didn't commit." He chuckled. "A little payback for letting me drown."

Colt's gut clenched like a fist. He was only focused on two words—*same scope*.

What the hell?

In out, in out, in out. Seth's not going to kill Colt. Brit tried to clear her mind of any negative thoughts. They were talking. That was good. Heated at times but still talking.

She knew it. Brit didn't have to look through the scope the minute she got into position to know what Colt was up to. It was called exposing yourself to the enemy. There were a handful of heroic stories of servicemen—mostly Army Rangers—exposing themselves to the enemy to protect fellow comrades during the Afghan War.

She wouldn't have expected anything less of Colt Rivers.

And he was expecting *this* Gentry not to fall apart on him. She wouldn't. But she needed a clear target to take the kill shot before Seth killed Colt. Seth—the sicko—was only giving her time to get into place with her scope. Its zoom lens would give Brit an up close and personal view of Colt's murder.

If the son of a bitch thought she was going to flip out—Brit wiped the sweat above her lip—he had made a critical error. His skull would be the next to explode.

After that she didn't give a damn about anything else. Although it would have been nice to have a witness.

Brit's phone rumbled in her back pocket. *Shit.* Who would be texting her? It sure as hell wasn't Colt. Reaching back to her jean pocket, she kept her sights on Colt and Seth through the scope and pulled it out. She set the phone down in front of her in her prone position. Her heart rate increased.

CJ: We have your back. What's your location?

Brit's fingers trembled as she texted back.

Brit: Fork Run recreation, cliff in northwest quadrant. You?

Brit's tense shoulders leveled off. Was he here? But how . . . Another text popped up.

CJ: Southwest entrance. Can you make him?

Her fingers scrabbled across the screen.

Brit: 50 yards out. Dark-haired one is friendly

Brit's mind spun. She was on administrative leave. They knew that. But she'd never been suspended. She still had all her police powers and statewide authority that came from being a Maryland state trooper.

Cmd. Wallace: We're going to try and talk him down first.

Brit tensed all over again. She wanted them here, wanted their support, and it looked like she had it—her last call-out notwithstanding. But this was Colt, the man she loved. Worse, she was married to the perp. He was unpredictable and desperate. With the commander now on scene, she had to take orders, which also meant he was the only one who could give the green light to take Seth out.

"Seth, it's Lieutenant Todd Wallace. How you doing, buddy?" The steady, even-keeled voice of a man Brit respected and had known for years emanated through the rustling coppery-colored treetops. Todd Wallace had also met her husband of three years several times. The Seth Gentry her team had been introduced to during award ceremonies, annual softball tournaments, and holiday parties was a likeable guy. They'd never met the real man behind the façade, until today.

"Long story, Wallace!" Seth called out, his usual demanding tone, softening, almost reflective.

Brit looked through her scope. Colt was still out in front with Seth using his body as a shield. If she didn't know better, she'd think Colt had four legs. Seth was that well-hidden, except for the gun positioned at the back of Colt's skull.

Now that she could see with clarity.

Brit chewed her bottom lip. Finding her on a cliff with an eye through the scope of a .223 semiautomatic rifle with every intention of putting a bullet in her husband's brain—a husband who was supposed to have been dead for the last seven months—would raise a few questions and doubts, especially about her current state of mind. They hadn't asked. But they had to wonder about this unlikely triangle and how a man named Colt Rivers—a fugitive she advised was a good guy—fit into the equation.

How much intel did they have?

Her biggest concern was Colt. Losing him *would* put her over the edge. She wouldn't kid herself about that fact. This was a huge dilemma. That bastard Seth didn't even have the black backpack with him. At least not that she could see. They stood in an opening, in a thick carpeting of freshly fallen leaves. It wasn't deep enough to bury a bag. So where the hell was it? Without the artifacts they—she and Colt—would be scrambling to prove their case to her team.

"I've got time, son." The older, wiser voice of her commander floated on the crisp breeze. "I'd like for you to put down the gun. The command bus is parked up the road with a hot cup of coffee waiting. We can have that talk."

Colt said something to Seth. Judging by his expression, it was an earnest gesture of some kind. Brit's lips formed a pout. Colt was honorable and kind. He'd known Seth under the most extreme circumstances—war. Before the incident that changed everything between the two, they had to have shared that band of brethren.

"Wish that were possible, Wallace." Seth readjusted the gun, nudging it below Colt's jawbone with enough force Colt's head tipped back.

Brit couldn't breathe. She turned the bill of her cap around, her heart thundering. She checked her phone lying directly in front of her on the moss-covered ledge she'd spread out on—no texts. Brit released the phone and placed her cheek against the stock and breathed. She glanced away from the scope, only using her eye, trying to get the natural point of aim. She didn't want to muscle the rifle. She then let her rifle drift to its natural point of aim and gazed through the scope. The crosshairs were aligned, the reticle dead center on Colt's forehead.

Not good.

Come on, baby, make a move.

Colt had put himself in this position. He had a plan. Now would be a good time to share it with her, though. Time was a precious commodity they didn't have. Colt's jaw tensed.

Brit settled in, keeping her eye glued to the scope. Her present and future were tied up with that ruggedly good-looking man who had defied the odds to right a wrong. With his face rough with whiskers since they'd left the comforts of Memory Maker, he reminded her of that stranger on the highway five days ago. Only he was more than that to her now, and unlike the desperation flitting in his eyes back then, there was only a cool resolve.

Don't give up on me, baby.

Her team was with her somewhere in the woods below. It was both reassuring and frightening at the same time. They were law enforcement. Colt was still a fugitive.

"Ten."

Shit.

Brit kept her eye in line with the scope and breathed in, then out, trying to keep a natural airflow, and her muscles relaxed. She didn't need anything interfering with her concentration. She'd have to call the shot between the pause in her breaths. That shot was up to Colt.

"Nine."

Damn it. Brit's heart raced. Colt's handsome face tensed. *Come on, baby, move your head.*

Brit's finger rested low on the trigger. Sweat beaded her forehead and her upper lip.

"Eight." The arrogant jut of Seth's chin made Brit's blood simmer. He was stretching out his count, trying to throw her off. He loved to be in control.

Colt remained calm and resolute.

Breathe. In and out, in and out.

She needed the green light.

"Seven . . . six."

Her breaths became shallow. Now he really was messing with her. *Fine.* If she got the shot she was taking it. What was one more shooting investigation?

Brit's phone rumbled on the bed of moss, and she turned away from the scope and a perfectly centered reticle to check the text.

Cmd. Wallace: You have the green light—take the shot.

Brilliant.

"Five."

Brit tested her sights again, placing the stock in the pocket of her shoulder. Her finger settled onto the trigger, her palm against the grip. She gave a rearward pull on the grip with her fingers to keep the rifle firmly seated when her thumb ran across a scratch in the finish of her rifle. She'd only noticed that imperfection one other time.

"Four."

Shit. In out, in out. Move your head, damn it.

Brit's clothes clung to her body, a wave of heat riding up her neck and into her face, and she kept breathing.

"Three."

Colt jerked his head to the right and Brit squeezed the trigger, pulling it back in one fluid motion, her heart in her throat. The moment of impact—a blessed relief when a grisly hole the size of a dime smacked Seth in the middle of his forehead. Seth's head swung back, his eyes wide in death, a round exploding from his gun.

Both Seth and Colt fell to the ground.

Brit let go of the rifle like it had turned to flames and jumped to her feet. The rifle, still attached by the strap, knocked her knee.

Oh my God, oh my God.

She grabbed her rifle and scooped up her phone. It must have been a reflex. She should have anticipated for that, but there was nothing she could have done. She had to take the shot. Brit traversed uneven rocks, her foot sliding. She dropped down onto a ledge. Her butt hit hard, the jolt searing up her spine.

She growled through the pain and kept lowering herself to the woodland floor, white-hot panic spreading across her chest. Her phone rumbled in her back pocket. She couldn't stop—not now. They could wait.

Members of her team moved through the woods along with other state troopers. Brit ran past them, dodging tree stumps and low-lying branches until it opened up to a clearing. Seth remained on the ground with CJ kneeling down next to him about twenty yards out in front.

"Where's Colt?" Heart pounding and out of breath, she came upon her teammate.

Wallace turned the corner of a boulder. "Brit." He reached out to her, waving her to him.

Brit nodded, her pulse beating like a tom-tom in her temples. "Where is he?" Her voice was breathless.

"He's gone."

Tears hit the back of her eyes and flowed down her cheeks. "He can't be."

Lieutenant Wallace's arms came around her. "Damn it, girl. Not dead. He was only grazed by the bullet. The *Army* took him."

"No, no, no, no, *no*." Brit pulled away and cupped her mouth with disbelief. "He's innocent. I can prove it."

"Regardless, he's gone."

Brit's head thrashed, scanning for signs of them. "H-How'd they know?"

"The accident investigator alerted them once they linked him to the car at the pileup."

Her brain imploded. All she cared about was seeing Colt. "Where'd they take him?"

His brows knotted over an authoritative straight nose. "Young lady, you're going to explain to me why one of my law enforcement officers has been harboring a fugitive. Because it sure looks to me like you were no hostage."

Crap. Had they come to rescue her? They must have connected Colt and Seth, thinking Colt had come for a wife who might know a thing or two about the artifacts. They would be right, too. Only she'd long since lost the title of hostage, and now she was losing her patience.

Brit took a deep breath, her nostrils flaring. "Not until you call that commander of the Army, with authority, and bring him back." She let her gun fall to her side and crossed her arms.

Commander Todd Wallace stared down his nose, his eyes two pinpricks tunneling into her.

Brit swallowed. She was in deep. What were a few more feet when digging her grave? "Sir?"

He scrubbed his face hard. "Damn it, Gentry." He unsnapped his cell from his hip and punched in a number. "Detain them."

Brit shook her head. "No. Bring them back."

He scowled at her and covered up his phone. "For what?"

Because she wanted to see him, and she needed them to help search for the missing bag. "I'll explain once you return Colt Rivers to me."

He shook his head, his eyes closing momentarily before his lids sprang open. He placed the phone to the side of his head. "Have the colonel call me on my cell ASAP." He ended the call and gave her a pointed look. "Let's have it."

Brit's body trembled. If she wasn't in fear of losing her job before, she was now.

Chapter Forty-Three

OLT SAT IN THE BACKSEAT OF AN ARMY SEDAN, PINE trees whizzing past his window. He expected to get extradited back to the USDB, but not at the lightning speed with which the soldiers retrieved him from the paramedic tending to his superficial wound.

He could still hear Brit's wispy voice floating through the trees while the MPs led him out of Fork Run and into their waiting car.

Where is he?

It just about tore him up. He shook his head. There'd never be another woman for him. Hell, there was only a jail cell in his future. Colt sat back, his chest heavy with regret and eyes glistening with loss. Homes flew by in a blur on Marsh Hill Road, along with the memory of the five days he'd spent with a gorgeous and heroic woman named Brit Gentry.

He'd never been more proud of anyone than he was of her today. He'd put her in a stressful situation. One that could rattle the most seasoned sniper. A smile touched his lips. She'd hit old Seth right between the eyes. Maybe he was being cold and insensitive, but he hated that son of a bitch. Colt could never walk away unscathed if Seth was involved. His throbbing jaw where the bullet from Seth's gun grazed him was proof of that. It had nothing on his broken heart, though.

He closed his eyes and leaned against the backseat where the MP had placed him with his hands cuffed behind his back. Though a big, strapping man who had suffered huge setbacks in his life, Colt wanted to weep.

Hell, he wanted to bawl like a baby.

There were no artifacts, only his word against Gentry's. They'd already read off a list of charges—escape, stolen car, kidnapping.

Okay, so maybe he was guilty of all those charges. But the one that had landed him behind bars in the first place was bullshit. Not that these guys, with their fresh crewcuts and Army garb, gave two craps he was innocent or that he'd been held at gunpoint. Colt winced. Not too long ago he'd held Brit at gunpoint. He'd been desperate, in pain, and wrong for frightening her that day on the highway. Although that charge could be enough to keep him in Maryland. *Damn.* For all he knew Brit would leave that little detail out.

Yep. That wouldn't go in her report. He was getting a one-way pass back to Leavenworth—no questions asked, until his hearing. But even that wouldn't be so bad; he'd get out eventually.

The real problem was that he'd shot Andi Hall. In the back. They must not have connected him to her murder. They would.

Colt's body slumped. He'd racked up more serious charges in the month he'd been out than the bogus one four years ago.

He'd never see her again.

A cellphone rang up in front. "Yes, sir. Entering 219, sir. . . Yes, sir."

Colt opened his eyes.

The soldier in the front passenger seat ended his call. He raised his finger, twirling it in the air. "Turn it around."

The driver made a quick U-turn.

Colt rocked to the right, his shoulder knocking into the soldier sitting next to him. "What the hell?"

They made the right turn onto Sang Run, then the left onto Marsh Hill. "What's up?" he called to the one riding shotgun.

He tilted his head back. "We're meeting the state police at a home on Marsh Hill Road called Memory Maker."

Colt sat up, his manic heartbeat pounding in his ears. He'd take the kidnapping rap if it got him a glimpse of Brit. He wanted to know how she was doing. In all likelihood she would be there. Memory Maker was part of the crime scene. He perked up. Hell, maybe they'd found Seth's hidey hole.

Although he doubted he'd left any artifacts behind.

Didn't matter. At this point Colt was resigned to his fate. His concerns lay with Brit. With all she'd endured the past seven months, this could be the toughest yet. Piercing Seth's brain like she was standing two feet away—and that was exactly how it looked through a scope—could induce one of her panic attacks. He only hoped she used the breathing techniques he'd shown her. It wasn't an easy thing—taking a life. It wasn't for him in Afghanistan. But there was one thing that Seth shared with the Taliban—he *was* the enemy. He was going to kill them if Brit hadn't taken the shot.

Colt's forehead creased. There was another shooting that remained unresolved—Crenshaw's. Something Gentry said still bothered him. It was right before the state police negotiator started to engage Seth. It wasn't until now that Colt had time to consider his cryptic words.

The sedan made the sharp left down the gravel drive of Memory Maker, the light of day disappearing behind the mountain. The swirl of red and blue emergency lights from state police marked and unmarked cruisers bounced off the main house and pool house complex. Colt squinted against the eerie purple tint of darkness settling in, while a flock of state troopers came and went from one building to another.

His pulse raced. A group—he guessed members of her S.T.A.T.E. Team—stood in some type of commando uniforms at the top of the ramp of the pool house complex. He searched for her familiar blond ponytail, his heart jackhammering in his chest when he spotted her in the doorway.

Colt's door opened, and the soldier from the front seat pulled him out by his elbow.

He eyed Colt. "Rivers, they want you in the pool house."

He led Colt up the wooden ramp where the congregation of special police forces had disbanded, along with Brit, and entered the tiled foyer. The heavy scent of chlorine from the pool one flight up permeated the air around him. The only thought he had at that moment was of Brit and the night they'd been that "normal" couple enjoying a movie and a bowl of popcorn. A smile played on his lips. They'd shared more than a war flick.

A trooper in full uniform, wearing a tan Stetson, walked toward them. "You can follow me. The commander wants to see him upstairs in the solarium."

As a group—the trooper in front and Colt sandwiched between two of the soldiers from the sedan—they climbed the stairs and then made the right out the door into the tropical palmed oasis where they'd tried their voodoo together.

Damn. He couldn't help but think this house had lived up to its name.

"Bring him over." The trooper's authoritarian voice and severe expression brooked no arguments. Colt was led with undo speed to the front of a teak table. Behind it stood, he guessed, some high-ranking officer based on his collar ornaments. He wore the same washed out olive commando uniform as Brit's team. *Great.* Probably her commander.

Yep.

Lieutenant T. Wallace as denoted on his brass name plate. Older and wiser, he'd hand Colt his ass for involving one of his officers in his escape.

Wallace lifted his chin. "Give us a minute."

The soldiers released Colt's elbows and stepped away.

Wallace eyed him speculatively. "You're only here because she"—his gaze traveled toward the glass windows of the pool and a blond female trooper with her team—"seems to think you're innocent."

As if she'd heard her name, Brit sneaked a peek over her shoulder.

Wallace dropped down in a chair behind the table, reviewing a map. "I've got men searching the area around Fork Run. If this backpack filled with ancient treasure exists, we'll be lucky to find it in the dark."

"Yes, sir." As much as he wanted to contradict Wallace, it would be in his *and* Brit's best interest if he remained respectful. He'd see how far that got him.

Wallace took a deep breath. "Did Seth Gentry offer you any clues as to the location of this panic room Brit's told me about?"

"Brit"—Colt cleared his throat—"I mean, Trooper Gentry and I believe it's behind the back staircase."

"What makes you think that—other than this brick wall and a door that goes to nowhere?"

"Seth Gentry alluded to it, sir. And I believe he's been holed up here since faking his death."

Another S.T.A.T.E. Team member walked up carrying the set of plans he and Brit had pored over a few nights ago. He handed them off. The lieutenant spread them out over the map of Fork Run. "Would said artifacts need a ventilation system?"

"That's my belief, sir."

"Uh huh." He cupped his chin. "I know a thing or two about schematics, and I don't see any ductwork that would lead me to believe there's a climate-controlled room."

The door swung open to the pool room, and Brit slipped out, her beautiful brown eyes transfixed on Colt. Her brows furrowed. "Lieutenant, with all due respect, I think those are a dummy set of plans."

He looked down his nose at her. "Something you were lacking about forty-five minutes ago."

A glance passed between Brit and her lieutenant. Colt imagined it centered more on a *lack* of respect.

Brit lowered her lashes. "Yes, sir."

Colt rolled his lips in, trying not to smile. He could only imagine what it took to get him back here.

Wallace scratched the side of his head. "Let's go check out this door." He nodded toward the soldiers. "Gentlemen, if you would escort Mr. Rivers down to the first floor."

A hand landed on Colt's biceps, and the soldier steered him toward the door. They led him back down the stairs where they waited for Wallace, Brit, and another member of her team who was talking to her and the trooper that led them up.

"Brit, show me this door," Wallace said in a stern voice.

"Yes, sir." She walked by Colt, giving him a quick glance, then proceeded down the short hall, past the staircase, and to the door.

They followed.

Brit reached for the knob, taking a deep breath.

He knew the feeling. This was it. If they couldn't prove the door a fake and locate this panic room of Seth's, they were screwed. Not to mention, they still didn't have the backpack filled with artifacts.

Hell, they might never find that.

Brit opened the door. The same stone remained. "We couldn't find the right pressure point."

Wallace shook his head. "Looks like a fuckup to me."

Colt hooked his chin toward Brit.

Her brows rose in question.

"Show him the door in the theater room."

Her eyes widened. "Ah, good point." She waved them back down the hall.

They piled into the theater room and down the carpeted steps to the bottom. The same brick ran left to right, top to bottom. "It's over here." She pressed into the wall, trying to find the exact pressure point that would open the stone-walled door.

"What exactly are you looking for?" Wallace gave her a curious gaze.

"It opens." She pressed some more, flustered. "I'm telling you, Lieutenant, it opens."

"Let me try." Wallace pressed in on the stone several times. "And you've seen it pop o—" The door sprung back, and they stepped out of the way.

"See." Brit pointed to the perfectly toothed stone that fit like a puzzle. "It's undetectable to the naked eye. He's got to have the same setup in the foyer."

Wallace nodded. "Makes sense."

They traveled again as a group until they all stood perplexed in front of the brick wall with the open door behind the staircase.

"Excuse me, Lieutenant Wallace." The MP released his grip on Colt's upper arm, stepping toward the door in question. "I've seen this before."

"You think you can open it?" Wallace gave him berth to work. "Be my guest."

"Thank you, sir." He smiled when he said it.

Probably some techno geek from the Science and Technology Division that got off on that shit.

The soldier stood in front of the door and pressed his hands all around the door frame. He angled his head at the jamb and the lock and pressed his finger inside the hole of the strike plate. Something clicked, and the wall started moving backward, creating the same effect as the door in the theater room, until it opened and cold air rushed out.

Brit drew her weapon on instinct, as did her teammate. "There's got to be a light." She reached in and fumbled with the inside wall. She flipped the switch, and bright light bathed the room.

"Brit." Wallace pulled her aside. "We'll check it out."

She frowned and moved aside, reholstering her weapon.

Wallace, troopers, and soldiers filed in.

Colt shook his head.

Let's all check out the freak's room.

On the flip side, that left him alone with Brit. Well, relatively alone, behind the staircase and away from the hubbub outside.

He hooked his chin toward her. "Come over here, beautiful."

Her eyes glistened with unshed tears, and she took the four steps toward him. Her shaky hand caressed his jaw. "He shot you."

"Grazed, and I'm fine. How are you?"

She shrugged. "Okay. I didn't have a choice."

"No, you didn't." He peered through the doorway to Seth's private lair. "This should be enough for them to drop that financial disclosure investigation."

"And for you, too."

"We'll see how fast government red tape works. I hope." His brows furrowed. "You tell them about Hall?"

"They told me. She's in trouble for something. When she didn't show up for roll call, they went looking for her."

"She dead?"

"*No,*" she said like it was a secret. "*Alive.* She told them we were headed west. I told Wallace she tried to kill us." She glanced back into the room. "You're not going to be charged."

Oh, yeah. His body relaxed incrementally. That was one less burden to deal with.

Brit pursed her lips. "I got the feeling there was something else he wanted to tell me."

"What?"

She shrugged and rolled her eyes. "Hell if I know. The superintendent called him and that was the end of that."

He gave her a tired smile. "I'm proud of you."

"For what? I got you shot."

"You saved my life." His eyes swept over her weary but pretty face. "I love you."

She caressed his arm. "I love you, too." She frowned. "But what are we going to do without the artifacts?"

"I don't know." He angled his head to get a look inside the room. They'd be out soon. "Listen, did you notice anything odd about Hall's rifle—the scope?"

She shook her head and frowned. "No. Why?"

"Did they say any more about the state's attorney's decision?"

"Honestly, I haven't thought about that. I was worried about you." She touched the wound under his jaw. "It's just a flesh wound, right?"

That was his girl. She'd been taking care of him and worrying about him since they entered the front door of Memory Maker. He smiled at that. Actually, she'd climbed in the window with every intention of locking him out.

"It's fine." He jerked his chin away from her probing fingers. "Think, babe. We don't have much time. That sick bastard was talking nonsense about the scope and how it was the same. It didn't make sense. Do you know what he meant by that?"

She chewed the inside of her lip. "I have no idea."

"Did anything seem different or the same from the last call-out you were on?" He didn't want to mention Crenshaw's name.

Brit pursed her lips. "Yeah. It's weird, but the gun felt the same."

"The same? Like how?"

She shrugged. "I don't know."

Voices floated toward the opening of the door. Wallace poked his head out. "I think you both are going to want to see this."

"Yes, sir." She leaned into Colt. "You go first."

With his hands behind his back, feeling every bit the criminal, Colt ducked inside. Soft white light glowed from wall sconces positioned strategically around the room. Calling it a room was an understatement. It was a damn royal palace with expensive wood accents and golden fleck walls. It had a living area, big screen TV, an office with several computers, full kitchen, and a master bedroom with marble bath.

Wallace directed one of his men over. "Get ahold of computer crimes. Let's find out what this bastard was up to."

Colt shook his head. "Try any black market buyer looking for priceless artifacts."

Wallace clucked his tongue. "There's that."

"Sir." A uniformed trooper pushed his way through. "One of the guys from Cumberland Barrack found this in a cave." He handed over a black backpack.

Wallace's shoulders dipped the instant he took the bag. "Shit. This has to weigh fifty pounds." He gave the trooper a quizzical look. "Did you open it?"

He smiled wide. "Tablet the size of Moses's, sir."

Brit burst out laughing.

Wallace sent her a look of reproof.

She rolled her pretty lips in. "Sorry, sir." Then she sneaked a peek at Colt and smiled.

It was what he wanted. But it wasn't everything. *Damn it.* They all seemed pleased with themselves.

Colt blew out an agitated breath. "Glad to hear you've solved the mystery. But your comrade Brit Gentry's facing manslaughter charges. What are you going to do about that?"

"*Shit.*" Wallace handed back the loot, looking like he'd forgotten his grandmother at the bus depot. "You were cleared this afternoon."

Chapter Forty-Four

"**M**OTIVE." LIEUTENTANT WALLACE CROSSED HIS arms. "It was what we were missing."

"Motive?" Brit's legs buckled, and she fell against Colt.

"*Christ*. Someone grab her." Colt pressed his thigh against Brit, struggling to keep her upright.

Wallace reached over and took hold of Brit's upper arms and steadied her. "You okay?" A pair of concerned blue eyes tunneled into her.

"N-no." Brit's heart strummed in her chest, and she jerked away. "Oh, my, *God*. You thought I intentionally killed Crenshaw."

"What?" He jerked his head back, his face twisting. "*No*. Let's go sit down." He released one of her arms but kept a steely grip on the other. "It's been a very fluid situation in the last forty-eight hours." He led her past Colt.

Brit nudged Colt in his side and hooked her head at him, motioning him to follow.

Colt fell in step behind them, his boots clomping on the tile floor, when something knocked into the wall.

"Get the fuck off me."

Colt's abrasive words echoing through the hall, in an otherwise calm environment, sliced through her like a jagged piece of glass. Brit swung back, her lieutenant's grip tightening on her upper arm.

One of the military police had Colt's rough whiskery cheek, ripe as an apple, smashed against the wall. Another charged past her from the front door on a rush of air.

"Sorry, Rivers," said the one with a blond crewcut. "We have our orders." They pulled Colt off the wall and dragged him toward her.

Colt struggled against them, cursing. "I need to know what's going on with her." His desperate green eyes clung to Brit's. "Then I don't care what you do with me." Still flushed and gritting his teeth, he thrashed against the MPs.

Brit jerked free of the lieutenant and stood in front of the open doorway leading down the ramp. "No. I want him to stay." She was breathing hard and glanced from Colt to her lieutenant. "Just until you explain to me—to us—what's going on."

Lt. Wallace raked his fingers through his short-cropped dark hair with silver running through it. "Yes. Fine." He waved the combative group into the theater room. "Take up a piece of wall, and, Mr. Rivers, I expect your full cooperation."

Colt shook the MPs off his arms and walked in without assistance. The lieutenant lowered his head, trying to hide a grin when the soldiers filed past empty-handed. Then he ushered her in next.

Brit slipped by him, trying to avoid eye contact.

He grabbed her arm before she cleared the doorway, holding her in place. "You *will* be giving me a full report about your dealings with Rivers. And it *will* be on my desk by eight hundred hours tomorrow morning."

Brit gulped. She'd told him what he needed to know back at Fork Run. Having to explain the intimate details of how she fell in love with a fugitive who was innocent—everyone seemed to forget that fact—was, well, embarrassing.

"Yes, sir." She stepped into the dimly lit theater.

"Have a seat on the first tier," he ordered.

Brit took a space on the corner end of the brown leather sofa, content to be in shadow. She wanted to avoid any more scrutiny. She wouldn't if the lieutenant realized the lights were set on a dimmer.

He passed the multitude of switches and dropped down next to her. "We got word this morning that an arrest—not yours—was going to be made for the murder of Beau Crenshaw."

"Murder?" Brit glanced from Lt. Wallace to Colt, who stood stoically on the second tier with an MP on either side of him, before she turned back to her commander. "This is the motive you were talking about." She cocked her head. "Do you know who would want him dead?"

Lt. Wallace rubbed his jaw and sighed. "Unfortunately, yes." His hand came down on her knee. "Things weren't adding up with the shooting, Brit. The trajectory was off. Yet you were the one who fired the shot. At least that's how it appeared."

"I was dealing with a lot that night, sir. I should have removed myself from the call-out."

His hand fell away, and he nodded. "Yeah, well, that husband of yours had you playing the blame game." His jaw tensed. "You understand that you had no choice today."

"Yes, sir." Seth had forced her to end his life. Husband or not. It was a clean shooting.

Lt. Wallace glanced at Colt. "If it's any consolation to you, we are working jointly with the Army on this investigation. When everything shakes out, you should be exonerated."

"One would hope," Colt said dryly.

Wallace reconnected with Brit. "Learning Crenshaw was a vet suffering from PTSD, I should have ordered you to stand down."

"I was upset, sir. But I was working through it. I didn't pull the trigger."

"I know that now, Brit. I'm just sorry it's taken over six weeks to clear you."

"If I didn't pull the trigger, then who did?"

"Right." His head dropped, and he rung his hands together like he was washing off the guilt. "Based on your position that night, the trajectory was slightly off. A lot of things could account for that—muscling the rifle for one."

Brit's brows furrowed. "With all due respect, sir, I didn't muscle my rifle."

He lifted his head, a pair of cutting crystal eyes held hers. "Figured you'd say that."

"But it's true."

He nodded. "It bothered me, too, when IAU came back with their original findings—your gun, your fingerprints, GSR on your hands, and no explanation as to the trajectory issue because, well, frankly, there was no other explanation."

"What changed?"

"From the way they told it to me, we have a sharp state's attorney. He wasn't buying the GSR patterns on your hands. You know there's a certain amount of blowback consistent with shooting a firearm. Yours was spotty, mostly on your hands and wrists, but nothing on your arms."

Brit had been so out of it, she'd never even considered the GSR. She'd just assumed it was consistent. She wouldn't have known definitively until the state's attorney reviewed the evidence and the final investigation report, which it appeared he had. Only her lawyer hadn't been notified of the findings.

Lt. Wallace scrubbed his face. "There's no denying the gunpowder residue existed. That's what was so baffling until IAU and the state's attorney's office went back and reexamined the evidence and re-interviewed everyone."

"They didn't interview me."

"They didn't have to."

"I don't understand."

"Before they got to you, they found that the Dorchester sheriff's deputy had activated his in-car camera."

Brit thought about that. He had parked directly behind them. CJ asked him to turn off his emergency equipment so that it wouldn't give up their location.

She pursed her lips. "The in-car camera is usually activated by his emergency lights."

He shrugged. "What can I tell you, Brit? Someone was watching over you that night, even if it felt like your own department had failed you."

"I knew you and the department would present the facts as they were."

"Sounds like they were wrong." Colt pushed off the wall.

"Whoa." One of the MPs grabbed his biceps.

"Relax." Colt looked down his nose at the MP. "There's not a whole hell of a lot I can do with my hands cuffed behind my back."

The MP grumbled something and let go.

"Can we get to the point?" Colt eyed his entourage. "I'm on a tight schedule."

Brit's pulse quickened, the air hard to breathe. She might be able to sway her lieutenant into keeping Colt around for a while. Seemed he harbored some guilt for what happened to her that night. Although the Army didn't owe her a damn thing. But they sure as hell owed Colt. He'd never get back those four years, and they—Colt and Brit—could only hope justice would prevail the second time around.

Brit gritted her teeth.

Oh, it would.

She was going to be the biggest pain in the ass the state police investigators had if they didn't wrap this thing up with the Army and get Colt out of prison.

Brit pinned Wallace. "Stop trying to protect me, and tell me who killed Crenshaw."

He took a deep breath. "Did you feel anything different about your rifle that night?"

Brit placed her elbows on her knees and leaned forward. It wasn't until today she noticed something. But it had nothing to do with *her* rifle. Colt had said something about Seth tonight—the scope.

Alarm spread through her like a flash fire, and Brit jumped to her feet. "Where's the rifle I used today?"

"What is it you're thinking?" Lt. Wallace said it like he was trying to coax it out of her.

"I-I don't know." Brit's mind scattered. All the moving parts were making it hard for her to focus on what had really happened. "I was looking through Andi's scope, then?" She squinted, not sure she was really believing what she was saying. "That night on the Crenshaw's farm." She cocked her head. "So I had Andi's rifle both times?"

Wallace nodded. "Your instincts are dead-on. You had Hall's rifle that night. It wasn't until the in-car camera tape that we put it together."

Brit held out her hands, focusing on her fingers. "When I was up on that cliff today my thumb ran across this scratch on the frame of the rifle. I didn't have time to process it then."

"Which is why you found the same imperfection in the gun tonight," Colt added.

Brit's eyes widened. "So she, what, had my gun by mistake?" Which could happen. They all had the same .223 rifles. Unless you had a distinguishing mark—which Andi would have known about—you'd have to check the serial number to tell them apart. It didn't make sense—the distinguishing mark. "So she shot Crenshaw by accident, then tried to cover her own ass by switching the guns?" Brit's hand flew to her mouth. "That's why she was grabbing my hands. She was trying to transfer the GSR to mine."

Lt. Wallace scrubbed his face. "That's what we believed at the time. An accidental shooting is one thing—but covering it up and tampering with evidence is criminal. We had planned to take her into custody quietly this morning at roll call."

Only Andi never made it there. "When did you find her?"

"Not long after Rivers shot her." Wallace's usual stern expression softened. "It's one of the reasons we got to Garrett County when we did."

She'd made Colt keep to the speed limit—her team had not.

Wallace eyed Colt speculatively. "We're not pressing charges. It's clear after hearing Brit's side of it and reviewing the surveillance video we now know exists, you shot her in self-defense."

Colt shrugged. "My only regret is Brit in all this."

Brit frowned. He'd been right not to trust Andi, and here she'd walked him straight into Cat Woman's den.

Wallace nodded his understanding and then clasped Brit's shoulder. "I got news a little over an hour ago that she was in recovery and talking."

"Lying through her teeth," Colt groused.

Wallace shot him an irritated look. "Mr. Rivers, you're still here because of Brit. One more comment and I'll have you escorted out." He then turned toward Brit. "Your father called. I figured I'd let you explain everything to him." Then he zeroed in on Colt with a hardened gaze. "Not sure how you're going to explain him to Joseph Dodd the retired state police commander."

If she'd never witnessed dueling stares before, she had now.

Brit beaded in on Colt, her message clear—*cool it.*

"I'm done." Colt shrugged and leaned against the wall. "Finish your story."

Brit gave him a wide-eyed stare. *Really?* He wasn't helping his case by giving her lieutenant the go-ahead. Innocent or not, he was the one still in handcuffs.

He lowered his head.

Okay, better.

This wasn't just about the two of them. She'd been so absorbed with herself and Colt, she'd forgotten about her commander in all this. The brass must be up his ass. Something like this could cost him his command. Brit gave Wallace her full attention. "I'm sorry for all that's happened."

"It's not your fault."

She didn't agree. She'd married the man. She should have been a better judge of character. "What were you going to say about Andi?"

"That she told the truth, finally. And one we never considered." He dropped back against the couch. "She swapped your gun before the call-out, Brit." His solid hand came down on her shoulder. "She shot Crenshaw in cold blood and switched the rifles back at the scene."

"But why?"

"Now *that* I hadn't figured out until you filled me in on Seth. Andi confirmed it at the hospital." He narrowed in on her. "Why didn't you share your concerns with me about this financial investigation?"

Brit shrugged. "I didn't want you to think I was making excuses. I should have been more proactive about our finances."

Colt pushed off the wall. "You need to tell him about the boating accident."

Brit's head fell, and she picked at her hands. "I was the one who was supposed to drown that night on the bay."

"What?" Lt. Wallace leaned forward, his arm coming around her.

Tears filled her eyes. The two people that were supposed to love her the most had plotted her death. "Seth and Andi. I guess Seth was supposed to throw me overboard and sail away during the storm." She wiped a tear from her face. "It backfired. He fell out instead."

"Stupid son of a bitch," Colt said under his breath.

Lt. Wallace shot Colt a disagreeable look. "Seems Andi left out that little detail."

Brit stood, the air in the theater room becoming heavy and too hard to breathe. She'd kept quiet about her investigation into Seth's finances and his past for several months. It was the holidays—Christmas, New Year's and Seth's annual lavish party at the house. She'd had too much to drink that night. Feeling sorry for herself, bundled in a winter coat outside on the back deck overlooking the bay until Andi showed up.

The lieutenant came to his feet, bending his head. "What are you thinking?"

"I told Andi I was investigating Seth and our unexplained wealth."

"You were a *threat*," Colt said, his voice razor sharp.

Brit sent him another warning with her eyes to tone it down.

Wallace caught her silently chastising Colt and chuckled. "No. He's right." He patted Brit's back. "Guess since killing you didn't work, they regrouped. Hall wanted to eliminate you any way she could. In her mind, and I'm assuming your husband's, it was a slam dunk. Having you fighting the judicial system, convicted, and then battling the arduous appeals process would have left no time to worry about some little agency financial disclosure statement that, honestly, would have been forgotten."

Brit's head dropped to her chest. She'd been their fall guy. Andi had pretended to be her friend and listened to the "woes of Brit" all the while gaining intelligence about her next move on Seth.

"I should have seen through her." Her voice was barely a whisper.

"*I* didn't see through her." Lt. Wallace shook her arm and dipped his head. "Stop beating yourself up. She fooled us all."

Brit bit her bottom lip and nodded. "Okay."

"All right, then." He released her. "I'm approving two weeks' vacation for you after I see that report." He cocked his head. "No showing up for training exercises, no listening in on the police scanner. You need to focus on Brit. You hear?"

Brit's mouth twisted with indecision. There was not much else for her to do. IAU would take care of the ongoing investigation on Andi. Her Chesapeake Beach home, Memory Maker, and the sailboat weren't legally hers. Eventually they'd all be confiscated. The thought of moving back with her parents made her groan.

Colt lurched. "You okay?"

"What's wrong?" Lt. Wallace peered down at her, his brows furrowing.

"Nothing." Brit waved them both away.

Her commander nodded. "One last thing. You'll have to be available for IAU if they need any more statements."

Yeah, yeah, yeah. He wasn't telling her something she didn't already know.

Lt. Wallace motioned toward the group against the wall. "How about we give these two five minutes."

The MPs looked at each other, then Rivers.

Brit held her breath. *Come on, you know he's just as much a victim in all this.*

The one closest to the door hooked his chin toward it. "We'll be outside."

Wallace followed them out, then turned back. "If you need to talk to the agency psychologist, we can set something up."

She shook her head. "Seen enough shrinks, Lieutenant."

"Gotcha." He winked and left the room, shutting the door.

Brit relaxed and stepped down to the second level where Colt stood with his hands cuffed behind his back. Although tired with dark circles beneath his eyes and lines bracketing his firm mouth, he was tougher than most men she knew. That was saying a lot, considering she worked in a paramilitary organization and was assigned to a specialized unit with all men, now that Andi wouldn't be coming back.

She placed her palms on his chest, his heartbeat strumming beneath her fingertips. "I wish you could touch me."

"You have no idea." He leaned back against the wall. "This thing could take months, even years to get resolved."

"I'll wait." She was prepared for that. It didn't matter.

"I know you say that now. The point is I don't expect you to."

Seriously? "Where's all this coming from?"

"It's not coming from anywhere. It's how I feel. How are you going to explain your relationship with me to your father?"

She hadn't really thought that far ahead. Her father was a reasonable man. He'd understand. "You saved my life. If we'd never met—"

He gave a hard laugh. "Don't make it sound like some fated star-crossed lover thing. I held a gun to your head. It's going to be in that report of yours you give to Wallace. Don't think for a minute your old man's not going to get a copy."

Brit stepped back, rubbing her temples. "Why are you being so difficult?"

"I just think you'd do better without me."

"And I think I can decide that for myself."

"Difference of opinion."

Brit squinted up at him, her fingers tightening into fists. "Then you are a liar. No more than twenty minutes ago you told me you loved me."

He shrugged. "I do love who you are. You saved my life, remember? I'll forever be in your debt."

Brit's nose flared, heat pinching her cheeks. "You're being a jerk."

The door popped open, and Brit jumped. One of the MPs stuck his head in.

Brit put up a finger. "Can you give us just one minute?" Her voice cracked.

"Ah." He looked from Colt standing stone-faced against the wall to Brit who could barely finish her sentence and shut the door.

Brit swung around. "Go ahead and play the martyr. But you telling me what I should do and me doing it are two different things." She turned on her heels. She wouldn't give him the benefit of seeing her cry. That she would do when she was alone. Although where could she go at this point? Memory Maker for now was a crime scene. Her home in Chesapeake Beach was probably one, too.

Fine. She'd drive her ass back to Annapolis and into her mother's arms.

She would tell her father about Colt before he saw her titillating report that would read more like a romance novel. He'd understand. She would then go to her room.

And she'd take it from there.

"Brit." Colt's voice was thin but direct.

She glanced over her shoulder, eyes glassy with emotion. All she wanted was him. She'd have waited. "I'll make sure your lawyer gets whatever he needs for your defense." She opened the door, swallowing a sob. "He's all yours."

"Brit," he called to her in a strangled voice.

With her heart in pieces, she walked out the door, a tear slipping down her cheek.

Colt Rivers would regret letting her go.

Chapter Forty-Five

*H*OW YOU DOING, SON?" GRAYSON RIVERS CALLED from outside the Ford pickup, several yards away, the sun glinting off the chrome grill.

Colt waved from behind the fence of the USDB, then shook the guard's hand. "Appreciate all you've done for me, Jack."

"Weren't nothing. You know that." The old guard with a slight gut took a cautious look around, then leaned in. "Just glad they never found out about the gun I smuggled in."

It had been the only thing Colt had lied about during his court proceedings.

"If there's anything you need, you know where to find me."

He opened the gate. "Montana. I'll be sure to look you up. Maybe we can go hunting."

Colt winked. "I got you covered."

With a clean pair of jeans, white tee, tan corduroy jacket, and cowboy boots his father had brought from home, Colt walked out the gate a free man but by no means whole. He and his father had talked numerous times during the eighteen months he remained behind bars, waiting for the military courts to exonerate him. Nothing too deep—ranch business mostly. Colt had mentioned a woman named Brit Gentry. Hadn't gone into great detail, except to say she'd saved his life more than once during those six days they were together.

Funny how, from time to time, he'd bring her up. Colt guessed he knew enough to be curious.

Colt strode toward his father. The man had taught him everything he knew and had stood beside him when most hadn't. He blinked back tears and hugged his old man. "I've missed you, Dad."

"I missed you, too, son." He pulled away, sniffed, and yanked a hanky from his back pocket and wiped his nose and eyes. "Let's get you on the road."

Colt headed for the passenger door.

"You want to drive?"

"Up to you."

"Ah, hell, why don't I take the first leg?"

"Sounds good." Colt hopped in.

Colt couldn't help but notice his father's gait. He wasn't as spry as he remembered him.

His father climbed in on a moan and sat down and started the truck.

Frowning, Colt reached over and squeezed his shoulder. "How about I drive?"

His father snorted. "Don't worry. They haven't taken my license away"—he winked—"yet."

Colt rubbed the back of his head. He'd left his father a huge burden. With time served, he'd been away a total of five and a half years. "You said you hired a ranch hand."

He nodded and pulled out. "Yep. The place has never run better."

"You mean since I left."

He laughed. "No, I mean ever."

Colt's brows rose. "How much you paying this ranch hand?"

"No money. I made a deal. Room and board."

Colt raked his hands through his hair. *Great.* The first thing on his list was to fire this wonder of a ranch hand. Eventually, he planned to expand. That took time. He needed to build a bunkhouse for the hands and a few hunting cabins for clients. After five and a half years in prison, he wasn't about to rub asses with some guy he didn't know from Adam in his own home while he built the damned bunkhouse.

Colt lifted his Stetson, ran his fingers through his hair, and dropped the hat on the backseat. "Glad to be a free man, Dad."

His father extended his old weathered hand and patted his knee. "Just wish your mother could be alive to see it."

A sigh escaped Colt's lips. It was one of many regrets. "Let's look to the future."

A smile curled his father's lips. "Oh, I already have."

Colt settled back along the bench seat of his father's old pickup. They had eighteen hours until they reached the ranch. There would be plenty of time to discuss business. They'd work something out—a severance package of some sort.

But he wasn't living with some hairy ass dude.

"Bella. *Damn it.*" Brit chased down the rambunctious chocolate Lab pup with her cowhide glove between her teeth. She ran, all paws, out the barn and into the glittering sunshine. Brit squinted at the narrow road with the snow-capped Mission Mountains anchored behind it and the gray pickup kicking up dust as it pulled in.

Shit.

Grayson had said dinnertime. She was still wearing her mucking boots, smelled of manure. *Err.* She brushed back the loose wisps from her flushed face and stopped, losing all track of the Lab when the driver's door swung open.

He didn't say a word. Colt only strode toward her, looking more handsome and Western with a Stetson in his hand. "You the new ranch hand?"

Brit glanced past Colt to Grayson, wide-eyed.

He laughed and waved her off. "I'll see ya'll at dinner." He hopped in his truck with more lightning speed than she'd seen in the past eight months since she'd been living on the ranch.

Brit straightened her shoulders. She'd pretty much put Colt on notice that she was going to do what she wanted. She just didn't know *what* at the time. But she figured, why not? Colt owed her big-time. She had no home after they'd confiscated the two she had—not Colt's fault. Nonetheless she needed a soft place to land. She'd done exactly what she'd promised herself that day in the movie theater with her heart in her hands. She was going to spend every free minute freeing a man who meant everything to her.

Even if he'd told her not to.

Colt's lawyer had said a solid year to get through the military court system after the state police had given him the case file on the investigation.

Seemed good a time as any to visit Montana. She always wanted to live out West, and there was a ranch in desperate need of upkeep. Grayson Rivers—after she'd explained her connection to his son—had been more than open to her suggestion of working the ranch for room and board.

Colt came up short when Bella ran in between them. "What's that?"

"Her name's"—Brit scooped up the eight-week-old puppy and kissed that furry brown head, her pulse beating like a tom-tom—"Bella."

Colt reached out and scratched the pup behind the ear, his gaze warm and content on Brit's face. "Can we call her Bell for short?"

"Ah, sure." Brit was still stuck on the word "we."

"So I hear my father's paying you room and board."

"That was the deal."

He rubbed his chin, his dark brows rising over a pair of inquiring green eyes. "Where are you sleeping?"

"The spare bedroom."

"Uh huh." He nodded toward the ranch house. "Who installed the window boxes?"

Brit swallowed and took in the log rancher with a green tin roof. When she'd arrived, the logs had needed to be cleaned, the chinking replaced. Now it shined like a new penny—a little more, she wanted to say "feminine," but on closer inspection she'd use the word "homey."

"Your father."

Colt snorted. "He plant the flowers, too?"

"*No.* I did."

He strode past her toward the front door.

Oh Lord. She wanted to ease him into the house. She'd done some redecorating—mostly furniture, lamps. She'd kept him in mind, even kept the leather rocker with the squeaky springs.

Brit put Bell down and caught up with him. "Wouldn't you like to see the barn first?"

"Nope." He swung open the door and walked in.

May was still chilly in the Rockies. It was one of the things she had to get used to—along with the snow. She had an inviting fire going and a pot of stew on the stove.

"You like stew, right?" She took his Stetson from him and hung it on the hat rack by the door.

"You know I do." His eyes scanned the great room with the new leather couches, wooden tables, and arts and crafts accents.

She gave him a quick smile. "I should check on dinner." She took a step toward the kitchen when he pulled her into his arms.

He was solid and warm and staring down at her. "My heart's beating a mile a minute." He placed her hand on his chest.

Sure enough, it was pumping away under that strong pec of his.

She'd taken a huge risk and made one crazy-ass assumption coming here without his knowledge. "Is that a bad thing?" Her voice quavered.

"No." It came out low and rough, and he caressed her face. "It's a good thing."

She nodded. "Your dad's been great."

"I knew he was up to something. But I would have never guessed all this."

"It's not too girly for you?"

"Nope." He gave her a teasing look. "Well, not if you plan on staying."

"What would my accommodations be?" She pursed her lips.

"You wouldn't be sleeping in the spare bedroom, I can tell you that." His hand slipped down to her lower back, and he pulled her snug against him. "What about your job?"

She remembered what he'd said during their private lunch at Unos. He'd shared his hopes and dreams with her. Dreams he believed would never be fulfilled. The thing was she shared his vision for the future. "The only thing

I want to see through a scope is wild game."

"Ah, a hunting lodge."

"What do you think? We could have a bunkhouse and cabins for our guests."

"You read my mind, beautiful." He kissed her on her head. "Wait right here." He released her and jogged into the master bedroom.

Brit placed her hands behind her back and angled her head to get a peek. Drawers slammed, something falling to the floor like boxes, and then he cursed.

"I'll be right out."

"Okay," she called back. *What on earth?*

He ducked out through the doorway of the bedroom, a sheepish grin tugging at his mouth and strode toward her. His arm slipped around her waist. His sharp green eyes held hers. "What are your plans for the next fifty years, Brit Gentry?"

She had a list. The first one was up to him. "I was thinking of changing my name—the last one."

"Ah." He pressed back a loose strand of hair behind her ear. "What do you think of Rivers?"

"It has a nice ring to it."

"Speaking of which." He reached into his pocket and flipped the top to a small black box. He pulled something out, dropped it inside the pocket of his jacket, and tossed the box on the leather sofa in the great room where Bell was rolling on the carpet with her ball. "Not a day goes by I don't regret how I handled things back at the lake."

"I know you didn't mean it."

"I wanted to call. But I figured you were moving on with your life."

"I was." She smiled up at him. "In Montana."

"You remembered that old chocolate Lab of mine?"

She nodded. "I wanted to give you everything you've been missing."

"You have." He bent his head and kissed her long and deep. Brit relaxed in his arms and kissed him back. She'd made the right decision.

Colt broke the kiss, his rugged hand cupping her face. "You're beautiful." His eyes shimmered with emotion under the recessed lights of the cabin.

Brit looped her hands around his neck. "You look relieved."

"More than you know." He gave her a quick peck on the lips and released her hands from his neck. He held them in his. They were wide, shades darker than hers, and trembling. "I think"—he hooked his chin over his shoulder at the Lab pup that was growling and wrestling with a plaid throw pillow on the corner of the couch—"that wild-ass dog needs a father."

"I'd have to marry you, then."

"Yeah, that's what I was thinking." Colt peered into the great room.

Bell pounced on the pillow and tore open a seam.

"The sooner the better. How does this Sunday sound?" He turned back and cocked his head, a smile playing on his lips. "You're Methodist, right?"

"Yes." Her voice was wispy and emotional, and she thought she might cry.

He bent down on one knee.

A tear slipped down Brit's cheek, and she wiped the corner of her eye with her palm.

"I went looking to settle a score. I found you instead, which made me angry."

"Why?" Brit caressed his smooth, clean-shaven cheek.

"He had everything I wanted."

"The wealth?" She just couldn't comprehend that.

"No, *you*. You were beautiful—are beautiful—and fierce. You came out here, wheedled your way into my father's heart."

"He told you that?"

"Brit, I've never seen him so happy."

Over the past several months, Grayson Rivers had become a second father to her. She just didn't know he felt the same way about her.

"And you?"

"Hell. I couldn't get out of that truck fast enough." He shook her hands in his. "I love you."

"I love you, too."

"I only wish I'd had time to pick out the perfect ring."

Brit wet her lips. "It doesn't matter. I'd accept one from a Cracker Jack box as long as it came from you."

He laughed. "How about my mother's for now?" He released her one hand and reached into his pocket. He pulled out a sparkling diamond solitaire in a platinum setting with matching diamond baguettes on either side.

Brit's breath caught. "It's beautiful."

She lifted her face to him. He was different on so many levels than the man she'd said goodbye to over a year and a half ago. She'd missed him. Just not the desperation that had lined his face during those days he'd been on the run. He smiled at her. It was relaxed and carefree. He seemed content—the kind of contentedness that came from familiar surroundings like being here with her in his home.

"There's no other ring I'd want."

Colt went down on bended knee. "Brittany Dodd Gentry, will you marry me?"

"Yes." Brit sniffed away her pesky tears. "Yes, I will marry you."

At home in a cozy Western cabin, surrounded by breathtaking vistas and a land rich with possibilities where they could start that family she had once only dared to hope for, Colt took her hand and slipped the ring on her finger.

His green eyes, filled with glassy emotion, swept over her. "I've waited for you all my life." Colt pulled her into his strong embrace and kissed her.

Brit kissed him back on that sensual mouth of his and smiled. She'd agree with him on that one point, but Colt Rivers had been wrong about one thing. They were every bit the star-crossed lovers. And their lives were meant to collide on that fateful day in October.

Shakespeare had nothing on their story.

She was here in Montana with him now, in a place she had always dreamed of living. He was the love of her life, the man of her dreams, and he was finally free.

Brit tingled with the kind of love that happens when you least expect it—the kind of love that stays.

I will love you, Colt, from now into eternity. .

Keep reading for and excerpt from P. J. O'Dwyer's next novel

DEADRISE

The second book in the
SATIN AND STEEL
Women of Law Enforcement Series

Available from Black Siren Books Fall 2016

DEADRISE

CHAPTER ONE

R OBBIE DUNCAN PACED THE WHITE TILES OF THE SOMERSET
County Commissioner's Station. She never expected to be back on
Smith Island. It was a lifetime ago when she left. If it wasn't for the
fact the man standing before the district commissioner was her father, she'd
have ignored his unexpected phone call at midnight.

But he was. And even though she hadn't seen or heard from him in ten
years, Terry Duncan, for all his shortcomings, still pulled at her heartstrings.

She should have written him off a long time ago. But tonight, standing
there in a powder blue, knit golf shirt snug against a slight pot belly, his
glasses perched on his thinning gray head that was speckled from age, he
looked every bit his sixty-seven years.

The court clerk motioned for him to move to a side table. He pulled his
glasses down to the tip of his nose, bent over to read and sign his release
form.

She remained toward the back, close to the doors as the sheriff's deputy led him to the property-held window to collect his belongings. After checking the contents of his wallet, he shoved it into the back pocket of his gray pants, and slid on his gold wedding band.

Why he gave a damn about that ring was anyone's guess. Lydia Duncan, Robbie's mother, chose to disappear twenty-six years ago.

Desertion Robbie was used to.

She didn't blame her father for her mother's disappearing act. She guessed Lydia Layton Duncan hadn't thought it through when she decided to marry a man below her upper-class upbringing. She should have known living on the only inhabited island in the Chesapeake, you either picked crabs or caught them. At a young age Robbie had accepted her father's livelihood. Crabs paid the mortgage on their small bungalow and put food in her mouth.

But damn it, this side action had nothing to do with earning a legitimate day's pay. It was the reason she'd disowned him six years ago. She'd been well on her way to achieving that dream job, and she couldn't afford to jeopardize her future. And now after landing that job three years ago, she wasn't about to let her father tarnish the reputation she'd worked hard to achieve. Her employer didn't know, and she intended to keep it that way.

"Hey, Dad."

"Long time." He smiled sheepishly and ambled toward her.

It would have been longer, but she bit her tongue and ignored his comment.

"I guess we missed the ferry?" Robbie pulled her car keys out from the pocket of her black blazer.

It was a rhetorical question. The ferry from Crisfield to Smith Island only ran twice a day, once at sunrise and then at sunset. Glancing at her watch, they had a two hour wait.

"You going back to the house?" He arched a furry white brow over the frame of his glasses.

She debated on whether or not to turn her back on him once she paid his bail. He was free for now. But staring into the hopeful gleam of her father's blue eyes maddened her to distraction. That was the one thing that made it impossible to deny she was Terry Duncan's daughter—she inherited those piercing baby blues. And at the moment, his were making it difficult to say no. Regardless of what he had done, he was still her father.

She'd stay but only until she found him a lawyer.

Pinning him with her own blue eyes, she nudged her black oblong glasses back against her nose. "You still have it?"

She just assumed he'd lost the house. He was never good at managing the little bit of money he did have. Terry Duncan always looked for the big payoff. That's another reason he found himself behind bars tonight. Running numbers, in his mind, was more lucrative than crabbing. Never mind he was breaking the law.

He peered over his glasses. "I don't need much. I kept it for you."

She ignored his last comment. Frankly, she didn't know what to say or how to respond. "It's too late to head back to D.C. I thought I'd see you to your door." Robbie shrugged. "Any place open to eat this early?"

"I have food at the house."

Robbie's eyes widened. If she was lucky growing up, she'd find enough peanut butter to make a sandwich—and jelly—forget it. Probably why she almost burned down their shack, trying to feed them both when she was eight.

"The ferry doesn't leave until six." She'd die of starvation by then.

"Griff said he'd give me"—he cleared his throat—"*us* a lift."

Griff? Robbie's stomach churned, and now food was the last thing she wanted.

"I thought—"

"He's back. Been back almost seven years."

Now she wanted to hide. He was the last person she'd expected to run into. From what she remembered of the tough-guy persona of Griffin Nash, he couldn't wait to shake the sand of Smith Island from his soles. Although it intrigued her he'd returned, and it appeared, to her mortification, the girl next door was going to be reacquainted with the "bad boy" who thought he was every girl's dream. Correction, he was, and he knew it, and that made him all the more irritating to her.

Roberta Duncan at fifteen, a freshman at Crisfield High was invisible to Griff. Overweight, an introvert, and the polar opposite of him, *she* actually wanted an education. He didn't know she existed. But embarrassingly enough, she was very aware of him.

Which made it all the more uncomfortable when Terry Duncan hired him the summer of her junior year. Because Robbie did the books for her father, she was subject to seeing Griff on occasion when they came back from a haul. He'd wink at her on purpose when he'd enter the cramped office on the dock, his green eyes agleam. The smile forming on his firm lips made her look away, the flush of embarrassment warm against her cheeks.

Basically, Griffin Nash was a self-absorbed jerk. He was all about having a good time. His three favorite pastimes included partying, womanizing, and carousing the thin ribbon of asphalt that wound its way through Ewell on a motorcycle he'd bought at a junkyard. Having a knack for mechanics, he fixed it up enough to ride. Since there weren't many motorized vehicles on the island, the advent of the bike made Griff even more desirable to the opposite sex.

That bike took him away from the island the day he graduated with no plans for the future and no education past the twelfth grade. Which made her wonder, what had the tall, broad-shouldered teen, sculpted like one of Michelangelo's statues, made of himself?

"Skip."

Robbie cringed. She recognized his voice. Griff called her father Skip. Short for skipper, since he'd worked her father's deadrise crab boat, the *Lydia*.

Robbie crushed the keys in her hand, the sharp points digging into her palm.

Terry Duncan never thought of renaming the boat, either.

"Griff." Terry raised his hand and waved him over.

Robbie stiffened. She needed to relax. She wasn't fifteen and enamored of a boy who enjoyed making her feel less than adequate. If anything, Griff Nash should mean nothing to the confident woman she had become. Besides, what could he possibly have accomplished in the eleven years since she'd seen him?

Robbie took a breath, pushed back her glasses, and turned. Her bottom lip dropped in wonderment, her mind trying to connect the boy she remembered to the man standing ten paces away. His jet black hair, usually worn long past his collar, was cut short and tight around his ears. But it wasn't the hair that had her straining for purchase on the tile floor of the commissioner's station. It was the tan uniform shirt, meticulously pressed, that hugged his muscled shoulders.

Robbie stared at his expansive chest and in particular the brass name plate that read "Nash" in black capital letters. She knew rank structure, and she knew what the gold bars affixed to his collar meant and the absurdity shocked her speechless.

Griff walked toward them, a black stripe along each side of his olive green pants, a sharp press line running down front and center of each muscled leg.

"Robbie?" he asked tentatively, a grin forming on those firm lips she remembered so well.

Robbie swallowed. "Y . . . yes."

God. Help save me from myself.

His grin now a full-fledged smile, he said, "You look great." Those sharp green eyes took her in from her dark hair that she wore tied back in a loose slipknot at the nape of her neck to the tip of her black pumps.

If he was looking for that chubby fifteen-year-old he was out of luck. She ran five miles a day and lifted weights. In her line of work she couldn't afford otherwise.

"Thanks."

The heat of his intense gaze stung her cheeks. He watched her closely and then put out his hand, which she didn't expect. She flinched before reciprocating the gesture.

His hand was dry and firm, the warmth of his skin making her a tad uneasy. "I appreciate you bailing out Skip," he said and glanced toward her father momentarily before turning back to her. He frowned. "I've warned him about the company he keeps."

That was ironic, Griffin Nash warning her father to stay out of trouble.

"He . . . he didn't tell me you were a trooper."

"Princess Anne Barrack Commander," Skip piped in.

Thanks, Dad.

What was it about Griff Nash that irked Robbie? Maybe it wasn't so much he was to die for gorgeous. Maybe it was because all those years ago it seemed her father took more of an interest in Griff than her. Just the way he announced his title. Did he ever think to brag a little about his daughter's accomplishments since leaving the island? Maybe her father hadn't seen her for years. But he knew what she did for a living.

Robbie nodded toward his collar ornaments. "Lieutenant Nash. You've been busy."

He shrugged and whispered, "I just know how to work the system."

Now that she could believe.

"Lieutenant." A slick-sleeved trooper—minus the chevrons on his upper arm, denoting rank—came through the door of the commissioner's station with a man in custody. "Got one to see the commissioner. And Grable's doing the Breathalyzer at the barrack."

Griff looked over his shoulder. "I'm heading out. If you need me call my cell."

"Yes, sir."

Robbie stepped forward, preparing to leave with just her father. "We can see you're busy. You don't need to—"

"I'm already heading that way. It's not a problem. My cruiser's parked outside."

They left the building as a threesome until they hit the parking lot. Robbie followed the olive and black Maryland State Police cruiser and the two dark heads above the headrest in front of her the twenty or so miles to the Crisfield dock. She wouldn't let it bother her that her father chose to ride with Griff. Her father was like a child in many ways. So being inside a cruiser with all its police gadgetry was probably a thrill. She rolled her eyes, and pulled her Honda into the parking space next to Nash, hoping no one would tamper with it. Disassembling her GPS, she opened the door and got out.

A shroud of clouds made the moon elusive. The darkness was something she needed to become accustomed to, unlike her condo in D.C. off Dupont Circle, which was well lit by streetlights. Skip and Griff headed down the small pier where a Department of Natural Resources patrol boat was docked. From what she understood, for now, the boat was a spare, and Griff had authority to use it to get himself for work.

Robbie locked her car, and then peered in the back window to check the backseat for anything valuable. She wanted to believe she was immune to theft, but she was a pragmatist. She grabbed the door handle one last time, making sure her car was locked, and stepped back to the rear of her Honda and popped the trunk.

Something told her Skip Duncan would get the best of her, and she was grateful she'd packed a bag. The thought of spending one night in the small house she grew up in put her on edge. It only reminded her how truly lonely she had been. She had long since stopped blaming herself for her mother's departure from her life, but the pain of worthlessness still nudged at her. Robbie sat the GPS in a little cutout of the trunk. She removed a small, but bulging, black travel bag and placed the strap over her shoulder when a warm hand pressed into her lower back, the weight against her shoulder being lifted off.

"I've got it." Griff slung it onto his shoulder. He nodded to her shoes. "You might want to take them off. The boards have a lot of gaps."

She peered past the flare of her black dress pants to her matching black Gucci pumps and then took a step back, meeting him stare for stare. "Okay? I appreciate the warning, but I can handle it."

There was no way in hell she was walking barefoot. If he meant to reduce her to a sniveling girly girl, he'd misjudged her quiet demeanor. Robbie reached up to his wide shoulder and slid the bag off and back onto hers. "Nash. I'm good." She shut the trunk and motioned for him to lead the way.

"You're sure?"

Damn it. He was laughing at her, maybe not with his mouth, but definitely with his eyes.

"I'm sure." She motioned again for him to precede her, but he held his ground.

Okay. Ladies first.

The weathered boards creaked with every step. With Griff behind her, the pier became a tightrope and the quicker she got off it, the less scrutiny she'd be under.

Water slick as oil splashed against the moorings below where a dark twin outboard was moored. Her father, already seated at the center console behind the wheel, leaned over the back of the seat. "Robbie, come on, girl. I'm starving."

That was her line, and she was moving just as fast as her high-heeled pumps allowed. The added attention only infuriated her. She picked up the pace and then stopped, completely immobile. Crap! She pulled her foot up from the heel lodged tight between the boards of the pier. But the heel remained rooted, causing her and her heavy overnight bag to list to the right. She didn't even want to hear, *I told you so.*

Not from Griff.

"You shouldn't have come, bright eyes," Griff whispered against her ear.

Robbie's stomach fluttered in that womanly way when she was attracted to the opposite sex. He knew exactly what he was doing. He'd called her that once before when they were young. Robbie took a deep breath. She had been unsure of boys at the age of fifteen. But at twenty-nine, she'd long since learned how to handle flirtatious men. His games weren't going to work on her now.

The weight of her bag slid off her shoulder, and strong arms lifted her from her shoes into his arms. "My—"

"I've got them," he said, and with minimal effort leaned down allowing her bottom to rest against his thighs while he yanked her shoes free. Griff handed her off to her father who steadied her once her bare feet hit the cold metal of the boat deck.

"Got her," Skip called out.

Griff untied the moorings and hopped in, dropping her shoes to the deck, the metal echoing hollow against the pitch of night.

"I'll turn her about," Skip called out as the boat purred to life. He hit the throttle, and the boat lurched.

Robbie flew forward, the gray decking of the boat growing closer. A strong hand gripped her arm.

"Find a seat," Griff ordered.

No . . . really? What did he think she was trying to do? Fall on her ass?

But rather than make a case for his domineering attitude, she grabbed the closest bench and sat, her back pressed against the rear seat of the boat. The icy spray of the bay dotted her face. Shoeless, she sat, her toenails painted in L'Oréal's Pink Fusion Coral, and she curled them under. Her once tidy hair pulled at the knot against her nape, escaping into flyaway wisps.

Griff and her father stood at the console talking. Their conversation left to her imagination. The twin motors, located directly behind her, revved at high speeds, drowning out their words.

She could handle this. But first she needed her shoes. She'd be kidding herself if she hadn't fantasized about meeting Nash someday in the future—but on her terms. Somehow windblown, barefoot, and struggling to put a pair of shoes on wasn't how she had pictured it. Those feelings of imperfection she'd suppressed for so long came screaming back, and she closed her ears and refused to listen. Spying her black pumps bumping along the deck, she inched forward off the bench. They were too far to snatch with her feet. She couldn't remember the last time she'd been on a boat, but the motion unnerved her. Standing was the last thing she should do. But they were so close.

Robbie concentrated. She took several deep breaths and pushed up to a standing position. The boat hit the water hard, and she hit the bench full-force with her bottom and grimaced when the pain shot up her spine.

Griff glanced over his shoulder, followed her line of sight, and smiled. He patted her father on the shoulder, said something that made Skip laugh, and the warm flush so easily provoked by Griff when she was a teen crept up her neck.

He grabbed her pumps and started toward her. Robbie swallowed and considered the inky black water surrounding her when he sat down next to her and handed over her shoes. "I meant what I said."

The pressure of his service weapon poked her hip, a reminder things had changed since she'd been gone.

Robbie slipped her shoes on and pushed away from his warm thigh pressed up against her leg. She eyed him speculatively. "He called me." She glanced at Skip.

With the motors running top speed—Skip enjoyed opening up on the bay—she was sure he couldn't hear their conversation. But still, this wasn't discreet. They were yelling to compete with the rumble of the motors in the back of the boat. Surprisingly, her father's attention was drawn dead ahead, which made sense, the obstacles at night in the bay could get you killed if you weren't paying attention.

Griff nodded toward Skip. "He told me. But Skip doesn't always think things through."

Like she didn't know that, but there was something in her father's voice when he'd called that Robbie couldn't ignore. "I'm here now. He needs a lawyer."

"I'll get him one." He moved closer and bent his head toward her. "Robbie, these guys play for keeps. Having you around is only going to make things worse for him."

Robbie gripped the bench. "Don't tell me my job."

"Are you here officially?"

The truth was no. They didn't know she was here. She didn't want them to know. "From what you're telling me, he needs protective custody."

"Answer the question."

She leveled her gaze on him. Of course, level for Griff had her craning her head up in an uncomfortable position. "Not officially."

He stood. "I'm turning this boat around. You're going home."

She grabbed his arm. "I'll pull rank on you. This is federal."

"You making it official, Special Agent Duncan?"

"Damn right."

A Personal Message from
P. J. O'Dwyer:

While it's thrilling to create that next complex character or never-saw-it-coming plot twist, I find hearing from readers the most rewarding. If you enjoyed this story or any of my other books, it would mean a great deal to me if you'd send a short email to introduce yourself and say hello. I always personally respond to my readers.

Please email me at pjodwyer@pjodwyer.com and introduce yourself, so I can personally thank you for trying my books. You will also receive notifications about future books, narrated titles in audiobook, updates, and contests.

I also hope you'll consider subscribing to my blog that's designed for both readers and authors at www.indieauthorsbrew.com.

Thank you!

A Message from
BLACK SIREN BOOKS

In an effort to support horse rescue organizations and their mission of rescue, rehabilitation, and education, P. J. O'Dwyer and Black Siren Books will donate a portion of all Fallon Sisters Trilogy book sales, and all future literary works purchased through www.pjodwyer.com or the publishing house of Black Siren Books, to horse rescues around the world.

ABOUT THE AUTHOR

Born in Washington, D.C., the oldest of five children, P. J. O'Dwyer was labeled the storyteller of the family and often accused of embellishing the truth. Her excuse? It made for a more interesting story. The proof was the laughter she received following her version of events.

After graduating from high school in the suburbs of Maryland, the faint urgings of her imaginative voice that said "you should write" were ignored. She opted to travel the world instead. Landing a job in the affluent business district of Bethesda, Maryland, as a travel counselor, she journeyed frequently to such places as Hawaii, the Bahamas, Paris, New Orleans, the Alaskan Inland Passage, and the Caribbean Islands.

Today, P. J. lives in western Howard County, Maryland, with her husband, Mark; teenage daughter, Katie; their cat, Scoot; and German Shepherd, FeFe in a farmhouse they built in 1998.

P. J. is learning that it takes a village to create a writer and is relieved to know she's not in this alone. She's an active member of Romance Writers of

America. She also participates in a critique group, which has been an invaluable experience with many friendships made and an abundance of helpful praise, and yes, criticism. But it's all good. Improving her craft is an ongoing process.

While creating that next complex character or never-saw-it-coming plot twist is thrilling, P. J. finds teaching the craft as an adjunct college professor the most rewarding. She's always eager to share her journey in the publishing world in hopes of inspiring her students to realize their own dreams of becoming a published author.

Writing is a passion that runs a close second to her family. When she's not writing, she enjoys spending time with family and friends, fits in her daily run with her husband, and tries heroically to keep up with her daughter Katie's social life. Who knew how demanding the life of a teenager could be, especially for Mom?

When asked where she gets her ideas for her stories, she laughs ruefully and says, "It helps being married to a cop." Actually, she admits, "Every day I find a wealth of possible stories and plots in the most unsuspected place—my daily life."

31872359R00241

Made in the USA
Middletown, DE
16 May 2016